Pride Publishing books by Rae Marks

Hart Consulting
Sweet Hart
Dash

Hart Consulting

DASH

RAE MARKS

Dash
ISBN # 978-1-83943-765-6
©Copyright Rae Marks 2022
Cover Art by Erin Dameron-Hill ©Copyright January 2022
Interior text design by Claire Siemaszkiewicz
Pride Publishing

Published in 2022 by Pride Publishing, United Kingdom.

Pride Publishing is an imprint of Totally Entwined Group Limited.

DASH

Chapter One

Nick

Nick's molars were getting sore. Yet he couldn't relax as he watched his brother, Bray, flirt with Ax. He never thought he'd lose respect for his twin, but there he was, clenching his jaw to keep the words in his throat.

"How does Sam do it?" Nick grumbled.

"Do what?"

Nick jumped. He'd been too caught up in what was in front of him and hadn't heard Sam walk into the gym of Hart Consulting, or, as the guys called it, HC. After leaving active duty, Nick had taken a few months off to spend time with his dad. Then, two months ago, he'd given in to his morbid curiosity and joined his older brother Mason's consulting firm.

"How do you stand back and watch them flirt like that?"

"It bothered me at first, but then I realized they've built a different kind of relationship. They are more like you and Bray than me and Bray."

Nick snorted. Sam was deluding himself. Bray and Ax had some sort of chemistry going on. Something had happened in Kiev — well, something besides Bray getting shot. Nick still didn't have authorization to read the reports on that op, since it was ongoing, and he was still in his six-month probation period.

At first Nick had thought Bray was stupid or crazy to join up with a bunch of assholes that hadn't watched his back and had let him get shot. Bray had just smiled and said he'd put himself in that situation, and that he'd do it all over again. *What is that supposed to mean?*

"I trust Bray." Sam squeezed Nick's shoulder.

All the guys were ex-military and most of them were queer, so Nick felt like one of the guys, sort of. He didn't have to watch his back or hide who he was. It was a relief. He felt comfortable with everyone... everyone except Ax.

"Hey, Magnum," Ax called out to Sam.

"Fucking call sign," Sam grumbled.

Nick nodded. His call sign was okay until he got the inevitable questions — 'what does Dash mean?' or 'how'd you get your handle?'. Nick sighed. "*Fucking call sign*" was right.

Now that he was out of the military, the guys mostly used the monikers they'd been saddled with in boot camp — or soon after — as just a nickname. It was banter now, not about making sure Nick never forgot the stupidest thing he'd done back then.

"Why don't you show your boyfriend how it's done?" Ax taunted.

Nick turned in time to see a wicked grin spread across Sam's face. Sam gave Nick's shoulder a final pat, kicked off his shoes and sauntered onto the mat where Ax and Bray had been sparring.

When Bray noticed Sam, there was no look of guilt, just awe — and a 'come hither' look that made Nick throw up in his mouth a little. Bray had found his place, his tribe. *He has also found the man of his dreams, apparently.*

Nick rolled his eyes at himself. There was no 'apparently' about it. The truth was that Nick was jealous. He probably turned green when he watched them. Yet there was still something with Ax and Bray, something that had Nick's gut tightening with anxiety.

Ax treated Bray differently than he treated everyone else and it had been that way since he and Bray had 'bonded' in Kiev. Sure, he teased Bray, but he was also viciously protective of him.

Maybe the feelings were all on Ax's side. Nick was so curious about the Kiev op that he stopped what he was doing to listen whenever anyone discussed it. He was like the office busybody, yet he couldn't help himself.

He was careful to keep his eyes on his brother and not trail Ax across the room like he was tempted to do. Ax saw right through him, and he hated it.

"You wanna spar, Nickel? I can show *you* how it's really done."

Ax's voice was low and teasing. Nick huffed out a frustrated breath, even as the cadence of the other man's voice had the hairs on the back of his neck standing at attention.

He worked hard to keep another part of his anatomy from standing at attention, too. Every time Ax used his nickname, Nick wanted to punch him in the face. It had been like that since they'd first met, though Nick wasn't completely sure why.

"I already know how it's done," Nick said.

He turned then and had to swallow down a groan. It was like a flashback to the first time he'd ever seen Ax. The man's entire body was glistening with the sweat of his workout. His white muscle shirt was practically see-through and glued to every dip and curve of the musculature from his chest to his waist.

His longish black hair was slicked back with sweat, though a few strands were hanging over his low-set brows. A drip of perspiration rolled down his temple and got caught in his beard scruff. Nick wondered what that scruff would feel like, what it would taste like against his tongue.

Ax's eyes were so light that the contrast against his caramel skin and black hair was almost startling. *Definitely striking.*

Ax was gorgeous...and the asshole knew it. He stood with a towel wrapped around his neck, one hand grasping each end. His feet were set wide apart in a confident stance.

It was exactly the way he'd looked the first time Nick had laid eyes on him. Only then, Ax had been giving Bray the same teasing look he was giving Nick. Ax hadn't even noticed Nick that first day, as he'd zeroed in on Bray. Nick had been jealous then as well. Was that why Ax calling him 'Nickel' from the start had pissed him off?

The thought left a bad taste in his mouth. No one was more important than his family. Well, the family that actually participated in his life. Mase was still a question mark.

"Not how *I* do it." Ax winked.

That wink did things to Nick's insides, but he kept his face emotionless. Ax couldn't see how he affected Nick because Ax flirted with everyone. Nick didn't delude himself into thinking he was special.

"I'll pass," Nick deadpanned with an eye-roll.

"Your loss, Nickel." Ax smirked as he turned to walk away.

"Asshole."

Nick whispered the word under his breath, but he apparently wasn't quiet enough, because Ax's laughter rang loud and clear as he sauntered away. Nick couldn't stay and watch what was happening on the mat. On the surface, sure, Sam and Bray were practicing tactical moves, mostly Krav Maga, jujutsu, aikido and judo, but really it was foreplay.

Bray had always been the shy one. Nick couldn't believe he was letting his boyfriend pin him to the mat and kiss him right in the middle of the gym where anyone working out could look over and see.

They weren't even in one of the private sparring rooms. It was like Bray was oblivious to the world around him, solely focused on Sam. Nick lengthened his stride toward the locker room as if trying to outrun the green-eyed monster.

The bathroom at HC was a million times better than any gym bathroom he'd ever been in, especially in the military. There was a row of about a dozen private shower stalls along one wall. Sure, there were lockers and sinks, urinals and toilet stalls, but the shower stalls were amazing.

No big room with a million shower heads circling one big drain. No more willing his dick down and trying not to look at all the naked men around him as they soaped up. The irony was that the guys at HC would be much more understanding if he popped a boner than anyone in the army would ever have been.

Nick punched in the code to his locker and pulled out his shower stuff. He turned and headed for one of the stalls but froze halfway across the floor when he heard a groan. He swallowed to get saliva past his dry, parched throat. He knew that voice. He also knew what the slap, slap, slap of skin meant.

Tiptoeing closer, Bray tried to listen to see if Ax was alone. Was he in there with another one of the guys or was he just rubbing one out in the shower—after sparring with Bray for thirty minutes? Nick's stomach bottomed out at the thought. Was Ax in there jacking off to thoughts of Bray?

Even that realization didn't deflate his cock when the sound of Ax's breaths echoed through the bathroom. Nick wondered if it was possible for his own dick to betray him as he locked the door to his private stall and began to undress. He turned on his shower to try to drown Ax out, but he didn't finish undressing and step in. He stayed and listened.

Just as Nick dropped his boxer briefs, Ax moaned out a soft "Ah, fuck," that had Nick strangling the base of his erection before his brain even realized what he was doing. He started moving his fist in time to the slapping of Ax's balls against his own hand.

Nick arched at the sound, and he wished more than anything that he could see exactly what Ax was doing to himself. Was he fingering himself as well? The thought had Nick stroking himself harder, faster.

"*Nnngh,*" Ax moaned before finally growling out his release. The sound alone had Nick spurting right along with him. He bit his lip to stifle the gasp that slipped out of his mouth.

"Was it good for you, too, Nickel?" Ax asked as the water shut off in the other stall.

All the lust and post-orgasmic bliss shriveled and died at Ax's words. Nick twitched with rage. Had Ax been putting on a show to embarrass him?

"Do you put on the same show every day at the same time? Was it meant for Bray or was it just first-come, first-served?"

"Why? You want a repeat performance?"

"You're an asshole," Nick said.

He stepped into the shower to wash away any evidence that Ax had turned him on.

"Glad you enjoyed it, but it was a onetime thing. Just needed to relieve a little tension. Enjoy your shower, Nickel."

Ax started whistling. A locker opened then slammed shut, and the off-key tune he was whistling got farther and farther away. Nick scrubbed himself raw in frustration.

He knew damn well he was going to have to work with Ax if he wanted to stay on the West Coast and be closer to his father. He wasn't sure they'd be able to pull off an op if they couldn't even stand to be in the same room together.

Ax was completely immature. It was up to Nick to be professional if he had any hope of getting assigned jobs closer to home so he could always spend his R&R with his family.

Resolving to be the bigger person, Nick tried to figure out a way to smooth things over with the asshole so he could get what he needed out of the situation. What was it about Ax that had him wound so tight?

Chapter Two

Ax

Ax's whole body hummed with satisfaction. He'd been picturing Nick bent over one of the weight benches as he'd stroked himself in the shower. When he'd heard a locker open and close, he'd peeked out and seen Nick through the tiny crack between the stall door and the wall.

Nick had gotten off right along with him. Ax had heard his gasp and groan. He wasn't sure why Nick was so determined to hate him, but the man could sure set his anger aside to beat off to the sounds of Ax in the shower.

Ax smiled.

He shouldn't push Nick's buttons, but there were just so many. Nick was strung way too tight. Ax had about a million more pounds of weight on his shoulders than the precious Nicholas Hart did, and yet he hadn't lost his sense of humor.

Ax whistled as he pushed the call button for the elevator. He'd considered waiting for Nick to get out of the shower, to try to see if his cheeks were still pink, either from embarrassment or just from getting off. But he'd spent enough time playing, so he headed back up to the second floor.

Just as the doors were about to slide closed, Chase called out for Ax to hold the elevator. Chase and a kid strolled toward him. Their building was secure, so Ax was curious about their visitor, especially if he was going to the second floor. First floor had low-level security, which by any other standards was high. The higher floors actually required security clearance.

"Who's your friend?" Ax asked as they stepped into the elevator.

"This is Max Freeman, our new tech guru. Max, this is Ax."

"Hey, we rhyme." Ax smiled.

"Jeez," Max groaned.

"You okay?" Chase asked.

Max nodded at Chase, but he did look a little queasy.

"Does everyone look like you two?"

Ax and Chase looked at each other. They looked nothing alike. Chase was all dark hair, light skin and light baby blues. Ax was dark—dark skin, dark hair, dark soul. Ax rolled his eyes at his own joke. His eyes were actually pretty light, considering his Latin heritage.

"We're not exactly twins, Maxie," Ax said.

"I mean tall and hot," Max said before his eyes widened.

Max slapped his forehead. When the elevator dinged and the doors slid open, Max hurried out, but Ax followed him and caught his shoulder.

"Hey." Ax lowered his voice to try to soothe the kid. "You may not be tall, but you're still hot."

Max dropped his hand and gaped. Ax gave his most encouraging smile. For some reason, the kid reminded him of his little brother, Diego.

"Don't fuck with the new recruit," Chase warned.

"I'm not fucking. Who's fucking? Look at him? Are you telling me he's not hot?"

Chase rolled his eyes but turned to assess Max. Max's ears turned red. He looked like a nerdy James Dean with his narrow cleft chin, his full lips and the eyebrows that were more like thick slashes above his gray eyes.

"You're plenty cute, Max," Chase said, "but a little young for me. And I'm seeing someone, so I try not to look too hard."

"See, Maxie? You fit right in."

"It's not 'Maxie'." He grumbled. "My handle is 'Sin'."

"Sin? Wait! *You're* Sin? You're the one who saved Bray's ass in Kiev?"

Ax couldn't believe this kid, who was probably eighteen, was Sin. *The* Sin. Without another word, Ax picked him up and gave him the biggest bear hug in the history of bear hugs. Ax swung the kid around in circles until they were both laughing.

"I can't believe it's you," Ax said as he set Max down.

"Excuse me."

Ax turned to see Nick stepping off the elevator. He looked even more grumpy than usual. *Is he really that pissed about what happened in the bathroom?*

"Hey, Nick," Max said.

"Hey, Max," Nick smiled. "They got you, too?"

Max gave a shy nod.

"Bray mentioned something, but I didn't think they'd be able to…"

Nick stopped and looked at Ax with a frown. Then he looked back at Max. All four of them ended up looking at each other as if they were trying to figure out who was who. Max apparently felt the need to fill the silence.

"I think HC will be able to use more of my hardware. The government is really interested in the software — or at least what I can do with it."

"When did you start?" Nick asked.

"Today, I guess." Max shrugged. "I'm supposed to meet someone named Wade."

"I'll show you where Wade is," Ax offered.

"I'll leave you to it, then." Chase gave Ax a pat on the arm and wandered into the bullpen.

"How long have you two known each other?" Nick asked.

"Depends on what you mean by 'know'," Ax teased. "I've known about Sin for about six months. I never met *Max* until today."

"I have no idea what the hell you're even talking about." Nick rolled his eyes but turned to Max. "It's great to see you, Max. If you need a sparring partner…Ax is your man. He'll, uh, 'show you how it's done'. Right, Ax?"

Nick stomped off down the hallway.

"Thanks, I think," Max muttered. "What's wrong with Nick? He's usually the life of the party."

"He's pissed at me, not you. So, you're Sin. Fuck. I thought you'd be older, kid."

"Yeah. I get that a lot, but I'm not exactly a kid. I mean, I'm twenty-four. I have a double masters in Math and Engineering."

"Don't sweat it. It's more of a vibe thing. Bray's a kid too."

"He and Nick are older than me. I, uh, skipped a few grades, and Bray always had my back all the way through high school. I mean, I stopped skipping grades so I could stay with him and Nick. The other kids were brutal."

"Yeah, sure you stayed with Nick and Bray for protection. It's not like those two are easy on the eyes or anything."

Max snorted and followed Ax into the bullpen. There were a few guys hanging around, but Ax took his charge directly to Wade's desk. Wade was just ending a call and turned to face them. When he saw Max, he stood with a smile on his face.

"Are you fucking kidding me right now?" Max whispered.

Ax's smile grew even wider. It looked like Wade did it for the kid. Wade was big, probably one of the biggest guys on the team. He was also the team leader, for all intents and purposes. He was six-foot-three and built like a boxer. His biceps were bigger than Sam's.

"Max, so glad you're here. We've all been dying to meet you. I don't want to overwhelm you, but we have a list of things we'd like your help with that's about a mile long."

"Yeah." Max stopped to clear his throat before continuing. "I'd be happy to look at you — I mean, look at it for you. Sorry, but I'm a little nervous."

"Don't be nervous. We've been chomping at the bit to see what you're willing to help us do."

"Anything," Max said. "I mean anything within reason that doesn't compromise any of my other contracts."

"Of course. In fact, the most important thing, the first thing on the list, is to have you help us locate a former brother in arms. We've lost track of Dakota and thought you could help out."

Ax patted Max on the arm and took a step back. He was in good hands and hopefully Max could help find Dakota. They'd been looking for him for a few months, since he hadn't contacted anyone at HC or even his own father.

When Max had a few minutes, Ax was going to pick his brain. If anyone could help Ax with his personal mission, it was Max.

Chapter Three

Nick

Nick had been summoned to the war room. All the guys worked in a huge bullpen with zero privacy. There were small offices on each floor if someone wanted quiet, but the war room seemed to be the place where everything really happened.

It definitely wasn't an office. It could easily fit their entire team of about twenty guys. Nick knocked once then entered when he was commanded to. Wade and Sam were in the room along with Ax. Everyone looked solemn.

Nick stiffened his spine and lifted his chin. If Ax had complained about him or was there to give him shit, Nick would give it right back.

"Nick, good." Wade said

Wade waved his hand at the chair across from him, the one right next to Ax. Nick pasted on a smile and sat next to the man who apparently had a thing for every guy who crossed his path.

"I assume you've been emailing with Mase?"

Nick was surprised by the question but nodded. He'd been going back and forth, trying to negotiate for Mase to visit their father since he was going to have some time stateside in the next few months.

Mase had staunchly refused. Nick was sick and tired of the tug-of-war going on in his family. He'd hoped bonding with Mase and his buddies would help. Nick had practically memorized Mase's last email.

Nick,

I get the point. You want me to see Dad, but you're judging my relationship through the lens of your relationship with him. It's not the same.

If you only got in touch with me on Dad's behalf, I'm not sure there's anything more to say. If you want us to get to know each other again, just you and me, I'm more than willing.

I won't be guilted or badgered into seeing him. Let me know what you decide.

M

Nick did want a relationship with Mase, but he hadn't yet responded. He just couldn't understand why Mase was being so stubborn. Bray had forgiven their father once he'd had the stroke.

Dad was sorry. He just wanted the chance to be able to say it in person. Technically Mase didn't have to accept his apology, though Nick was pretty sure that one look at their father—and the toll this had all taken on him—and Mase would probably forgive him.

Their big, strong father was a shell of the man he used to be. Anyone who knew him before would look at him now and pity him at least a little, even Mase.

"Then you know he'll be here for a few months. He's been pretending to drag his feet, telling his chain of command he won't exactly be welcome here. But they finally talked him into coming stateside."

It took Nick a moment to remember what they were talking about. He nodded. He hadn't known Mase had been dragging his feet. It made sense for his cover story, but it still pissed Nick off a little. He could have already been there but was delaying?

"Kozak, his superior, has promised him that Sam will help pave the way. This is great news for us, as we can provide support and backup for Mase, at least while he's here."

"Is that why you called me in? To update me?"

"You've requested West Coast ops, which means you'll be working a lot with Ax and Colt."

"Colt?" Ax snorted.

Nick wasn't sure what was wrong with Colt. He seemed like a decent operator.

"Colt handles West Coast too, and you two have different styles. It'll be good for Nick to work with as many operators as he can to try to find his own style." Sam said.

"For the first few assignments, you'll be with Ax." Wade said. "He has more HC ops under his belt than anyone else."

"Ax's specialty is Northern California. He grew up there," Sam said.

Nick wasn't sure why they were trying to sell him on Ax's qualifications. Ax was probably a good operator. He likely thought he was an amazing operator.

"We have a lead on a mark attending a gala in DC." Wade continued. "If successful, it will lead to an op in San Francisco in the next few weeks. I put you in for this op but wanted to make sure you're ready, because you'll be heading west maybe days after Mase is finally back on US soil."

Nick's only hesitation on taking the assignment was that he'd be working with Ax. They were giving him an out, but if he took it, they might have him working with Mase.

He wasn't sure he could do that and not be distracted by all the other crap going on in their family. It was a case of two shitty choices.

"I'm fine taking the assignment. My brother and I have a lot to talk about, but it won't be appropriate to do so while on an op."

Wade's eyebrows lifted in surprise, but he nodded. He seemed to approve of Nick's decision, even if he hadn't expected so much honesty.

"Mase should be arriving in a few days. The gala is on Saturday. That gives you and Ax four days to get your background memorized. I suggest you work together, though your background is more as business associates."

"Do I still need to bring a date to the gala?" Ax asked.

"Yes. Nick will be your right-hand man, but a date will look even better. For this op, the younger the girl, the better off we'll be. Think depraved."

Nick held back a snort. He was sure Ax would have no problem being depraved.

"I have someone in mind. She'll be perfect. Young and stacked."

The way Ax said that had Nick's gut clenching. He'd heard Ax swung both ways. Now he was going to get to witness it. *Hooray.*

"Is that all?" Nick asked.

"For now. There may be another meeting in DC, and there will be at least a few days in San Francisco to arrange a meeting with the lawyer we're hoping to take down."

Nick nodded and stood. He lifted his hand because saluting was ingrained, but he curled it into a fist and pulled it back to his side. Sam stood and patted his arm.

"It takes a while to assimilate to civilian life. Longer still when you're taking orders similar to military ones."

Nick gave him a grateful smile. He'd expected Ax to make fun of him, but Ax and Wade had stepped aside to talk about something else. Nick took the opportunity to get out of there and head up to his 'apartment' on the fourth floor.

He hadn't been in his room for five minutes before the knock came. He was sure Ax had sought him out. He was expecting him to gloat or tease about Nick being 'under his command'. But when he opened the door, it was Bray on the other side.

"Your first op," Bray said as Nick stepped back to allow him in. "Sam said you didn't seem excited. Are you having second thoughts about being here?"

There were no windows in the room. None of the rooms on the fourth floor had windows. They were safe, sure, but Nick liked to see the skyline. He started to pace.

"Mase'll be here in a few days," Nick said.

"I know. It's probably weird for him. I don't think he's been back at all in the two years he's been undercover."

"He won't see Dad."

Bray didn't answer right away. Nick turned to him and could tell he was weighing his words.

"It's not as simple for him to forgive as it was for you."

"Or for you?" Nick asked.

"It wasn't simple for me at all. It's like a pendulum. I swing back and forth—he didn't really mean it, but he was so cruel, but he didn't fully understand my point of view—but he didn't try to understand either. Some days I think I've fully forgiven him, then another emotion or memory pops up and I have to deal with that to get back to forgiveness."

"But he *didn't* mean it."

"Nick, he made Mase choose between being a part of the family or being his true self. He *did* mean it. He was callous. He was better with me than with Mase and better with you than with either of us, so please, please don't act like we all had the same experience and you're the only one who's big enough to fully forgive him."

Nick swallowed his retort down his burning throat. He kept trying to remind himself that their father had been less supportive of his brothers. He just had a hard time imagining it.

"He fully embraced the idea when you came out, because he knew what the alternative would be," Bray said.

Nick wanted to argue, but he knew it was true. Their father had admitted it.

"I understand Dad's sorry, but you can't just back up, say 'oops, I didn't mean it,' and expect all the pain you caused to disappear. You can't un-break a glass. You have to put it back together piece by piece and the cracks will always be there, even if you do."

"I just... He's dying. Can't Mase give him one dying wish? What could he have possibly said that would have Mase passing up the chance to say goodbye?"

Bray looked down at the floor. He licked his lips like he did when he was nervous. It was that fucking Kiev job. Bray knew something, something he wouldn't, or couldn't, tell Nick.

"If or when you get a chance to talk to Mase, listen with an open mind. Maybe you'll understand."

"How can I trust Mase will tell me the truth when you haven't even really told me what Dad said to you? You didn't tell me at the time, and you still haven't told me. Why didn't you tell me you came out to him?"

"Honestly? A big part of me hoped that maybe he had learned his lesson and that maybe he would be different with you. But then when he was, I felt cast aside, like I wasn't as important. I didn't know it would tear apart *our* relationship as well."

"Because you didn't tell me why you wouldn't talk to him. I thought *you* were being callous and cruel."

"I've never been callous or cruel if I could help it. Telling you what he said to me would be both those things."

"But you were willing to let me be pissed at you."

Bray shrugged as he said, "I've always tried to do what's right, to have integrity. I wish I could say Dad taught me that, but it was Mase who taught me."

Nick wanted to refute it. He searched his mind to try to find an argument against it, but he couldn't. Mase had been rebellious, sure, but he'd always been honest. And he'd always been kind to his little brothers until he'd disappeared. Their father wasn't perfect. He was used to getting his own way at any cost. The right or wrong of it didn't weigh heavily on his decisions.

In Nick's mind, no matter what words their father had used, they had been words said in anger. He was still their father, and he was dying. *Why not grant a dying man his last wish?*

Chapter Four

Ax

"Oh, the irony," Ax grumbled as he walked into the ballroom with Lena on his arm.

Nick was a couple of paces behind him. It probably looked to an outsider like Nick was deferring to him, when really Ax was pretty sure Nick was dragging his feet because he was pissed.

What exactly he was pissed about this time was a mystery. It could be that Nick didn't like playing second fiddle or that he didn't really want to work with Ax at all. Ax didn't mean to poke the bear, but it was just too easy. Right from the start, Nick had had it in for him, and he had no idea why.

Ax had even resorted to asking Bray if he'd been talking shit to his brother. Bray had sworn he'd never mentioned Ax in their conversations and that if he had, he'd have mentioned how Ax had always had his back. He wasn't even sure why it mattered that the kid couldn't stand the sight of him — yet it bothered him.

"What's ironic?" Lena asked.

Nick snorted behind them.

It wasn't that Lena was stupid. She was brilliant. She just didn't know that she was a prop in their current mission. She had no idea he was undercover as part of a human trafficking ring. There was no way she could see the irony of them attending a gala where the sole purpose was to raise money to end human trafficking.

Ax had told her he was trying to make an ex jealous so she'd hang all over him and look at him like he was her dream pair of Manolos on clearance for seventy-five percent off and in her size.

His cover was that he was working his way up in Lucien's organization after being Sam's sidekick for a year. He was taking over day-to-day operations for the West Coast.

California was by far the biggest business in human trafficking in the US. It would be a coup to be in charge of just that state, let alone the whole West Coast. They had a few low-level names and they'd busted up a few rinky-dink rings, but the one they were after was organized, international and *big*.

Ax could practically hear the eye-roll Nick was giving behind them as Lena moved closer to Ax and wrapped both her arms around his left arm. She was a good kid, the baby sister of a guy he'd served with. Luckily, Lena looked nothing like Saint.

Not that Zayne 'Saint' Archer was a bad-looking guy. Ax would totally call him hot if it didn't make him want to heave. Saint was like a brother to him. But he wouldn't make a good-looking woman, that was for sure.

Lena would be just Ax's type if she was old enough to drink—and if he hadn't been jacking off to thoughts of the sourpuss behind them every fucking night. Maybe he'd become a masochist—always chasing, never catching. That was how he felt with his personal mission and that was how he was beginning to feel with Nick.

"Loco, your mark is dead ahead, stage left at the bar," Sam whispered through the mic in his ear.

Ax looked up and saw him. William Campbell. He was a lawyer from San Francisco, and Ax's goal would be to get a meeting, to buy some 'merchandise' and see if he'd be willing to do business with Lucien.

It was arranged that Ax would be sitting at Campbell's table. There had only been two spots available, so Nick was relegated to sitting with Sam and Bray and listening through the earpiece buried down his ear canal.

Campbell's date was surprisingly close to his own age and seemed very confident. Though when Ax and Lena sat at his table, the guy was totally eye-fucking poor Lena.

By the time hors d'oeuvres were served, Ax could feel by Lena's stiffness how uncomfortable she was with the attention. He did his best to keep her under his arm and even tried to lean forward to block the guy's view.

Campbell's date, who turned out to be his wife, seemed completely oblivious. Ax was just about to excuse both himself and Lena when Campbell's wife asked the very question he'd been waiting for.

"What do you do, Mr. Hernandez?"

Ax breathed a sigh of relief as he again leaned forward to give Mrs. Campbell his attention. He also blocked her husband's view in the process.

"I'm actually getting ready to move to the West Coast. I work for Bernard Industries. I'm the new VP in charge of West Coast operations."

"Bernard." Campbell finally leaned back a little. "That name sounds familiar. Lucien Bernard?"

"Yes." Ax acted surprised. "You know him? I think he's here this evening."

Ax knew damn well he was. Lucien Bernard was HC operative Jazz, and he'd spent the last few years building up that fake persona. He had a reputation for being a cold bastard who trusted almost no one, so rising in his organization was rare.

"No. Not personally. I've heard the name. I wouldn't mind meeting the man."

Campbell gave Ax a look. It almost made him sick that this guy was giving him a look of approval. It took balls of steel for a trafficker to show up and mingle with the enemy in the nation's capitol. It looked like Campbell was holding back laughter at the irony of it as well.

"Will you be making your home base in California, perhaps?" Campbell smirked.

"Yes. I'll be mostly in San Francisco, though I'll need to be in San Diego a lot as well."

"That's unique," Mrs. Campbell said. "Most people go between San Francisco and LA."

Ax cleared his throat as if he were slightly uncomfortable. "Our business is unique," Ax replied.

Campbell snorted.

The conversation moved on, with Campbell talking a lot about himself and his well-to-do clients. When the women excused themselves, Campbell asked Ax to bring Lena to see him in San Francisco.

"Unfortunately, Lena's only arm candy. My last girl was unwilling to move with me, so we had to part ways."

"And Lena?"

"She has a crush on me, but her family is too overbearing for my tastes. Military family. Plus, she's a little too accommodating. I like a woman with more fight," Ax said with a wink.

Ax was thinking more of Nick as the words about a fighter fell from his lips. Lena was as sweet as they came. She was probably so good that Ax would be way too much for her, even if he were interested.

"Ahh," Campbell leaned back and nodded in understanding.

Ax was glad he hadn't used Lena's last name in introductions. He was also glad he hadn't introduced her by her full name, Lenore. If Campbell did sniff around for her, she'd be impossible to find.

"Well, I have plenty of friends I can introduce you to. We have similar tastes, I think."

Ax raised an eyebrow at Campbell, because his wife looked nothing like Lena. Campbell laughed heartily.

"Don't judge my wife. Ellen is as loyal as a Labrador. Lena, though, is definitely my type." Campbell pressed his business card into Ax's hand.

"I can help you meet someone local when you're in San Francisco," Campbell promised. "I know all the right people to help you find exactly what you're looking for."

"I have no problem finding bed partners," Ax scoffed.

"I'm sure in your travels you find plenty of average women, but if you want something truly unique, give me a call. I'll introduce you to a few very special women."

Ax didn't even have to pretend to be intrigued. Campbell obviously knew that someone in Ax's position would have no shortage of options, partners both willing and not-so-willing. And yet he was saying he had something better. The idea made Ax sick to his stomach, but he smiled and nodded in agreement as he stuffed the card into the pocket of his tuxedo jacket.

As soon as Lena sat back down, Jett's voice came over Ax's comm device.

"Ten-forty-five, all report. Mayday. Ten-twenty-two, report to the hotel room. Ten-sixty-seven."

Ax heard the codes come through his earpiece. He wouldn't normally report, since he wasn't alone, but he needed to get his ass up to the hotel room. He hated the ten codes. He knew them, but if someone was going to insert a Mayday, anyone listening would know there was trouble.

But the last two codes, the 'report to the hotel room' and 'all units must comply', had Ax moving to get Lena out of the room. If their cover was blown, he needed to get her to safety immediately.

"Lena, let's go check out the silent auction to see if there's anything you'd like to bid on."

Ax took a breath and told himself to relax. He threw Campbell a wink as he led Lena away. He leaned close to her for appearances but was surreptitiously checking the room for his team.

"There's a problem I have to check out," he whispered in Lena's ear as he led her to the elevator.

The went to the eighteenth floor, then took two flights down to make sure they weren't being followed and also just in case anyone was watching their elevator.

When he knocked on room sixteen-o-three, Jett opened the door and Ax rushed in. He didn't see anything going on the main room of the suite. Jett nodded toward the bedroom.

"Wait here," Ax told Lena as he opened the bedroom door.

Jazz was passed out on the bed. Ax turned to Jett for an explanation, but he looked pointedly at Lena. *Fuck.* They couldn't talk openly in front of her.

Just then, someone else knocked on the door. Jett rushed to get the door as Lena stood bewildered in the living room of the suite. Ax went farther into the bedroom to check Jazz's vitals.

Sam, Mase, Mitch, Nick and Bray all came rushing into the bedroom at once, looking around for a threat. Mitch stepped out and quietly closed the door. Ax was grateful Mitch would sit out there with Lena so he could help figure out what the fuck was going on.

Mase went to the bed and lifted Jazz's wrist, checking his pulse as Ax had just done. Ax opened his mouth to let Mase know he was fine but stopped himself at the gentle way Mase was touching Jazz, looking at him.

Ax had never seen the two men together, but only a blind man could miss that there was something between them. Hell, even a blind man would feel the emotions emanating from Mase. There was mostly fear and anger but also tenderness.

"Okay. What happened?" Sam asked.

"He's been roofied. He could tell there was something wrong with his drink, but he'd already taken a few sips. He didn't want to rush out immediately, so he walked around for a few minutes. He also kept taking little sips so that whoever drugged him would see him drinking."

"Fucking Jazz," Mase grumbled.

"That means he trusted you to get him here safely," Sam told Jett.

"We tried to figure out if anyone was watching him to see if they could take advantage of him in his drugged state. I stayed back, pretended to be distracted, but no one approached him," Jett said.

They all stood watching Mase check Jazz over as Jett explained the situation. Ax found his gaze kept snagging on Nick. Nick's eyes never left his older brother.

"We didn't see anyone watching," Jett continued, "but something startled Jazz. He saw something or someone and said it was time to go. He was starting to feel the effects by then and he said something about never wanting to see 'that fucking coward's face' again as long as he lived. His lips were a lot looser because of the drugs, so I got him the hell out of there and sent out a Mayday."

"We need to find out who the fuck did this." Mase stood and took two strides.

He didn't get past Sam.

"Savage," Sam called Mase by his handle as he grabbed his biceps. "Take a breath. You can't exactly go down there and start questioning people like a police officer."

"The mafia works surprisingly like the cops in these scenarios," Mase said.

"We're not in Kiev," Sam said.

"It's Jazz," was all Mase said in response.

"And he hasn't needed protection for ten years," Sam said quietly.

Ax looked at Jett to see if he had any sort of understanding of the code they were speaking. He gave Ax a shrug. Jett had been on the team longer than Ax by at least a year, but neither of them seemed to have enough history to know what had happened ten years before.

Mase nodded but didn't otherwise respond as he started pacing the room. Sam held out his hand, and as if he could read the man's mind, Bray pulled out his phone and handed it over. *What the fuck is it with all this telepathy all of a sudden?*

"Sin, I am so fucking glad you just signed up with us. We need you."

As Sam explained the situation to Max, Ax watched Nick. Bray had moved to his side, and they were talking quietly as they both watched their older brother pace.

After a few moments, Jazz thrashed on the bed a little and called out for Mase, who was kneeling by his side in an instant.

"Jazz," Mase breathed.

There was so much anguish and longing in that one word that Ax had to look away for a moment. His gaze landed on Nick, who was watching the scene unfold with what Ax suspected might be horror. No one wanted to watch their sibling fawn all over their lover.

"Mase, he was here." Jazz's words were slurred but understandable.

"Who, Jazzy? Who was here?"

"He was here, Savage. I work so hard," Jazz whined.

"I know you do."

"So hard to avoid him. I'm never where he is. Why was he here, Savage?"

"Who?"

"He's the reason. He's why I'm so fucked up. He's why I could never, will never… I'm so fucked up."

If Ax had thought Mase's voice was full of anguish, it had nothing on the tortured words that were spilling from Jazz's mouth. Bray stepped up behind Mase and put a hand of support on his shoulder. Nick stood back, wringing his hands as if he wanted to do the same but wasn't sure it would be welcomed.

"It was the bartender," Sam said. "Sin found it on the CCTV. We'll question him and try to find out where this started."

"I'll do it," Mase said.

"Stand the fuck down, Savage," Sam said. "He wants you. You stay with him. Jett is his bodyguard, so he stays. Ax and I will go."

Ax gave Sam a nod of confirmation. Mitch might be Sam's new pretend bodyguard, but he and Ax had worked closely together for over a year. They could read each other.

Chapter Five

Nick

Nick felt like he was drowning. His emotions swirled around him like an undertow, pulling him below the surface. He knew that deep down he loved Mase, but he hadn't liked him, not for a long time.

The story their father told was that when Mase had told Dad he was bisexual, Dad had asked Mase to only date women. Sure, that had been a dick move, but was it bad enough to walk away from his entire family as Mase had done?

Nick knew that wasn't the entirety of the argument between Mase and their father, but that had been the basis of the request. Their dad said that all the blame was on his shoulders, even though Mase had been the one to walk away. Nick had doubted that.

But here, now, listening to Mase beg Jazz to give him a name, Nick knew. Asking Mase to only date women was just as bad as asking Nick or Bray to stay firmly in the closet. He wasn't sure how long Mase and Jazz had been in love, but from the sound of it, it had been at least ten years.

If their father had asked Mase to give up the man he loved, Nick couldn't blame him for walking away. He just wished Mase had sent out a few feelers once Nick and Bray had been old enough to make their own choices.

Mase knelt near the bed, his face close to Jazz's, his intense gaze focused on the man passed out there. Bray rubbed Mase's shoulders. Jazz was in and out of consciousness, mostly just acting three sheets to the wind.

"Jazzy, please give me a name."

"I hate it when you call me that," Jazz slurred.

"I know." Mase chuckled then sobered. "Tell me his name, Jazzy."

"He's untouchable," was all Jazz got out before he passed out again.

"Fuck." The word was loud and drawn out as Mase pulled at his hair in frustration.

He sounded like a wounded animal. His breathing was fast and choppy. Rage throbbed from him, yet he was so gentle as he brushed Jazz's hair back from his forehead. Nick's throat burned and his eyes stung as he watched.

Mase had always been rough and aggressive but so tender with the people he loved. He'd been kind to his little brothers. Nick had somehow blocked that out.

Unable to stand back and watch but also unable to step forward and offer comfort like Bray, Nick silently slipped out of the bedroom. Ax's date, Lena, was sitting quietly on the sofa as she stared at her phone.

This situation wasn't a hell of a lot more comfortable than what was going on in the bedroom, but at least he could pretend to ignore Ax's date. Nick sat on the sofa opposite Lena. She looked up and gave him a smile.

"You get relegated to the couch too?" she asked.

"What?"

"Oh, y'know. I have no security clearance or whatever, so I'm sitting out here pretending I'm totally fine with it. Looks like you're in the same boat."

"I wasn't kicked out. No point staying in there. It's not like you can interrogate a guy who's passed out."

"Probably not too effective," she agreed.

Mitch was standing quietly by the door, and after a moment, Jett stepped out of the room as well and sat on the same sofa as Nick.

"You have any idea?" Jett asked as he flicked his head toward the bedroom.

Nick shook his head.

"Poor Mase," Jett whispered before clearing his throat and starting a conversation with Lena.

Before long, Lena and Jett were flirting back and forth. Nick wasn't sure why he was surprised. Jett was gorgeous in a square-jawed, baby-face, 'aw, shucks, ma'am' kind of way. Nick had maybe assumed that pretty much all the guys on the team were queer. Ax was bi, so maybe Jett was too. Not that it mattered, of course, except the dude was flirting with his teammate's date.

It got to the point where Nick felt like an intruder, just as he had in the bedroom. He stood to pace but ended up stepping out onto the balcony. After a moment, Mitch joined him.

"Everything okay?" Mitch asked.

"With me or with Jazz?"

"Both, I guess. Whichever needs asking. I respect Jazz, so I hope everything's all good there, but I know I'd be rushing out for a doc if things were really bad."

"Sorry you were odd man out. Jazz got roofied."

"Sam gave me the condensed version on his way out. How's Mase taking it?"

"Does everyone know about those two?"

Mitch huffed out a laugh and shook his head. "I'm not sure those two know about those two. I...uh...I've known Mase for a while. We served together before he left the military."

"That's a polite way of putting it," Nick said.

"They were wrong," Mitch shrugged. "Jazz thought there was something fishy about the whole thing. I agree. Doesn't really matter, since I think we all ended up where we were meant to be, but Mase has always been protective of Jazz, and the opposite's true as well."

Nick was pretty sure that even in his drugged state, Jazz was holding tight to the name of the guy who might have drugged him and surely fucked him up just as he'd said.

"How long have you known Mase?"

"'Bout ten years, give or take. Met him when I signed up to be a Ranger. I hadn't actually been in the army that long. We served together for six years before he left. I left not long after."

"Had Mase already met Sam and Jazz?"

"Oh yeah. Sam, Mase and Kota were in it together from the start. Jazz wasn't long behind and they included me and a few of the other guys that have joined HC."

Nick nodded. So, no one knew what had happened ten years ago except Mase, Jazz, Sam and some guy named Kota. *Just my luck.* Although maybe he didn't want to know.

"So you were close with Jazz as well?"

"Sure… We all hung out when we had time. He'd already moved on to Delta by the time I became a Green Beret."

Nick hadn't known that Jazz had been in Delta Force, but it made sense. Now he was working somewhere else with the government. Nick wasn't completely sure, but it was probably the CIA, because the DEA mostly stayed on US soil. Jazz was good at his job too, if he was still keeping all his secrets, even in a hindered state.

When the door to the suite opened, Nick and Mitch hurried back inside. Sam gave them both a hard look as he and Ax headed back to the bedroom. Jett jumped up as well. Mitch stayed out in the living room with Lena again as Nick followed the other guys back into the bedroom and closed the door.

Maybe it was petty, but there was something about closing that girl out of their private conversation that made Nick feel just a little better. He rolled his eyes at his own cattiness.

Mase stood when they all entered the room, but then he sat on the edge of the bed next to Jazz.

"We found the bartender. He said he was told it was a practical joke and that Jazz had done the same to the guy who'd paid him to do it."

"He didn't see through a bullshit story like that?" Mase demanded.

"When the guy offered him five thousand dollars, he must have decided it was worth it," Sam said.

"All the more reason to be suspicious," Bray said.

"I agree, but the guy seemed legit, and he handed over the money to us as an apology and to beg us not to turn him in. Said he couldn't afford to lose his license. I told him he'd be hearing from us about identifying the guy who paid him. He told us it was a young blond guy. Said he was 'built like a brick shithouse', but that's not very descriptive. It also doesn't particularly fit anyone we know who would want Jazz in a vulnerable position."

Nick didn't have a whole list of people who would want to harm Jazz, but he knew Sacha Clement was Jazz's biggest competition. Clement was an older, skinny brunet, not to say he didn't have a young blond stud working for him.

"What about the guy he's scared of?" Nick asked.

Everyone turned to look at him. He kept his eyes on Ax. He couldn't look at his brother, not while he suggested anything to do with Jazz's past. Ax nodded encouragingly, which surprised the hell out of Nick.

"Can Sin run a quick search to see if anyone on the guest list has ever served with Jazz? I mean, I assume it would be someone he served with." Nick stumbled at the end.

"Or someone he went to school with," Sam added. "Jazz was ROTC, just like me, so it could be someone from college, someone who hurt him before we knew him."

Nick looked at Mase just in time to watch his brother's eyes close as he probably imagined the worst. Maybe he wasn't too far off. Nick had never met Jazz before the gala, but he guessed the guy probably wasn't scared of much.

"Good thinking, kid," Sam said as lifted his phone to call Max again.

"Since everything's under control, I need to get Lena home. It's getting late," Ax said.

Sam gave Ax a nod and told him to meet back at HC when he was done. Ax gave Nick a pat on the arm as he walked past. Nick hated how that simple touch made him feel like he'd done a good job.

Chapter Six

Ax

"Z's probably awake if you want to come in and say hello," Lena said.

"Sure."

"Before we go in, I was just curious. Is…is Jett seeing anyone?"

"Jett? Oh, honey, he's a sweet guy, but he's a vet, and your brother will kill him as soon as he sees him."

"Z doesn't have to know everything." She huffed out a breath and stomped to the front door.

"I am *so* not down with lying to your brother."

"No need to lie. It's not like I asked you for his number or anything."

Ax had no doubt that Jett had given her his number as soon as he'd discovered she was a beard for the op. At least Ax could claim ignorance, even though Z would still blame him if she got her heart broken.

Lena unlocked the door of the small house she shared with her brother in Woodbridge. Luckily that area of Virginia was right on his way home from the gala they'd attended in DC.

"Lena, that you?"

"Yeah...and Ax."

Ax followed Lena into the house, even though Zayne had yet to give any response to his presence. He was sitting on the sofa...in the dark.

"You're worse than both our parents put together," Lena complained. "This wasn't even a date. There was no need to wait up in the dark to try to catch me giving someone a kiss goodnight on the porch."

"I wasn't," Z said but he didn't move to say hello to Ax.

"Night, Ax. Thanks for letting me rub elbows and all that. Hopefully it will help with my internship."

Lena gave Ax a quick hug and whispered low, "See if you can get him to crack a smile."

Ax nodded but said louder, "Just not Mrs. Campbell. Her husband's a shady character."

"As if I didn't know that by the creepy way he looked at...women," she said quickly, probably so her brother wouldn't know the geezer had been eye-fucking her.

Lena walked down the back hallway. When Z still didn't say anything, Ax made himself at home and collapsed down next to him on the sofa.

"Alissa left me," he finally said.

"Z, I didn't know. Lena didn't say anything, and you sure as shit haven't been talking to me."

"She left me for another soldier, one still on active duty, one who 'isn't missing any parts'."

"Did she say that?"

Z shrugged. "I didn't know she was so shallow. I mean, it's a pinky. Who the fuck needs a pinky

45

anyway? What are they really for?" Z gave Ax the side-eye, but there was a smirk on his face. "It's not just a pinky. I lost part of my foot too."

Ax knew most of Z's injuries. He'd been there through it all with Z. They'd been on the same team, on the same mission. Ax had been lucky enough to walk away with a few cuts and bruises.

"I'd still fuck you if you swung both ways," Ax said.

"There's scarring all up my left side."

"I'd still fuck you if you swung both ways," Ax said again.

"They had to do skin grafts, and they took chunks of skin to use on my hand — chunks out of my thigh."

"And yet, you're still a handsome motherfucker. Maybe I'm just not shallow, but I'd still fuck you."

"Shut the fuck up," Z groused, but he was smiling. "Now what the fuck did you get my sister involved in?"

"Nothing. I mean, there was this lawyer, Campbell, who she should stay far, far away from, but everyone else she was introduced to would probably be a decent contact for her."

"Campbell," Z repeated as if committing it to memory.

"He's a lawyer from the West Coast but a total misogynist."

"Not even a DC lawyer?"

"Nope."

Z nodded at that, but there was something dark lingering in his eyes, something Ax didn't like to see one bit, so he stretched back, kicked his legs up on the table and settled in.

"How 'bout we have a death match on your PlayStation?"

"You don't have to babysit me."

Ax rolled his eyes and threw one of the controllers into Z's lap.

"I had a shit night. Looks like you did, too. Let's just lose ourselves in a game for a few, all right? I can count on one finger the number of guys from our old unit who were willing to talk to me after they found out I was bi, and I'm looking at him. So, not babysitting. Maintaining a friendship."

"You had a shit night?" Z asked as he powered up the PlayStation.

"Yeah. A buddy on my team, it's looking like he has PTSD."

"Join the club," Z said.

"Yeah, well...there are a few guys on my team facing the aftereffects of serving. You should come by sometime, meet some of them."

"I'm not in the mood to share war stories," Z said.

Ax sighed and leaned back on the sofa. That wasn't what it would be like at all, but how did he explain that to someone right in the middle of their suffering?

"No matter what Alissa said, most of us come back with some baggage. Where I am, these guys I'm working with, I feel like I fit right in, baggage and all. I just thought you could fit in too."

Z nodded but didn't otherwise respond.

"I wish I could come by more—"

"Don't even start." Z cut him off. "I know what you're doing. I can only imagine how your every waking thought is focused on...I mean, if anything happened to my family. Don't mind me, Ax. I'm just having a pity party over here. I'll get over it soon enough."

Ax nodded and gave him a shoulder bump. He needed to stop by more often and make sure his friend was doing okay. He should drag him out of the house and get him to meet a few guys from the team. He imagined Z and Wade might have a lot in common.

* * * *

It was three in the morning by the time Ax rolled into HC. He'd received a text from Sam about a short debrief in the morning but also an assurance that Jazz was fine. He hadn't felt tired after the drive home from Z's house, so he'd changed out of his tuxedo and into gym shorts and a muscle shirt.

It was hard watching Z suffer. Alissa was an asshole to leave him because of the scars he'd got protecting her freedom. It pissed Ax off. The world was a horrible place, and people like Z went out there and risked their lives trying to make things a little safer.

When he got down to the gym, Ax went directly over to the heavy bag and began to tape his hands. He needed to hit something, to wear himself out so he could get a few hours of sleep before he had to debrief and probably work on the new timeline for this op around Campbell.

He'd be traveling with Nick as his 'personal assistant' and probably a 'bodyguard'. The last thing he fucking needed was Nicholas Hart in his pocket and in his face.

Ax tried to keep his anger at bay. Most of the time, he laughed so he wouldn't cry or scream. He'd spend the last two years, eleven months and thirteen days with one sole focus. Nick was a distraction — and Ax couldn't afford a distraction.

They were coming up on the three-year anniversary, and Ax felt no closer to solving the puzzle than he had been three years ago. That wasn't fully true. At least he was moving in a forward direction, taking guys off the street, making new contacts who might help him find out what had really happened.

"Date didn't end the way you wanted it to?"

Ax closed his eyes for just a second. He tried to rein himself in and ignore Nick as he went full force at the bag.

"That bad, huh?" Nick's taunting voice was a little closer this time.

"Go to bed, Nickel," Ax gritted through his teeth.

He flicked his gaze sideways and caught Nick smirking at him. This was not a smart place to be with his mood and thoughts where they were, so he turned away and started pulling the tape off his hands.

He was on the razor's edge and he knew it, so he ignored Nick's baiting and prepared to do something he never did—retreat. Of course, it would have to be Nick he'd run into at almost four a.m.

"Don't take it out on me if your date was smart enough not to fall for your bullshit."

"You think I left Jazz like that to go off and stick it to Lena?"

"I wouldn't put it past you," Nick said from behind him.

Ax must have moved faster than Nick had expected, since he didn't even fight him. He had Nick flat on his back on one of the sparring mats in less than two seconds. He was breathing hard from his workout and his anger as he looked down at a surprised Nick. He held both Nick's wrists in one hand and his neck in the other. Ax's weight pressed down on the smaller man.

"Don't fuck with me tonight, Nickel. I'm on the edge, and I have more training than you do."

"You just fight dirtier," Nick gasped out.

"Yeah, like I said, more training. I would not go fuck some chick while Jazz was drugged. I also would not fuck my best friend's little sister."

"Get off me."

"Did you hear what I fucking said? Did it sink in? Go back to bed, Nick, or stay on the other side of the gym. You can bait me all you want when we head West."

"I'm not going anywhere with you after you threw me under the bus."

"I don't know what the fuck you're talking about."

"I got reamed for telling one Lenore Archer that Jazz was passed out," Nick said as he struggled to free himself.

Ax kept his hold, but he was going to have to let go or they'd have a problem in a minute. He didn't think his body was capable of getting hard when he was in one of these moods. Yet there he was, his cock twitching to life against his will because a certain Hart brother was writhing beneath him.

"You damn well shouldn't have told her. She needs to be able to honestly say she knew nothing that happened. She's an innocent bystander in all this. I shouldn't have brought her."

He was going to talk to Sam about putting someone on her. Putting someone—who was *not* Jett Lowell—on her six to tail her for a month or so to make sure Campbell didn't find her. He hadn't realized that Campbell considered himself some kind of connoisseur. Most traffickers just took what they could get.

"I'm sure you could have called one of your fuck buddies to be your date."

"You jealous, Nickel?"

"No. I—"

Ax did the dumbest thing he'd ever done in his entire life. Instead of backing away from Nick Hart, he pressed down. He groaned when he found Nick just as hard as he was. Their dicks rubbed together and Nick gasped. *Yeah, it's good.*

There were sparks of something arcing between them. Ax was pretty sure it was hatred, at least on Nick's side. Ax didn't have much experience being attracted to someone he despised, but Nick looked like he was struggling with exactly that conundrum at that moment. Ax leaned down to whisper in Nick's ear.

"Sometimes angry sex is the best."

When he let Nick's hands go, they fell to Ax's ass and pressed him down harder as he ground against Nick again and again. He would have laughed if he hadn't been pushing his tongue into Nick's mouth.

He'd wanted Nick from the moment he'd seen him, and Nick had hated him at least that long.

The kiss was sharp and biting. Ax cupped the back of Nick's head to get a better angle but didn't gentle the kiss at all. Nick's fingers were so deep in Ax's ass cheeks that he'd probably be able to get the kid's fingerprints off him.

The grinding was as frantic as the kiss. Ax was already close, so he slowed down a little, since he couldn't back off with Nick pulling him closer. He thought maybe he'd scared Nick. But by the way Nick was alternating between sucking his tongue and biting Ax's bottom lip, he was with him all the way.

Ax would have given just about anything in that moment to have a rubber and some lube, but he hadn't planned on seeing anyone in the gym, let alone getting down and dirty on the sparring mats.

Insinuating his hand between them, Ax released Nick's erection from the confines of his shorts. Nick had some excellent girth. He was definitely a handful in more than one sense of the word.

Nick growled and began thrusting frantically into Ax's hand. *The selfish little prick.* Ax pulled away and Nick protested until he realized what Ax was up to. In seconds, he had Nick back in hand. They both pulled in a breath as their bare cocks touched.

Ax swiped some pre-cum from where they were both leaking to use for natural lube as he started pumping his hand over their dicks. Nick was panting, his pupils blown, his neck arched. Ax bit back any pretty words he might have used in any other circumstance and gripped them both tighter.

Nick whined and his hips started pumping so hard that he almost threw Ax off him. Ax adjusted his weight and quickened the speed of his thrusts.

"Please," Nick whispered.

That was all it took to throw Ax over the edge. He leaned close and bit down on Nick's neck to keep from screaming his lungs out. The release was cathartic. It wore him out more than punching the heavy bag. As soon as Ax's teeth sank into Nick's skin, he followed Ax over. His body bowed off the floor and convulsed as he spurted his release between them.

Ax licked at the red indentations his teeth had left in Nick's smooth skin. They both panted but didn't move. He took that as a sign that at least Nick wasn't disgusted.

Ax took a deep breath. His mood wasn't black anymore and he was unbelievably grateful for that. Ax tucked himself away before finally rolling off Nick. He lay on his back, looking at the ceiling and still panting.

"Fuck, I needed that," Ax said.

When he didn't hear a response, Ax turned to look at Nick. He was fingering the welt on his neck as he stared, unseeing, at the ceiling.

"You like it rough, don't you Nickel?"

Nick's hand dropped from his neck as his gaze speared Ax.

"I told you I could show you how it's done."

Ax reached over to run a fingertip along the bite mark, but Nick pushed his hand away and stood from the mat. Ax sighed. He teased. It was part of who he was. He wasn't sure why Nick had such an issue with it. Ax rubbed his hands over his face.

"Nick…" he started, but realized Nick was already gone.

Chapter Seven

Nick

If Ax could just keep his mouth shut, Nick might almost be able to explain his attraction to the asshole. He couldn't believe he'd let Ax jack him off. He definitely couldn't believe it was probably the best orgasm he'd ever had.

No one had ever pounced on him, ripped his shorts down and tugged on him so hard that his cock might get bruised. No one have ever wanted him that badly — or just wanted to get off that badly. For Ax, it seemed to be a proximity thing.

Nick had just been lucky enough to be the closest cock — or maybe the closest human, since Ax was bi. Letting Ax touch him had been beyond stupid. He traced his fingertips over the bite mark on his neck. His body was stupid enough to want to do it all over again.

Nick went up to his room and tried to get some sleep, but his mind kept going back to that sparring mat. His dick kept tenting his sheets, but he refused to get himself off to thoughts of Ax.

After a few hours of tossing and turning, Nick got up and headed back down to the gym. This time, he avoided the sparring mats, even though Ax was nowhere to be seen. It had been quick, but the sex had been so hot that he'd probably get at least a semi every time he walked by the damn things.

Ax had been taking out his aggression on the heavy bag, but Nick usually preferred to run. Headphones on, he cranked up the treadmill and tried to run away from every memory he and Ax had created earlier that morning.

By the time he headed for the showers, Nick was drenched in sweat and pissed that he would probably be able to fall into bed and sleep, but it was eight a.m., so there was no chance that was happening.

When he stepped out of the shower, Nick felt relatively normal again. His muscles ached, but from exercise this time. He didn't want every twinge to remind him of Ax.

He needed to back out of the op. Sure, he wanted West Coast, but Ax had a monopoly on West Coast ops. Nick didn't want to work with a team lead who went over his head without even addressing the situation with him. He needed to be able to trust his teammates.

Nick hadn't said Jazz was drugged. It wasn't like he'd compromised the op or anyone's safety. All Lena knew was that Jazz had passed out. People drank too much all the time.

Ax wasn't scheduled to debrief until this morning, so he would have had to call Wade to make him aware of whatever it was Lena had told him.

"Hey," Mitch said as he caught up with Nick in the hallway.

"Hey."

Nick was *so* not in the mood to chitchat, but Mitch seemed awkward. He was normally a confident guy, but he was stiffer than usual.

"I hope you're not pissed at me," Mitch said.

"Pissed? Why would I be pissed at you?"

Mitch shrugged. "I'm good at my job, but I've lost friends because of my honesty before."

"Your honesty? Did you say something last night that I don't remember?"

"No, but Wade and Sam didn't seem happy that you told Miss Archer about Jazz."

"Wait," Nick stopped dead in the hall. "*You're* the one who told Wade?"

"Well, yeah. In my debrief. I was worried she might infer Jazz had been drugged. I wanted to make sure Wade and Sam knew. She's an innocent bystander. She shouldn't know anything about our op, anything that might put her in danger. Honestly, Ax probably shouldn't have brought her with him to the room."

Nick could get behind that statement one hundred percent. In fact, Ax shouldn't have brought her to the gala at all if she was his precious best friend's younger sister. Then again, Jett had sent out a Mayday and demanded all team members respond.

"I'm not mad. I just would have appreciated a heads-up."

"Oh, well, we can't discuss anything before debrief." Mitch said. "My goal wasn't to throw you under the bus."

Nick paused at the wording, since he'd said the exact same phrase when he'd thought it had been Ax who'd told Wade what he'd said.

"Debriefs happen like that for a reason," Mitch continued, "so our memories are fresh and not affected by others."

"I get that, but when we were out on the balcony, or later, after Ax and Lena were gone, you could have addressed it with me directly. I'm open to feedback. Then I could have been the one to tell Wade and Sam — or at least I would have realized it was worth mentioning."

Nick rubbed his neck. He'd been blindsided when they'd asked him about it.

"It wasn't like I was trying to hide it," Nick said. "I would have at least mentioned it so it wouldn't have appeared like I was trying to gloss over something I didn't realize was a big deal. I would have felt like you had my back."

"All right," Mitch said with a nod. "I can do that. I don't want you to think I'm grading you or trying to be team lead when it's not my op. I try not to give opinions. Sam almost kicked my ass for my opinion on his behavior after the op in Spain with your brother."

"Yeah, I bet." Nick laughed. "I'm not pissed at you. I mean, it sucks that I got reamed after my first op — and a mini op at that — but I should have kept my mouth shut."

"And I should have reminded you of the potential to put a civilian at risk, so you didn't say anything else. So we're cool?"

"Yeah, we're cool."

Mitch gave him a bright smile and a pat on the shoulder before heading off in a different direction.

Nick blew out a breath. He didn't like the fact that he'd fucked up on his first op, but he really didn't like the fact that he was a hypocrite. He'd been considering declining an op when he thought Ax had reported him. But when he'd realized it had been Mitch and listened to why Mitch had done it, he could understand.

If he searched hard enough, he would find that he'd been looking for a reason to back off ops that included Ax. He didn't like being laughed at, and Ax always seemed to be doing just that.

Nick took the stairs instead of the elevator as he made his way to the second floor. He paused on the landing and wondered if coming to work for Mase's company had been the right move.

He was worried about his dad, but he also couldn't be without a job indefinitely. He hoped his father had some more time left. If he thought his dad was really going to die soon, he would have delayed getting a job. Dad seemed to be moving past each hiccup in his path.

Nick was really the only one their father had. Sure, Bray had forgiven him, but their relationship was strained at best. Mase responded to Nick's emails, but he didn't want to hear anything about their dad at all.

When he heard the door on the landing above him open and slam shut, Nick started making his way up to the second floor. He opened the door from the stairwell just as Bray stepped off the elevator.

"You get any sleep?" Nick asked.

"A few hours," Bray said, but the dark circles under his bloodshot eyes told a different story. "You?"

Nick shrugged. He didn't want to lie, but he also didn't want to tell his brother he hadn't slept a wink. Bray sighed and tugged Nick by the arm into one of the private work rooms.

"You look as bad as I feel," Bray said when he shut the door.

"I was just thinking the same thing about you," Nick admitted. "How's Jazz? Have you seen him?"

"Yeah. Dee's been hovering over him. She gave him some godawful drink this morning, but it seems like it might have helped. I'm not sure he remembers much about last night."

"If he was coherent enough to hold back names, he probably remembers some of it."

"That might have been his training kicking in. Max found a name."

Nick closed his eyes against the memories of their brother begging Jazz for a name.

"Do you think Jazz is the reason Mase came out to Dad?" Nick asked.

"What do you mean?"

"Dad told me. He told me he asked Mase to stick to girls because he was bi, but I thought…"

"Great minds," Bray said. "I wondered the same thing, if Mase had come out because he'd been in love with a guy. But I don't think it could be Jazz. I think Jazz is a year or two younger than Mase, and Dee says he lived with her in Louisiana until he went off to college."

Nick nodded. He hadn't gotten friendly with Jazz's grandmother, Dee, but all the other guys seemed to treat her like a surrogate grandma.

"How long do you think he's been in love with him then?" Nick asked.

Bray shrugged. They both knew it was at least ten years. Nick couldn't imagine pining after someone that long. He also couldn't imagine choosing to work with someone when being around them hurt as much as being around Jazz obviously hurt Mase.

"What's the name?" Nick asked.

"Martin Coleman. He's an up-and-coming politician. He's a congressman for Texas. His father is a senator from Texas."

"Shit. No wonder Jazz kept his mouth shut. Charles Coleman?"

Bray nodded. The guy was a right-wing conservative who still called anal sex 'sodomy' and thought it should be a crime. He was trying to move the great state of Texas back into the 1950s, even as most other states were finally embracing the new millennium.

"What's Mase gonna do?" Nick asked.

"Not sure. Max hasn't told him yet. Mase wouldn't leave Jazz's side until he was better, but then…I think they had a fight or something and he left. He's meeting with some of Kozak's contacts. Seems his people have some connections in the nation's capitol."

Nick nodded.

"Don't tell anyone about Coleman, okay? I only know because Max told Sam and me together. I mean it's not officially part of an op, but you suggested getting Max involved and he came through."

"Pretty damn quick."

"Sometimes I'm scared of how smart he is," Bray admitted.

"Good thing he's on our side."

"Yeah. Hopefully he's smarter than whoever the other guys have in their pocket."

Nick couldn't imagine anyone smarter than Max, but he also would never have imagined one person who could do all that Max could.

Nick and Bray made their way out to the bullpen. Nick walked over to speak with Wade and get an update on the timeline. Wade informed him that he would be heading to San Francisco with Ax and Jett within seventy-two hours.

They were just wrapping things up when Max approached Wade's desk. The poor kid looked awkward and unsure. He used to have that same look whenever he approached Bray. It was like he was gearing up to face rejection. Nick gave him an encouraging smile and a nod.

Nick had always wondered why Max hadn't bitten the bullet and asked Bray out. Maybe he figured they were better as friends, but it seemed Max had a new crush.

Nick squashed the relief he felt that Max had set his sights on Wade. Max cleared his throat and Wade turned to see who was behind him.

"Max," Wade said, "what can I do for you?"

"I didn't mean to interrupt."

"You're not." Nick said. "We were just wrapping up."

Nick stood to leave as Max stuttered on.

"I, um, created a program to improve your video surveillance."

"Already?" Wade asked.

"Yes. I also found Dakota Strickland."

"Fuck. That was fast. Let me get Sam up here...and Jazz. I'll see if Mase can maybe join by phone. We all want to know about Kota. We'll want to see everything you found."

"Okay. I can go get my laptop, but I also need to ask a question."

"Shoot," Wade said as he started typing out something on his phone, probably a text to Sam.

"Is it against company policy for teammates to have a" — Max stopped to clear his throat — "romantic relationship?"

Nick choked on his own spit and started coughing. Max moved around the desk and patted him on the back as he continued on his tirade.

"I wasn't sure. I mean, I know that Bray and Sam are seeing each other, but that all started before Bray was technically part of the HC team. I didn't know if it was kosher for" — Max paused and looked at Nick for a moment before continuing on — "well, for two teammates to start seeing each other."

Nick was a sympathetic guy but he was no empath. That was more Bray's style. Yet there he was, cringing because he was so embarrassed on Max's behalf.

He was sure Max was going to ask Wade out and probably be shot down right in the middle of the bullpen. He wanted to stop his friend from getting hurt, so he reached out to touch Max's arm, but stopped dead when he saw what he would have sworn was interest in Wade's eyes. Wade cleared his throat.

"It's not against company policy. We would want to know upfront because it might compromise a mission."

"Of course," Max agreed. "Thank you."

Max turned and gave Nick a relieved smile. He patted Nick's arm and turned to walk away. Nick and Wade both watched him go with open mouths. It seemed they'd both expected him to use the knowledge immediately.

They also snapped their mouths shut when Max approached Ax. Nick swallowed thickly and his gaze dropped just in time to see Wade's nostrils flare.

Nick didn't want to watch what happened next. His eyes lifted of their own accord just in time to see Ax laugh and nod.

"Fuck," Wade whispered.

Nick could only grunt in agreement.

Chapter Eight

Ax

"Ax." Max pulled him aside as soon as he made it to the bullpen.

"What's up?"

"I...uh...I created this program to make the surveillance more efficient both in and around the building..."

"Wow. Already? I guess I shouldn't be surprised by anything you can do."

"Thanks, but I saw something you might not want drawn to anyone's attention. I would have given it to Nick, but Wade was right there."

Ax looked over Max's shoulder and saw that both Wade and Nick were watching them. They also both looked shell-shocked. Max had probably just awed them with his brilliance.

"Nick?" Ax asked. *Why would he give something to him that was for Nick?*

"Yeah." Max cleared his throat. "In the gym, early this morning…"

Ax's eyes widened as he realized what Max had seen.

"I honestly forgot about the cameras. Normally, I'd just brazen it out, but I really appreciate you keeping this under your hat. I'm not sure Nick would be okay with the brazen approach."

"It's not like he has anything to regret. It was the hottest thing I've ever seen. Better than porn."

Ax couldn't hold back the laugh that burst out of him at Max's comment. It was by far one of the hottest encounters he'd ever had.

"I deleted the footage from all the servers, but I put it on this drive in case…well, some people like to make movies or whatever. I didn't know if you and Nick…"

"Fuck. You're gonna kill me," Ax groaned.

He would love to see the video, but no way was he going to watch it without Nick knowing it existed. He was a hundred percent sure that Nick would want any evidence of them together erased. Ax would never use it against Nick, but the memories of that morning were already in his spank bank for future use, even if Nick hated his guts.

Ax gave Max's shoulder a squeeze and a nod as he thanked him. Max discreetly passed him the USB drive and walked away with a smile and a wave. As Ax approached Wade's desk, both Wade and Nick frowned at him.

"Hey" Ax said. "I'm here for my debrief as scheduled."

Wade looked at him for a long moment before finally nodding.

"Nick and I were just going over the timeline. Let's get that nailed down. I'll have Dee schedule your accommodations in San Francisco for arrival in forty-eight hours. You'll be staying in a penthouse condo you just purchased under your alias in Nob Hill. There are five bedrooms, all with private baths, so it'll be a cushy situation for the three of you heading out."

Ax nodded. He'd stayed in some of the most expensive hotels in Europe and some of the shittiest motels in the US. He'd take luxury every day of the week if he had his choice.

"You good, Nick?" Wade asked.

Nick nodded but didn't look at Ax. *No surprise there.* He turned on his heel and left.

"Let's get to it," Wade said as he stood and made his way to the war room.

Chase joined them to take notes and ask additional questions, since Sam and Jazz had both been on the op as well. They made their way through the debrief quickly and efficiently until the last question.

"Why did you feel it necessary to take Lenore up to the room?" Wade asked.

"It was a Mayday. No one was available to watch over her, and I didn't want her telling Campbell any truths about herself. He doesn't know her real first or last name. He doesn't know where she lives or what she does. I needed to keep it that way."

"It was a public place, Ax —"

"Do you know what type of 'human capital' he trades in?"

"Of course. He doesn't seem to do a lot of business, but he makes a shitload on each 'transaction'."

"From what he was telling me, he caters to people's tastes. If he thought Lena was what one of his clients was looking for, he'd risk a lot more to get her if she was worth a few million. He's no snatch-and-grab op. I think he looks for people with specific traits. If I'd known that beforehand, I wouldn't have brought Lena at all."

Wade sighed. Ax tried not to be bothered by the disappointment in Wade's eyes. It had really been his only option, and Wade had been the one to tell him to bring a beautiful woman.

"I get that it's tough when we have to make accommodations. There was a Mayday, and you hustled upstairs. Knowing how many other operators were there, it might have been better to have put Lenore in an Uber and sent her home."

Ax bit back the urge to say, "Yes, sir." They weren't in the military anymore and he would have wanted to wait there with Lena to make sure she got in the Uber and safely away from Campbell.

"I'll try to consider all options next time," Ax conceded.

With a nod, Wade signaled to Chase that they were done. There was a knock on the door. Chase went to answer it, and as he left the room, Sam and Jazz came in.

"Max already found Kota?" Sam asked.

"He ran up to get his laptop so he can show us everything he found."

"You need anything else from me?" Ax asked.

Wade gave him a long, assessing look but shook his head. Ax stood and left the room just as Max was approaching. Ax gave him a wink as he passed by.

When he slipped his hand into his pocket, Ax fingered the USB. He should probably talk to Nick about the fact that they'd been caught on surveillance, even though they were now safe from everyone finding out and teasing them mercilessly.

When he didn't see Nick in the bullpen, he decided to head up to the fourth floor and seek him out. He probably owed him an apology, but he admitted to himself he wouldn't be able to choke out the words. When the elevator doors opened, Dee came walking down the hall.

"Mornin', Cher," she said.

"You spend all night taking care of your wayward grandson?"

"Wayward," she chuckled. "*Pauvre ti bête*. He was sick as a dog."

"He looked fine just now. Good thing you were here to take care of him."

Dee gave him a nod of agreement.

"You look tired, Abuelita," Ax said. "Let me take you down to your room." He'd called her 'grandma' since he'd been working at HC and she treated all the boys like adopted grandsons, but Jazz would always be her heart.

"I hate elevators," she sighed but stepped in with him.

"That's a lot of stairs when you've been up all night."

"*C'est vrais*," she sighed. "I wish I had a cure for his nightmares."

"I wish you had a cure for all our nightmares."

Dee smiled as she reached up and patted his cheek.

"You'll never look love in the eye and run away, Cher."

Ax didn't know what to say to that, so he laid his hand over hers for a moment. He didn't know Jazz's whole story, but he knew he hadn't had an easy life.

Dee couldn't have either, raising her grandson after his mom had died.

He also knew Dee's son had died serving in the military, but he didn't know much beyond that. She'd told him tons of stories about Jazz's childhood, but she didn't really talk about either of her children.

After escorting Dee to her apartment on the first floor, Ax looked around for Nick. When he didn't find him, he figured he'd give him space. They'd be holed up together once they were in San Francisco. They'd get a chance to talk then.

For now, it was back to the grindstone. He had a personal mission that was always at the forefront of his mind…Cherie. When they got back from San Francisco, he was hoping to pull Max aside and get some advice on how to proceed.

He was chomping at the bit to pick Max's brain, but every time he went to find the kid, he was in meetings. Everyone wanted his time. It wasn't like Ax could pull him out of a business meeting to ask for help on a personal level, no matter how badly he wanted to.

Instead, Ax did what he normally would. He spent every free waking hour looking, asking questions where he could, anonymously visiting chat rooms and forums—always searching for information.

Chapter Nine

Nick

Nick did his best to ignore Ax on the cross-country flight. He'd wanted to give him the cold shoulder, but Ax had promptly fallen asleep as soon as they'd been in the air.

Nick was back to wanting to quit this stupid job. Ax was such a dick. Who had sex with someone then accepted a date with someone else just a few hours later? The only thing keeping him from actually quitting was his refusal to make such big life decisions based on one asshole.

Plus, he was sort of feeling like he might want to get to know Mase a little better, and this was his best chance without having to seek him out. Working together might just help them build a relationship organically. He was still hoping to talk Mase into at least one face-to-face visit with their dad.

When they landed, Jett went to pick up their rental car while Ax and Nick waited for their luggage. Nick wanted to be pissed at Ax, but he looked a little green around the gills. He was tight where he was usually relaxed.

He had circles under his eyes, despite having slept the entire six-hour flight. Add that to his middle-of-the-night workout and Nick realized that he probably wasn't getting much sleep. For a man who seemed to have an easy life living for free in HC, even though he scooped up all the high-paying assignments, today he seemed to have the world on his shoulders.

"Ruby?" a woman yelled across the baggage area.

Ax stiffened beside him. Nick looked up to see him cringe before peeking over his shoulder. An older woman ran over and started speaking to him rapidly in Spanish. Nick only caught part of the conversation because his Spanish was rusty, but she seemed pissed that she hadn't known he was in town.

"I have work," Ax bit out.

"Were you going to come to San Francisco without even a visit to your family?"

The family resemblance was striking, so she was obviously Ax's mother, and Nick could tell she'd once been a beautiful young woman, but the tension lines around her mouth made her look probably every year of her age. Tears gathered in her eyes as she looked imploringly at Ax. It ripped Nick's heart out. He could never stand to see his mother cry.

"It's my fault," Nick said before Ax could hurt his mother's feelings even more. "I didn't —"

"Is this your boyfriend?" she asked Ax.

Nick had been about to say that he hadn't left any time in the schedule for Ax to have any personal time. But Ax's mother zeroed in on him, and the hope shining from her eyes tore what was left of his heart to shreds.

He could tell Ax was about to dash his mother's hopes. Nick did the only thing he could think of. He slipped his hand into Ax's and twined their fingers together. He wasn't sure how such a sweet woman had raised such a coldhearted dickhead, but Nick wouldn't be the one to make the woman cry.

"It's new. I wanted to join Ax on his business trip, but I wasn't sure I was ready to meet his family."

Before he even got the whole sentence out, the woman was hugging him and whispering how happy she was to meet him into his ear. Nick awkwardly wrapped his free arm around her and patted her back. She also told Nick to make sure Ax got more rest. By the time she pulled back, Nick's face was flaming. *Did Ax's mother just tell him to lay off the sex?*

"I'm Marcella, Rubio's mom. Call me 'Cella'."

"It's a pleasure to meet you, Cella. I'm Nick."

"Mom, what are you doing at the airport?"

"I was dropping off your Uncle Leo. He just came for a visit and is flying back to Arizona."

"Then why are you in the baggage claim?"

Cella suddenly seemed unable to look Ax or Nick in the eye. Nick had no idea what it was all about, but there was tension flowing from Ax in waves and he squeezed Nick's hand so hard that Nick grunted.

"Mom…"

Ax's voice was rough and weak. Nick looked up. Any anger he felt toward Ax eased a little. There was so much pain in his eyes that Nick could almost feel it right along with him. He looked tortured.

"You'll stay with us," Cella announced.

"Mom, we can't stay at your house. We're here on business."

"It's *your* house. You bought it, and you can stay in it."

"Mom—"

"We're here with another of Ax—I mean Rubio's—business partners. He's going to be picking us up at any moment."

"But surely you can save the company some money and stay with us for at least a night or two?"

"We'll see, Mama."

"We'll talk about it tonight at dinner," she said as she wrapped her arms around Ax.

Ax closed his eyes as if both relishing and hating his mother's touch. Nick imagined that was how Bray felt about their father. He couldn't help but wonder about the family dynamic that caused the pain in Ax's family.

Ax opened his mouth and Nick just knew in this guts that Ax was going to refuse to even see his family. Nick might not be able to bring his own family back together, but he'd do his best to throw this one into the same room.

"Let us know what time," Nick said.

"Ruby knows. He knows the time and place. See you tonight."

Cella reached up to pat Ax's cheek before hurrying off. Had she known that Ax was on the verge of telling her they wouldn't come?

"Why the fuck did you do that?" Ax growled as he turned to Nick. There was still pain in his eyes, even though he tried to hide it behind the anger.

Nick shrugged. "I couldn't watch you break your mom's heart."

"I already did that three years ago," Ax said as he yanked one of their suitcases off the baggage carousel. "What if you just put her in danger? I don't want anyone attaching her to my alias."

Nick licked his lips. "Can't we find a way to make sure they're still safe but not heartbroken?"

Ax shook his head.

Nick pulled off his bag and Jett's. Ax remained silent while they moved out to the curb where Jett was already waiting. He'd thought Ax was so easygoing, but now his body was stiff as a board.

As soon as they got to the luxury condo, Ax closed himself in the master bedroom. Nick took one of the guest rooms a little farther down the hall and Jett took the 'servants' quarters' closest to the front door, since he was on security detail.

With five bedrooms and eight bathrooms in the pricey condo, it was fancier than Nick would have expected. Then again, if that Campbell guy wanted someone with money, they needed him to be impressed by Ax's address.

Nick settled into his room, since they'd be there for about a week—maybe longer, depending on how fast they could make things move to get a look into Campbell's organization.

Once unpacked, he called his dad then his mom to check in. With nothing left to do, he walked around the condo, checking everything out. When he found Jett relaxing on a couch in front of a huge projector TV, he plopped down and tried to relax along with him.

His mind kept going back to Ax and their interaction with his mom. Love for his mother had been apparent in everything he said and did, but it seemed painful for him to be around her. *Why?*

"You wanna order in some grub?" Jett asked.

Nick opened his mouth to answer when he heard a bitter voice booming into the room from behind them.

"He can't. He roped us into dinner with my folks by pretending to be my boyfriend."

Jett's eyes popped wide as he looked back at Ax to see if he was joking, then at Nick. Nick shrugged, even though he wanted punch Ax in the throat.

"I couldn't break his mom's heart. She probably thinks his only relationship is with his hand."

Jett gave a snorted laugh, but the smile fell from his face when he looked back at Ax. Nick didn't need to look behind himself to know Ax wasn't smiling. He could feel the tension from across the room.

"Let's go, Nickel. We have to make sure we're not being followed, so we have to leave early."

Nick rolled his eyes but stood from the sofa. *I'm sure to be punished for trying to do something nice.*

Chapter Ten

Ax

The closer they got to his parents' house, the more tempting it was to turn the car around and just...leave. After dropping his uncle off at the airport, his mom had stayed and walked around the arrival baggage claim — like she'd chance a glimpse of Cherie returning home after almost three years?

That was what killed him, the hope. The hope in his parents' eyes that they'd find her, that Ax would find her like he'd promised them three fucking years ago.

He'd tried calling his mom to cancel. This whole thing was a bad idea. It had been the hope in her voice that had him swallowing down his objections and agreeing to come. He felt the need to make everything up to his parents, to make up for the fact that he could have done something to prevent what had happened.

Every day his sister Cherie was gone was like a year, and yet he pretended to go on with his life. He acted like everything was fine.

But she was always there in his dreams, crying out to him, screaming his name. Most of his nights were spent searching. His days were spent searching, too, but searching for the scum who took people like Cherie away from their families. It was the only thing that eased the pain.

"I didn't realize how painful it would be for you to be around your family. Your mom seemed fine with you dating a guy. Is it your dad?"

"Can we just *not*? Besides, we're here," Ax said as he pulled the car into the driveway of his parents' house.

Nick whistled as he stepped out of the car and shut the door. Ax looked at the house. He'd wanted a safe place for Diego and a beautiful place for Cherie to come back to. He didn't want his parents to worry about rent or money. There was still a big Cherie-sized hole in his plan.

"You bought this place for your folks? No wonder you jump on every assignment."

There wasn't censure in Nick's remark, so Ax let it go. He had enough to deal with. He hadn't been home in six months. He'd tried to come see Diego, but it was so hard to sit down with his family and not rage or sob or… Ax tried to pack away all the powerful emotions so he wouldn't end up falling apart in front of everyone.

The front door opened before they even set foot on the path that led from the driveway. Ax's mom stood there with a huge smile on her face. She'd clearly been worried he'd cancel. He almost had about a dozen times. She had no idea that his presence could put her in danger.

"Come in. Come in." She gave Nick a hug, then Ax. "Dinner's ready. I made ceviche, arroz con pollo, baleadas, licuados con mango and arroz con leche."

Ax groaned. He'd have to eat it all since they were his favorites, but his stomach felt tight and sick.

"I don't understand anything you just said except ceviche, but I love that, so I think I'll be okay," Nick said.

"Two desserts?" Ax complained.

His mom smiled and patted him on the cheek. She seemed actually happy. He was sure it was an act for Nick's sake, but the smile seemed real. It reached her eyes. How could she be happy he was there instead of out searching?

"What's baleadas?" Nick asked. "Is it testicles? I won't eat testicles, even if your mom went out of her way to make them."

Ax smiled. A real smile, and he would have laughed if he wasn't nauseated.

"Relax. It's like a burrito."

"I know pollo is chicken."

"She made things she knows I like — chicken and rice, ceviche, burritos, mango smoothie and rice pudding."

"She went all out. Sounds amazing."

"Yeah, amazing."

Nick gave him a side-eye and headed into the house. Ax's mom introduced Nick to his father and his brother Diego. Diego looked about two inches taller than the last time Ax had seen him.

The table was set and ready. His mom had probably been pacing by the front door looking for his headlights. Ax sighed as they sat down at the table. His mom was an amazing cook. The food was so good that Ax found himself eating more than he thought he would.

His dad seemed relaxed, but he caught Diego casting sullen looks around the table. Nick didn't seem to notice anything as he shoveled food into his face and made embarrassing sex noises.

"This is amazing," Nick said.

Ax's mom beamed as she patted Nick's hand, the hand that wasn't busy stuffing his face.

"Next time I'll make nacatamale, sopa de caracol and tres leche."

"It's been a while since I've spoken any Spanish. So soup of some kind and milk?" Nick asked.

"It's like a tamale, then seafood soup and three-milk cake."

"Cake? I'm in." Nick nodded.

Ax wanted to kick him under the table. His mom was trying to use food to lure Nick back, and Ax right along with him. Everyone seemed to be talking around Ax like they knew he was about to explode.

"How long have you been dating?" Diego asked.

Ax looked over at his dad. He knew he was lucky. Fernando Guttierez wasn't his biological father. He'd met Ax's mom when she had already been pregnant and was fleeing her abusive husband in Honduras. She'd escaped to America with hopes of a better life, and she'd found it.

Still, in the Latin culture, there were a lot of preconceived notions about homosexuality. Ax was bi but Nando had never cared. He'd loved Ax regardless. He'd never treated him as anything less than his own son, even after Cherie and Diego had been born.

Ax always thought of Cherie when he came to his parents' house, even though she'd never lived there. She was always in the back of his mind, but when he was with his family, it was like he was drowning in guilt and regret. He had to escape to be able to breathe, to move forward and do what he needed to do.

"We've known each other about six months, but only recently have we started seeing each other," Nick said.

Ax almost snorted. He might have gotten his hands on Nick, but he sure as hell hadn't seen much of anything. Nick probably regretted even going that far.

"You work together?" Dad asked.

"Yeah. I just joined HC. I left the military a few months ago. Both my brothers work at HC, so — "

"Mase, his older brother, started HC when he left the army. Most the guys there are former military," Ax added.

"And you do corporate security too?" Dad asked Nick.

"I'm still learning the ropes," Nick hedged. "I'm trying to stay on the West Coast so I can be closer to my parents."

Nick's gaze shot to Ax, as if just realizing he was painting himself as a fabulous son when Ax was a horrible one who avoided his family at all costs.

"My dad is having a lot of health problems. It's part of the reason I didn't re-up in the army and moved over to IRR."

Nick didn't even realize he'd stepped in it again. Ax had left the army for family reasons as well. He'd planned to make the military his career. He'd dutifully sent money home to help his parents and wanted to continue to do so. The army made that a better possibility.

"What's IRR?" Diego asked when the silence stretched out too long.

Nick looked around at everyone at the table before answering. He probably wondered why Diego didn't know, since Ax had done the same thing. The truth was that Diego didn't know, but his parents did. They'd encouraged him to choose the reserves so he'd at least draw some pay, but he'd wanted to devote all his time to finding Cherie.

"Technically when you sign up for the army, you sign up for eight years. After four or six, you can move over to the Reserves or to Individual Ready Reservist. I chose IRR so I wouldn't have to go in except for one weekend a month and a couple weeks each year. I could still be pulled back in, but it's up to me to stay in good shape and keep my skills sharp."

"Will corporate security help you keep your skills sharp?" Mom asked.

Ax was ready to call a halt to all the questions so his parents wouldn't figure out he'd lied about the dangers of his job. Nick continued on before he could.

"Corporate security? No. But working with a bunch of guys in the same situation or even those who've served out all their time will. I have access to a shooting range just as consistently as I did in the army, and I spar with guys like Sam and Wade, who were elite soldiers. I never got to spar with Delta Force or Navy SEALs when I was a First Lieutenant."

"These are the men you work with?" Ax's mother demanded as she looked at him.

Ax nodded but didn't add anything. His mother looked at him for a long time before finally looking away. *She knows.* Nick had tried to alleviate their worries, but now his mother would worry more. He'd made himself seem like a desk jockey, and Nick had all but obliterated that.

Ax shoved food into his mouth but tasted nothing. Nick and Diego kept trying to carry the conversation past the awkward silences, but Ax just wanted to throw up. He'd disappointed his parents...again.

"What concert?" his mother asked a few moments later.

"Not a concert, a music festival. I was going to go with some friends."

"No," his mother said immediately and with finality.

"Cella," his father chided.

"No," she said again, just as firmly.

"I'm sixteen. One of the other kids going is fourteen."

"Your age doesn't change the answer." His mother stood from the table and started clearing dinner dishes.

"Ax." Diego looked at him with a plea for help in his eyes.

Ax looked at his brother. About eighty percent of people pulled into human trafficking were women. But more than that, the majority were Latino, and minors tended to be more vulnerable. Ax knew all the statistics, and his parents did too.

Without answering Diego, Ax looked down at his half-eaten dinner. He couldn't be part of this conversation. Diego wouldn't want his opinion on this.

"This is ridiculous. I'm a brown belt in karate and you still won't let me go to a freaking music festival? I can take care of myself. I won't end up like—"

"Enough," Ax roared as he stood from the table so quickly that his chair fell back.

He was breathing as if he'd run a marathon. Maybe he was having a heart attack, but he couldn't handle Diego acting like what happened had been Cherie's fault. It wasn't, and no one could guarantee the same thing wouldn't happen to Diego.

Without another word, Ax turned and left the house. He was slamming the car door shut when he remembered Nick. He'd give him exactly two minutes before leaving his ass behind.

Chapter Eleven

Nick

Nick sat there with his fork halfway to his mouth. Dinner had been tense and awkward, but Ax walking out because his brother wanted to go to a concert seemed a tiny bit over the top.

His mouth still open, Nick looked around at each of Ax's family members before laying his fork down and closing his trap.

"Uh," he said as he stood and rubbed the back of his neck, "thanks for dinner, Cella. It was delicious, but I'd better go make sure Ax is okay."

"Here." Cella stepped forward and handed him a heavy bag that he had no doubt was full of food. "Take this with you. Here's my phone number. Text me when you get back to the hotel, okay?"

Nodding, Nick said another quick thank you as he turned and hurried out of the kitchen.

"Why did you bring that up in front of your brother?" Nando asked. "That's the surest way to get him to leave."

"I didn't want him to leave. I thought he'd be on my side," Diego said. "I wouldn't let what happened —"

"Nobody *lets* that happen," Cella chided.

"Mama, I didn't mean —"

"Go to your room, Diego," Nando said quietly as Nick slipped out of the front door.

Nick hurried to the car that Ax had already started and had idling in the driveway. As soon as his door was closed, the car screeched back out of the driveway. Nick set the bag of food at his feet as he put his seatbelt on. The way Ax was driving, he might actually need it.

The air in the car was so heavy with a mix of bad emotions that Nick thought he might choke. He shot a few sideways glances at Ax. His thick eyebrows were normally pretty low and gave him a little bit of an intimidating look, but he was usually smirking, which made him approachable.

If Nick didn't know what he was usually like, he might be a little scared by the murderous look on Ax's face. He kept gripping and releasing the steering wheel. This mood was probably what had sent him to the heavy bag at three in the morning.

Nick wasn't Ax's biggest fan. He'd been downright rude to his own loving family, but it was obvious something else was going on and Nick couldn't bear to see him suffer.

"Okay, so maybe you were right about not going to your parents' for dinner. It's too soon in our relationship."

Ax turned and gave Nick a dead stare for about two seconds before he smirked and shook his head. Nick breathed a sigh of relief. He was the reason they'd ended up in that tense situation, so he was glad he could at least get Ax to crack a smile.

"I never figured you'd be one to break tension with humor," Ax said.

"You obviously know nothing about me."

"Guess I don't know much, but I do know what you sound like when you get off."

Nick bit the inside of his cheek to keep from reacting. Ax was goading him. Instead of responding, Nick looked out of the window.

Ax didn't head directly to The Bay Bridge as Nick expected him to. He drove through parts of Oakland Nick wouldn't want to walk through alone during the day, let alone at night. Ax had his eyes trained out of the window, and all Nick could think about was the fight he'd overheard.

Something terrible had happened in Ax's family. They'd lost someone, and though Nick's dad was still alive and his death wouldn't be horrific, Nick was still in a constant state of mourning as he waited for the worst. It seemed like Ax was still in mourning too. Maybe his loss was very recent—or maybe he felt like he'd lost someone who was still around.

Nick let Ax stew as they made their way to the condo. When they got back, Nick put the bag of food in the fridge while Ax stomped off to his room. It hadn't taken long for Nick to realize that the bag hadn't been full of leftovers. Cella had made an entire second meal and had it ready to go for Ax to take home. He also sent her a quick text to let her know they were back safe.

"What's all that?" Jett asked as he came in to get a juice from the fridge.

"Ax's mom sent it home. You should try some. She's an amazing cook."

"Yeah? What's in there?"

"Well, we didn't get around to dessert, but there was mention of rice pudding."

"Ooh, I'm in."

They pulled the bag of food out of the fridge and dug around inside until they found the pudding.

"So what's Ax's family like?" Jett asked.

"Nice, maybe a little overprotective. Typical family."

"Yeah? I guess I pictured Ax coming from a family of practical jokers."

"They seemed normal."

Although as Nick said it, he realized that maybe that wasn't Ax's real family. Maybe they had been full of jokes and laughter before whatever happened had taken place.

As they finished off their dessert, Nick felt bad that Ax hadn't been able to have any of what was obviously one of his favorites. Deciding to be the bigger man, he warmed another bowl, carried it to Ax's room and knocked on the door.

"Yeah," Ax called from inside.

Nick opened the door. Ax was in nothing but sleep pants. Nick licked his dry lips as he approached him. Ax was at the desk, tapping away on his laptop.

"What?" he asked without lifting his eyes from the screen.

Nick swallowed down his snarky retort and took a deep breath as he stepped farther into the room. He made his way over to Ax and set down the bowl.

"Your mom sent home food. I thought you might want some dessert, since you didn't get a chance to finish dinner."

"You my mother now?"

Ax still didn't look up from what he was typing. His brows were pinched together as he scowled down at the computer.

"No, but it wouldn't hurt to let her know you got home safe. She seemed really worried about—"

"All she does is fucking worry. It doesn't do any good."

Ax pushed away from the desk and started pacing back and forth in front of the floor-to-ceiling glass doors that led to the balcony.

"Look… If you want to talk about—"

"You think talking will change one fucking thing? If you want to help me relieve some stress, drop your pants and we'll fuck it away. Otherwise, get out."

"I'm not a fucking *Fleshlight*. If you want relief so bad, use your hand. Too bad Jett's straight or you could call him in here and order him to his knees, but I'm not just a hole."

"I didn't say you were, but you sure seemed to get off on hate sex."

The words pierced Nick in the chest, way too close to his heart for his liking. Ax hated him?

"Is that what that was?" Nick asked.

"Why I want someone who hates me is beyond me," Ax said.

"I don't hate you."

"Yes, you do. That's why you're so conflicted about the hard-on you have for me."

Nick had to admit that his dick was definitely interested in a repeat of the other morning, but he didn't hate Ax. He didn't know how he felt. Maybe he didn't want to feel anything, because he knew he wouldn't be able to keep Ax's attention for long.

"Who says I have such a hard-on for you?"

Ax turned to Nick with a smirk. With a flick of his wrist, he pulled the string on his pants and they fell to the floor. He stood there gloriously naked. Nick hadn't been able to see much the other night, but he was memorizing everything now.

Ax was gorgeous. His caramel skin was stretched tight over his well-defined abs. A light dusting of dark hair fanned out over his pecs. His abs were bare but for a small happy trail that led from his belly button to the thatch of close-cropped hair surrounding his big, very hard cock.

Nick's pants tightened as his eyes took in every detail, but he didn't make it past Ax's crotch. He knew Ax's legs were muscular, but he just couldn't look down any farther.

Ax's dick was long and thick as it arched up and bobbed in the air. It had to be close to eight inches long. Nick's ass twitched in interest.

"Like what you see? Hop on."

"What if it's *your* ass I want?" Nick quipped.

Ax's smile grew as he slowly turned around. Nick tried to swallow to get some moisture in his parched throat as he watched all Ax's muscles flex and jump as he moved. He gave Nick one last grin over his shoulder before bending at the waist and grabbing his ankles.

Nick gasped. Ax's pucker was a tempting, dark ring of color. From where Nick was standing, his ass looked hairless. It wasn't that Nick was opposed to hair, but fuck if his mouth didn't water at the sight.

Unable to resist, Nick reached down and pressed against his erection. Like a zombie, he took a few steps closer. As he did, Ax spread his legs a little farther.

"You're…" Nick stopped to clear his throat. "You're vers?"

"I guess you could say I'm the ultimate vers. I like men, I like women, I like to top, I like to bottom, I like giving head, I like receiving head. I just like sex in most forms."

"And rimming?" Nick asked as he stepped closer.

"Rimming?" Ax twisted around to look up at Nick.

"Yeah, rimming."

Nick wasn't too experienced with rimming. It was intimate, not something someone did with a hookup, in his opinion, but saliva was pooling in his mouth as he moved to kneel behind Ax. The fact that it seemed to make Ax a little uncomfortable was just a bonus.

Chapter Twelve

Ax

"Like I said, most any form of sex."

"Mm-m," Nick agreed as he reached up and pulled Ax's ass cheeks apart.

Ax had been goading him. He'd been pissed at Nick for agreeing to dinner with his folks. He'd been pissed at himself for giving in because it wasn't safe. He'd been pissed the whole thing had gone to hell because Diego wanted to be a normal fucking teenager.

But now, maybe he'd gone too far. He felt exposed, raw, vulnerable. A few guys had given him cursory licks as they'd prepped him for fucking, but no one had ever looked at him like he could be dessert—like Nick had looked at him as he'd stepped closer.

Ax bit back a whimper. *I don't fucking whimper.* But when Nick leaned in and rasped his tongue slowly over Ax's opening, the high-pitched noise that came out couldn't be described any other way.

Nick pulled back and feathered a fingertip over Ax's pucker. *Has that patch of skin always been so sensitive?* He couldn't remember.

The next time Nick leaned forward, there was no cursory lick, no gentle warning. This time his flexed tongue sought entrance. Ax gasped. Pre-cum dripped from the tip of his cock and started to pool on the hardwood floor between his feet. Gibberish spouted from his lips.

He was going to come. With barely any penetration and not a finger to his dick, Ax was going to shoot all over the floor. The warning tingle started to spread from the base of his spine when Nick pulled back.

"Don't fucking stop," Ax begged, though it came out like a demand.

"Might want to grab on to something. This won't be gentle."

Straightening up, Ax took two big strides and bent over the bed. He heard the crinkle of the condom wrapper that must have come from Nick's pocket but didn't look back. He needed this release but he couldn't bear to see hatred in Nick's eyes. He usually let it roll off him, but he was too raw after being with his family.

When Nick started to prep him with lube, Ax bit out a terse, "Don't." He wanted this to be a punishing fuck. He didn't want hearts and flowers, because as soon as he came, Nick would hate him all over again. He had to remember that. This wasn't romance. This was punishment.

Ax fluttered his eyelids with relief when he felt the broad head of Nick's cock at his entrance. He still hadn't gotten to see Nick naked.

The burn as Nick entered grounded him. Nick didn't seem to be as long as his was, but his cock was thick and it split Ax open. Nick moved forward at a slow pace. He was being gentle, and Ax couldn't handle it, so he pressed back in one quick thrust until he felt Nick's balls against his own.

"Fuck," Nick groaned. "Tight."

Ax squeezed his inner muscles. The burn inside him intensified and Nick sucked a breath in through his teeth. Ax pulled forward but Nick grabbed his hips.

"Wait a sec. Give yourself a chance to adjust," Nick said.

Instead, Ax gave his hips a sharp flick backward until Nick was balls deep again.

"Quit topping from the bottom," Nick growled as he ground himself against Ax's ass.

Ax could feel Nick's pubes against the cheeks of his ass as he rotated his hips. Nick pulled back then snapped his hips forward. Ax arched his back and moaned. That was what he needed, the pain and the pleasure. That was his relationship with Nick in a nutshell.

Nick reached forward and grabbed Ax's shoulders as he started a rough rhythm, pulling almost all the way out and slamming back home. The friction was amazing. Ax fisted his hands in the sheets and tried to hold on. Nick's thrusts got so hard, so vigorous that Ax was soon plastered to the mattress.

The soft sheets felt cool against his hot dick. Ax started humping the bed, but then he and Nick both gasped as it changed the angle. Nick was suddenly pounding his prostate and Ax's muscles wound even tighter around Nick.

The friction of the bed under him and the pressure of Nick against that magic spot inside him was just too much. Ax humped harder and Nick thrust faster until a guttural groan burst from Ax as he shot all over himself and the bed. Nick was only a second behind.

Ax collapsed onto the mattress. When he turned, Nick was holding on to one of the bedposts for support as he panted. Ax couldn't say why exactly that pissed him off — maybe because he'd wanted to feel the weight of Nick on top of him, maybe because he wanted to fuck Nick so good that he wouldn't have the forethought to hold back from falling down drunk from sex. Before his orgasm had even subsided, Nick was trying to keep his distance. *Fuck that.*

"Thanks for the fuck," Ax slurred out. "I really needed it. Better than a massage."

Nick's nostrils flared as he looked down and met Ax's gaze. Ax gave him a wink. Without a word, Nick pulled off the condom, stuffed his dick back into his pants and left the room. The door shut with a quiet click.

The post-orgasm buzz was completely gone, so Ax got up and jumped into the shower. Any tension the sex had relieved came back in full force.

It was still early in the evening and Ax was in town, so he got dressed and decided to check out his old stomping grounds. As he headed for the door, Jett stopped him.

"What did you say to him?"

"What do you mean?"

"Nick. He said he was going to bring you some of the rice pudding your mom made, then a few minutes ago, he came stomping out and shut himself in his room."

Ax shrugged. He wasn't about to tell Jett they'd fucked.

"What's up with you? You're usually the one who's chill. This op has you more skittish than a feral cat."

"I have an errand to run. I'll be back in a few hours."

"This an official errand?"

"Nope. Personal."

"Be careful. Anyone could follow you from the building."

"I didn't let anyone follow me to my parents' house and I won't let anyone get the jump on me now, either."

Jett shrugged as Ax walked away. Technically he shouldn't be doing anything personal. He could thank Nick for agreeing to see his family.

If it were anything else, he'd just stay put, but if he didn't get out of the condo, he might punch something — or someone. And he needed to check on a few personal things, since he was in San Francisco. He'd told HC when they'd brought him on that his personal mission was his first priority. Revenge was what he was looking for, but he had to find out who he was fighting in order to take them down.

Not wanting to take the luxury SUV they'd rented to the neighborhood he was going to, Ax snuck out of the back of the building and darted a few blocks away before ordering a car to come pick him up.

Once the driver had dropped him off, he wasted no time squealing off and turning away from the street where Ax had grown up. The old apartment building looked exactly the same as it had when he'd lived there ten years before — the same as it had when he'd moved his parents out two-and-a-half years before, the same as it had when he'd checked up on the place six months ago.

Ax blew out a breath and swallowed past the bile that always tried to come up when he went back home.

His parents had always been saving to get a better place, but three kids were expensive. Diego had slept in their parents' room until Ax had moved out. Ax had slept on a pullout in the living room and Cherie had been in the tiny, closet-sized second bedroom.

He ran up the stairs two at a time. When he got to the third floor, he pulled out his key. There was still one hidden in the stairwell. If Cherie ever made it back, she'd know right where it was and be able to safely get into their old apartment.

Turning the key, Ax's heart leapt into his throat when he heard someone moving around inside. His pulse was racing with hope. He held his breath and swung the door open.

"Get the fuck out," a man's voice said as soon as Ax opened the door.

A man and a woman were sitting at the old table where his family used to eat dinner. The man had a tourniquet around the woman's arm and was ready to shoot her up. He stood from the table, ready to fight. The guy didn't even care that Ax had a good forty pounds of muscle on him.

"You a cop?" The woman demanded.

"No. This is my apartment. Get the fuck out," Ax snarled.

"We rented this place through the week," the woman said.

Ax's blood pressure was rising. He could hear the thump, thump, thump of his heartbeat in his ears. He'd only ever been so ready to explode once before in his life.

"I'm calling the cops. You two better be gone by the time I get back."

The woman looked like she wanted to argue, but the guy told her to keep her mouth shut and pack her things or the cops would come and take their score away.

Ax didn't stay to hear them argue. He flew down the stairs to the first floor and pounded on the apartment manager's door. If it was still Joe Aguilar, he was dead. He knew exactly why Ax kept the apartment. He'd been the manager when Cherie had been taken.

"It's nine o'clock at night. This better be a fucking..." Joe said.

When he saw Ax, Joe tried to shut the door. Ax shoved the wood panel so hard that it threw Joe back.

"Fuck. My nose," Joe whined as he covered his face with his hands.

"Why are there people shooting up in my apartment, Joe?"

"That place just sits empty all the time. You're barely ever here."

"That's not your concern. I pay my rent on time every month. I'm in the fucking military. We have lawyers who sue people for this shit."

"Why are you keeping the apartment anyway? It's been years. She's never coming back."

The way he said it had something lighting up inside Ax — a fear and a hope. Ax picked Joe up off the ground and lifted him by his shirt.

"What do you know about it?" Ax whispered low and deadly right in Joe's face.

"N-nothing."

Ax tilted his head to the side and looked straight into Joe's eyes. There was fear there, but was there deception? Ax had a sinking feeling that he'd left a resource untapped for three fucking years.

"You'd better tell me what you know or I won't bother with the lawyers. I have connections. No one will ever find your body, and no one will ever fucking miss you."

Joe's Adam's apple bobbed as he swallowed. Blood dripped from his broken nose. His harsh breathing was the only sound in the room as Ax waited for an answer.

Joe started with the shake of his head, "I don't—"

Ax kneed him in the balls. Joe groaned. He figured Joe deserved at least that for making extra money off him and making the apartment unsafe if Cherie ever did return.

While Joe was still gasping for breath, Ax spun him around and threw him face first against the wall. He pulled Joe's arm up his back almost to the breaking point as he started whispering in his ear.

"They teach you a lot in the military. I know right where to give a kidney punch. At best you'll be pissing blood for days. At worst, they'll shut down and you'll die a slow, painful death while I sit and watch."

"Torres," Joe choked out.

"What?"

"Shawn Torres was sniffing around after your sister before she disappeared. He's been moving up around here, working for a guy named Silva, Danny Silva."

"They get women to hook? Is that why they took Cherise?" he asked, using his sister's full name.

"I don't know. I don't even know if he had anything to do with Cherise. I just saw her brushing him off a couple times."

Ax's insides boiled with rage. He'd gone to school with Shawn. The guy was at least ten years older than Cherie, and she'd still been a child when she'd been taken.

"I don't believe you. When I came to talk to you right after she was taken, you said you hadn't seen anything. Why didn't you mention it then?"

"Look… I thought he was just dealing. I didn't know he was selling chicks until one of them killed him."

"What?"

"It was all over the news. This girl killed him, but she claimed it was self-defense because he'd snatched her. That's what had me connecting the dots to your sister. I swear I wasn't hiding anything."

Torres is dead? Ax would definitely verify that, but at least he had a new name—Danny Silva. When he let Joe drop to the floor, something insidious came to life inside him and he .wanted to kill the man for not speaking up sooner—for not coming forward when Ax might have been able to do something, for taking advantage of his knowledge of the situation and renting out the apartment Ax paid for.

"If I come back again and find anyone in that apartment—including you—you won't get off so easy."

"You won't," Joe wheezed as Ax left the apartment.

Chapter Thirteen

Nick

After a shower that didn't make him feel much cleaner, Nick paced his room. He felt like the world's biggest douche. He'd been pissed for two days that Ax had treated him like a fast fuck but was going to go out on a date with Max. *Max and Ax. Stupidest fucking couple name ever.*

It wasn't like Nick was stealing Ax from Max. Hell, Ax was still treating him like a booty call. Nick had also hooked up with Ax first. Max had only asked him out, and they hadn't actually gone yet. He figured he shouldn't feel too guilty.

The thing that was niggling at him was the fact that Max hadn't even crossed his mind until he'd already come deep inside Ax's tight ass. He'd come so hard, in fact, that he'd almost collapsed to his knees. He would have too if he hadn't grabbed on to the bedpost to keep himself upright.

He'd been about to let himself lean forward and feel Ax's sweat-slick skin against his when Ax had tensed. That tightening of his muscles had brought Nick out of his post-orgasmic haze and he'd remembered why he was so pissed at Ax in the first place.

Then Ax had had the nerve to thank him, like Nick had provided a service. He'd walked out of that room with fisted hands. He'd wanted to wring Ax's neck.

He had nothing to be ashamed of. Ax had goaded him on. If Ax was going to do that while still making dates with other people, that was none of Nick's concern...except he was going to have to tell Max. He didn't want Max to be looking at Ax with hearts in his eyes when Ax was just after sex.

Done spinning himself in circles, Nick left his room. He couldn't avoid Ax forever and he didn't want to be stuck in his room all night, so he went out into the entertainment room. Jett was playing video games on the huge projector screen.

"Wanna play?" Jett asked without looking back.

"Sure."

Nick plopped down next to him on the sofa and picked a controller up off the table. He welcomed the distraction.

* * * *

When a door slammed somewhere in the distance, Nick blinked and looked at the clock. He and Jett had been playing nonstop for almost two hours.

There was a crash out in one of the main rooms and something shattered.

"Fuck." Ax's voice sounded lazy, almost slurred.

Nick and Jett looked at each other before scrambling off the sofa and hurrying out to the large open living area of the condo.

Ax was on the floor. A side table was overturned. Broken glass and liquid were pooled around him. He looked angry and confused as he lay there.

"Did he leave?" Nick whispered.

"Said he had a personal errand. Didn't know it was to go get drunk off his ass."

They both stood there for a moment before Jett sighed.

"Get him to bed. Make him drink, like, a gallon of water. I'll clean up the mess."

"Maybe you should get him to bed. He hates me," Nick said.

Jett snorted.

"If you think he's sending you looks of hate, you haven't had enough sex in your life."

Nick opened his mouth to speak but didn't want to tell Jett that Ax might be attracted to Nick, but that didn't mean he didn't hate him. With a sigh, Nick gave in.

"Watch him for a sec while I go get my shoes on," Nick said as he hurried to his room.

When he came back, Jett had pulled Ax up off the floor. Nick was afraid of what would come out of Ax's mouth because of what they'd just done.

"I need a favor," Ax told Jett. "I need you to run two names...Shawn Torres and Danny Silva. I need to know if they're only into drugs and hooking or if they're deeper into trafficking."

"Sure. I'll do it first thing in the —"

"Tonight," Ax said.

"Okay. I'll get right on it," Jett said as he made eye contact with Nick over Ax's shoulder and gave him a little nod.

"Why don't you go get cleaned up while Jett runs those names?" Nick asked.

He grabbed Ax's elbow and steered him toward his bedroom. Ax seemed too drunk to argue. When they got to his room, Nick helped Ax remove his wet pants. He tried to avert his gaze as he helped Ax out of his wet boxer briefs and into clean ones.

He'd be sticky in the morning, but that wasn't Nick's concern, and he sure as hell wasn't going to help Ax take a shower.

"I was too late," Ax whispered.

Nick looked up from his crouched position as he snapped Ax's clean underwear into place. He was surprised to see so much remorse in Ax's eyes.

"You're not too late," Nick soothed, though he didn't know what they were talking about.

He was sure Ax was just doing a little drunk blathering until he saw moisture gather along his lower lids. He tried to steel himself. The last thing he needed to feel for Ax was any kind of sympathy.

"I am. He said Shawn was dead. What if he was the one?"

"Who said Shawn was dead?"

"Joe. He never said anything when I asked him before, but this time, he said Shawn was hanging around. What if he was scoping her? What if he knew something and I'll never get to ask him now because he's dead?"

"Then you keep looking. You get her back."

"You're so naïve. If Shawn's dead, what do you think the chances are she's still alive?"

Nick wanted to ask Ax who he was talking about. He assumed a sister, considering what had happened with his family earlier that night. Ax plopped his ass on the bed and promptly fell backward.

"There's a chance," Nick said.

"I left. I got out as soon as I could. I fucking knew him. I knew it was something I could have prevented if I hadn't left. I'm so fucking selfish."

Nick wanted to argue, but he didn't really know much about Ax, not to mention that Nick had been thinking he *was* selfish. No matter how drunk Ax was, Nick wasn't going to lie.

"I don't know that you could have prevented anything," he said with honesty.

Ax snorted and rolled away. There was a loud sniffle and Ax swiped his arm over his eyes. Nick stood and turned away from the temptation to comfort him. He'd been a total dick just a few hours earlier. When Ax had been quiet for a few moments, Nick turned back and covered him with the duvet from his bed.

"Cherie," Ax whispered as his eyes fluttered closed.

Nick's heart broke a little. Maybe he could give Ax a little leeway to be a jerk because he was dealing with so much on the inside. Nick shook his head at his own thoughts. He was trying to make excuses for the fact that he was still attracted to Ax after everything he'd done.

Jett came in with a pitcher of water and a laptop. He gently set the pitcher on the nightstand next to Ax and got a glass from the bathroom.

"Go ahead and get some rest. I'll sit with him and make him drink while I look up those names," Jett said as he pulled a chair closer to the bed.

Nick didn't want to leave. He needed to shake himself loose of the strange tie he had to the loyal asshole passed out in the bed. He didn't have a reason to stay, however, so he made his way to his room, settled into his bed and tried to get to sleep.

After an hour of tossing and turning and thinking about the paradox that was Ax, Nick finally fell asleep.

Chapter Fourteen

Ax

Ax's head felt like it would fall right off his shoulders if he sat up, so he groaned and covered his head with a pillow. He remembered Jett waking him up and shoving water down his throat, but before that, things were fuzzy.

He'd left Joe in a heap on the floor then he had gone up and cleaned the apartment. After that, he'd stopped at the liquor store at the end of the street and bought way too much Scotch.

The driver had huffed when he'd started drinking right there in the car, but Ax hadn't given any fucks what the driver thought. He'd been dropped off a few blocks from the condo, made his way up to the top floor and sat outside the front door as he'd emptied the first bottle. The second bottle had ended up all over the floor when he'd tripped over a table. The look of censure on Nick's face was the last thing he clearly remembered.

Guilt cramped his guts as his stomach roiled. Two names blared to the front of his memory like a neon sign, and Ax sat up in bed. He realized his mistake a moment too late as he jumped out of bed and ran for the toilet. When his stomach was empty and his head was throbbing in time with his heartbeat, Ax called out.

"Jett. Jett, get your ass in here."

"Dude," Jett said from the doorway, "I'm not the kind of friend to hold your hair and rub your back while you puke. I'm more the 'shut the door and not smell the vomit' kinda friend."

"I'm done puking. I remember asking you to check a couple names for me. Was that real or did I dream it?"

"I got all the info."

"Tell me."

"Ax, why don't you finish up, and when you feel better — ?"

"Tell me," Ax said, louder this time.

"Fine," Jett sighed. "Shawn Torres, the one who went to high school with you, was killed two months ago. A woman stabbed him four times, but it was ruled self-defense because he'd kidnapped her. She was sixteen. She's been reunited with her mother."

"And Silva?"

"Prison. He's doing some serious prison time for dealing and trafficking. You said this is personal, but Ax, it seems like business."

"It's my business but don't worry. Wade won't care you ran a couple names for me."

"That wasn't what I was worried about." Jett said.

Ax wondered what the chances were that he could get in to see Silva in prison. Maybe he could talk to Wade and see if they could pull some strings.

"Where's Silva? He in San Quinten?" Ax asked.

"No. He's in Arizona."

"Fuck."

It just wouldn't be his luck to have the guy right there where he could possibly see him within a day or two. Ax pulled himself up off the floor and stumbled back into his bedroom. He made it to the bed just in time to collapse. His head continued to throb as he poured another glass of water and drank it down.

When he looked up, he saw Nick standing in the doorway holding a tablet to his chest and looking at Ax like he was a bug under a microscope. The last thing he needed at the moment was another dose of judgement.

"What?" Ax bit out before refilling his glass.

"We got an appointment with Campbell for this afternoon. Will you be up for it?"

"I'm fine. I just need to take a shower. What time is it?"

"It's nine," Jett said.

"And the meeting?"

"At two this afternoon," Nick said.

Ax nodded then downed another glass of water. Being hungover wasn't necessarily a bad thing. People in this business liked it when others were using. If they didn't use, it gave them a sense of power, and if they did use, then they felt a strange sense of camaraderie.

He had a few hours to get his shit together. Without another word, he stood, slowly made his way to the bathroom and quietly closed the door.

* * * *

Ax was still feeling a little rough when they arrived at William Campbell's law office. The place was more opulent than the penthouse the team was using to impress him and others like him.

Campbell wasn't their main reason to be on the West Coast. The guy wasn't a big player, but he was making more money than a lot of the groups that were taking ten times the amount of people that Campbell was.

It was guys like Campbell who didn't get caught. They were a small operation that flew under the government's radar. He wasn't dealing drugs and he didn't take enough women to draw a lot of attention.

Add to that the fact that the guy was a wealthy, high-powered attorney who was supposedly an ally to women. He and his firm had a reputation for going after companies that exploited women. Yet in the privacy of his own home, he was one of the worst offenders.

Those were the conundrums they faced. Campbell had helped thousands of women get justice against companies or men who had victimized them. And yet he was helping other men to privately and systematically violate females.

His wife was a very wealthy philanthropist who wholeheartedly supported his work. She had no idea that in the privacy of a secret estate, he was housing and grooming women to be slaves to the men who paid him unbelievable sums of money.

"Mr. Hernandez?"

Ax looked up from his tablet to find a cute brunet twink in a custom suit looking at him expectantly. Ax stood and nodded once. The assistant's eyes widened a fraction when Nick and Jett also stood.

Ax sent the twink a smile and the guy actually preened a little. His green eyes were bright and beautiful. His hair was perfectly styled. He had a flawless complexion, and his full lips gave his face an almost feminine beauty.

"I'm Peter Thornton, Mr. Campbell's personal assistant."

Thornton actually fluttered his eyelashes. He probably didn't get a lot of clients who showed any interest. Ax pretended to lose himself for a moment before turning and introducing his companions.

"This is my PA, Nick Andrews, and my security, Jett Clifton."

Ax could swear he heard Peter whisper Jett's name. Ax just barely held back from rolling his eyes. Sure, Jett was a sexy name, and the guy who went with it was a sexy beast with a boy-next-door vibe, but he was also straight as an arrow.

Thornton must have had a decent gaydar, because he immediately turned professional and polite to Jett. Nick, on the other hand, got just as much of a thorough perusal as Ax had.

"I'll escort you to Mr. Campbell's office," Thornton said as he began walking.

They all followed. When they reached an office at the back corner of the top floor, Thornton stopped and turned with flourish. Ax wondered if the guy was a dancer. Normally he'd be all over a graceful twink like him, but instead, his focus kept pulling back to the blond next to him.

"Mr. Campbell is expecting you, but he likes his first meeting with clients to be private."

Thornton gave a meaningful look to Nick and Jett. Ax was used to this. After all, he used to pretend to be the muscle or the assistant or both.

"Mr. Andrews would be more than happy to wait out here with you, but I don't go anywhere without protection."

Ax heard Nick's indignant huff. Thornton's sharp eyes turned to Nick as well, like he was taking him in, calculating. Ax didn't like men or women who were calculating or conniving. He wondered how much Campbell's assistant knew about Ax's real purpose and Campbell's little side business.

"Does Jett have a weapon?" Peter asked with concern.

"Of course," Ax scoffed. "What kind of protection would he be without a weapon?"

Thornton looked at Jett again and licked his lips. Ax barely restrained another eye-roll. Thornton was obviously having a fantasy where he got to frisk Jett and discover all his 'weapons'. After a moment, he cleared his throat and gave a nod.

"One moment," he said as he went to his desk and picked up his phone.

He turned away from Ax as he no doubt was having a little conversation with Campbell. The conversation didn't seem heated, so Ax was guessing Campbell wasn't too surprised about the request.

In all honesty, Ax would have been willing to leave Jett waiting too, but this was more of a power play. Nick was the only one without a weapon, as it wouldn't fit his cover. It was well known in these circles that Ax had guarded Sam, so it wouldn't be surprising for him to carry as well. All three of them also had cameras and undetectable listening devices in a small pin on the lapel of each of their suits.

Thornton hung up the phone and turned to Ax with a smile.

"Mr. Campbell is ready for you and Jett, Mr. Hernandez. I'll keep Mr. Andrews company."

Ax chuckled a little that he had used all last names except for Jett. Jett was probably relieved he would be in the office and Nick would be the one rebuffing the twink's advances.

The door to the office was ajar, so when Ax knocked, it slid open a little. He pushed it open and stepped in. Campbell stood from his desk and came to meet him. *Another power play.*

"Ax. I'm so glad you took me up on my offer."

"I have to admit that intrigue is the only thing that brought me here."

Campbell chuckled as he motioned for Ax to take a seat in front of a large, ornate desk. Campbell motioned for Jett to sit as well, but Jett shook his head and stood at attention with his back to the wall and his eyes toward the door.

"Are you getting settled in? Some people have difficulty with the time change."

"I stayed up late last night celebrating, so I'll have to tell you how I'm assimilating once I actually try to go to bed at a decent hour."

"You went out celebrating?"

Campbell's brows drew together in seeming confusion. Ax smirked a little, because Campbell had tipped his hand. He was watching Ax, and Ax had obviously gotten away with his subterfuge when he'd snuck out both times the day before.

"Technically I stayed in, but that doesn't mean I didn't celebrate."

At that, Campbell's brows lifted as he likely understood Ax was just talking about sex. The crazy part was that it wasn't fully a lie. Memories of the sex he'd had would have kept him up all night if he hadn't gotten drunk off his ass and passed out.

"You trust your man?" Campbell nodded toward Jett.

"I used to be in Jett's shoes. I watched Sam Wheeler's back until I proved myself. This is Jett's chance to do the same."

Campbell nodded in understanding.

"If there's one thing I've learned, it's that having someone you trust at your back allows you to focus completely on the business at hand," Ax said.

"Mr. Wheeler taught you this?"

"Yes. He learned from Bernard himself. Our organization is growing, but we don't want to grow so quickly that we start adding people we don't fully trust."

"Very wise," Campbell nodded.

"I must admit" — Ax leaned back in his chair — "I'm very curious why you invited me here. Technically, one might say we're competitors."

"Not at all. In fact, I was hoping we might consider working together."

"I'm not sure how possible that is. Like I said, we're very careful about trusting new additions to our team."

"I wouldn't join your team, per se. Sometimes I have a difficult time procuring what my clients are looking for, and wealthy clients are rarely patient. They pay for convenience and urgency."

Ax nodded. Now he knew exactly where this was going. Campbell was looking to tap into their supply. Ax was going to have to find a reason to delay decision-making. Working within the US, they'd need the approval of about fifty government agencies to actually break the law.

Outside the country, it was a lot easier, but within the borders, they had to be very careful. They contracted with the government, but they were no longer actually employed by Uncle Sam.

"So you need to expand your inventory?" Ax guessed.

Campbell inclined his head in confirmation.

"You're new to the area and I know a lot of available women I might introduce you to. What do you like?"

Ax snorted. "I'm what you might call a hedonist. I believe in pleasure, especially *my* pleasure. I'm also a pragmatist. I like to get off and I'm usually pretty laissez-faire about who's doing the pleasuring."

"Meaning men or women?"

Ax shrugged as he spoke the lie. "I prefer women, but I'll take whatever turns me on."

Ax would say he was a four on the Kinsey scale, which put him more on the homosexual side. He definitely preferred men to women, but only a little more than slightly. If he had to choose one over the other, he'd definitely choose men. Luckily, he'd never had to choose.

"Bernard seems to prefer being surrounded by homosexual or bisexual men. Is he gay?"

"I've never asked. And I've never seen him with someone, so I'm not sure about his sexuality."

"I'm not judging," Campbell was quick to say. "I'm just interested."

"In our business, it never serves to judge," Ax agreed.

Campbell chuckled and gave Ax a nod. He steepled his hands in front of him and seemed to reassess Ax.

"If you could describe your perfect woman, what would she look like?" Campbell asked.

Without thought, Ax began describing his sister. It was what he did by default because he'd been looking for her for so long.

"That makes things easy for you. There are so many Latin women you work with, I'm sure."

"I'm a busy man. When I don't have time, I like someone who knows the score and is simply willing to do as I say. When I have time to play…I like someone who isn't as inclined to do as she's told."

Campbell laughed. "I know just what you mean. I have a gift for you. Let's call it a gift of good faith. If you like it, I'd appreciate you putting in a good word with Mr. Bernard and hopefully a meeting."

"If I come to trust you, I can guarantee a meeting with Sam. Sam is now over the entire US. Bernard is over the whole company, but he mainly handles Europe."

"I have no problem working my way up. Your European product is what I'm most interested in. Many of my clients are very particular about things like…color. It sometimes makes it much more difficult for me to procure what they demand."

So he needs a lot of white women. That makes sense. If he was working with local groups, he'd run into mostly Latinas. Ax had just made Campbell's job very easy, as far as a 'gift' was concerned.

"Why don't you come to my estate tomorrow evening? Feel free to bring protection" — Campbell nodded toward Jett — "but I just want to set expectations that my estate is heavily guarded." Campbell handed Ax a card with an address.

"Then I'll be bringing my PA as well."

"Your PA?"

"Yes. *Your* PA only allowed Jett into this meeting, but I would prefer to bring Nick as well. They're both looking to move up in our company and both are...equipped to watch my back as necessary."

"Fine, fine. Bring both." Campbell waved off any concern.

Chapter Fifteen

Nick

"Does he know?" Peter asked as he gave Nick a bottle of water.

"Know?"

"Does your boss know you have the hots for him?"

"Actually, my boss and I don't get along all that well. I'm working my way up in the company, despite him."

"Mm-m, that sexual tension between you two was off the charts."

"He's not interested," Nick said. "And neither am I, for that matter. He's kind of a prick. Shit, don't tell him I said that."

"Your secret's safe with me." Peter winked.

Nick hoped that was true, and he hoped Peter would tell him a thing or two about Campbell in return. Nick pasted on an embarrassed smile and Peter sat next to him on the cushy leather sofa outside Campbell's office.

"Thanks. He's giving me a real hard time. It should be me in there, not Jett. I don't get him sometimes."

"He's probably harder on you because he's fighting his tendencies," Peter patted his arm.

"Tendencies?"

"Yeah. His queer tendencies. If he hasn't fucked you yet, it's because he's running from those tendencies. He's bi. I could have sworn there was something between you, some sexual knowledge."

"I walked in when he was stepping out of the shower." Nick gave the guy a partial truth.

"That could be it. Anyway, I have a perfectly tuned gaydar. That's how I know you're gay and that crazy hot hunk of man meat who did zero talking is pretty much straight."

"You're basically right on the money. How'd you do that?" Nick tried to insert awe into his voice, even though he was only slightly intrigued.

"Honestly? I come from a family of con artists."

Nick widened his eyes at the honesty of that statement.

"I try to use my powers for good, though. It's all about reading body language, cues and tells."

"For good, huh?" Nick asked a little suspiciously. "What do you know about me?"

"Hmm-m." Peter scratched his chin dramatically. "You come from money, you're not an only child but I'd say you don't have any sisters."

"That's pretty good. I do have brothers."

"I'd say you're also a middle child."

Nick nodded. He was technically only a few minutes older than Bray, but still qualified as a middle child.

"You don't look like a Nix, maybe a Nico?" Peter tapped his index finger on the side of his chin in thought.

Nick shook his head, but he was fighting back a smile.

"Hmmm...Nicky, Nicolo, Cole, Nicksie, Nickiboo, Nibbles?"

"Nibbles?"

"No? What about Snick, Snickers, Knickers, Nickel, Pickle—" Peter stopped mid-tirade. "Ah, so Nickel it is. Cute."

"Where do you come up with this stuff?" Nick asked with a laugh. "Snickers? Really?"

Peter shrugged. "It worked."

"Is that how you work? You badger people until they tell you the truth?"

"You didn't tell me anything, at least not verbally."

Nick realized he hadn't. Peter had watched him as he'd listed off names and seen him light up with recognition or humiliation at the name 'Nickel'.

"It's not an uncommon nickname for Nicholas and you don't look like a Nicky, so it's a good fit, but my guess is you hate the name."

"You got me. I don't really want to talk about my nickname," Nick grumbled. "Tell me something about Ax."

"It's easier if I can actually talk to him, but I'd say he's a loner. I think he might like to be in charge, until he doesn't."

Nick frowned in confusion. That last sentence didn't make much sense, but Ax definitely was a loner.

"I bet Campbell finds your talents useful. Is that why you work for him?"

Nick tried to steer the conversation back onto the rails and in the direction he needed it to go. Peter instantly turned serious.

"Mr. Campbell helped my sister when she was getting sexually harassed at work. He won her case. During the investigation, I noticed he had a hard time keeping a personal assistant." Peter leaned in and lowered his voice. "He says the women couldn't handle seeing what his clients are going through. I mean, as a woman, it would be hard. But as killer as Mr. Campbell is in the courtroom, he's a flirt. I'd bet my law degree he cheats on his wife. He's also very demanding."

"And you're okay with him cheating?"

"It's not like I help him cheat. It's a feeling. I could be wrong. I know he'd be willing to cheat on her by how he flirts, but I don't know for a fact he's done it. I try to assume positive intent. He does a lot of good things."

Nick was taken aback. Unless he was an amazing actor, Peter had no idea what Campbell was up to behind the scenes. It seemed he had a few doubts about Campbell but was trying to go only with what he saw.

"So you worked here before he helped your sister?" Nick asked.

"Not here. I was interning at another firm while I finished law school. After he helped Keira, Mr. Campbell was grumbling about losing another PA, so I offered my services."

"Wow. And you seem protective of him."

"Yeah. He does a lot of good. Once I pass the bar, I'm going to become an associate here. It's a win-win."

"Huh," Nick huffed. He wondered why this meeting with Ax wasn't suspicious. "So all his clients are women?"

"No. He takes on a few very wealthy clients like your boss, and that allows him to take on pro bono cases like my sister's."

"And that's what you want to do?"

"Definitely. Although I won't aim for women. Campbell has that covered. I'm going to focus on other marginalized populations, mainly queer people who are exploited or victims of prejudice or sexism."

"That sounds like a really noble cause."

"Thanks." Peter hesitated for a moment before continuing. "I, uh, I heard Mr. Campbell mention you just moved here, so—"

"I didn't," Nick said.

"You didn't?"

"Technically Ax—Mr. Hernandez—did. I'm not sure how long I'll last in this job or how long I'll be in San Francisco. Why did you just look guilty when you said that, anyway?"

"See? You're good at looking for cues." Peter gave Nick a smug smile. "You were also spot on. I heard him talking to one of the associates about the ritzy condo Mr. Hernandez just purchased. Technically, I wasn't actually a part of the conversation, but Mr. Campbell did seem the teensiest bit impressed at the choice of locale."

"That's got nothing to do with me." Nick shrugged.

"Well, while you're here, if you need a tour guide, feel free to give me a call." He handed Nick his card.

"Not sure how much free time the bossman will give me."

"Even so. I'm open to being the meat in your hunk sandwich." Peter gave a wink.

Nick smiled at him because he was just so over the top. He also seemed on the up and up. Nick would need to check out his story about his sister needing Campbell as a lawyer, but he felt really bad for Peter. He thought he was such a great reader of people, but boy did he have the wool over his eyes — that or he was the best actor Nick had ever seen in his life.

"So, you know all about Ax. Is there anything I need to know about Campbell?"

Peter wrinkled his nose with distaste and shrugged.

"Am I supposed to know what that means?"

"Is your boss only interested in his skill as a lawyer? Because he's really a shark. He's the best."

"Probably. I mean, Ax will want to know he can trust the guy."

"Well, unless you're his wife, you can trust him."

"Aren't you going to lose him business if you're telling all his perspective clients this?"

Peter snorted. "I don't tell anyone this. I have no proof. It's just something I know, and I like you. All the guys who come in here are total zeros on the Kinsey scale. And I want you to be able to keep your job, so you can tell all this to your hot boss and maybe he'll let loose on the reins he's holding when it comes to you. If he does, I want all the dirty, dirty details — or to join in the fun."

Nick smiled. No way would he tell Peter about him and Ax. The guy was nuts. Peter turned over the card he'd given Nick and pointed out his personal cell number before sauntering back to his desk with only a wink over his shoulder. Within minutes, Ax was stepping out of Campbell's office. As they passed by Peter's desk, Peter gave Nick a wave.

"Call me if you want that tour of the city," Peter sing-songed.

Ax turned and gave Nick a look like he'd done something wrong. Nick sighed. Ax would have flirted with Peter too, although Nick hadn't actually had to work for it.

They all remained fully in character until they pulled out of the underground parking and headed back to the condo. Ax didn't turn from the window, so Nick was a little startled when he spoke.

"You get any intel out of Thornton?"

Nick was glad Ax wasn't looking at him, because he couldn't help the smile that spread as he thought of the crazy shit that had fallen from Peter's mouth.

"He's a little bit of a mystery," Nick said.

"So he didn't give you anything?"

"Oh, he did. I'm just trying to figure out if he's the world's best liar or if he's really what he says he is, because if he is, Campbell's got him snowed."

"What do you mean?"

"He knew where all three of us fell, sexuality-wise."

"Big deal," Ax scoffed.

"He knew there was negative tension between you and me."

"That's not really a secret," Jett reasoned.

"Yeah, but I'm sure both of us were trying to act like we were just professional colleagues. He knew there was anger between us."

This time, Ax did turn enough to give Nick a little side-eye. Nick didn't want to try to read what the look meant, so he turned toward Jett in the front seat.

"He also admitted that he comes from a family of con artists but tries to 'use his power for good'. He's graduating from law school. Campbell took his sister's case pro-bono, so when he needed a PA, Peter offered."

"Peter? So he tells you he's a con artist and that makes you believe everything he says?" Ax asked, his tone condescending.

"I didn't say I believed him, but why would he tell me he was a con artist if he was trying to con me? There are two reasons I can think of — one, he's being honest, or two, he thought it would benefit him in some way. Usually if you're a con artist, that's the last thing you'd actually admit to people. He also said something interesting about Campbell."

That had Ax's attention.

"I asked if all his clients were women and Peter said that Campbell took on a few wealthy clients to be able to afford to help those who couldn't pay him. He said most of the men who visit Campbell are zero on the Kinsey scale. He also said that he got the feeling Campbell was a manwhore who cheats on his wife."

"He got the feeling?" Ax asked.

"He said he'd never actually seen any of Campbell's women, but he just knew he wasn't faithful to his wife by how he looked at and treated other women."

"What's a Kinsey scale?" Jett asked.

"Only a zero on the scale would even ask that," Ax teased.

"It's a sexuality spectrum," Nick explained. "Zero is totally heterosexual and a six is totally homosexual. There's also an X category for asexual people. Most people fall in the one to five area. I'm a five. I have found women physically attractive before, but I identify as gay and don't really have a desire to have sex with women."

"So most of Campbell's clients are super-hetero?" Jett asked.

"I'm not sure Peter can tell where people lie on the Kinsey scale, even if he does have gaydar as finely tuned as he says. He just meant that all Campbell's wealthy clients are all hetero men. He also said something about the way Campbell looks at single women. I think Peter wants to believe what he sees, but part of him knows there's something else going on."

"And he just so happens to want to date you. What a coincidence," Ax said.

"Actually, he thought there was something between the two of us." Nick gestured between himself and Ax. "He offered to be the meat in our sandwich."

Jett laughed, but Ax gave Nick a look he couldn't decipher. There had obviously been some kind of sexual tension between them or they wouldn't have fucked, so Peter *had* noticed something.

"What happened with Campbell?" Nick asked to ease the tense silence in the back seat.

"He has a 'gift' for me. He wants to tap into our supply because he needs more white women, from the sounds of it. He wants some of the women he thinks we're pulling from Europe."

"So he's going to give you one of his female treasures in good faith?" Nick asked.

The very thought had bile creeping up his throat. Would he expect Ax to fuck her in front of him? Nick knew that sometimes they'd have to break some laws — but having sex with someone against their will? The very idea was disgusting and add onto that the little seed of jealousy that sprouted and grew in Nick's mind.

"Am I on the sidelines for that too?" Nick asked. "I'm not going to learn anything if —"

"You get to come with tomorrow." Ax said.

Nick had been prepared to argue and be shot down, so he simply shut his mouth as he tried to take in the fact that he would actually get to take part.

Nick's phone pinged as they pulled into the underground garage.

Chapter Sixteen

Ax

As soon as they were back in the condo, Ax shut himself in the office and did his own research on Shawn Torres and Danny Silva.

For now, he needed to figure out how he could get to Silva. It wasn't like visiting someone who was in prison for trafficking would blow his cover. He'd have to discuss it with Wade. Maybe one of the guys who wasn't undercover could give Danny a visit.

Even thinking the word 'blow' had Ax's mind wandering to Nick. He rubbed his forehead and tried to get back to the job at hand.

He'd learned a few hacking skills in his search for his sister. He didn't want to get his hopes up, because she could be dead. He knew that was easily a possibility, but she'd been so beautiful and fresh-faced. She would have made a lot of money if they'd tried to sell her.

If she was alive, Ax was going to find her. It didn't matter what country she was in or how locked up she was, he was going to find her and bring her home. He had a rehab facility in mind already if they had her hooked on drugs.

He had a therapist ready to go, too. It would all be in place, no matter how long it took him to find her. Then maybe he'd be able to look his parents in the eye again.

Ax's phone pinged and he saw it was a message from his mother, inviting him and Nick to dinner again. Just as he was determined to push Nick back out of his mind, there was a knock at the door.

Ax didn't even get a chance to respond before the door pushed open and Nick walked in carrying a tray. Just from the smell that hit his nose, Ax could tell it was his mother's cooking. His stomach growled.

"You haven't eaten anything today and it's almost dinnertime," Nick said as he set the tray on the desk.

"Thanks."

"Your mom had an entire meal for about ten ready to go. She handed it over before I left the house."

"I saw the bag when you got in the car."

"Your mom's an amazing cook."

Ax grunted in agreement as he started shoveling food into his mouth.

"Okay." Nick drew out the word to about eight syllables. "Let us know if you need anything."

"Has Peter Thornton contacted you?"

"No. I didn't give him my number. He gave me his. Did you want me to contact him?"

Ax gritted his teeth. The angry ball in the pit of his stomach felt a little like jealousy.

"Not right now. We'll see how tomorrow goes."

Nick nodded but seemed hesitant to leave. Ax didn't mind him lingering, and that was exactly why he needed to go.

"Anything else?" Ax asked.

"I, uh…" Nick rubbed the back of his neck. "After dinner, your mom asked me to text her when we got home safe. I didn't think a boyfriend would refuse, so I did. She texted me today to invite us to dinner again."

Ax would normally be irate at the Nick's presumption. There was a little anger there, because he didn't want his parents knowing what his job really entailed. But he also knew his mom wouldn't have invited them back if she hadn't liked Nick. Something about that warmed him, even though it shouldn't.

"I got the same text," Ax admitted.

"I can tell her I'm sick. I don't want to make things awkward."

"Things are already awkward. Don't act like you didn't notice."

"Does that mean you want to go?" Nick asked.

Ax sighed.

"It's too bad you can't meet them in a neutral territory." Nick suggested.

"It's not the place, it's…" *The guilt*, he thought. "It's all the history we have hanging over us like a dark cloud."

"Still, it's their home, their comfort zone, their territory. If you feel a little like an outsider, neutral territory puts you on a more equal footing."

Ax nodded. He hadn't really thought of it like that. He'd assumed that because it wasn't his childhood home, it was more of a neutral territory, but Nick was right. It was their comfort zone, not his. There wasn't much he could do about that while he had to keep his cover.

"Why don't you tell them I'm embarrassed or sick or whatever?" Nick said. "That way you can at least push it off for a few days. You have enough on your plate right now. You don't need the distraction of family drama."

Ax nodded as he shoveled more food into his mouth. He didn't tell Nick that his 'family drama' was always there in the background. He'd just learned how to turn the volume down on it so he could get other shit done — other things that just might lead him to where he had been trying to go before he'd joined HC.

Nick turned to leave, but Ax called him back. He couldn't quite look him in the eye, but he appreciated Nick's willingness to take the fall.

"Thanks," Ax said.

"Sure," Nick said before walking out and closing the door.

Ax went back to his dinner. As he tried to form a response to his mom, he put his fork down. His appetite was gone.

He tried to get back to work, but after an hour of more dead ends, he took his half-finished plate of dinner and headed toward the kitchen. On the way, he heard Nick and Jett playing video games in the entertainment room.

"Fuck," Jett yelled. "You killed me."

"That's the point," Nick shot back.

"I had no idea you could be such a stone-cold hard ass."

"Now you know."

Ax heard them both chuckling. Straightening his shoulders, he moved past and dumped the remains of his dinner into the compost bin. Jett was straight. There was no reason to be jealous of him — except, for some reason, he had an easy camaraderie with Nick. When Jett teased, Nick teased right back. Ax hadn't even known he had a sense of humor. Whenever he was around Ax, Nick had a stick up his ass. It had been that way since day one.

When Ax got back to his desk, he did a little checking on Peter Thornton and discovered that he was probably telling Nick the truth—or at least a partial truth about himself.

Thornton's father was currently in jail and his mother had recently been released early, due to good behavior. His mother's sister and her husband had taken custody of Peter because both his parents had ended up in jail when he was fifteen. He had seven siblings, all of them older and all boys, except one younger sister, who'd also ended up with the same aunt and uncle until she was eighteen.

Every single one of them had a record except the youngest two. Three of the eight children were also currently serving time. None of them had ever done anything with drugs or trafficking. All the charges were about fraud, embezzlement, identity theft, exploitation of the elderly and extortion.

Ax wasn't ready to trust the guy, but it did seem like he might be telling the truth about his history, at least. His present was still undetermined.

What did look interesting were his financials. Thornton had graduated with honors from Berkeley Law School and was currently studying for the bar. The guy had almost a hundred thousand dollars in student loans, something that would not have been necessary if he were truly in Campbell's inner circle.

Ax also found the case Campbell had worked on for Peter's sister Kiera. She had been awarded almost a million dollars because there had been some email evidence of the harassment, which she'd reported to HR, and she had replies from HR advising that it was a first-time offense so no disciplinary action would be taken.

The poor girl had asked for a transfer, which had been denied. The boss had apparently touched her one time too many and she'd slapped him. He'd called 'foul' and tried to press assault charges. Ax rolled his eyes at the idiocy and conceit of the asshole. Ax also set his name aside to investigate later.

Ax skimmed through the court documents. Kiera had admitted that the email exchanges and the transfer request had been submitted on the advice of her brother. Campbell had sure done a good job fighting for her. The man was such a dichotomy, defending women by day while exploiting and abusing them at night.

It was probably the most brilliant cover. Who would suspect him, even if they did have a few misgivings about the man? That might be exactly where Thornton fell. Campbell had fought for his sister and supported all the right charities, so if he flirted a little too hard or Thornton's instinct told him something might be off, Ax could understand him putting those to the back of his mind — or Thornton knew everything and was unscrupulous, but that didn't seem to add up.

Kiera had purchased a small house outside Berkeley with her winnings and Peter lived there with her. His student loan payments were consistent with his salary but had kicked up once his sister bought the house, since they had no rent. He wasn't ready to consider Thornton an ally, but he would avoid letting the kid lose his license to practice before he even got it.

When Ax looked at the clock, he realized it was after midnight. He'd spent hours checking on Thornton when it hadn't been necessary. Part of him had wanted to show Nick he'd been wrong to even consider that the man might be innocent.

He'd wasted time he could have been working on his own research, and that had the guilt flooding back in. Cherie was out there, the third anniversary was closing in and he needed to spend every spare moment he had finding her. If she was alive — Ax took a deep breath at that thought — she was counting on him.

The guilt and shame closed in on him like they sometimes did. They were a weight in the center of his chest, making it hard to breathe. Ax headed for the bar in the main living room. He wasn't normally a big drinker, but lately it seemed like he was on fire and needed something to numb the pain.

He could barely keep his head above water between work and searching for Cherie. Add to that the demands his parents wanted to pile on top — then there was Nick, who was entirely too distracting and contrary. It was all just too much.

Grabbing a crystal bottle from the full bar, Ax took it to the room where he'd seen Nick and Jett playing games. The room was quiet and empty now, so he collapsed onto the sofa, opened the bottle and took a swig.

Not wanting to pass out on the sofa, Ax stood and made his way down the hall toward the master suite until he heard Nick talking to someone.

Chapter Seventeen

Nick

"How are you feeling?" Nick asked.

"Same as yesterday," his dad said.

"That sounds like a complaint, but I'll take it as a win."

"I was thinking…"

"That's never good." Nick joked.

"The doctor cleared me to fly if I take the nurse with me. I could charter a plane and—"

"No," Nick said.

"Nick, he's back on American soil. I need to make the first move like I should have years ago."

"No."

"You realize I'm not a child." His father chuckled. "I can actually do this since I've been medically cleared."

"I'm handling it." Nick gritted the lie out through his teeth. He shouldn't have told his father Mase was going to be in the US.

Mase had no interest in discussing their father or his health. Nick understood, sort of, but he didn't understand why his brother wasn't even willing to hear Dad out. He knew Dad's health was deteriorating.

And yet, if Nick put himself in Mase's shoes... He stopped himself. He tried not to see things from Mase's perspective very often, because it didn't help to be angry at his father.

"I know you're trying, Nick, but maybe he needs to see me make the effort."

"Just give me a little more time, okay?"

"Do you think there's a chance he'll at least see me? Even if it's to curse my name?"

The hope in his father's voice cut Nick to pieces. His father was a confident, commanding, take-no-prisoners type of guy. At least he had been.

"I think it's possible, but just give me more time."

"All right." His father sighed. "It's just that I have nothing to do but sit back and ruminate on all my regrets."

"Maybe you should read a book," Nick quipped.

His dad chuckled again. "Maybe I should."

"I'll send you some."

"Will you be able to visit again soon, Nickel?"

His dad had rarely used that nickname when Nick had been growing up. Nick had heard him tell his mom probably a thousand times that Nick was worth far more than a nickel. Their mom would just shake her head and tell him even a nickel could be priceless if it had sentimental value.

"Yes. As soon as I get some R&R."

"Okay, then. Talk to you tomorrow. I love you."

"I love you too, Dad."

With a sigh, Nick ended the call and threw his phone down on the bed next to him. He rubbed his hands over his face. He had to figure out how to keep his dad from flying to Virginia.

"Your dad on your case?"

Nick turned to see Ax leaning against the doorway, half in the dark of the hall. He tensed up as he realized Ax had heard his conversation. He hadn't really discussed Mase with his father, had he? His dad had thrown out that crazy idea, but Nick couldn't remember saying Mase's name. He didn't want anything getting back to his brother.

"More the other way around." Nick didn't know why he felt the need to defend his dad, but he did.

"You're getting on his case? Sounded like he was pushing you to do something you didn't want to do."

Nick stood and turned to face Ax. He got the loyalty to Mase that all the guys had, but there were at least two sides to every story.

"On the contrary. I was telling him not to do something foolish."

"Foolish? Who says that?" Ax laughed as he moved into the room.

"Me, apparently," Nick said, but he smiled at how old-fashioned it sounded. "Look... I know you guys all hate my dad, but—"

"I don't hate your dad," Ax said.

"You don't?"

"No. I don't know him, so how can I hate him? I'm not sure I like him, though, at least from what I know."

"What exactly do you know?" Nick demanded.

Neither his father nor Bray had been very specific on the details of Mase's departure from the family. All Nick really knew was that there had been a fight when their dad had found out Mase was bisexual. Their dad had asked Mase to leave. Mase had and he'd never come back.

"I don't know any specifics. I just know your family turned their back on Mase when you guys found out he was bi."

"We did not." Nick blew out a breath. "At least Bray and I didn't. My mom didn't either, which is pretty much why my parents got divorced."

"I haven't even met your mom, but I like her already."

"Tearing the family apart even more isn't always the best answer," Nick said.

"I get that," Ax said quietly, "but sometimes you just can't fix what's broken, so you have to start fresh in order to move on. Sometimes we just can't forgive and forget."

Nick nodded but didn't say anything. They both stood there, lost in thought, not quite looking at each other.

"I noticed you call your dad every day. You two seem close."

"I'm all he has," Nick said.

"Really? I remember Bray risking his ass to get a message from your dad to Mase."

"It's different with Bray. He's selfless with everyone. He'll go see my dad, but it's mostly because he wanted to make amends before Dad dies. I'm the who checks up on him every day, I'm the one who stuck around to make sure he was okay and I'm the one who watched him fade away."

"Seems to me he treated each of you three a little differently, so it would make sense you treat him differently."

"I know he made mistakes, but he learned from them. He's changed. He feels remorse, regret. He's not without a conscience. That is what's killing him."

"What's killing him? Mase?" Ax asked.

"Not Mase. It's the whole situation. He had a family, then it shattered. He changed long before his stroke. He seemed to melt away, bit by bit. He's still in love with my mom, but he has to watch her be married to someone else. He missed half of Mase's life. Bray didn't speak to him for years. Do you know what it's like to keep paying for one mistake you made years ago?"

Nick's voice rose as he ended his tirade. His dad wasn't perfect, but didn't he even deserve the chance to apologize?

"I know exactly what that's like," Ax said.

Nick looked at him and realized by the haunted look on his face that Ax did know. He and Nick's dad could be matching book ends. Ax's punishment may not have been as long, but it was sharper.

"Unfortunately," Ax said, "some mistakes set things in motion you can't fix or take back. Sometimes one mistake can cause a lifetime of pain, and only the person who was wronged can decide if forgiveness will ever be granted."

Nick moved before he even realized it. Ax was carrying a burden Nick didn't fully understand, but he felt for him. He wondered if Ax would let anybody share that burden. Ax's eyelids were drooping.

"You should really go to bed," Nick said.

As he walked toward Ax, the light reflected off something in Ax's hand. A bottle dangled from his fingers. It had been in the dark, but as it swayed it caught the light. Nick wondered if the liquor was why Ax had been so honest.

"Are you drunk?" Nick asked.

"Not yet." He smiled and took a few more gulps of the amber liquid.

With a shake of his head, Nick took the bottle. Ax tried to grab it back, but his depth perception was off and he missed. Nick felt a little pissed and embarrassed that he'd just bared his soul to someone who might be three sheets to the wind.

"You need to sleep this off. If you don't get rest, you're going to make a mistake and get us all killed."

"I won't," Ax said. "Won't let anything happen to me until I find…what I'm looking for." He shrugged.

Nick's heart squeezed in his chest at the thought of something happening to Ax. He shook the thought right out of his head.

"And what about the rest of us? Are we safe until you find what you're looking for?"

Ax stared off into the distance and didn't answer.

"You drink too much," Nick complained as he grabbed Ax's arm and steered him toward his room.

"Was it Kiev — or do you just hate me on principle?" Ax asked.

"I don't hate you."

Ax snorted.

"I don't. I just don't particularly like you."

But the words felt like a lie as they fell from his lips. Nick did like Ax, probably a little too much. And he was coming to respect him too.

"Yeah…from the moment we met. You had it in for me right away," Ax said.

When he remembered their first meeting, Nick's stomach tightened uncomfortably. "You were making fun of us. You called Bray 'Hot Cakes'. What kind of name is that?"

"It's a perfect name for someone enamored with pancakes."

"Pancakes?"

"He didn't tell you the story?" Ax asked.

"If it happened in Kiev, he didn't tell me anything. Said it was classified."

Ax snorted again.

"Are you saying it isn't classified?"

"The mission is. Your brother's love for pancakes isn't. It's probably a good thing you don't know what I did in Kiev. You'd hate me even more."

"What did you do?"

"It's classified."

Nick smiled, despite himself.

"Did you make a pass at my brother?"

Nick immediately regretted asking the question. His tone was way too concerned for his liking, and it was none of his business, even if something had happened between him and Ax.

"Bray's adorable. We were all a little surprised by his arrival, and he sure is good-looking, but he had eyes for Sam from the very beginning. I'm the reason they're together, but also the reason Bray was shot. It makes me feel like a dumbass and a cupid all at the same time."

Nick gave a relieved laugh as he eased Ax down on the bed. Ax immediately fell back and closed his eyes. Nick watched him for a moment, thinking he was already passed out, until he spoke.

"He doesn't have your sinful mouth, though," Ax mumbled.

"What?"

Ax opened his eyes, and they had that look, like he was getting ready to zing Nick with an insult again. He smirked a little as he looked Nick over.

"You have any idea how many times I've imagined those lush lips stretched around my cock?"

Mutely, Nick shook his head.

"I've lost fucking count. That's how many."

Nick groaned. If Ax wasn't so drunk, Nick would be crawling into the bed to show him exactly what it would look like, despite the fact that he shouldn't even do it if Ax were sober.

"You're drunk," Nick said.

"Not too drunk to get it up." Ax nodded toward the tented crotch of his pants.

"Is it even possible for you to get that dunk?"

"Not with you around," Ax grumbled.

Why that warmed Nick from the inside out, he couldn't exactly say. Ax was a mess. Ax was an asshole. Ax had accepted a date with Max. That stray thought had Nick's guts tightening again.

"It's not just me or you wouldn't be going out with Max. I think you're just horny."

Ax had closed his eyes, but they popped open again and he looked adorably baffled. "Max?"

"Yeah. He asked you out."

"He did? How did I miss that?"

"The morning after the gala fiasco with Jazz, he asked Wade if it was against company policy for operators to date each other, then he marched over and asked you out. Wade and I both watched you nod and laugh."

Ax's eyebrows pulled together in confusion as he seemed to think hard about what Nick had said. Ax burst out laughing. Nick wanted to punch him in his smiling face for finding it so amusing. Ax sobered and turned to Nick.

"Does Wade think he asked me out too?"

"Didn't he?"

Ax laughed even harder. "Man, no wonder he had a such a stick up his ass in my debrief."

"Why do I suddenly feel like we're speaking two languages?" Nick asked.

Ax scooted back and pressed himself against the headboard as he sat up. He was still chuckling as he reached over, opened the drawer of the nightstand and pulled something out. When he straightened up, he tossed it at Nick. Nick caught it against his chest and looked down at the little USB drive.

"Max wasn't asking about dating so he could ask me out. He was asking because he knew there was already something going on between the two of us."

"What?"

"Something he caught on tape."

Nick was horrified as he looked down at the USB drive in his hand. He hadn't even known there were cameras in the gym, although it made sense there would be cameras almost everywhere in HC.

"That's right. His first order of business was to make sure our security was as tight and hack-proof as possible. He was creating some sort of program for security footage when he came across a video of us frotting in the gym in the wee hours of the morning."

"And this?" Nick held up the digital drive between his thumb and forefinger.

"He didn't know if we'd have any interest in watching it. He saved that copy before deleting it from the servers."

"Oh, thank God." Nick sagged in relief.

The last thing he needed was for both of his brothers to know about — or, God forbid, watch — the little anger fuck session they'd had on the mats in the gym.

"So no interest in watching it? Max said it was hot."

"You…you didn't watch it?"

Nick didn't know why he felt disappointed. Wouldn't it be creepy for Ax to be watching them when Nick had no knowledge of the video? And yet, he liked the idea of Ax getting off to thoughts of him—or even videos of him.

"Nah. If we were dating, you can bet I would have saved it onto my hard drive, but with the way things are…" Ax waved his hand between the two of them as if that explained it all. "I figured you wouldn't want me watching us having hate sex, even if Max said it was hot."

Nick didn't like the way Ax described what had happened. It had been hot. Both times with Ax had been the hottest sex he'd ever had, but Ax kept talking about 'hate', and that didn't sit right with Nick.

"I keep telling you I don't hate you. I just don't like you calling me 'Nickel'."

"It's how I first thought of you," Ax admitted. "Bray called you Nickel from the start."

"But you know I don't like it."

"That was just a bonus. The first time we met, you were on my case. That's still true to this day. I was sure Bray told you I was the reason he got shot, but now that you said he didn't, I'm even more curious why you were gunning for me as soon as we met."

Nick thought back on the day they'd met. Enough time had passed that he could objectively look back and realize that his snark that day had come from a few things. His dad had recently had another mini stroke, Bray had been shot but was going to join up with HC anyway and Mase was still refusing to meet with their father.

And to top it all off, the hottest guy he'd ever seen in his life was flirting with his brother and hadn't even acknowledged Nick. Then Ax had suggested Bray might be joining HC to trail after him. That had been the last straw.

Bray would have been crazy to join HC just to follow his crush—especially a crush as cocky as Ax had been that day.

"I might not have been at my best that day. I didn't want Bray to join HC after being shot on one of your ops."

"I get that."

"You mentioned he might be joining up to follow you around, so that didn't make me like you very much either."

"I was joking that he was joining to be around Sam, not me."

That made more sense now, as Nick thought about it. The antagonism between him and Ax had just spiraled from there. Sure, he would have preferred a different kind of relationship with Ax, but Ax *was* a little bit of an asshole.

"I'm sorry about the first day we met," Nick said.

"Finally, I get what I'm owed."

"I think you owe me an apology too."

"What for?"

"For being an asshole that day and every day since."

"I'm sorry you think I'm an asshole," Ax said.

Nick shook his head, but he was smiling. It felt like something had settled a little between them. That seemed to ease some of the tightness in his shoulders.

"You should probably get some sleep," Nick said after the silence between them drew out.

"You wanna stay and cuddle?" Ax smiled.

Nick almost gave in. Almost. But Ax was still at least a little drunk and Nick was sure it would lead to more than cuddling.

"Maybe when you're sober," he said instead.

Nick brought Ax a pitcher of water with a glass and a few aspirin before heading to his own room. He lay on his bed in the dark and went over the revelations from Ax's drunken tirade. As he was falling asleep, he realized to his chagrin that he did like Ax a lot more than he should.

Chapter Eighteen

Ax

When Ax woke up, he didn't have a hangover, but he felt completely out of sorts. He remembered the night before a little too clearly. Now that he and Nick weren't frenemies having hate sex, he didn't really know where that left them or how to act around Nick, so he ended up avoiding both his teammates for as long as possible.

He'd gotten a text from William Campbell asking them to be at his estate in Sonoma at six p.m. It was a weeknight in San Francisco, so traffic could take ninety minutes or it could take three hours. It was anyone's guess.

Around lunchtime, Ax couldn't take his growling stomach anymore. He trekked to the kitchen to see if any of his mom's leftovers were still in the fridge. When he came around the corner, Ax found Nick and Jett already there, laughing and joking as they prepared lunch together.

Ax's steps faltered as he felt a strong urge to turn and head back to the office until they were done with their lunch. One of them would probably seek him out to join them anyway, though, so he stayed where he was.

As he entered the kitchen, Ax reminded himself that Jett was straight, so it was stupid to be pissed about the easy rapport he had with Nick. It was also stupid because Nick wasn't his in the first place, regardless of Jett.

"I didn't know you could cook, Jett," Ax said.

Both men stopped what they were doing and turned to look at Ax.

"Actually, I'm a great cook. My mom taught me how to take care of myself. Can't say the same for Nick," Jett joked.

Ax looked at Nick for the first time, and Nick gave him a shy, unsure smile. Apparently Nick didn't know where they stood either. He was pretty sure that if they were naked in the same room, they'd know exactly. Ax shook away that thought and returned Nick's smile.

"I feel like I'm missing a story here," Ax said.

"Nick burned some of your mom's precious leftovers. We were just putting together the last of them. You want some?"

Ax nodded and went to the cupboard to grab himself a plate.

"I'd love some of your mom's recipes, especially the tamales. Or if she wanted to send over another load of food, I wouldn't be opposed."

"I'll ask about the recipes," Ax said.

As they sat down and ate together at the table, Ax watched Nick and Jett. He didn't really understand why Nick was okay with Jett teasing him. Nick was actually doing a lot of his own teasing.

"I'm going to find out what 'Dash' means," Jett threatened.

"What's 'Dash'?" Ax asked.

Nick turned red all the way to his ears, which intrigued Ax all the more.

"It was my call sign. And good luck finding out. Bray will never tell, and only a few other guys know the real story."

Ax was surprised he hadn't known Nick's handle. He was usually the one who sniffed out things like that. Maybe it was a good thing he hadn't, since the name seemed to embarrass him even more than 'Nickel'.

"It's got something to do with running naked or getting caught naked," Ax guessed.

"Like streaking?" Jett asked.

"Probably," Ax agreed.

"You guys are so far off the mark," Nick said.

"Maybe he's a minute man." Jett nudged Nick with his elbow. "Maybe he *dashes* to the finish line without taking care of his partner."

"I know that's not true," Ax mumbled.

"So I was right," Jett almost yelled. "I knew it was sexual tension. Shit, I'm glad you two got that out of the way. You both seem a lot calmer today."

The tips of Nick's ears were red again, but when he looked at Ax, there was no anger there at what he'd let slip. If anything, it looked like Nick might actually be up for another round together. Ax cleared his throat.

"Maybe it's an acronym," Ax suggested.

Nick froze in the process of scooping food up with his fork. It only lasted a second. It looked just a little like hesitation, but Ax knew he'd just stumbled onto a truth.

"Maybe," Jett agreed.

Ax decided to go easy on Nick, so he changed the subject to the plan for the evening. They had Max's camera buttons with audio that would be undetectable, and they would all be armed, since Campbell had practically told him it was allowed.

After lunch, they had a secure call with Wade and Sam to discuss everything. Once they had an approved plan, they all went to shower and get ready for the evening.

They left at four p.m., so it gave them a little extra time in case there was any kind of hold-up. Ax wasn't too concerned. Campbell was obviously having them watched, so he'd know when they left. Ax and Nick waited in front of the building so they'd be seen while Jett retrieved the car from the underground garage.

It was just a few minutes after six when they buzzed the gate of the large private vineyard owned by Campbell. The wrought-iron gates slid open, and Jett drove the car through.

"Looks like any other vineyard, and yet it gives me the creeps," Nick said as they drove past all the rows of grape vines.

Jett grunted in agreement.

"You think his wife even knows about this place?" Nick asked.

"No," Ax and Jett said at the same time.

"That's what I thought," Nick said.

"Are you nervous?" Ax whispered.

Nick gave him an assessing sideways glance. Ax had no intention of teasing him, though he was pretty sure that was what Nick was worried about.

"I've seen death and blood," Nick said. "I may be gay, and I may not have a sister or anything..."

Nick paused for a moment and gave Ax a look. Ax wasn't sure what the look meant. Had his face shown the punch to the gut he'd felt when Nick had said the word 'sister'?

"But I do have an amazing mother who taught me to respect all humans in all forms. I've never seen anyone tortured or enslaved. They showed me pictures and stuff in training, but this is real life. My only concern is that my face might betray a little of the horror I'm sure to feel bursting out from the inside."

"You've got a pretty good poker face," Ax said. "Just remember that the only way to protect and hopefully save some of these women — or at least women like them — is to put their safety above your feelings. The success of these ops depends on all of us. We can joke and talk shit during down times, but when we're on, it's all about saving the lives of people who are taken against their will. We are their only voice, their only chance for freedom."

Nick nodded and was looking at Ax in an intense way, like he was absorbing the very truth of his words. Ax took a deep breath and told his body to back the fuck down. Having Nick's sole focus like that was a powerful aphrodisiac.

"It's easy to want to burst in there and save the ten or twenty women he has locked up, but he'll just replace them. They'll just take more women and hide them in a different place. The only way to really end this is to work our way to the top of each ring and make sure every last fucker is in jail — no deals, no pleas…jail. For the rest of their fucking lives, if I have anything to say about it."

"I get that. Thanks. Keep the end in mind. I'll try to remember that."

Jett pulled to a stop under a large portico that covered the main stairs of the mini-mansion at the end of the drive. Ax and Nick waited for Jett to open the back door.

There was a man standing beside the front door and Ax had counted six more walking the grounds as they drove up. Campbell was doing very well for himself.

Ax handed over the card Campbell had given him in his office. The man looked down at the card then looked back up at Ax. Ax gave him a confident smirk. The guy backed up and opened the front door for them. They were led to a room at the back of the house that looked to be a comfortable sitting area.

Ax and Nick were seated at a small table with a variety of hors d'oeuvres and a few types of caviar. A man came in to offer wine and advised that Mr. Campbell was running a little behind. Ax went immediately for the caviar. He liked the salty taste of it, though he was never willing to pay his own money to buy it. He figured it went along with his cover that he'd have expensive taste.

He and Nick talked about the move as Jett plucked a book off the shelf and thumbed through it, his gaze flicking toward the guard at the door every few seconds. As Nick scanned through his phone and they discussed fictitious meetings, Ax knew Jett was quietly setting the tiny pin cameras Max had given them into the spines of the books.

They would be undetectable unless someone actually took the book out and read it. Even then, it would probably be passed right over. Max had assured them that even though it had audio and video, it wouldn't show up on a scan of the room.

When he was done with the bookshelf, Jett walked around the room looking like he was checking security, but he was probably placing a few additional pins. They would only last up to seventy-two hours of actual recording. Overall, they could last days or weeks, depending upon how often they were sound-activated. But it would give them insight into Campbell's operation at least from the room they were in and the entryway, where Jett had hopefully placed another pin or two.

The harder part would be to see if Jett could get the second device installed. It was a faceplate that snugly fit over any outlet and could draw power to stay on indefinitely. They'd taken a risk that his outlets would be either white or almond. The outlets were almond, so if Jett could get one or two outlets placed, they'd have unlimited access to this room until someone figured out about the covers. That could take months…or even years.

Max was giving them a technical edge that they'd never even dreamed of having before he and Bray had used that same edge to drop Bray in the middle of a shitstorm. Now that they had an address, Max had also been able to tap into the security for the house, so he was watching the feed and said he'd be able to splice out anything where Jett looked suspicious, doctor it and set it right back into their servers.

"Ax," Campbell said as he stepped through the door, "I'm so sorry I'm late. I got tied up in court then stuck in traffic."

"Don't worry about it, Campbell. The caviar and wine kept me occupied," Ax joked.

"Please, call me Bill. The wine is from the vineyard. I hope you like it. It's just a little side project, really, but I do love wine."

Ax nodded, not knowing what else to say.

"I won't drag things out any further than necessary. I'm excited to see how you like your gift."

There was something in his voice that had the hair on the back of Ax's neck rising. An idea popped into his mind that maybe Campbell knew exactly who he was and had Cherie.

There was no way that was true, but he didn't take another breath until the door behind Campbell opened and a young girl, about fifteen years old, was led into the room. The guard had her by the bicep and roughly pulled her to a large cushion on the floor at the opposite corner of the room from where they sat.

The girl yanked her arm away from the man before huffing and plopping down where she was told. There was no doubt that the girl would one day be a beautiful woman, but Ax simply saw a girl. He smiled at her spunk. If she was fifteen, as he'd guessed, she was the same age Cherie had been when she had been taken.

"This is Mona. You said you liked spirit. This one has loads of it," Campbell said with a smirk as he took in Ax's smile.

Wanting to appear a little eager, Ax stood and walked over to the girl. She looked straight ahead as he approached from the side. She gave him a quick side glance before looking ahead again. He slowly walked all the way around the large pillow she sat upon, taking in her youth and obvious inexperience.

He squatted down next to her and told her in Spanish that she was very beautiful. She turned and looked at him for a long moment. He tried to show her with his eyes that he could be trusted, but she shook her head, gave him a sardonic smile and told him that it was a curse and now she knew why they said, "Beauty is pain."

Ax laughed. She watched him warily but didn't look away. This girl reminded him so much of his sister that his heart felt lighter and heavier than it had in years. It was almost like he was getting to save Cherie, because even if Campbell now told him he had to pay for this girl, he would...whatever the cost.

He'd pay any price to save someone who wasn't yet broken. Then again, he'd probably pay even more for someone who already was, someone who wouldn't last much longer in this life.

"*La vida es dolor,*" he said.

Life is pain — it was a line from one of his sister's all-time favorite movies. He'd watched *Princess Bride* with her thousands of times. She said it was the best kind of fairytale. Ax hoped Cherie could have the kind of faith Princess Buttercup did at the end of the story. He might not be her prince, but he was her brother, and he was coming for her, no matter how long it took. And nothing would stop him.

The girl scrunched her eyebrows together in confusion before turning and staring straight ahead. He belatedly realized she probably thought he was warning her about what she was in for. She was much too young for the reference, but it was too late to back out now.

"What did you say to her?" Campbell asked when Ax returned to the table where Nick sat.

"I told her she was beautiful."

"She didn't seem pleased," Campbell said.

"No, she didn't," Ax smiled.

"I think you're even more sadistic than I thought, Hernandez."

Ax shrugged and sat in his chair. They all watched her as she sat like a statue. She was young but full of pride and dignity. Ax was proud of how she held herself.

"This one may be a runner," Ax told Jett.

"We have an insurance policy we offer our clients. I didn't add that to Mona yet, but I can if you like. You can test it out. It may be another way we can help each other."

"Insurance?"

Ax's stomach cramped with worry. In his past experience, what handlers and pimps used as 'insurance' was getting their slaves hooked on drugs, so they had to keep coming back for more. It was how they kept them from asking johns to help them escape or trying to keep some of the money they earned.

"Why don't we go to my office for a moment?" Campbell asked.

With a flick of his head, Campbell let one of the guards know it was time to take Mona away. Ax moved to stand, but Campbell put a hand on his shoulder. Ax's stomach rolled at the mere sight of the douche touching her, but he remained still.

"They're just going to get her ready to go. She'll meet us in my office. I'm so glad you approve of my choice."

"I do." Ax said.

They were all quiet as they walked through the hallways. There were a couple of men stationed at key points in the house. Most just nodded to Campbell as he walked by. Finally, he opened a door and they all stepped into a large, opulent office with a great view of the entire vineyard.

"A few years ago, I obtained a client who is a doctor. He's quite the sadist. I'm not into that sort of thing, but I don't judge. We do our best to train the women not to run. But his first purchases only lasted weeks. The first two ran. The third killed herself. He learned not to have any prescription bottles in the apartment he keeps for his toy."

Ax could feel the stiffness of Nick's posture beside him. He shot a glance at him, but his appearance was that of a professional personal assistant. Ax was pissed at himself for letting Nick's emotions distract him from the task at hand.

He fucking wanted to soothe the man for having to act like it didn't sicken him that Campbell had a client who was likely torturing innocent girls.

"As a heart surgeon," Campbell continued, "he had an idea. He inserted an ICD under her skin that he had an engineer friend modify."

"An ICD?" Ax asked.

"It's an internal defibrillator. It tracks the heart and sends shocks if the heartbeat becomes irregular. Inside a person with a perfectly functional heart, it will do nothing. My client had a remote added so he could send electric pulses to the heart on command."

Ax lifted his hand to cover his mouth. At the last second, he caught himself. He rubbed his fingers back and forth across his chin and hoped he appeared to be in thought. He really just needed to keep the food he'd just swallowed from coming back up. His first thought was Cherie. The chances of Campbell having been the one to take her were slim, but something like that would be a reason she wouldn't be able to escape or try to contact them.

"And this can work from anywhere?" Nick asked when Ax took too long to reply. "Talk about cutting edge."

Campbell smiled at Nick. The man was excited about this device. Pride shone from him as if he'd thought of the idea and implemented it as well.

"Yes. It's our most effective deterrent."

"How far can it reach? Miles?" Ax asked.

This caused Campbell to deflate a little.

"No. In truth, you would need to be less than fifty feet away in order to make it work. But we aren't dealing with educated women, are we? A few low-grade zaps and the woman understands the consequences of running away. We haven't had one with the insurance policy even try."

Ax tapped his fingers against his lips. He was still thinking about Cherie.

"It seems a little risky."

"Risky?" Campbell scoffed.

"Yes. If a client pays hundreds of thousands of dollars for a woman and she gets zapped on accident in a week or a day, he's going to come back looking for compensation."

"And we'd give it to him. It might take a while if his tastes are rare, but we would compensate him."

Ax nodded.

"We've been doing this for a few years, and we've never had an issue. I could make my physician friend available if you needed an insurance policy or if you wanted to incorporate him into your organization as well. It would be more lucrative for him than actually practicing medicine."

"I think we might be interested in that, but only for a few test cases in the beginning."

Campbell smiled and nodded.

Ax smiled in return as he thought of meeting the doctor and cutting the man's heart out with a spoon. Campbell patted his desk as if he'd gotten exactly what he wanted from the meeting.

"I can practically see the numbers calculating in your head," Campbell said. "I think you will serve your boss well. Though I don't wish to actually be incorporated into your organization, I would like to have a good working relationship."

Chapter Nineteen

Nick

Nick watched Ax and Campbell's discussion. Ax was excited about something. Nick could feel it, and Campbell apparently could too.

Nick wondered if this new turn of disgusting events had tipped him off about something regarding Cherie. He wondered how much Ax knew about her disappearance.

"This is very interesting technology. I'll talk to Sam."

"And Mr. Bernard, of course," Campbell said.

"Yes. He'll make the ultimate decision, but I have a feeling he'll be willing to work with you. This could definitely add to our business. Will it be possible to meet with this doctor of yours at some point? I can guarantee Sam will want to see how this all works."

"That can all be arranged."

"I can't help but wonder where your tastes lean," Ax said. "I'm willing to bet they're rare."

"My tastes are unusual. I, of course, appreciate women in all shapes and forms, but my preference was something my family found…unacceptable."

"Now I'm even more intrigued," Ax said.

Campbell pulled out his phone and typed something before putting it back in his pocket.

"I'd love for you to meet Akifa while you're waiting for Mona to pack her things."

Nick wondered what the hell was really happening to Mona while she 'packed her things'. There was no way they'd showered her with gifts. They'd obviously expect whoever bought her to do that…or not.

A moment later, the office door opened and a woman with skin as dark as ebony walked in. She was dressed in a cream-colored pantsuit that was open almost to her navel. Her hair was intricately plaited across her scalp and fell in long, thick braids to her waist. Her fingernails and toenails were painted bright red, as were her lips.

When she saw Campbell, she smiled, showing bright, white teeth that contrasted starkly with such dark skin. There was no question she was beautiful, but even as she smiled, her dark brown eyes were dead.

"My dear… My friend Mr. Hernandez wanted to see my prize possession. This is Akifa. It took me years to find her."

Nick felt unbearably uncomfortable. His skin was hot with embarrassment on the girl's behalf at being treated like a car rather than a human. The girl was obviously young. There was no way she was older than sixteen. She was probably younger than that, but he just couldn't bring himself to think about it too closely.

He was beginning to understand Ax a bit better. How unbearable would it be to look into the dead eyes of this beautiful girl and see his own sister?

"She is a rare beauty," Ax agreed.

"I had to find her myself. No one had anything like her. It was how I started all this," Campbell waved his hands around the room. "I knew there had to be a market for rare beauties. Even with my connections in DC, I couldn't find what I was looking for. Now I help others in my situation."

Nick didn't understand why the man didn't just find a Black woman to love and marry. He lived in one of the most liberal and progressive cities in the country. Plenty of people had a type. If his type was black women, who would care?

Nick didn't know who he was attached to politically. Maybe it had something to do with that or the girl's age. It would be more accurate to say that Campbell's type was Black girls. Campbell dismissed the girl and she left quickly and happily.

Campbell herded them out of the large office, and they found Mona waiting for them next to one of the guards by the front door.

She was dressed in a little sundress that she was practically bursting out of. She pulled at the hem as the men said their goodbyes. There was a small suitcase beside her that Jett took as they all walked through the front door.

Nick sat in the front seat with Jett and Ax sat in the back with Mona. The mood in the car was tense and stilted.

"Were you able to pack all your things?" Ax asked when the silence had gone on too long.

"I don't have any things anymore. That's just a bunch of stuff that makes it look like they treated me with any decency. It was all a diversion so they could remove the chastity belt they made me wear."

"Chastity belt?" Ax asked.

"Yes. Apparently, bossman doesn't trust his men to keep me pure, but that didn't stop them from touching the 'goods'."

Mona grumbled the last part under her breath, but they'd all heard it. Nick could tell by how Jett was clenching and unclenching his fingers around the steering wheel.

"I hope we can get along," Ax said. He ignored her snort and continued. "I'll give you a few days to get settled in and we'll get to know each other."

"Oh, I'm sure we will," she said.

The girl had guts. Nick liked her. Campbell had treated her like cattle and yet she didn't hold back. Maybe she was trying to figure out how she'd be treated now. Or maybe she was a spy for Campbell. They'd discussed that possibility.

"Look." Ax's voice took on a rough tone. "I'm not sure how things went in that place, but I like to be respected. I don't like to use my size and strength, but I will if I have to. I like your spirit, but not enough that I'll be willing to deal with a bunch of shit."

"So, if I talk too much, you'll just pass me along? Big deal. You could always just let me off anywhere and maybe I can find my mom."

"Honey, your mom's probably the one who sold you to him."

Nick looked back when he heard the smack of skin on skin. Ax was holding his cheek and fighting a smile.

He liked her too. Nick could tell by the twitch of his lips, but he grabbed her wrists and held them down. She struggled against his hold, but he kept her still.

"She was missing before they even took me, asshole. She loves me. She would never have done anything like that. She was the kind of mom who would sell herself to save me, not the other way around."

"You need to calm down, Mona," Nick said.

He had his gun in his hand and her eyes widened slightly when she saw it. She pulled back from Ax and sat back against her door with her hands in her lap. She seemed so small and alone. Nick put his gun away to stop himself from giving her any comfort.

"My name's Ramona, not Mona," she whispered. "Ramona Ruiz."

She said her whole name like a talisman, like it was something she was afraid she'd forget. Nick wanted to give her a fucking hug. It was going to be so hard to keep their cover going in the penthouse.

Nick sent Max a secure email asking him to check to see if anyone had reported Ramona Ruiz missing in the Bay Area. Max's reply was instant, and he asked Nick how far back to look. Nick asked for six months.

Before they were pulling into the garage, Max had replied that there was no missing persons report for Ramona Ruiz, but there was only one Ramona Ruiz under the age of forty in Oakland, California. She was last listed as attending Oakland Technical High School. Her age, fourteen. Nick closed his eyes in disgust.

Behind his lids, he could tell when they drove under the building. The light he'd seen through his eyelids disappeared. He wondered if it gave Ramona a sense of doom. She was a child.

Nick knew the statistics of what he'd be facing, knew a lot of the people taken were minors, but this was the first one he'd met, and it was gut wrenching. His sympathy for the girl was so strong that he felt frozen. Part of him wanted to run so far away from this job, from this assignment, but he couldn't.

Now that he'd seen it, he couldn't bury his head in the sand. He had to fight for these kids who had no skills to escape. All they could do was try to survive their circumstances. But he could help his brothers and this team do more. His mind kept drifting back to Ax calling his sister's name. There had to be something they could do to help there, as well.

When Jett turned off the engine, Nick opened his eyes and burst out of the car to take a few deep breaths. Needing something to do, he opened the trunk and retrieved the small suitcase Ramona had brought with her.

"Leave the suitcase," Ax said as he got out of the car.

"But she'll want—"

"I said leave it," Ax said.

"She'll at least need toiletries," Nick argued.

"Are you questioning me?" Ax's voice was low and deadly.

Nick was about to argue but looked at Ramona. She was watching the dynamics between the two of them. With a sigh, Nick set the suitcase back in the trunk and closed it.

Ax took Ramona's wrist and led her to the elevator. She kept looking at Nick under her lashes. Did she see him as an ally? That wouldn't be the end of the world. Although, if she was a spy and he showed weakness, he'd be pulled off the op.

Nick looked at Ax as he tried to figure out if he wanted off this assignment. The elevator doors opened to the penthouse and Jett locked the private elevator to the top floor for the evening.

"I'll show Ramona to her room. Nick, please bring her a toothbrush and a shirt she can sleep in."

With that command, Ax led Ramona away. Nick gritted his teeth and got a new toothbrush from the amenities in the bathroom. He took a T-shirt from his closet, since Ax's clothes would be much too big for the girl. As he approached the room they'd designated for her, Nick heard them talking.

"I get my own room? Are you locking me in, too?"

"There's no need to lock you in. The elevator and stairway are locked unless you have the code. If you're hungry, there's food in the kitchen. If you want to watch TV, there's one here or there's a larger one in the entertainment room."

"Are you trying to lure me in? I'm not used to wealth, but I'm not impressed by it either."

"I'm not doing anything. We can make this introduction hard, or we can make it easy. You were a gift, but I'm not a monster." Ax said.

"I guess we'll see, won't we?"

Before Ax could respond, Nick knocked once and pushed open the door that sat ajar. They both turned to look at him. He didn't know why he was jealous. There was no way in hell Ax was going to touch the girl. She was a child. They all knew that. Yet she now belonged to Ax.

"Toothbrush," Nick said helplessly as he held it up.

Ramona huffed and turned away from them both. Ax gave Nick a shrug as he headed toward the door. Ramona walked to the window and looked out.

"Let one of us know if you need anything else," Ax said.

She didn't respond. Ax told Nick he needed to speak with him in his office, then left the room. Nick was about to follow him but remembered belatedly that he still held her toothbrush and shirt.

"I'll just set your toothbrush here on the bed," Nick said. "And here's a shirt you can wear to sleep. We'll probably have to figure out your clothes situation."

"Why not just make me walk around naked?" Ramona asked as she spun to face him.

"I'm not sure Ax would like everyone seeing what's his," Nick said.

"I'm not sure if he'd mind if you saw me naked. You're gay, right?"

"I am."

"I could tell. You look at me like you're trying to figure out why the other men are looking at me the way they are."

"I know why. I can see beauty even if it doesn't turn me on. I was trying to figure out why Ax was being so patient with you."

It was a lie, but it might give her some comfort to think that Ax might be kind to her because she was special. She looked intrigued by his answer.

"You want him? You can have him," she said.

"I do okay on my own." Nick smiled. "I don't need hand-me-downs, thanks."

She smiled at him, but the grin fell from her lips after about two seconds.

"You help him. You do this same thing to vulnerable people," she said.

This was something Nick thought he had prepared himself for, to pretend to be a monster so he could blend in with other monsters. But in the face of an innocent child, it was something completely different. Nick pictured what Ax's sister might look like and imagined what he did now might save her or someone like her.

"I do what needs to be done," Nick said with a frown. "Have a good night."

"Yeah, right. I have so much to look forward to."

Nick didn't respond as he left the room but heard the lock click into place once Ramona shut the door. Why the hell did he want to defend himself to her so badly? He felt a pull to the girl. He wanted to protect her, soothe her. Nick shook the urge away and went to Ax's office.

Chapter Twenty

Ax

"We're about to start checking the feed from Campbell's house." Wade said. "So far, we've checked the office feed. His office has been empty since you left. Sin will also keep an eye on the security footage, but there's no audio on it."

"They gave us a suitcase for her, but we left that in the trunk of the car. She says the stuff in it isn't hers."

"Ramona Ruiz," Wade confirmed. "Nick sent Sin a message. He's already found her. It looks like it's her."

Ax was surprised that Nick had already reached out with intel. Then again, he'd known Max a long time and would be comfortable keeping him in the loop.

"She said her mom went missing before she did."

"The mother named on her birth certificate is Lluvia Ruiz and her father is Ernesto Ruiz. Sin is trying to see what he can find, but we've sort of loaded him down. Everyone's got something for him to do. We're trying to triage."

"I get it," Ax said as he wondered if the poor kid would have any time to help him with his personal project. "We just need to figure out how far we go with this act and the girl. How old is she, sixteen?"

"Fourteen," Wade said. "Campbell swept for bugs once you left but didn't find anything. I guess I should specify that they swept the room you were in for bugs. They didn't even sweep the hallway, so we can confirm by what's said there that they didn't find any of our devices."

"Sin's some sort of genius." Ax said.

"Never figured a nerdy genius would be your type," Wade said.

Ax bit back the laugh that bubbled up inside him. Maybe it would do the man good to be a little jealous. Wade was too confident. He bordered on cocky.

"I don't have a type. You know that."

Wade's only response was a quiet grunt on the other end of the line. Ax shook his head at the man. If he wanted Max, maybe he should just ask him out. Even if Ax did go out with him, it would be casual, not exclusive.

"We'll keep an ear on Campbell tonight and touch base tomorrow. For now, just keep up the appearance that you're in control of your men."

"Ten-four," Ax said. "Out," he added before ending the call.

When he looked up, Nick was standing in the doorway, watching him. They stared at each other for a few seconds before Nick strolled into the room.

"Don't look at me like that," Ax said as he rubbed his eyes.

"Like what?"

"Like you're surprised I'm an asshole. You've thought so from the moment we met."

Nick shook his head but smiled.

"Look… If you want to get the girl some clothes, head out in the morning and buy her a few things. It's not like we have anything on the books for the next few days. Just don't let her doe eyes pull you in and get you to do something stupid or I'll have your ass."

Nick smirked at Ax's wording. "Yeah, okay. I'll go get her a few things. I'll need to get her size."

"I'm a size six," Ramona said.

They both turned to see her standing in the doorway. She gave Nick a shy smile. There was a spark of hope in her eyes. She was hoping for him to be her hero, but he couldn't unless she was really the victim she was claiming to be.

"I don't have any toothpaste." She shrugged with a smile.

Nick escorted Ramona to get toothpaste. Maybe they *should* lock her in her room. Ax shook his head. They couldn't make her afraid, even if she was a spy for Campbell. In the end, she was a child and a victim, even if she'd been tricked into helping her captor.

Ax looked at his phone. It wasn't even eleven p.m., but he figured he'd take his laptop to his room and see if he could get some work done on Cherie's case. Just as he was settling down in bed, there was a knock at the door.

"Yeah," he said as he pulled the blanket up to his chest in case it was Ramona.

Nick stuck his head in and smiled. That was all it took for Ax's pulse to jump. Ax took a deep breath and casually propped up his knees so Nick wouldn't see how easily he affected him. Was it stupid of him to hope Nick was sneaking into his room for a booty call?

"I got the rest of Ramona's size info," Nick said.

Since Ax had witnessed part of it, he nodded.

"Also…" Nick stepped into the room and closed the door.

Heat spread through Ax as Nick came a little closer.

"Your mom texted me," Nick said.

That had Ax's sex fantasy evaporating. He rubbed the heels of his hands over his tired, stinging eyes. He really couldn't deal with the feelings his family brought up. He looked at Nick. He was still in his suit from the meeting with Campbell and he filled it out in the best possible way.

"Just handle it for me, okay? Tell her whatever will keep her happy. I can't deal with telling her you're not really my boyfriend, and I can't exactly pop over for dinner with Ramona here in the condo. That wouldn't be fair to Jett."

"I get it. I'm willing to help, but—"

"If you want to help, take off your clothes."

Nick went still. Then he licked his lips.

"Lock the door," Ax said.

Even though Nick's breath was coming faster and his pupils were dilating, Ax was still expecting a refusal until Nick turned and did as he'd asked. Ax pulled in a surprised breath when the lock snicked into place. His hard-on went from a semi to a full throbbing erection with that small scrape of metal on metal. Hopefully Nick would be naked and underneath him soon.

When he spun to face Ax again, Nick pulled at the knot in his tie. Ax smiled and sat up as he set his computer on the nightstand.

"It's my turn to top," Ax said conversationally.

"Lucky for you, I'm vers." Nick threw his tie on the bench at the foot of the bed and began to unbutton his shirt.

"Lucky is definitely what I'll be feeling when I push inside that sweet little ass."

"You like trying to shock me," Nick said.

"I like to be honest."

"Is that what that is?"

Nick always turned Ax on. From the moment they'd met, he'd made Ax's body yearn, but this was new. It was different. Every time they'd come together, it had been fueled by anger and need. This was simply want.

Before, he'd had to practically goad Nick into sex. This time it had been a simple request. It was like Nick was agreeing that there was something between them, and it was heady.

Ax knew this was temporary. It had to be, but fuck if he didn't feel hopeful that maybe — just maybe — Nick might see something redeemable in him. Maybe that was why he was slowly removing his clothes without taking his eyes from Ax's.

Ax stood from the bed and dug through his suitcase to find the lube and condoms he knew were there. By the time he turned back around, Nick was naked, his cock hard and flushed. Ax pushed his sleep pants off his hips and let them fall to the floor.

He gave Nick a wicked smile as he moved toward him. He felt lighter, happier, because he could feel that Nick wanted this too. They weren't fighting or pushing each other. They were both smiling.

Nick's bottom lip was so full and plump and tempting. When he was close enough, Ax leaned and gently bit it, pulling it with his teeth.

Nick groaned and skimmed his hands down Ax's back. He cupped Ax's ass cheeks before pulling them apart. Ax smiled as he let go of Nick's lips. He shook his head.

"It's my turn to top," he reminded Nick.

"Is that what we're doing? Taking turns?"

"Since we're both willing to top and bottom, it only seems fair."

Nick laughed and leaned in to kiss Ax. He opened his mouth and tangled their tongues together. The kiss was playful. Though it was still hungry, it was gentler than their previous kisses, but just as hot.

Ax stepped forward. The move aligned their cocks and they groaned into each other's mouths. Ax cupped the back of Nick's head even as Nick used his grip on Ax's ass to press them more firmly together.

Before long, they were both humping frantically as the kiss burned out of control. Ax pulled back, panting for breath as he watched Nick lick his red, swollen lower lip.

"On the bed," Ax demanded.

"Oooh, bossy."

"Impatient. I've been imagining that tight ass since the day we met."

"Since we met?"

Ax hadn't meant to admit so much, but he truly was impatient. He wanted to see Nick's hole stretching around his dick. A little regretfully, Ax looked at Nick's mouth. He'd had plenty of fantasies about those swollen lips stretched around his length as well.

"I said, on the bed."

"Mm-m. I think I like impatient Ax. That little growl in your voice makes my cock twitch," Nick teased.

Ax paused. This was the first time Nick had teased him playfully. It felt like he was with the real Nick, not the bitter, angry Nick that Ax seemed to bring out.

He wanted to bottle up this light feeling and store it away for the times when it felt like there was a boa constrictor around his chest. Ax shook off the thought and watched as Nick fell back and bounced on the bed. He laughed at the sight.

"Roll over," Ax said.

Nick did, then he got on his hands and knees and stuck his peach-shaped ass in the air. Ax ran a hand over one of the cheeks before gripping one in each hand and spreading him for his view.

"Your ass is perfection." Ax rasped.

"So I've been told," Nick said with a smirk over his shoulder.

Ax smiled up at him. He ran a fingertip over Nick's opening and watched a shiver snake up his spine as he groaned. Ax leaned forward and licked along Nick's back. Goosebumps fanned out to either side of the wet line he'd created.

When Ax leaned in and circled Nick's pucker with his tongue, Nick gasped. The hole under Ax's tongue spasmed. He pulled back long enough to watch a drip of pre-cum fall onto his sheets.

"Don't fucking stop," Nick demanded.

"Who's bossy now?"

"Please," Nick amended.

In answer, Ax dove in with his tongue pointed. Nick whimpered and pressed back against Ax's face. Ax tried to smile at the reaction but couldn't with his tongue out. As he ate at Nick's opening, Ax blindly reached for the lube with his free hand.

Flicking the cap open, he poured a little on his fingers. When he pulled back, Nick whined in protest. Ax chuckled as he used his thumb to spread the liquid around.

"Why are you going torturously slow?" Nick asked.

"I told you. Your ass is perfection," Ax reminded him.

"I'd rather it be irresistible. I, uh, haven't bottomed in a while, so don't go too fast, but faster than this would be good."

"Topping from the bottom?" Ax asked as he pressed his thumb inside.

"Fuck," Nick groaned.

"Too much?"

"Not enough. Want your cock or your tongue or just...just more."

Ax smiled at Nick losing his words. He pushed in farther and Nick gasped when he pressed hard against his prostate before rubbing back and forth. Soon he had three fingers stretching Nick wide.

"If you keep that up, I'm coming now."

Ax gently pulled his fingers out and ripped open the condom wrapper. He watched Nick swing his ass from side to side as he grunted impatiently. Ax rolled the rubber on and lubed up before pressing himself to Nick's pucker. When he pressed in, Nick grunted and sucked in a breath.

"Too much?"

"Just go slow," Nick said.

Ax pulled back. He didn't want to hurt Nick. With a whine, Nick looked back over his shoulder. When he saw Ax standing back, his covered cock straight out in front of him, Nick licked his bottom lip and his cock jumped with excitement.

"What's wrong?" Nick asked.

"Nothing. I was just thinking that since you like topping from the bottom, why don't you bottom from the top?"

"What?" Nick laughed.

"Trade me places."

Nick scrambled up and Ax lay down on his back. He used his thumb to lift his erection off his stomach and point it toward the ceiling. Nick's eyes didn't leave Ax's crotch as he crawled up on the bed.

"I thought you liked to be in charge," Nick said as he knee-walked over Ax's body.

"I do, but you said it's been a while. It'll be better for you if you can control it."

"That's almost...sweet," Nick smiled down at Ax.

That smile was sweet, too, and it had Ax feeling things in places other than his dick. He cleared his throat and ran a hand up Nick's abs. Nick shivered as he wrapped his hand around the base of Ax's cock and pressed it to his opening.

Ax didn't usually let guys ride him. He didn't usually let guys top him either. Then again, he'd never attacked a guy and rutted up against him until they'd both come, either. He was allowing Nick to affect him in ways that made him uncomfortable.

Then all the thoughts left Ax's head when the warmth of Nick's body enveloped him. He fisted his hands in the sheets next to Nick's bent knees to keep from thrusting up into the tight heat.

Nick dropped his head back as his ass slowly descended. Ax's focus moved down Nick's luscious body. He let his hands glide along his solid thighs, over his six-pack, all the way up to his defined pecs and shoulders.

Then Ax did something else he didn't really do. He clasped his hands at the back of Nick's neck and pulled him down for a hungry kiss. When Nick pulled back slightly to get some air, Ax sucked on his bottom lip, the one he found so tempting.

When Nick's channel tightened around his cock, Ax smiled, still keeping Nick's lip captive between his teeth. He started experimenting, letting Nick's tight, clenching ass tell him what he liked.

Nick liked Ax's mouth on him. It didn't seem to matter if it was on his mouth, his neck or his nipples. Nick liked it all. Ax did too, and he usually wasn't big on kissing, but the hungry kisses Nick gave had him close to blowing his load.

Ax rolled them over, so he was on top. He scooped his arms under Nick's knees and spread his legs up and out. He looked down and watched his cock disappear into Nick's body. It was so hot that his balls drew up and a tingling began at the base of his spine.

"Fuck. I'm not going to last," Ax warned.

"Good. I'm close too," Nick panted.

Ax looked down into Nick's eyes and could see a desperation there that drove him. He picked up his pace and began to pound into Nick. His back arched, Nick bit his bottom lip and squeezed his ass cheeks tighter. He was reaching for his orgasm, but Ax wanted it to come on its own, so he pulled back until only the head of his dick was still inside Nick and he stopped.

"Don't fuck with me now," Nick demanded. "I'm almost there."

"I'll give you what you need," Ax said.

After another hesitation, Ax slammed all the way home. Nick gasped, then he groaned and whined and egged Ax on with little flicks of his hips. Ax held him still as he changed his angle until Nick opened his mouth but no sound came out. Ax knew then that he was pegging his prostate.

Nick's eyes went wide, his pupils blown so wide that Ax could barely see any of the blue of his irises. Nick didn't close his eyes or turn his head like a woman would. Ax had never fucked a man in this position, so he didn't know what a man would do, but Nick kept his gaze locked on Ax's.

Ax couldn't tear his eyes away, so he blindly reached down and grabbed Nick's cock. He stroked him once, twice and on the third stroke, Nick erupted between them. Ax watched his eyes roll back slightly as his lids fluttered.

It was the sexiest fucking thing Ax had ever seen in his life and it threw him high over the edge. His abs jerked, his legs weakened and his muscles spasmed as his body tried to deal with such acute pleasure. It exploded from him like a starburst.

Even as he still floated on the cloud of his orgasm, Ax started to worry. How did it get better every time he was with Nick? It had never been this good the second or third time he'd been with someone. Then again, he usually didn't care if he liked or respected the person he fucked. He felt both for Nick.

"Fuck," Ax said as his dick gave one last spasm before he gently pulled out.

"Yeah," Nick sighed and began to close his eyes as he curled up like a tired cat in the middle of Ax's bed. It wasn't a good idea for Nick to stay. If Ramona came to his room for any reason, it wouldn't look good.

He could always say he was using Nick to give Ramona a few days to adjust, but it was still a bad idea.

When Ax came back to the bed after throwing away the used rubber, he watched Nick.

Nick moaned a little in his sleep. Ax smiled as he climbed into the bed. He'd give Nick a few minutes to rest.

Chapter Twenty-One

Nick

Nick's back was sweaty and hot. Something hard was poking his ass. When he tried to stretch, the warm arms that were wrapped around him tightened. The fog of sleep cleared from his brain and he smiled as he remembered where he was.

There was a change in Ax's breathing as he slowly woke up. As he did, he again pressed his morning wood into the cheek of Nick's ass. Nick's smile grew, even as his ass ached a little from the sex the night before.

"Morning," Ax said softly next to his ear.

A thrill ran down Nick's spine when Ax thrust his hips forward again. His voice was raspy and sexy from sleep. Nick pressed his ass back, putting pressure on Ax's erection. Ax groaned and lightly bit Nick's shoulder.

He wouldn't mind waking up like this more often, but he wasn't sure that was a possibility. Last night had been more of a fun coming-together and less of the angry sex they'd had previously. It wasn't like Nick would knock the angry sex, but he would sure take the cuddling that came with the fun kind.

"You playing possum?" Ax asked.

"No. Just enjoying your cock in my ass."

"You mean 'on' your ass. If you want it *in* your ass, I'd be more than happy to oblige."

Nick was just about to take him up on the offer when there was a knock at the door. Nick looked at the clock. It was only six forty-three a.m.

"Ax," Jett said through the door, "is your phone off? Sam wants a meeting and he said your phone is going straight to voicemail."

Behind him, Ax scrambled out of bed and searched for his phone. Nick sighed as he too got up and put his pants on.

"My phone died. Sorry, Jett," Ax said.

"No problem. Thought it must've been something like that. I'll go round up Nick," Jett said.

"Nick's right here," Ax said. "He just heard everything you said."

Nick froze with his pants halfway up his thighs. It wasn't like he was embarrassed about having been with Ax—or wanting to be with him again, for that matter. He was more surprised that Ax was so blasé about it. He'd figured Ax would want to keep their rendezvous a secret. Nick actually felt something inside him break free at the honesty.

Nick looked up at Ax, who raised an eyebrow at him. *Is he waiting for me to get pissed? That isn't going to happen.* Instead, Nick gave him a wink and a smile as he pulled his pants the rest of the way up.

"Finally," Jett mumbled. "Does this mean you two won't be at each other's throats anymore?"

"No guarantees," Nick said.

Ax chuckled as he pulled on a shirt.

"Any signs of life from our guest?" Ax asked.

"Nope…unless you count some light snoring."

"Give us ten minutes," Ax said.

"Sure thing, boss," Jett said.

Nick was picking up the rest of his clothes and heading for the door when Ax grabbed his arm. Nick gave Ax a questioning look.

"We have ten minutes," Ax said. "I can get off in five with some decent…visual stimulation. If we do it in the shower, we can kill two birds."

The smile seemed to burst from somewhere deep inside Nick before it spread across his face. He dropped all the clothes he'd just gathered and unbuttoned his pants as he headed for the bathroom. Ax laughed as he followed him in.

It didn't even take five minutes of them jerking each other with some body wash before they were done and clean. They panted as any evidence they'd just jacked off washed down the drain. Ax turned off the water and Nick quickly dried himself before heading to his own room for clean clothes.

By the time he walked into the office, Ax and Jett were already there. They'd installed a camera outside Ramona's door, so they'd be alerted if she came out of her room.

Nick blushed when Jett gave him a knowing grin as Ax dialed for the secure line. It was Wade who answered, but that wasn't too much of a surprise. Because Ax's phone was charging, he was calling on a line from the condo, so they had to go through security protocol.

"HC," Wade said.

"Hotel Charlie three-eight-six-four-two-seven lima oscar ten-eighteen," Ax responded.

"Hotel Charlie four-eight-seven-four-three-two lima alpha ten-five," Wade responded.

"I've got you on speaker." Ax said. "What's the latest?"

"We've been getting a lot of feed from Campbell. It's safe to say your visitor is a victim. Last night Campbell had another client come to pick up his...purchase. Let's just say this man wasn't as civilized as you were and demanded to test the merchandise right then and there."

At Nick's quick intake of breath, Ax looked over at him. Ax looked as green as Nick felt.

"Please tell me Sin wasn't the one to —" Ax started.

"It was me," Wade said.

"Why don't I feel any better?" Ax grumbled.

Wade wouldn't want to see that any more than Max would, but Nick was sure Wade had seen worse. Max wasn't even military. Wade was the only one on the team — beside Max — who wasn't army. Wade was a former Navy SEAL. The dude was former Team Six, best of the best, yet he'd probably puked after watching that, just like Nick would have.

"I look at it as ammunition in the archives. The client was a certain wealthy philanthropist with strong political ties. We need to get eyes in Campbell's lair in DC. We might get enough ammo that I could probably become President."

"First gay President...or maybe not. Who the hell knows what they do in private?" Ax said.

"I'm not joking, Ax. Let's make this happen," Wade said.

"I'll work on it." Ax sighed.

"The second visitor was much more interesting. The feed Jett was able to get in the office is gold on this one. We have an ID on the surgeon doing the implants."

"Don't give me a name. If you do, I'll be tempted to make him holey," Ax said.

"Holy?" Nick asked.

"Yeah, as in full of holes."

Nick shook his head at Ax.

"I get it," Wade said. "But you may come face to face with this guy, so pull up your big girl panties. We need to find a way to take this guy out that will make it seem like you had no involvement."

"Then you should do something before Ax meets him," Jett said. "That way he can claim ignorance, since Campbell never gave a name."

"I'll put it in motion, but I don't know when Campbell plans on introducing you. The surgeon was pissed he was cut out of the meeting. Apparently, he gets to sample each girl he implants the defibrillator into…with only a few exceptions."

"That's why Ramona was safe," Ax said. "Her biggest selling point was apparently her virginity."

"The surgeon wasn't happy about that, either. This guy's a monster. He makes millions but spends it faster than he can make it. He's champing at the bit to meet you and Jazz and sell his services, because he's in over his head. He has some pretty nefarious ties, so it would be easy to make it look like his debts are being called."

"I'll delay a meeting," Ax said.

"What about Ramona?" Nick asked.

"Sin thinks he found her mom, but…in the morgue. She'd need to go identify the body and I'm not sure she's up for that," Wade said.

Nick couldn't even imagine what that would be like. He was about to lose his father. He was struggling to keep it all together and he still had a mom who loved him unconditionally. If he lost both his parents…and Ramona wasn't even close to eighteen.

She was all alone in the world. If there was anyone who needed someone like his mom, it was Ramona. She might end up tossed into a system that would do little to protect her from something similar happening again.

"She needs someone to talk to, probably a woman." Nick said. "She's not going to trust any of us, even if we do tell her who we are."

"I can try to find her a local therapist," Wade suggested.

"Or I could have my mom fly up here," Nick offered.

"She's a civilian." Ax flung his hand out as if punctuating his sentence.

"So are we," Wade said. "Even government ops sometimes involve civilians, but Nick, are you sure you want to pull your mom into this?"

"She knows the basics of what we're doing. She hates it and yet she loves us for doing it. She's the most compassionate person I know. She's also a woman. And she'll keep things quieter than any therapist."

Bray had broken down and told her why he wanted to work with Mase even after being shot. She hadn't liked it, but she'd understood. She'd cried and declared all her boys heroes when Nick had joined up too. She'd also told them they'd better keep each other safe.

"Campbell is having this place watched," Ax reminded him.

"And we've been sneaking in and out unnoticed daily. We could also meet somewhere else. We could make it look like my mom was some etiquette teacher or something. There are a million ways we can get this girl support, and she's going to need it. She's going to need someone to be with her when she sobs because her mom is dead, and I don't think she'll trust any of us to do it."

Wade sighed over the phone. He could practically hear him shaking his head at the suggestion.

"Warn your mom about the situation…the entire situation. And don't think I'll be keeping this from either of your brothers."

"Like they can tell my mom what to do," Nick scoffed.

"I'll want to clear it with Mase and Jazz before giving the final go-ahead, but reach out to your mom and see if she's even willing to do something so crazy. This case is getting all FUBAR," Wade grumbled.

"Any more instructions, boss?" Ax asked.

Nick looked up when he heard the strain in Ax's voice. He was looking at Nick like he wanted to kill him. The morning had gone so well, and now it looked like they might be back to fighting.

"Keep me apprised," Wade said.

"Ten-four," Ax said before disconnecting the call.

They sat there looking at each other. Jett stood from the seat next to Nick and patted him on the shoulder before heading out of the room without a word. *Traitor.* Nick stood as well.

"Your mom could be in danger if she comes up here," Ax growled.

"I can do my best to make sure she's not. If she knew a girl was in the clutches of a monster and was about to be thrown into the game of Russian roulette they call the foster care system, I'd be the one in danger for standing by and letting it happen."

"That girl's not ending up in foster care," Ax said.

"You gonna adopt her?"

Ax pressed his lips into a thin line but didn't respond.

"She has no one else. There's no family out there looking for her, ready to keep her safe."

Ax's jaw worked. Nick was sure they were both thinking about how lucky Cherie was to have someone looking for her day and night.

"Fine," Ax ground out. "Call her, but warn her to keep quiet and that we'll have to sneak her in."

"Agreed. I'll do whatever it takes to keep my mom safe."

Ax snorted at that, but Nick let it be and got up to leave the room.

"I'm going to go get some clothes for Ramona. I'll be back in a bit," Nick said.

"Check for tails. Maybe let them tail you so can see if you can figure out who's watching the building and from where."

Nick nodded and left before Ax could question him further. He replied to the text Ax's mom had sent him, then sent a secure email to Max to see if he could help figure out who was watching the building.

Next, Nick called his mom, then his dad. He didn't tell his father what he'd asked his mother to do. It didn't matter that his parents had been divorced for years. His dad thought he had a say in his mom's life. He refused to have his dad anxious about something he had no control over.

He got a frantic call from Bray — and likely Mom did too — but ultimately, Sam and Jazz left the final decision up to his mom, so she bought a ticket.

Chapter Twenty-Two

Ax

Ax paced the office for twenty minutes before breaking down and calling Max. He was edgy knowing that Nick was going to offer for his mom to come visit them.

"Sin City," Max answered.

"Sounds more like a porn shop than a tech shop," Ax said.

"It's a habit."

"It's funny. Why's 'Sin' your handle, anyway?"

"It's not as cool as it sounds. A couple guys in college called me a Super Intel Nerd. It sorta stuck."

"Hmm, such nerdy beginnings, and yet in the end, it sounds so sexy."

"What can I do for you, Ax?"

Ax sat back from his desk and looked down at the patterns in the wood. He didn't want to tell Nick's friend that he didn't agree with Nick's decision to pull his mom in.

In truth, Ax was a little jealous of Nick's trust in his mom to make her own decision. Ax would never allow his parents to play even a minor role in what he was doing. He'd lost his sister, and that was enough.

He was also envious of Nick's selflessness, though he might be a little less likely to offer if he'd lost someone the way Ax had. But he was putting Ramona's mental welfare before any selfish desire to keep his mom far away from danger.

"I need you to check into how many men Campbell has watching this building."

"Already on it. Nick emailed me and Wade approved everything. I have one target following Nick as we speak."

"As we speak?"

"Yeah. He's going to the pharmacy nearby to get some things for your visitor. Then he'll come back, and I'll watch the target and all other angles while Nick sneaks out the back to make sure the back delivery entrance is a safe route to come and go."

Ax relaxed back in his seat as relief filled him. Nick was taking every precaution. It was smart. Ax needed to have more trust in him.

"Nick needs to learn to keep his team in the loop," Ax said.

"Oh, I think he just feels comfortable asking me for things. We've known each other a long time."

"I get it. I'm glad he feels comfortable, but we all need to know what's going on."

"We're both new to this protocol. We'll learn. My instinct is to always help or fix, especially for Bray and Nick."

"I'm glad they have you, Sin. Just let everyone else know what's going on. We're in precarious situations, and sometimes not knowing can put someone in danger."

"You're talking about Kiev," Max sighed.

"No. I'm talking about unknown situations. We're constantly facing the unknown, so we all need every bit of intel that's available."

"That's fair," Max said. "I've been analyzing security footage for all three-hundred-sixty degrees around the building. I've only seen two cars parked on the street at opposing intervals that are probably surveilling. There's nothing to indicate anyone is watching the service entrance you've been using to slip out."

"That's basically what we figured. Campbell doesn't see us as a threat. He's just watching his ass, making sure we are who we say we are."

"Looks like. Either way, I have the license plate and the name of the owner. His driver's license photo looks like the guy trailing Nick."

Something inside Ax tightened at the thought of Nick being tailed without backup. Nick could most definitely take care of himself. Then again, Ax had once had those same thoughts about Cherie.

"The guy following Nick... Does he have a military background?"

There was a flurry of clicking before Max answered.

"No. Petty crimes. He does own a gun—well, probably more than one—but he has a concealed carry permit in Nevada."

That didn't make Ax feel any better. Nick could hold his own one-on-one, especially against some paid thug, but a gun? Ax blew out a breath. Nick was an excellent shot. Ax had watched him, had looked at the logs at

HC. The army taught soldiers how to avoid being shot. He just hoped Nick had listened that day.

"Okay, Nick's heading back to your building," Max said.

"And the tail?"

"He's pretty obvious if it's so easy for me to spot him, since I don't have military training."

"Can you shoot?" Ax asked, wanting to keep Max on the line until Nick was safe inside the building.

There was laughter floating over the line.

"I'll take that as a no," Ax smiled.

"Do FPSs count?"

Ax laughed, and it was a laugh that helped relieve all the tension in his body. He was going to have to teach Max how to take care of himself.

"First-person shooters definitely do *not* count. Video games don't teach warfare. When we get back there, I'm going to ask for your help with something. In return, I'll teach you how to defend yourself and how to shoot."

"You're going to teach me how to fight? That's sweet, Ax, but you have no idea how clumsy I am. There's a reason I only swim for exercise. It's safe."

"Clumsy or not, I'll teach you some defense moves and how to handle a gun."

"Show me some moves first. After you see me in motion, you won't want a gun in my hands, I promise. What did you want my help with?"

Before Ax could even begin to answer. Max was clicking away and jumped back into the conversation.

"Nick's in the front door. Tail's back in his car."

Ax breathed a sigh of relief. Nick would probably pop into the apartment to drop off whatever he'd bought. Ax decided he was going to send Jett with him when he went back out. Ax could handle Ramona on his own. The girl hadn't even woken up yet—or if she had, she hadn't left her room. He was just about to say goodbye to Max when he continued on.

"And he's out the back. The man in the car's on his phone to someone. Think you can get Jett down there with a tracker so we can see where he goes?"

"Sure." Ax sighed.

He couldn't send Jett after Nick when they had the perfect opportunity to find out more about Campbell's operation.

"Great. I'm going to go back over the video surveillance and see what I find. I won't let Viv walk into a dangerous situation."

"Viv?"

"Nick's mom."

Ax nodded, even though Max couldn't see him.

"And when you get back, you can *try* to teach me how to fight and I'll help you with whatever you need, even if you fail epically in the teaching department."

"It's a deal," Ax agreed as he ended the call.

Ax sent Jett out to track the car. When he came back up, Jett brought the bag Nick had apparently dropped off with the concierge when he came through the building.

Taking the bag, Ax knocked on Ramona's door. He heard some rustling around in the room, but it took a while for the door finally open. Ramona was wearing the shirt Nick had given her the night before, but Ax also caught glimpses of the dress she'd worn from Campbell's house hanging just below the hem.

"Can I come in for a moment?" Ax asked.

"Do I have a choice?"

"Not really." Ax shrugged.

Ramona flounced away from the door, leaving it open for him to walk through. She went over to the window, staying far away from the bed.

"We picked some things up for you." Ax set the pharmacy bag on the bed, and Nick's out now picking up some clothes that will be more comfortable for you to wear."

"Comfortable or revealing? Because no matter what guys think, they are not the same thing."

'I'm pretty sure Nick will get you some things that are comfortable. I didn't exactly tell him what to buy, but he figured you'd need your own things."

When there was no response, Ax took a moment to look around the room. She'd obviously been up when he'd knocked, and he wondered what she'd been doing with no access to a computer or a phone. The corner of a book was peeking out from under her pillow.

Since her back was turned, Ax eased over to the top of the bed and gently lifted her pillow enough to see that she'd been reading *Anne of Green Gables*. The sight of that book slapped Ax in the face with the reality that Ramona was just a child.

After replacing the pillow, Ax decided to give her a little hope. He didn't have approval to tell her who he was just yet, but it looked like she was innocent in all this.

"You said something yesterday that had me curious," Ax said.

"Which thing would that be?"

He smiled at the lack of enthusiasm in her tone. She was such a teenager.

"You said your mother was missing before you ended up with Campbell. Was she taken as well? Maybe I could find out if she's available for —"

Ramona whipped around and looked at him.

"Don't," she said as tears gathered along her lower lashes.

"Don't what?"

"Don't try to play the nice guy to get me to like you. You're not going to find my mom. You're not going to do anything but use and abuse me."

"Damn, I love your spirit, kid," Ax said. "You remind me of someone who was very important to me."

"Past tense. Did you run her off or kill her or something?" Ramona said.

She was trying to be a little shit, but the accusation hit too close to home. He hoped Cherie was still alive. From his perspective, she wouldn't be better off dead, but if she'd ended up somewhere that was horrible and she'd... Ax shook his head.

"I'm not going to make promises I can't keep, but if you give me her name, I can see if I can at least find out what happened to her."

Ramona looked at him for a very long time. She reminded him of a feral dog hiding in the bushes. Ax was holding a big juicy steak and she was trying to decide if she trusted him enough to come out of the bushes to take a bite.

"Lluvia Ruiz. Her name is Lluvia Elaina Ruiz."

Ax put on his best poker face. Max had been right. Chances were that this girl's mom was dead, and she now had no one in the world to protect her. That wouldn't do...not at all.

Then he remembered Nick and what he'd offered. Nick had felt that protective surge for Ramona that Ax was feeling now. They'd find a way out for her.

Chapter Twenty-Three

Nick

"Nick?"

Nick turned at the sound of his name. Ax's mother stood by the front door of the coffee shop on the street level of the mall. His heart hurt for her when her face fell with the realization that Ax hadn't come.

"Mrs. Guttierez," Nick said.

"Please, I asked you to call me Cella."

"Cella, I didn't tell Ax I was meeting you. I told him you texted me, but he was too busy with work to even wonder what the text said."

Nick looked around and realized that even though he'd zigged and zagged, even though Max had said he wasn't being followed, and even though he'd circled the large shopping mall twice to be sure before going inside, he didn't want to risk being overheard. He couldn't risk Ax's family being tied to what they were doing.

"Can I get you something?" Nick asked as he guided her to an open table in the back corner.

"I'll have a vanilla latte, if you don't mind."

Nick got her a single shot and himself a double. He watched everyone walking by the window as he waited for the coffee. He tried to relax when no one even glanced in.

"Thank you," Cella said, when he handed her the coffee.

"It's not a problem."

They each took a sip. She gave him an awkward smile.

"I know you were hoping I could be some sort of bridge between you and Ax, and I wish I could, but he barely opens up to me."

"He's always been self-contained." She covered his hand with hers. "He's always covered hurt with jokes."

"He still does." Nick smiled.

Cella gave Nick a knowing look, one he couldn't return. She was looking at him as some sort of prospective mate for her son. There was no way Ax was thinking long-term.

"Ax has a laser focus," Nick said. "He works all day and spends all night searching and researching."

"He told you?" Cella gripped his hand hard as her voice went high with surprise.

"About Cherie? Yes and no. He didn't come out and tell me was happened. When he gets anxious and worried, sometimes he gets drunk. He'll say her name and talk about her a little. I had to divine who she was, since he's bi, but I figured it out."

"I feel like I've lost two children. Diego is all I have left, and he's sick of my hovering."

Nick nodded, because he'd seen the argument.

"Ax is angry with me. He blames me, and there's nothing I can do to apologize."

From what Nick had seen, Ax was too busy blaming himself to blame his family. Nick turned his hand over, so his palm was against Cella's, and he gave her hand a squeeze.

"Why would Ax blame you?"

Tears pooled so quickly in her eyes that it surprised Nick. She shook her head and used her free hand to wipe them away.

"It might be my fault. I was married before I met Nando. My ex-husband is powerful in Honduras. What if he found me? What if he took Cherie?"

"Is she his daughter?"

"No, but Ruby... I left him as soon as I found out I was pregnant. I couldn't let my child become like him if he was a boy or endure him if she was a girl. So I ran. I had a friend who married an American, and she told me to just get to Mexico."

She grimaced at a memory but went on.

"I sent her every cent I had. It was a gamble, but I had to try. I secretly sold what I could and took any money I'd stashed away for emergencies and sent it in chunks to her. I sold all my jewelry and sent that money to her as well. I took nothing with me. You see, my husband was in the military, and they would check me before I left the compound."

Nick wondered if she was telling him a secret that even her children didn't know.

"I had the clothes on my back and enough money for groceries. I used that to buy a change of clothes and a bus ticket. Every town I stopped at, I would contact my friend and she would wire me some money to get to the next place, so I wouldn't have to carry cash with me.

"I was sure he'd find me and drag me back, but I had to try. When I got to Mexico, she was there with her husband. They had some documents to get me over the border. She said I just needed to make sure to have the baby in America so he would be a citizen.

"I stayed with her in San Diego, but I began to worry it was too close to the border. I met Nando through my friend. His brother had sponsored him to come from Mexico. He was so unlike any man I'd ever known."

Cella smiled, probably at a memory of her husband. Nick stayed quiet and allowed her a happy thought. After a moment, the smile fell away.

"He was looking for me. My husband was looking for me. He had tracked me to Mexico but didn't find me in California. I panicked and began to pack, but then I went into labor. Nando was there. He was there from the first day Ruby was born. He listed himself as the father on the birth certificate because he had his green card. He promised me that if anything happened, he'd raise Ruby."

"Does Ax, I mean Ruby, know? Does he know about his biological father?" Nick asked.

"He knows. Nando said he had a right to know. We told him when he was fourteen. I brought it up when Cherie went missing, but he said he was worried it was something worse than revenge. I know he's right.

"Part of me knows that Geo would never do something like that without getting credit for it, but it's the only hope I have, the only lead I have. I wanted to go back to Honduras to look, but Nando said he wouldn't let me go alone. If something happened to both of us, there would be no one left for Diego."

She closed her eyes, and there was defeat and desperation in her posture.

"I'm not telling you that you should go to Honduras, but Ax would take care of Diego. He'd always have family."

"If we don't find Cherie by the time Diego is eighteen, I'll go back. I'll make sure she's not there as quietly as I can. We hired a private detective and he hired someone who was supposed to look in Honduras, but the man took our money and disappeared."

Nick had an idea, but he didn't want to give Cella any hope.

"Do you have a picture of Cherie?"

Cella smiled and nodded. She pulled a card from stack in her purse and handed it to Nick. It was a small, business-card-size photograph. The girl in the photo was stunning, her smile happy and radiant. Along the bottom of the picture were stats on Cherie — her age, the date of her disappearance, a phone number to call and an offer of a reward for information that brought her home. Nick stuffed it into his wallet.

"This is what you do? You canvas the city with these?"

"When I have time, while Nando's at work and Diego's at school."

"Do you have a digital version you can send me?"

Cella nodded and pulled out her phone. Nick started forming the email as she searched through her photos. By the time he got the picture, he attached it to the email and sent it to Max.

"Could you... Could you try to get Ax to give us another chance? To come to dinner again?"

"Cella —"

"I'm only asking you to try. I lost two children three years ago. It's just that one of them chose to leave and one of them didn't. I miss my son just as much as I miss my daughter."

"I'll talk to him," Nick promised.

"I'll let you get to your shopping. I just..."

"I understand," Nick said as he stood.

He did understand. He felt the same way with Mase. He had to keep trying any way he could to get Dad and Mase to make up before anything else happened to their father. If only he could find a way to do that without risking his own relationship with Mase.

Cella stood and wrapped her arms around Nick. She gave him a tight hug before pulling back. Reaching up, she patted his cheek.

"Thank you. I know you can't force him but thank you for trying."

With one last pat to his cheek, she released him and turned to leave. Nick sat back down for a few moments, drinking his coffee, before his phone rang. He left the shop as he answered.

"Nickel Arcade," Nick answered.

There was silence on the other end of the line before Max laughed. Nick smiled as he pulled open the door to the mall and entered. It was close to ten, so most of the stores would be opening soon.

"I never thought I'd hear you joke about that nickname," Max said.

"I guess you're rubbing off on me with your Sin City."

"Nick, this request you sent, it could take me days."

"I don't care what it takes. It's a personal request."

"I get that, but three years? Most places don't have security footage that old unless a crime was committed, and even then, they could take it off their servers."

"Please, just check airports as far back as you can — more than three years if it's available."

Nick cleared his throat. He was embarrassed that Max had surely heard the desperation in his voice. The thought of Nick's mom going to Honduras sent a chill down his spine.

"I'll check what I can. I'll try to just keep the search going and let you know what I find."

"Thanks." Nick almost said Max instead of Sin, but stopped himself in time. "You're a great friend, Sin, and I'm so glad you're the one watching our backs."

"I… Thanks, Nick."

"Later," Nick said.

He quickly disconnected the call to cover his and Max's embarrassment. Nick had always liked Max, always protected him, but mostly because Bray had. They hadn't exactly been close.

Nick made his way through some shops, buying a few outfits for Ramona, including a couple of bras, panties and shoes. He'd never picked out women's underwear, so he'd asked for help. The girl who helped him had been kind but had also assumed the undergarments were for him. He'd ended up buying Ramona bras that would bring out his blue eyes.

Nick chuckled as he left the mall. He knew some guys were into that. He even had a straight friend who liked to wear women's underwear. It was just funny that the woman had assumed that, rather than him buying it for his girlfriend. As he trekked back to the apartment, Nick called his mom.

"Nick, is everything okay? How's Ramona?"

"I haven't seen her today. I just ran out to get her some actual clothes."

"What does that mean? Did she not arrive… clothed?"

"She had a dress on, but basically that was it."

"I just can't wrap my head around this. I have a flight for this afternoon. I wanted to fly up earlier, but—"

"Mom," Nick interrupted, "relax. I'm so grateful you're willing to do this."

"Like there's any other option," she scoffed.

"Just remember not to talk about Ramona or why you're coming to San Francisco. These aren't people who like you discussing their business. They're very dangerous."

His mother sighed in exasperation. His concern was real, though. His mother was a social butterfly. She made new friends everywhere she went. Bray was the most like her—guileless, naïve, optimistic and yet stubborn as hell when he needed to be.

"I won't speak a word. I haven't discussed it with anyone but Gil...and Bray...and Mase, but that's it. I can keep a secret. Believe me."

There was something about the way she said it that had Nick wondering if that applied to him. With a shake of his head, he let the thought go. His mother was also fiercely loyal and true—another trait she'd passed on to Bray.

"Send your itinerary to that secure email address I sent you. It will either be me or Jett who picks you up at the airport."

"I can't wait to meet her. Love you," she said as she disconnected the call.

Chapter Twenty-Four

Ax

Ax had left his office door open to keep an ear out for Nick's return. Wade and Sam had given him the go-ahead to tell Ramona she was safe and break the news about her mother.

Ax wondered if it would be better for Nick's mom to break the news when she arrived. He shook his head. It might be better for Ramona, but it wasn't fair to Nick's mom.

When he heard Nick's voice, Ax came out of his office. Nick was talking to Jett as he moved through the main room of the penthouse.

"What the hell did you buy?" Jett asked.

"Women need more stuff than men do. They need options. I wasn't just going to buy her one thing."

Jett threw up his arms and shook his head in bewilderment. Nick gave Ax a smile but continued through the condo toward Ramona's room. Ax followed and quietly updated him as they approached

Ramona's door. Ax knocked, since Nick's hands were full.

"Hey, Squirt," Nick said through the door, "is that dress getting uncomfortable yet?"

Ramona answered the door much more quickly to Nick than she had to Ax, but he couldn't blame her. She pulled open the door with a smirk on her face, but her eyes went wide when she took in all the packages Nick carried.

Ax followed Nick into her room when she opened the door all the way. Nick laid all the packages on her bed then turned to give Ax a look of commiseration.

"I need to talk to you, Ramona," Ax said.

She hesitated before making eye contact with him, but her chin was high when she did.

"I was checking on your mother. The name you gave me." Ax cleared his throat at the look of hope in her eyes he was about to dash.

"I'm so sorry, Squirt," Nick said when Ax found he couldn't tell the girl her mom was dead. "There's a police report that your mom was killed."

The hope was snuffed out and replaced with sheer anguish. That was what his mother's eyes looked like when she talked about Cherie. It was why Ax couldn't bear to watch.

The fight was totally gone from Ramona. She looked at Ax after a moment, suspicion in her gaze. He'd figured she might doubt him, but he didn't want to have to show her the photo Max had sent.

"We have something else to explain," Ax said. "Please, sit down."

"I'll stand."

"She's not going to believe this part, either," Nick sighed.

"I was thinking I'd have your...Vivian tell her, but I didn't want to put that on her."

"Stop talking about me like I'm not here," Ramona yelled. "You're just trying to get me to trust you, but I don't. You're lying."

Tears ran unchecked down her cheeks as she panted from her outburst. Nick moved away from Ramona to give her space. He backed all the way up until he stood next to Ax. When their eyes met, Ax saw the sympathy he felt reflected in Nick's gaze. Ax gave him a smile to try to reassure him.

"You two are together, aren't you?" Ramona asked.

Ax turned and looked at her. She was swiping her knuckles under her eyes and looking at them with surprise. Ax wrapped his arm around Nick and nodded. Nick looked up at him in shock, but Ax was going with his instincts. She'd trusted Nick because he was gay. Maybe she'd be more willing to believe what they said.

"If we're being honest here," Ax said, "I don't want to have sex with children."

"Then why buy me?" She asked.

"I didn't. Technically you were a gift, because Campbell wants to do business with my boss."

"Why didn't you tell me this yesterday?"

"We didn't know if you were working with Campbell," Nick said.

"I would never do anything for him willingly," she said.

"We had to be sure," Ax said. "Anything you know about how they run that 'vineyard' would be helpful to us."

"Can you get the other girls out?"

"I can't guarantee you anything like that. If we go in and take girls right now, they'd just move and they'd know it was us. We need to dismantle the whole operation," Ax explained.

"But those girls... Some were younger than me."

"And if we go get them, what about the hundreds or thousands of other girls they'll take after them who we won't be able to find out about because we'll be made? It's a horrible choice with no real winners, but it's a choice we have to make every day."

Ramona looked at the floor but nodded. "I'll help any way I can," she said as she wrapped her arms around her middle.

Nick was right—she needed someone to talk to, someone to comfort her. None of the guys there were the ones to do it, either. Hopefully Vivian was as maternal as his mom was. Ramona could probably use a mother hen hovering over her right now.

"We'll give you some space," Ax said. "Let us know if there's anything you need."

Ramona didn't respond in any way except to collapse onto the mattress as he and Nick slipped out of the room.

"We're together now?" Nick whispered as Ax closed Ramona's door.

"I didn't say we were engaged or anything."

Why were Ax's cheeks burning? And why did Nick thinking it was all some joke make him want to ask what the hell was so funny?

"Are you saying you don't want me, Nickel?"

"I didn't say that. You know I want you. I just didn't know we were an item."

Ax shrugged.

"You wanna be my boyfriend, Ruby?" Nick teased.

"When did you get so annoying?"

Nick laughed in response.

"Are you seeing anyone else?" Ax asked.

"Like who, Jett?" Nick laughed again.

"I mean, like in SoCal," Ax said.

Nick's smile dropped from his face as he assessed Ax. Ax felt like a bug under a microscope. He wasn't even sure what he was asking

, but the thought of Nick with someone else made his insides burn. Why did Nick find it so amusing?

"I wouldn't be sleeping with you if I was seeing someone," Nick said.

"What about fuck buddies?"

"You're my only fuck buddy." Nick raised an eyebrow at Ax, as if willing him to disagree with the term.

"We're *not* fuck buddies. My mom is practically planning our wedding," Ax said as he headed for his office.

"Wait. Hold up. You can't say something like that and walk away." Nick was hot on his tail when he entered his office.

"Say what?" Ax asked as he plopped down in his office chair.

"You don't blame me for your mom's delusions, do you? I did that to spare her feelings."

"I don't blame you."

"Are you saying you don't want me to have any other fuck buddies?" Nick smirked.

Ax licked his lips as he thought about his response. He sure as hell didn't like the idea of Nick screwing anyone else while he was with him. *With me? When did I start using those terms?*

He looked at Nick, who had his hands on his hips as he waited for Ax to answer. If Ax gave his typical response, that he didn't care, Nick was just stubborn enough to go find someone else to fuck. That thought didn't sit right with Ax.

"Yes," he finally ground out.

"So, you want to be exclusive fuck buddies?"

Ax growled and pulled at his hair.

Nick laughed. "I'm just clarifying where we stand."

"What is it you want? Do you want to be boyfriends?"

"I wouldn't mind going out on a date to see if we could be compatible outside the bedroom."

Ax bit back his automatic response that he didn't have time to date. It was what he'd told every other damn person he'd slept with over the last three years, but he couldn't really believe Nick was admitting he actually liked him.

They were also in a unique situation where Ax probably could make time for him and still do everything he needed to do, especially if Max could give him some direction.

"I can't exactly go parading around San Francisco with you after accepting Ramona. When we get back to Richmond, we could go out and grab something to eat," Ax said.

"You sweep me right off my feet." Nick smiled. "We'll see if I still like your ass when we get back to Virginia."

"Oh, you'll still like my ass. It's the rest of me you might not like."

Nick shook his head but laughed. "I'm heading out to pick up my mom, unless you think it'd be better if Jett did."

"That's fine," Ax said. "Take the second car Wade had delivered, so there's no chance of our friend out front seeing you."

"Ten-four. Max will also be keeping an eye out."

"Just…be careful."

"Aw" — Nick batted his stupidly adorable eye-lashes — "are you worried about me?"

"I'm worried about your mom, asshole. You should be able to take care of yourself. Now get outta here."

He threw a pen at Nick, who easily dodged it and hustled out of the door. Ax leaned back in his chair. It took him a few minutes to realize that he was smiling and didn't feel quite so weighed down.

Chapter Twenty-Five

Nick

"Nick."

Nick turned to see his mom approaching the baggage claim. He greeted her with a hug. He'd had his mom fly into San Jose, as it was the farthest airport from the city and therefore the least likely that Campbell or any of his associates might use.

"How many bags are we looking for?" he asked.

"One. I didn't know how long I'd be staying, but it's San Francisco. Anything I didn't bring, I can find here."

Nick shook his head at his mother. "You can't go out and about. If you need something, I'll get it for you. I'm not sure how much you'll leave the condo where we're staying."

"Okay." She shrugged as they made our way out of the airport. "So," she said when he was pulling out of the parking structure.

"So?"

"So tell me about this smile you're sporting? I haven't seen it in a while."

Nick rolled his eyes but noticed when he looked in the rearview mirror that he was still smiling. Ax wanted to see where this went. It could end up going exactly nowhere, but it could also go somewhere.

"Oh-ho," she said. "Who is he? Do I get to meet him?"

"Who said it was a guy?"

"I did, and I'm right."

He'd eventually give in to her antics and tell her, but it was also fun to tease her for a while. And when his mom started car dancing to the song on the radio, he turned the volume of the music up rather than get embarrassed.

Ever since Mase had started responding to her emails, she'd become so happy. Mase had been gone for so long that Nick had forgotten how much fun his mom could be. She'd been loving but much more subdued when she'd lost touch with one of her children.

Nick had many memories of his carefree, charismatic mother, but they'd been lost somewhere on the edge of his consciousness until now.

Dad blamed himself for Mase's departure. They'd fought when mom had been out of town, probably visiting family. Nick couldn't remember. He did remember how angry he'd been at Mase, how abandoned he'd felt. He'd never stopped to think about how his mom had been affected.

In his selfish nine-year-old mind, he'd only considered things from his perspective. And a few years later, he'd been angry at his mom for further ripping their family apart by leaving his father. Now that he saw the difference in her, he realized how much it had bothered her and how hard it must have been, especially after what he'd seen of Ax's family.

"What's that look for?" she asked.

"I like seeing you so happy. It's been a while since I've seen this side of you."

Her smile dimmed a little, but she reached over and squeezed his arm. They were quiet as Nick drove. It wasn't an uncomfortable silence, but he felt bad for taking even a bit of his mom's happiness. She was there to do him a favor—and a pretty grim one at that.

She raised her brows when he drove into the delivery entrance of the garage but didn't say anything. Nick helped her unload her luggage and settled her into one of the guest rooms before introducing her to Ax and Jett.

"I never knew it was dark brooding looks that would have my Nickel chasing his tail," she said when she saw Ax.

"Mom," Nick scolded quietly.

"Mrs. Hart? You're not how I pictured you at all."

"Please, call me Viv. And what did Nick say about me? That I'm old?"

"I'm Ax," he said. "And it wasn't Nick who described you but Bray."

"Oh no. Then you thought I'd be a demure angel?"

"Something like that. I guess I should have known. Bray's a hopeless romantic and an eternal optimist."

"I won't knock either of those qualities. That and his tenacity has brought our family back together," she said.

Ax nodded.

"And this is Jett." Nick waved a hand in Jett's direction.

"Mrs. Hart."

"Please call me Viv."

"She's also not Hart anymore. She's Vivian Freiberg," Nick said.

"Hart-Freiberg, actually," she reminded him.

Her tone had been a little haughty. It was how she sounded when his dad reminded her that she wasn't a Hart anymore and she could no longer tell him what to do. Yet he always ended up grumbling and doing what she asked.

"I didn't mean anything by it. You know I like Gil."

She nodded and gave him a small smile. He did like his stepdad. Gil was soft-spoken and kind. Their father called him 'the lawyer', like that made him scum, but Gil was an estate attorney. The guy made a fortune creating trusts for rich people and donated his time and expertise as a CPA to help people with tax issues who couldn't afford to pay someone. He wasn't an ambulance chaser.

"Where is she?" His mom was practically bouncing in anticipation. "I can't wait to meet her."

"Mom, she's been through a trauma. She's not ready to be your shopping buddy or whatever."

"You said she's smart and funny and gorgeous. She'll fit right in with the rest of my children." His mom gave him a wink.

Nick rolled his eyes, but they all turned when Ramona said, "You told your mom I was smart?"

Nick nodded and shrugged at the same time.

"You're smart enough to survive and bide your time," Nick said.

"I knew you hated me when I was talking to you at Campbell's," Ax said. "It was coming off you in waves, but you kept your cool. Plus, you asked all the right questions. You were hesitant to believe we were on your side but also looked at it logically. Smart."

Ramona nodded. She had her arms wrapped around herself. Nick's mom walked tentatively toward her.

"Hi, I'm Viv, Nick's mom. He told me all about you and I flew up here so we could meet. Can I... Would you let me hug you? I'm so sorry to hear about your mom and —"

That was all Viv got out before Ramona flew into her arms. It hadn't even occurred to Nick that she might need a hug. He'd assumed she wouldn't want anyone to touch her. Maybe it was because she was a woman, maybe it was because she'd asked or maybe it was because she was a mom. Either way, Nick was glad Ramona had someone she felt comfortable with.

* * * *

"Is your mom still in with Ramona?" Ax asked.

His mom and Ramona had come out for dinner, the first meal they'd actually gotten Ramona to eat. She'd also opened up a little and told them some of what she knew about Campbell's organization.

"I wouldn't be surprised if my mom sleeps in Ramona's room while she's here," Nick said.

"Sounds like your mom wants to take Ramona back down south with her."

Nick nodded. She was determined. Wade was checking to see if they could put her under a false name with equally false documents, giving Nick's mom and stepdad custody of Ramona.

"Your stepdad's down with that?" Ax asked.

"You don't know Gil. He's head over heels for my mom."

"If he's okay with it, I think it might be the best thing for her, to get her out of this area, to give her a new start."

Nick nodded as they walked down the hallway to their rooms. He wondered if Ax was right and he'd just put his family in danger. He sure as hell hoped none of the traffickers that worked with Campbell would find out Ramona was living with his parents.

"I was thinking that I'd have Jett head down to Southern California with them, if they get clearance to leave," Ax said.

Nick turned to Ax as they walked down the hallway. It was a thoughtful gesture, one Nick hadn't even been aware he could request. Ax's eyebrows were raised in question. Instead of answering, Nick laughed and shook his head as he backed Ax into the master bedroom and shut the door behind him.

"I think it's my turn to top." Nick smiled.

"Oh, well, taking turns doesn't mean we're going to have to keep track of who topped last, does it?"

"You're just saying that because you want to top again." Nick laughed.

"True. But still, we should just go with it and not keep score."

Nick liked both, but his preference was usually to bottom if he trusted who he was with. It surprised the hell out of him, but he trusted Ax more than anyone he'd dated recently.

"You gonna take your clothes off or do you need me to do it for you?" Ax asked.

"Are you always so bossy in bed?"

"I'm a take-charge kind of guy, if you haven't noticed."

Nick had noticed. He pulled his shirt off, unbuttoned the jeans he'd worn to the airport and kicked off his shoes. He pushed down his underwear with his pants, yanked them off and threw them both over his shoulder.

Ax was naked, hard and pulling condoms and lube out of the bedside drawer when Nick crawled to the middle of the mattress. He got on his hands and knees, but Ax easily flipped him onto his back and pulled him so his ass was dangling over the edge of the bed.

Ax glided a lubed finger over his opening as he hovered above Nick. He nipped at Nick's lower lip as his thumb circled Nick's entrance.

"I'll tell you what," Ax whispered. "If I come before you, you get to come in my ass."

With those words between them, Ax pressed his finger slowly inside Nick. He curled his hips in as the sting turned to a slight burn.

"Then no touching my cock."

"Challenge accepted." Ax smiled as he pumped his finger in and out.

Nick moved his ass back and forth on the bed as Ax grazed his prostate. He was so hard that his dick curved up and started leaking below his belly button. Ax looked down at Nick's erection and licked his lips.

"You're not being fair," Nick complained.

"What? I like how you taste."

"Fuck. Don't say shit like that," Nick groaned.

Ax pressed a second finger inside him. Nick looked up to find Ax multitasking. He was stretching Nick with one hand and putting a condom on with the other. Nick hadn't even heard the tear of the wrapper.

As he watched Ax suit up one-handed, he wondered what it would feel like if Ax fucked him bare. Nick was taken aback by his own stray thought. He'd never had sex without a rubber. He'd never trusted anyone enough or been in a relationship that long.

When he felt the tip of Ax's cock at his entrance, he tried to relax. Ax was big, but he'd taken him before and it had felt amazing. Ax leaned over him as he pressed in farther.

"So fucking tight. Do you have any idea how amazing you feel as your body tries to suck my cock in farther?"

"I fucked your tight ass. I know exactly how it feels." Nick groaned.

Ax paused in his forward progression to smile down at Nick.

"I really like this teasing Nickel," Ax said.

Nick smiled and shook his head at Ax for saying that right in the middle of sex. It was sweet and adorable. It had Nick's pounding heart fluttering.

"Are we going to talk all night or are you doing this to draw it out so I come before you do?" Nick asked.

Ax laughed heartily and Nick could feel the vibration of it inside him. He liked that. Ax began pressing forward again. Nick squeezed his inner muscles, making Ax groan as he started to pump in and out.

The friction was amazing, but the thought of winning their challenge hovered at the back of Nick's mind. He used every trick he had. He rotated his hips a little, he pulsed his inner muscles and he looked Ax deep in the eye. All the things he liked, all the things that put him over the edge, he did.

"So fuckin' sexy," Ax said as he leaned down and pressed a kiss to Nick's lips.

The kiss went from sweet to dirty within a breath. Ax was fucking Nick's mouth with his tongue as thoroughly as he was fucking his ass. But he didn't do it in the same rhythm. Nick had to divide his attention between the two onslaughts and the challenge slipped from his mind.

Nick wrapped his arms around Ax's shoulders, holding him close as they continued to kiss. After a few moments, Ax pulled back, panting.

"Fuck, Nickel," he was breathless. "I wanted to last longer, but you're so fucking tight, so fucking sweet. Your peach of an ass is going to suck me dry. I'm so close."

All Ax's dirty talk was pulling Nick right to the edge. *Who doesn't want to hear how hot he is?* But it was the way Ax looked him dead in the eye while he said it, the way Ax seemed surprised by it that had Nick curling his toes.

"I can't get enough," Ax said.

And it was that statement and Ax pegging his prostate that had Nick pulsing and shooting between them. Even more than the friction and stretch of Ax's big dick, even more than the way he flicked his hips at just the right angle, even more than his addicting kisses, it was the surprise in Ax's statement that had Nick flying. It made it seem like this was something Ax had never had before.

"Fucking hell," Ax growled as he slammed in one last time and groaned so loud it could be classified as a scream.

Ax collapsed on top of him, panting. Nick smiled at the ceiling because Ax didn't pull away.

"Guess I lost." Nick pouted.

"Are you fucking kidding me?" Ax bit his ear a little. "You came hands free. That's the sexiest fucking thing I've ever seen in my life. I'd say we both won."

He hadn't realized he'd come without touching his dick. That had never happened to him before. It had been an amazing orgasm too. Ax's statement was on a loop in his head. *Sexiest fucking thing I've ever seen.* Nick could live with that.

Chapter Twenty-Six

Ax

Ax woke up alone. That in and of itself wasn't rare or even unwelcome. It was the fact that in that moment between sleep and awake, he'd reached for Nick. That was what had woken him up, finding the other side of the bed empty.

Every time he had sex with Nick, it was some of the best sex he'd ever had. Nick had come without a finger to his cock. And though that had been Ax's goal, he'd been sure Nick would hold back just to win the game.

After scrubbing his hands over his face, Ax sat up and looked around. Nick's clothes were gone. He stumbled out of bed and took a quick shower before heading to the kitchen for some coffee, but paused when he heard voices.

"It's a big responsibility," Nick said.

"Nickel, I raised three boys. I think that qualifies me to finish raising one girl. Seems her mom did most of the work anyway."

"She's not just any girl. She's had a trauma. I mean, having your mom die is a trauma, but then being kidnapped and raped and who knows what kind of torture…"

"She told me a few things about what happened, but I can afford the best therapists. I already care about her. I have the time and the inclination to help her. It's amazing, really, that she's got such a good head on her shoulders after everything that's happened."

"What if Ax needs her to pretend to be his plaything?"

There was a pause.

"She's willing to help in any way she can. There's one boy in particular she was sorry to leave. He's…the boy is only eight years old. His name is Raymond Snow. They changed it to Robby because it sounded more innocent."

"Shit," Nick said.

"I know you told her you can't break everyone out, but Raymond is the youngest one there. The man who's supposed to buy him is from Chicago."

"I'll tell Sam and Wade, but I can't guarantee anything."

"I know. She wasn't even going to tell you. She told me what you said about taking down the whole organization but, Nickel…eight years old."

"I know, Mom. I know."

Nick didn't mention what he and Ax both knew, that he wasn't the youngest girl or boy they'd heard of being sold…not by a long shot. Ax made some noise as he approached the kitchen. When he walked in, Viv was in the circle of Nick's arms.

"Morning," Ax said as he headed for the coffee machine.

"Morning," Nick said with a smile over his mom's head.

Viv discreetly wiped her eyes after letting go of Nick.

"Good morning, Ax," Viv said.

Ax's phone beeped. He looked at the message then smiled as he sent docs to the secure printer in his office.

"Looks like you girls should be good to travel by end of day," Ax said.

"What does that mean? I have custody of Ramona?" Viv asked.

"Well, we have documents that say you do. We can't go through the regular channels or the people who took her might track her."

"But if we have fake documents, that won't give her a lot of security," Viv argued.

"Technically, they're 'official' fake docs. The government's in the loop on this."

Viv bit her bottom lip, much like her son had a tendency to do, but nodded. She started to walk out of the kitchen but turned around.

"What if she became emancipated?"

"She'd have to prove she can support herself financially —"

"That's taken care of," Viv interrupted. "Gil already formed a trust for her."

Ax looked at Nick, who didn't seem surprised in the slightest. *Who are these people?*

"She'd still have to use the fake docs," Ax told her. "I know she's proud of her name, but she can't be Ramona Ruiz, at least not for a while. She'd end up putting you and your husband at risk."

"All right." Viv sighed. "What's her new name?"

Ax looked at the email Wade had sent. "Rosalia Perez."

"Soon to be Freiberg." Nick smiled as he stepped closer to his mom.

"Only if she wants it," Viv said.

"She could be a Hart, like her new brothers." Nick gave his mom a nudge.

Viv turned to Nick with fresh tears and thanked him for the offer. Nick hugged her close while she cried. She told Nick she'd give Ramona the choice as she left the kitchen wiping her eyes.

"My mom caught me sneaking out of your room this morning." Nick gave Ax a sexy smirk.

"What did she think about that?"

"She said she wasn't surprised."

They both stood there, smiling at each other. Nick cleared his throat.

"I promised my mom I'd go buy Ramon— Uh, I mean 'Rosalia', a suitcase. It didn't seem urgent, but now that they have the docs, she's going to want to fly home as soon as possible."

Ax nodded.

Nick gave him one last knowing grin, then headed out of the kitchen.

"Hey, boss," Jett said as he came in the kitchen for a coffee refill.

"Jett, just the man I wanted to see."

"What's up?"

"Wade came through with the paperwork, so Viv and Ramona are going to fly back home."

"Did Wade clear me to go with them?"

"Yep. Nick and I will be heading East in a day or two anyway. You'll meet us back up here in a week or in Virginia, depending on if we hear from Campbell.

We'll have to assess how long to keep security on the Freibergs."

"Sounds good. I'll get packed up."

After refilling his mug, Jett left the kitchen. Ax went to his office and tried to get some work done, but a thought kept poking through every time he tried to concentrate. He was going to have Nick to himself for a few days until they headed back to Virginia.

Normally, Ax would be pushing to head back to HC. He'd made better contact with Campbell than they'd hoped for. They'd actually rescued one of the girls.

He thought back to the name Viv had given Nick...Raymond Snow. He spent the next hour researching the kid as much as he could. His mom was local, but he didn't find a current address for her. That usually meant homeless or renting a room. Her last address had been in Oakland. Raymond's grandmother was looking for him. She had his picture all over social media websites.

There hadn't been an Amber Alert for him, so he could probably be moved out of state at any time. Kid was cute as a button too, with his red hair and freckles.

Ax sent Wade and Max a secure email with all the intel he'd gathered on Raymond 'Robby' Snow and asked if there was anything that had been heard on the audio about him. Within minutes, he received a call from Wade.

"That was quick," Ax said when he answered.

"I wanted to let you know we've called in Ghost to handle the doctor."

Ax froze in place for a moment. He'd heard a lot about the man whose call sign was Ghost, but he'd never met him. If all the bullshit the guys spoke was to be believed, the man was a legend. He could appear and disappear without a trace. He was also one of the most elite soldiers the army had ever had. He'd been a Night Stalker.

"Will he need anything from us?" Ax asked.

"He's not exactly a team player. He's technically not even part of our team, but Jazz called in a favor. I think he's hoping Ghost will join us once he sees our mission."

"How long will it take Ghost to get up to speed?"

"He already is. He's on his way to SFO right now. I'll need you to stay put for another forty-eight hours. Hopefully Campbell won't contact you before then for a meeting. If he does, delay."

"Is that all?"

"No. When Sin was giving Ghost the intel for the op just now, your data on Mr. Snow came through."

Wade's tone sounded harsh, angry.

"It was just additional intel, not specifically a request for action."

"Yeah well, wrong place, wrong time. Ghost said he'll take care of the retrieval as well. Fuck. I hope he doesn't get caught."

"I thought he was a legend," Ax said.

"Even a legend can slip up if he takes too much on or gets emotionally involved."

"I'm here to support him in any way. Jett is going south with Mrs. Hart-Freiberg and Rosalia as discussed."

"All right," Wade said.

A weary sigh came over the phone. In their recent ops, surprises kept popping up and Wade was ultimately in charge. He handled all logistics. He was really good at his job, but it couldn't be easy. Most the guys on the team were renegades. That was why they hadn't really fit in the military. Well, that and the fact that most were queer.

"Send intel on the travel arrangements for Jett and keep in touch."

"Ten-four," Ax said before ending the call.

He knew Wade wasn't happy with the turn of events, but Ax couldn't bring himself to feel guilty that one more kid would be broken free. He hoped Ghost didn't get caught.

Chapter Twenty-Seven

Nick

Nick hadn't thought his mom would be there and gone in a little more than twenty-four hours. But it was best to get Rosalia away as soon as possible. He'd said his goodbyes at the condo, since Jett was going with them.

He wasn't exactly disappointed to have some time completely alone with Ax, but the past few days had been such a whirlwind that he needed time to step back and just...just be.

He checked in on his dad, sent a text to Bray then went to find Ax. He hit the jackpot. Ax was in the first place he looked.

"I knew you'd be in the office," Nick said.

"Workday's not quite over yet."

"It is for most people, people who don't work sixteen hours a day."

"There's still a lot to be done. We have an operator coming in to take care of the doctor."

Nick nodded. He was relieved it was happening but didn't really want to talk shop. He rested his hip on the edge of the desk as he started unbuttoning his shirt. Ax watched his fingers work for a moment.

"What exactly are you doing?" Ax asked.

"I was thinking I'd get naked and maybe test out that little lap pool in the gym. Or maybe the hot tub. I hadn't really decided yet."

"If you take your clothes off, you won't even make it to the door."

"Are you going to tackle me?" Nick laughed.

"I won't need to tackle you."

"I'm intrigued," Nick said.

He pulled off his shirt and let it drop to the floor. Next, he unbuttoned and unzipped his pants. When they were around his ankles, he pushed his boxer briefs down to join them. His cock was already half hard, plumping up thick and proud.

Ax licked his lips and stood from his chair. Nick wasn't sure if he could make good on his threat to walk away when Ax's gaze was locked on his dick. Ax lowered to his knees and took Nick's cock in his hand.

"I think it's probably your turn to top," Ax said.

He leaned forward and sucked Nick's crown into his mouth. Nick reached behind, using his arms to support himself on the desk as his knees went weak. Without much preamble, Ax swallowed him down and sucked hard.

"I'm not missing out on topping again because you make me come too fast," Nick said.

Ax chuckled around his cock and the vibrations made the base of his spine tingle. How could he already be that close?

Then Ax started a hard, fast rhythm. Nick tried to think about the most unsexy things he could imagine. Just as Nick was about to come down his throat, Ax pulled off, leaving Nick panting, his cock as hard as a spike.

"I want you in a bed," Nick said.

"You've had me in a bed."

"Not on your back."

Ax smiled as he stood. He pulled off his shirt as he strode from the room. Nick bent down to pull his wallet from his pocket, then followed the trail of clothes down the hall until he found Ax in his bedroom.

Nick smiled as he pulled the condom and lube from his wallet then dropped it on the floor. He tossed the rubber onto the mattress as he ripped the lube open with his teeth.

Ax was in the middle of the bed on his back, his erection curving up to drip pre-cum just beneath his navel.

This was the first time it felt real with Ax, the first time they hadn't come together like a flash of lightening only to burn down whatever they touched.

When Nick poured a little lube on his fingers, Ax pulled his knees up toward his chest. Nick groaned as Ax's ass cheeks spread, showing off the deep mocha color of his pucker.

With gentle fingers, Nick circled Ax's opening. He blew out a harsh breath when he watched the muscles clench and unclench.

Nick pushed a little lube inside. Ax punched out a loud 'fuck' when Nick pulled out, pressed in two fingers and went directly for his prostate as he stretched him.

"I'm ready." Ax's tone was impatient, and his voice had a raspy quality.

Nick was beyond ready, especially to do this slowly and face to face. He ripped open the condom wrapper and rolled it down his length, slathering the rest of the lube over himself.

It felt different now, not to be rushed, to be testing out actually having a relationship. As soon as he lined himself up, Nick looked into Ax's eyes. He held there for a minute as neither of them said anything, neither egging the other on.

When he breached Ax's hole, Ax groaned and spread his legs wider. Though he longed to look down and watch himself disappear into the other man, he couldn't tear his gaze from Ax's face.

Nick leaned down and nipped at Ax's lower lip. Ax opened for him and he pressed in to taste and tease. He entered Ax slowly as they kissed lazily. When his balls pressed against Ax's ass, Nick pulled back then pressed forward, swallowing Ax's grunts.

He lifted his head to take a breath, but Ax let one of his legs go and used the freed hand to bring Nick back for another kiss.

They continued like that, slow but intense. Ax's body squeezed him so tight that Nick paused each time their bodies met.

When he kissed his way down Ax's jaw, Ax planted one foot on the bed and thrust his pelvis up in perfect sync with Nick.

"Is this a contest to see how long we can last?" Ax panted the words.

Nick smiled down at him. "If it is, it looks like I'm winning."

Ax smirked, but the look lost its edge when his eyes rolled back the next time Nick thrust into him.

"I like this flirtatious Nickel," Ax said. "He's sexy as hell and pretty good in bed."

Nick laughed. It broke the serious intensity that had been building but didn't ruin the intimacy of the moment.

He increased his speed, finally taking the time to look down and watch his length disappear into Ax's tight ass. He groaned.

Ax reached between them, but Nick pushed his hand away. He wanted to be the one to push Ax over the edge. He grasped the base of Ax's shaft but didn't jack him.

Instead, he changed the angle of his thrusts until Ax sucked in a breath that came back out as a moan.

Bingo.

Nick pegged that spot again and again. Ax grasped Nick's hip, squeezing.

"Oh, fuck," Ax rasped.

Nick flicked his focus up and took in Ax's expression. His lips were parted, his lids at half-mast, his breathing heavy and his neck arched back a little — yet their eyes met and held.

What Nick saw in Ax's gaze had his balls drawing up tight. Along with the hunger and lust was a flicker of wonder and maybe even affection.

"Please," Ax whispered.

Nick jacked him once, twice, then felt the hot spurt of Ax's ejaculate landing on his chest and abs. Nick's body convulsed, his muscles spasming as embarrassingly high-pitched grunts burst from his lungs while his own cum shot into the condom.

When they finally settled, Nick felt more naked than he ever had in his entire life. He wasn't sure when he'd closed his eyes, but when he opened them, he saw the same questions in Ax's gaze that he felt bubbling inside himself.

He would have stayed inside Ax for hours — or at least a few more minutes — but the condom needed to be dealt with.

"I'll be right back," Nick said.

He hurried to the bathroom and tossed the rubber into the trash. He went back and forth only a moment before wetting a small towel and stepping back into the bedroom to do something he'd always considered a little hokey.

"What the fuck is this?" Ax picked something up off the floor near Nick's wallet.

It took a moment for Nick to focus on what Ax was holding, but when he did, all the warmth he'd been feeling drained from his body, leaving him cold.

Ax was looking at a picture of his sister.

"Where the fuck did you get this?" Ax asked when Nick didn't answer his first question.

Nick gripped the damp towel in his hand as he tried to find the best thing to say.

"Answer me," Ax demanded.

"Your mother gave it to me."

"At her house? Why would she — ?"

"Not at her house. I met her for coffee."

"You went behind my back?"

"No, I didn't. I — "

"Then what the fuck else do you call it?" Ax yelled.

"I call it keeping your family happy, like you asked me to," Nick yelled back.

"That's not what I meant, and you know it. Keep your fucking nose out of my business."

"She hands them out to strangers, Ax. It's not like I had to crack a code to get one. I asked her what Cherie looked like."

"Don't say her name. You don't get to say her name." The words came out through Ax's clenched teeth, his voice low and deadly.

Nick swallowed. The warm rag in his hand was now cold against his skin. He wanted to cover himself but was too proud to do it, so he stood there naked, his hands at his sides. "Your mom said she lost two children the day Cherie was taken. She said she missed you. I was just trying to help your family."

"Like you tried to help yours? Why don't you worry about your own fucking family and leave mine alone?"

Ax curled his hand around the photo and stood. He walked past Nick.

"I don't need your help. In fact, all this has proven was that I was getting sidetracked by a piece of ass. I need to double down and move forward with my own plans."

"A piece of ass?" Nick repeated.

"What?" Ax threw his hand out. "Did you really think this was a happily ever after? This was mutual gratification and now it's over."

Ax walked into the bathroom and closed the door with a quiet click.

Nick picked up his wallet and went in search of his clothes. He felt like he had a hole in his stomach or his chest…maybe both. All he knew was that he needed to get the hell out of there before he walked back into that room and punched Ax in the face.

Within fifteen minutes, Nick was packed and taking the elevator down to the garage. He called Wade on the way to the airport and told him he needed to head south and check on his dad. Luckily, Wade didn't give him any pushback since they'd done what they needed to do.

He was in line at the ticket counter, credit card in hand, when his phone rang. For a second, he let himself think maybe Ax was calling to apologize, but it was Max's alias, Sin, that popped up on the screen of his phone.

"What's up, Sin?"

"Nick." Max was almost breathless.

"Can I help you?" the woman at the counter asked.

Nick waved her away and stepped out of line.

"What is it, Sin?"

"Wh-who is this girl? Was she taken? Is she one of the victims?"

"You found her," Nick breathed.

Nick's stomach dropped. Ax had been searching for years, probably following leads that had turned into dead ends, but Max had found her in less than twenty-four hours.

"I got a hit, multiple hits. She has traveled from Texas to DC multiple times in the last twelve months."

"She's been so close?"

"Nick, who is she? I looked up the name she's traveling under and it's bogus."

Nick walked farther away from the line. He walked all the way outside and made sure no one was around before answering.

"This isn't common knowledge," Nick said.

"I get it, but you have no idea who... Just tell me who she is."

"She's Ax's sister."

"Fuck. Fuckity fuck," Max yelled.

"But we found her. You found her."

Nick expected Max to gloat a little, or demur even. He was confident in his skill but usually humble about the results. Since he and Nick teased each other, it could go either way. But Max didn't say anything. All the feelings of elation Nick felt plummeted.

"Has something happened? Did something happen to her?"

"No. I mean, not that I know of. I'm trying to get into the security system where she's staying."

"Okay, so some rich asshole has her? We have to—"

"Not just some rich asshole, Nick. He's a goddamned fucking US Congressman."

"What? Who?"

"Daniel Meyers, Congressman for 'The Great State of Texas'—one of the many whose platform is family values."

It would be so easy, so, so easy, to walk away. Ax didn't want his help. Ax didn't want anyone's help. He could let Max make the decision. Nick considered it and realized it wouldn't actually be so easy. It wasn't just about Ax. It was about his whole family, none of whom had given up on finding Cherie, even after years had passed.

"Sin, tell me we can get her out. I don't care if she's with the President himself. She was taken, sold, exploited. Get Wade on the line."

Chapter Twenty-Eight

Ax

Ax woke with a start. His head was resting on his hands on top of the desk he'd remained at after he'd yelled at Nick. He figured he owed Nick an apology. He'd overreacted.

But how could he explain to the guy he was falling for — the guy who until recently had thought he was a piece of shit — that it was his own fault his sister had been taken?

After what Nick had said about his mom losing two kids that day? Talk about an arrow to the heart. But he couldn't look evil in the eye then go home and pretend everything was what it used to be. If his mom knew he could have taken steps to prevent what had happened, she wouldn't feel the way she did.

And what could Nick do that Ax hadn't already done? He'd chased dead end after dead end. Max was his last hope.

Ax checked his phone. *Four in the morning.* He couldn't exactly go apologize now. He'd need to wait until Nick woke up. With a sigh, Ax got up and tried to stretch the kinks out of his back. He picked up his laptop and headed for his room. At least if he fell asleep in front of his laptop again, he'd actually be in bed.

So many things ran through his mind. How many opportunities had he missed? The things Joe had told him… Was it too little, too late? Instead of hanging around and worrying about fucking Nick, he should be heading to Arizona to try to talk to Silva.

He only had one other lead. Hopefully Max could help him get some new intel. Ax wasn't completely sure what Max was capable of, but as soon as he got back, he was going to find out.

As he walked by Nick's room, Ax noticed the door was open. He peeked in but didn't see Nick. He also didn't see any of Nick's things strewn about the room, so he checked the en suite bathroom and closet. All Nick's things were gone.

The guilt weighing down on Ax's shoulders got ten pounds heavier. He tried to call Nick, but it went straight to voicemail. Ax didn't know if the phone was really off or if Nick had blocked him. He hoped Nick wouldn't go AWOL and had contacted Wade. He pulled up Wade's number. It was after seven on the East Coast, so he made the call.

"Ax, I was going to wait a few more hours to call you."

"I'm up. I guess I'm all alone here?"

"Nick was on his way to see his dad, but we have a development in Houston. I need you on a flight ASAP. I was going to plan for a ten a.m. flight, but since we're on the line now, let's get you booked."

"I'm packing up right now," Ax said.

He wasn't sure how he felt about meeting up with Nick again. Sure, he owed him an apology, but maybe it would have been better to let things settle for a few days. They could hopefully move past this attraction and find a way to be colleagues.

"Either Mitch or Colt will meet you at the airport."

"Ten-four. Out," Ax disconnected the call.

He wanted to know what the hell was going on. It had to be an emergency. Jazz had some ties to Texas, so Ax was worried it might be something to do with that. It seemed they'd called in the cavalry.

This was putting all his plans to shit once again. As he arrived at San Francisco airport, Ax got a text from his mom asking him to please bring Nick to dinner again.

"Fuck," he muttered as he turned in the rental car.

Just one more way he was letting his family down. Ax formed and deleted about twenty different responses to his mother. By the time he landed in Texas, he still hadn't sent one.

"Hey, Loco."

Ax looked up to see Colt waiting for him when he walked past the security gate. Ax smiled at the use of his handle. He was no longer that crazy eighteen-year-old kid who'd joined up, but it brought back some pretty good memories.

"Reaper, what the hell's going on?" Ax asked Colt as they made their way to the parking garage. "Is this an all hands?"

"It is." Colt gave Ax a quick side glance then avoided eye contact. "Everyone who's not under deep cover is here."

"Why?"

Colt licked his lips but didn't respond. He pointed Ax to a blue rental then clicked the fob to unlock the doors and pop the trunk. Ax let Colt take his bag and throw it in the back. When he closed it, Ax caught him before he turned to get in the car.

"What's going on, Colt?"

Colt sighed and finally met Ax's eyes.

"Intel is changing from minute to minute. I don't have the full scope, just the gist. Wade will be the one to let us know where we stand when we get to the hotel, okay?"

Ax ran his tongue over his teeth as he thought about it. It made sense, but Ax was suspicious about Colt avoiding eye contact with him. *Has Nick started bad-mouthing me?*

The drive was quiet and tense, which just had Ax's anxiety levels rising. He and Colt were both pretty easygoing and liked to joke around with each other. Colt kept giving him glances and it was making Ax edgy.

By the time they had his luggage out of the car and approached the hotel room, Ax was ready to explode. Something was up and he couldn't help but point all his frustration in Nick's direction. Maybe he wasn't going to apologize after all.

The presidential suite of the hotel was their command center. There were people and computers everywhere. At the center of it all was Max, who had two laptops in front of him.

Wade was pacing by the window to the balcony and talking quietly on his cell phone. Sam and Bray were cuddled together on a sofa. Clay was stretched out on one of the other sofas. Mitch and Chase were taking up the two chairs, and Nick was sitting next to Max on his own laptop. The only guys missing were Jazz, Mase, Jett, Brody and Finn. Ax figured somebody had to keep the home fires burning.

When Wade spotted Ax, he quickly ended his call and stuffed his cell into his pocket. All the air seemed to leave the room as everyone looked at Ax — everyone but Nick. Anger flared to life in his chest. Had Nick really gone and tattled to everyone about what had happened between them?

Max quickly turned back to his computer and everyone else seemed to follow suit. All of a sudden it was the opposite, like everyone was pretending he wasn't even in the room.

"Ax." Wade smiled.

His shoulders slumped in relief that at least someone seemed friendly.

"Let's go in here. I need to update you on where we are. Max, can you join us? We'll need your intel."

"Yeah, sure," Max said as he scooped up one of his laptops.

They ended up in a sitting area of the master suite, each of them in their own cushy chair. Max opened his laptop, set it on the table near them and began typing once again. The quiet stretched out, but Ax refused to be the one to fill it.

"Fuck," Wade finally said. "How the hell do you start a conversation like this?"

"Just rip off the Band-Aid," Ax said.

He was pretty suspicious about what was going on. It would have been ridiculous to call him all the way to Texas to fire him.

Wade leaned forward. He placed a hand on Ax's knee and looked him straight in the eye. "I think we found her."

And just like that, all the air left Ax's lungs. He tried to breathe—he really tried—but nothing happened. His body was frozen. There was no way Wade was talking about Cherie.

"We think we found Cherie. We think she's right here in Houston. Breathe, Ax."

Wade stood and slapped Ax on the back. The move was so jarring and unexpected that it caused Ax to suck in a breath.

"It really looks like her," Max said. "But she's older, so we wanted you to ID her before we up and kidnap her."

"Let me—" Ax's voice cracked. He had to clear his throat. "Let me see her," he demanded.

Max turned his computer and showed some still images of a surveillance video that looked to be from an airport. *It's her.* It was her. It was Cherie. Ax would bet both his life and the lives of all his family on it.

There she was, walking through an airport. Part of him wondered why she didn't just run up to someone and ask for help, but he knew. He knew the mind games traffickers and owners played.

"It's…" Ax's voice came out in a hoarse whisper. He had to swallow past the burning lump in his throat. "It's her. That's her. When did you have time to…? How did you…?"

"We have a plan," Wade said. "There's little-to-no security today because Meyers is out of town until tomorrow. Tonight's the night to act."

"Wait." Ax's voice came out louder than he'd planned. "Who's Meyers?"

"Daniel Meyers. Congressman Daniel Meyers. He's the one who purchased her. We think he's her original purchaser, because Max was able to find evidence she's been traveling back and forth with him to DC for over two years."

Ax tried to absorb all this, but he wanted to laugh and throw up at the same time. They'd found her. Where she'd ended up might be his worst fear realized, but they'd found her.

"How? How did you know what she looked like?"

Wade turned to Max.

"Uh, well." Max's eyes darted to the door that led to the main room of the suite. "I got access to her photo about twenty-four hours ago. I told...uh, what I mean is I thought it would take a lot longer to find her. I didn't realize she'd traveled so recently and frequently."

Max wrung his hands a little as he spoke. Ax knew Max was nervous, but he was too stunned to placate him.

"Anyway, I got a hit within a few hours—then another and another. She usually travels with most of the household staff, so it took me a while to work out where she was and who she was living with. But a few times, it was just her, the congressman and a bodyguard."

Twenty-four hours? Nick had done this. He'd met with Ax's mom, got Cherie's picture and fucking found her. Ax wanted to be angry at Nick for interfering, but he simply couldn't. Because of Nick, they'd found her. Even after Ax had been a royal asshole, Nick had put this in motion.

"I've hacked into the security footage at his house in Memorial Park." Max continued. "The place is huge, but I think he's passing her off as a maid, so she's actually living in the same house as his wife."

Ax leaned back in his chair and stared at the ceiling. He wanted to kick his own ass. He may not have had the skills to hack in somewhere and use some facial recognition software, but he hadn't fully realized it was possible. He'd been waiting to ask Max for help when Nick had just waltzed right in and done it for him.

Nick was the reason they were there. Nick was the reason he was going to go get Cherie and bring her home…at any cost. And he'd done all this even after Ax had said some pretty horrible things…things he hadn't really meant.

"I think we've lost him," Max whispered.

Tears slipped down Ax's temples, only to get absorbed into his hair. It was all too much. Nick was too much. Max was too much. All the guys who'd dropped what they were doing and answered an 'all hands' for an op that was in no way company business. It was all too much.

"Give him a minute. It's all sinking in. He's been after this intel for three years."

"Three years?" Max said as if something had just clicked into place.

"We only just hooked you onto our team, Max. We were counting on our clients to provide us with the intel in most cases. Being as the government is our biggest client, that's worked so far, but we're taking on more private clients now."

Max and Wade continued to talk in hushed tones, but Ax tuned them out. So many things were flashing through his mind. *How much will my sister have changed? Will she recognize me with my longer hair and beard scruff? Will I have to drag her out of there?*

How many unspeakable things had happened to her? Would she be able to overcome it? How would she take reconciling with their parents? How would their parents take it? How did he break this to his parents in a way that didn't give them a heart attack?

He'd never know any of it if he didn't go get her.

"How do we do this? How do we bring Cherie home?"

Chapter Twenty-Nine

Nick

"Okay." Wade clapped his hands then rubbed them together. "Tonight's the night. Meyers is out of town until tomorrow, so this is our best bet. He doesn't have travel plans again that we know of for another three weeks. We're not willing to wait that long. Let's talk logistics. Max?"

"Daniel Meyers and his wife, Melissa Gaffling-Meyers, live in a twenty-thousand-square-foot home in an exclusive gated community called Stablewood. I'll be able to get you access. The Meyers children are both currently away at college. That still leaves Mrs. Meyers, two security guards, five full-time staff and Cherise in the home, at least during the day."

Nick glanced at Ax when Max said his sister's full name. Ax closed his eyes one beat too long, but then focused back on Max. Nick tried to do the same.

"This house is going to be a piece of cake. There are more than ten doors on the ground floor, most of them in the back and all of them French-style doors with glass panels. It will be easy to see what you're up against. I have plenty of pictures of the house from all angles."

"We'll be more interested in where everyone is inside and if you've noticed any patterns," Wade said.

"I have a program working on that. So far, at least yesterday, the staff worked from about eight a.m. to about six p.m., with the exception of Cherise and the chef, who begin work at seven a.m. and work until dinner is served at five-thirty. There are two other household staff who live in the home — the house manager, a woman named Vicky Lopez, and her assistant, Adriana Martinez."

"Are all the rooms right next to each other?" Mitch asked.

Max pulled up the blueprint of the house. "Here on the east side of the kitchen are the staff living quarters. There are four bedrooms there — two on each side of the hallway. The last bedroom looks like it's used for the security staff to take shifts sleeping. One of them may be sleeping directly across the hall from where Cherise is."

Nick had been poring over the plans for most of the morning with Max. He knew the blueprints by heart. He knew the security staff, their names and their backgrounds.

Max had gone back over their detail for the thirty days that were stored on the server of the security company. They knew that the guards had a schedule and most likely knew who would be working that evening. One of the guards, an Eric Carter, would take a few extra breaks and head to the front corner of the house where he was least likely to be seen and have a smoke break.

Cherie's room had glass French doors that led to the backyard. Max and Nick had seen Meyers enter through those doors multiple times in the dark of night.

"We're in luck when it comes to getting into the backyard," Wade said, pulling Nick out of his revery.

"Yes," Max agreed. "Meyers has a corner lot, so his only shared fence—with the neighbor to the west—is in the backyard and very heavily wooded. I can handle all security footage from both Meyer's security and the neighbors, so you only have to make sure not to be seen by any actual people."

"This is the best entry point." Wade pointed to a section of the map. "It should shield you from being seen climbing the fence."

"Two-thirds of the house is backed right up to those trees, but you'll have to sneak past the wide open and very well-lit pool area that takes up the last third of the backyard. Cherise's room is right here." Max circled a spot on the monitor with a few clicks of the mouse.

Nick chanced another look at Ax. His eyes were narrowed at the red circle on the screen, but he looked like he was about to pass out.

"Max and I will stay here at our temporary command post. Everyone else will be on the ground. Sam will be driving the plumbing van and Bray will be a lookout."

"That's too many cooks in the kitchen," Ax said.

"Ax—" Wade chided.

"No," Ax said. "Just me and Sam and we can get this done."

"No," Wade said.

"You don't get to decide—"

"Yes, I do. I'm the one who does logistics. I'm also the objective one of the two of us. Your emotions are involved. We're treating this as we would any extraction."

"You'd send four men, tops, for an extraction."

"And more helping hands isn't a bad thing. This isn't the army, Ax. We're not fighting to be top dog here. We're not all trying to lead the team. Every man in this room, every man who's worked with you and joked with you over the last two years, is invested in this. Their only goal in this will be for the op to succeed. We're going to bring Cherise home."

Ax's chest rose and fell in quick succession. His throat worked as his mouth opened, but only a whispered sob came out.

"We're bringing Cherise home," Wade said again.

Ax turned and ran into the bedroom like his ass was on fire. The door slammed behind him and all the men in the room heard the muted sob.

Without thought to how it looked or whether he'd be welcome, Nick rushed after Ax. There were still remnants of anger and hurt at what he'd said the day before, but he couldn't stand back and watch the man suffer.

After Nick quietly opened and closed the door to the bedroom, he turned to find Ax in a ball on the floor. His fists were against his mouth as he tried to muffle his sobs.

He rubbed a hand down Ax's back, but there was no response. Nick knelt next to Ax and wrapped his arms around him. After a moment, Ax turned and buried his face in Nick's chest. The sobs came more freely. Nick's heart cracked open as he tightened his hold.

He didn't offer platitudes, because he wasn't sure how things were going to go. They weren't out of the woods yet. Instead, Nick concentrated on offering comfort to a man he was truly worried he'd gone and fallen for.

After what could have been ten minutes or an hour, Ax seemed to quiet. He took in a ragged breath and pulled back. Nick let him go. They sat and stared at each other for a few seconds.

"Thank you," Ax said, his voice rough and hoarse from crying.

There were a million things Nick wanted to say, a million questions he wanted to ask, but now wasn't the time. There was only one thing Ax needed to hear.

"You're welcome."

"I'm sorry about what I said. I've had one goal for three years, and that was to bring my family back together. Everything else was peripheral. But that's no excuse for what I said. I'm sorry."

"Let's just concentrate on getting your sister back."

Ax looked at Nick for a long moment before nodding. Nick gave him a weak smile and stood. They had plans to perfect before nightfall.

Chapter Thirty

Ax

Ax was short of breath. His heart was racing and his pits were sweaty. He'd never been so nervous heading out for an op. He'd been more confident on his first mission than he was in that moment.

Nothing could go wrong. Nothing could botch this job. If Meyers got wind of anything and hid Cherie somewhere, Ax would... He would...

He took a deep, calming breath. No way would one of those snot-nosed security guards get Cherie out of that house without them knowing. He had Max on his side now, and that in and of itself inspired confidence.

They could all hear Max over their earpieces as he click-clacked on his laptop and slurped whatever it was he was drinking.

When they arrived at the security fence for the private community where Meyers lived, Max gave Sam a code that had the gate sliding open. Ax's shoulders relaxed the tiniest bit. Sam drove past Meyers' house, turned the corner and parked exactly where Wade had told him to.

The passenger side of the van was so close to the trees and shrubs that the six of them didn't even need to crouch down before disappearing into the overgrowth and jumping the fence.

Clay stayed on the outside to catch Cherie if they had to throw her over. Colt stayed just inside it to keep a lookout. Mitch and Chase followed Ax and Nick farther into the backyard.

It was overkill. They all knew it. This could have been done with two to three people, but now that they were there, Ax was glad for the support. If they had to shoot their way out, Meyers' security detail would be totally outnumbered.

Max stayed in their ears the whole time. He told them when he spotted them and noted the times so he could go back later and delete any evidence—not that Ax would care.

He'd happily go to jail for breaking and entering once Cherie was safe at home, but he had to protect his teammates from that fate, and Max would do that.

He was a little off-center with Nick, though, and Nick was his partner in this op. He'd been a total douche and yet Nick had still gotten this mission going. Nick had been the one to put Max on the case in the first place and he'd comforted Ax when he'd fallen apart in the middle of the briefing.

Mitch stayed at the corner of the house where they emerged from the trees. As a team, Ax, Nick and Chase crouched and snuck along the back of the house. Max was leading them, telling them there was no one walking around inside. They only had one guard to worry about, since Meyers was out of town. The other two men were with him.

"Guard has just gone out to the front corner for his smoke break," Max said through the comm.

Ax motioned for Chase to guard the other corner of the house. Ax crouched outside the door. He had all his tools to pick the lock, but he tried the knob since he knew that Meyers had a tendency to come in through the door.

When it opened, Ax slipped silently inside as Nick kept watch. The lights from the pool lit the room enough for him to see that Cherie was in bed asleep. He stood for a moment to just take her in.

Crouching next to her bed, Ax whispered her name. "Cherie."

"I thought you were still out of town," she groaned sleepily.

"I'm not the asshole. It's Rubio. I need you to keep quiet."

As soon as he whispered his name, Cherie jackknifed in the bed and flipped on her bedside lamp. Eyes wide, she silently stared at him.

"You need to be quiet," he warned.

She opened her mouth. Just as his hand twitched to cover it, she licked her lips and closed it again. They continued to look at each other. He could see the differences in her now.

"How...how...?"

"Don't worry about how. We're leaving. I'm taking you home."

"No—"

"I don't care what kind of mind games that bastard has played on you. If you need to kick and scream because he's made you think he loves you or some shit, then fine. I'm still taking you out of here."

"Ruby, no." She grabbed his arm.

"Cherie, I'm not going back to Mom and Dad and telling them I found you but you wouldn't come home. You're coming. I'm going to take care of everything. We just—"

"Rubio, you're not listening to me. I. Can't. Leave."

"Cherie—"

"Look around the room, Ruby. *Really* look."

Ax did as she said. There were photos all over the place. He squinted at a few then stood to get a closer look.

"Where are they? Where are Mom and Dad and Diego?"

Ax's stomach roiled as he looked at the pictures. They were all recent, within the last few months. They were all of his family. When he came to her dresser, he noticed a pile of new photos. They needed to find out who had these photos and delete them all.

"Sin?" Ax said as he touched his earpiece.

"I'm trying not to eavesdrop, but I was listening for security. Only I can hear you…well, and Wade."

"The bastard has surveillance on my family. Find out who's been watching them."

"I'm on it. I'll find out who and make sure every digital pic is deleted."

"I still want the name." Ax said.

"You got it." Max said.

"Who are you talking to?" Cherie asked.

"My team. We're all here to protect you."

"Ruby, I can't go. You need to leave. There's a guard, and if he—"

"I know. I know every fucking detail about this house."

"But you didn't know he was watching them. He'll hurt them, Ruby, and he'll get away with it, too," she said.

"I know who he is."

Ax paced back and forth in the room. He could kick his own ass for not making sure everything was in place. It had seemed like such low-hanging fruit.

"Sin, can you delay his flight?"

"I'll see what I can do."

"Do we have any audio devices?" Ax asked.

"In the van," Wade said. "Didn't think you'd need it, but there are two in the bag Sam brought."

"I need them."

"Fuck," Wade growled.

Ax listened to his team talk. Max told Sam, and Bray threw the plug devices to Colt, who was running them in. Ax looked at Cherie. The thing that killed him the most was that he didn't know if he could trust his own sister, but he knew deep down that she loved him and wanted to go home.

She said she was staying to protect their parents, but things got twisted when people were in a situation like she was.

There was a tiny knock at the door. Ax pulled it open and Nick handed him two plug covers that would allow them to see and hear what was happening in Cherie's room. Ax plugged them into the most visible outlets.

"These will allow us to hear what's going on in your room. I'm going to get Mom and Dad someplace safe. I'm going to find out who's been following them, then

I'm coming back. It will take less than forty-eight hours."

"He'll be back by then," she argued.

"I don't give a flying fuck. I'm getting you out of this house if I have to shoot my way out. Get him to talk to you if he comes in here. Get him to admit to everything you can. Don't be obvious but see what you can get him to cop to in casual conversation."

Cherie nodded.

"I'll be back in less than forty-eight hours."

Ax's stomach was lead. His eyes stung and his throat burned, but he gave her a tight squeeze and walked to the door. When he turned back, Cherie wasn't looking at him but at the pictures on her dresser. Her arms were wrapped around her shoulders.

Ax opened the door and Nick was there like an excited puppy. There was anticipation in his eyes and a smile on his lips. Ax wanted to punch him. Maybe not Nick specifically, but a rage was burning inside him.

The smile dropped from Nick's lips as he took in Ax's face. Then there was confusion, then anger. Nick pushed past Ax into the room.

"No way," Nick said. "No fucking way. I don't care if she said she wanted to stay. You've spent three years tirelessly searching for her and…"

Nick stopped when he saw Cherie's posture. She looked scared, torn. Then Nick made a slow circle in the room. Ax knew what he was seeing. Nick slowly closed his eyes and Ax heard "fuck," fall in a whisper from his mouth.

"Sin." Nick touched his earpiece.

Ax could hear Max respond.

"Check on Ax's family right-fucking-now."

"Their house is secure," Max confirmed.

"What do you want to do?" Nick asked.

"Everyone's here," Ax said. "Everyone is here, and my parents are vulnerable. I can't…"

Nick nodded and squeezed his arm. Then Nick slipped silently back out of the door to let Ax say his goodbyes. He turned to Cherie. He was afraid to touch her. She used to run and jump at him when she'd been little, and now he was afraid to touch her.

Ax put a finger under her chin and lifted her face so she met his gaze. He looked deep into her eyes. They weren't the same. She wasn't the same, but she was still Cherie.

"I'll be back in twenty-four hours if I can get them out that fast. Otherwise, it will be forty-eight, but I *am* coming back. I'll never let you go again."

Ax touched her cheek. She didn't cringe or pull away, but she didn't lean into it as she once would have, either.

Before he fell apart at the thoughts of what she'd endured, Ax turned and left the room. He quietly closed the door behind him. He didn't hear a lock engage. She left it open. And that made him sick all over again.

Nick put a hand on his shoulder, but Ax couldn't handle any sympathy. He couldn't handle anything at all, so he hunched down and hurried along the wall. Nick updated the team that they were falling back.

Somewhere deep inside, Ax was grateful, but at that moment he wanted to howl, so he kept his mouth shut as they all regrouped and headed out.

"What is it?" Sam asked as soon as they were in the van.

Ax covered his eyes and shook his head. He heard Nick quietly explain everything as Sam drove them back to the hotel, as they drove away from Cherie. That was all Ax could concentrate on.

He heard everyone talking, making plans, but he couldn't pay attention to the words. He'd left her there. She was still in hell, and it was all his fault.

Chapter Thirty-One

Nick

"We need a team to go out and get Nando, Cella and Diego," Nick said.

"Agreed," Wade said through the phone.

Nick could hear the click-clack of Max typing in the background. The echo of Wade's voice told Nick he was on speakerphone.

Ax was basically catatonic. Nick understood. Through the glass doors, he'd watched Ax's expression morph from delighted joy to anger to despair. Yet he'd still been shocked when Ax had come out empty-handed.

If Nick had been asked to describe Cherie, the phrase he would have used would have been 'beaten down'. The surveillance photos of her family plastered all over her room were scary as fuck for so many reasons.

"What about The Ghost?" Nick asked.

"Not 'The' Ghost, just Ghost." Wade said. "He's still in the Bay Area."

"How fast can he get over to Oakland Hills? We need him to keep an eye on Ax's family until the team gets there."

"Let's hold off on pulling Ghost from his current op," Wade said.

"Nick, calm down. The house is secure." Max said.

Nick tried to take a deep breath. He didn't know why he was in such a panic. The rest of Ax's family were safe. He was just emotionally involved, and he needed to take a step back. But just to make sure...

"Sin, can you track all their phones? Just keep tabs on them?"

"Give me two minutes."

"As soon as you guys get back here, Mitch and Chase will head to the airport. We already have their flights. Ax just needs to decide if he wants them to come here or go directly to Virginia."

Nick turned to Ax. He was staring blindly out of the window. His chest rose and fell jaggedly like he was struggling to breathe. He looked ready to burst at the seams.

"Here," Nick said.

"Okay. Max is gathering evidence on Meyers."

"What about delaying his return home?"

"I have him delayed, but there are other flights and other airlines. I can't create weather to delay all flights, and though I could put a virus in the airport's system, I don't have enough time to create one, especially one that would leave no trace back to me. I can't flag him because he's a fucking Congressman. Plus, I get why we're doing this, but I try to do good with my powers and — "

"Sin, it's me. I get it. I wouldn't ask you to take down an airport or an airline unless millions of lives were at stake, okay?"

Nick heard Max's sigh of relief.

"Okay," Wade said. "By the time you get back here—"

"Shit," Max growled.

"What?" Nick and Wade said at the same time.

"Diego must have snuck out. He's not at home," Max said.

"How did you know, Nick?" Wade asked

"Gut instinct," Nick answered.

"Get me the coordinates of the cell phone. Is he on the move?" Wade asked.

"No, not currently," Max said.

"I'll have Ghost there in less than an hour."

Nick looked at Ax again. He wasn't paying attention to the conversation at all or he would have been firing questions left and right. Nick wasn't sure he'd made the right decision bringing Ax's family to Texas instead of Virginia, but figured they'd want to see Cherie as soon as she was rescued. He remembered Ramona reaching for his mother.

When the van pulled into a parking spot in the garage beneath the hotel, everyone got out—everyone but Ax. He just sat there looking at the carpet of the van.

Nick placed a hand on his forearm. Ax's body jolted and he looked up then around, as if wondering where everyone had gone.

"We need to re-eval and figure out what happens next."

"I'm going back as soon as my parents are safe, even if I have to bust in there," Ax said as he pushed past

Nick and made his way to the elevator where everyone was waiting for them.

Nick sighed and followed along. *It's going to be a long twenty-four hours.*

Chapter Thirty-Two

Ax

It was like being in a dream or an alternate reality. Ax had fantasized about finding Cherie a million times in a million different ways. Most times she was alive. In his nightmares, she'd been dead. Never, not in even one of those scenarios, had he ever pictured anything that might make him leave her behind.

He would have died to free her. There would have been nothing to stop him. He would have stormed into whatever situation he found her in. But there he was, empty-handed, even though he'd seen her, talked to her, touched her.

When they entered the hotel suite, Wade and Max were both hunched over the screen of Max's laptop as if it held the secrets to the universe. Hell, knowing Max, maybe it did.

"He's almost there," Wade said.

"Is it a residential address?" Nick asked.

"Negative," Wade said.

"There are over two hundred cell phones pinging from that place. Looks like a party or a rave." Max said.

Ax felt like he was under water. What the fuck was everyone talking about? He thought they had come to help him get Cherie.

"Why are we watching cell phones at a rave?" he asked.

Wade, Max and Nick all looked at each other before turning to him. A silent conversation seemed to ensue before Wade stood from hunching over Max.

"It looks like Diego snuck out of the house to go to a party."

Ax's knees weakened before he locked them in place. It was happening again. His parents didn't know where Diego was. The helplessness he felt had anger surging through his blood. He'd trained, researched, made contacts and joined HC to avoid feeling helpless like this again.

"We've got Ghost on the way to pick him up and sit on your parents until Mitch and Chase can get there to bring them back here."

"Here?" Ax felt a little dizzy.

"Yeah, Nick said to bring them here."

Ax looked at Nick. Nick was bringing his family to ground zero? His nostrils flared as he clenched his hands into fists. He took a step forward, but before he could take another, two arms wrapped around him from behind and pinned his fists to his sides.

He struggled against the binding, but Wade was stronger. Wade probably thought he was about to crack, and maybe he was. He wasn't going to hit Nick — at least, that hadn't been his goal. He had been ready to get right in his face, though.

"Let. Me. Go," Ax growled.

"What are you doing, brother?" Wade whispered in his ear. "You'll hate yourself if you do it."

Ax opened his mouth to let Wade know he could yell at Nick if he wanted to. Nick spoke before he could.

"Let him go," Nick said.

"You sure about that?" Wade asked. "He'll outmatch you."

"He's just had to make the worst decision of his life," Nick said.

Ax tried to break free, but now it was to get out of the room. His skin felt too tight and his chest was on fire. Why the hell would Nick welcome Ax attacking him?

What kind of asshole did it make Ax that he'd even think to take it out on the person he loved most in the room? *Loved?* Any fight left in Ax drained out of his feet.

"Wade, he had to leave her behind," Nick said quietly. "He's angry, but he won't hurt me."

Nick's faith in Ax made him want beat his own ass. His body loosened, and Wade set his feet back on the floor before leaning in to speak quietly and calmly.

"Nick's the only reason we know Diego snuck out. He's the one who asked Max to track their cell phones."

When Wade let Ax go, he crumpled to the ground. His throat was on fire. Hands clenched, he lifted them and screamed. This time he had no one to hate but himself. Again, he screamed. So much rage had been building inside him. Now that a little had escaped, he couldn't seem to hold any back.

This time when two arms wrapped around him, it was in a hug, and Ax had no doubt about whose arms they were. He was humiliated by his behavior both before and after he collapsed to the ground.

Nick held him and rocked from side to side. He whispered quiet words in Ax's ear as he raged, yelled and cried.

Ax didn't know how much time had passed, but eventually, his breathing slowed and steadied. Nick was still wrapped around him like a monkey. He didn't deserve the sympathy or the care Nick was giving.

When he looked up, he realized he'd cleared the room. Everyone was gone but the two of them. The first thing that popped into Ax's head was Diego.

"I have to find out about Diego." Ax moved to stand, but Nick knocked him back. "What the fuck?"

"You need to calm down and take a few deep breaths."

The anger that had tamped down in Ax flared back to life. "I'll do whatever I need to do to keep my family safe."

"Those guys in there? They're your family too. They dropped everything to come out here and help you get your sister back. Fighting with them is reckless and selfish."

"I need to know if they found Diego."

"They found Diego. Max texted me. Ghost has him and is going to sit on your parents until Mitch and Chase get there, which will be in a matter of hours."

The tension in Ax's shoulders relaxed, but Nick didn't let him up. Nick watched him with a wariness in his eyes. Ax had lost any trust he'd built between them, but he couldn't worry about that now.

"I wasn't going to hit you," he said.

"I know, but sometimes words hurt worse than a punch. You need to stop letting this fear and anger boiling inside you explode out and hurt the people who care about you."

Nick let go of Ax and stood. Ax looked at the ceiling as a million conflicting thoughts rolled through his mind like a tornado.

"If you really need to hit something, maybe we could stand a mattress against a wall or something."

"I'm not touching a bare hotel mattress. Are you fucking kidding me?"

Nick laughed. Ax hadn't meant to be funny, but he could see what Nick found amusing. Nick continued to laugh. He laughed so hard that Ax began to grin as well as he sat up.

Nick had a gorgeous smile. He spread his full lips wide, revealing not-quite-perfect teeth as he shook his head and kept laughing.

"That was your first thought?" Nick asked.

Ax shrugged.

"I'll tell everyone they can come back in," Nick said as he started typing on his phone.

Ax was hesitant to face all the guys. He was ashamed of his behavior, embarrassed by his meltdown. He wondered why there was no judgement from Nick.

The same couldn't be said of Bray. When everyone made their way back into the suite, Bray narrowed his eyes at Ax. He was taken aback for a minute because Bray was such a sweetheart. Ax hadn't been sure he'd been capable of getting angry — until now, anyway.

"I'm sorry," Ax said to the room at large.

He owed Nick an individual apology and also a thank you, but that would have to wait. For now, they needed to change their plans and figure out a way to get Cherie out while Meyers was home.

Mitch and Chase had already left, and though Ax would have preferred his parents go directly to

Virginia, he could understand why Nick had made the decision to bring them to Texas. Maybe it was the best thing for Cherie, to be surrounded by the family who loved her.

They were discussing so many things that when the mention of delaying Daniel Meyers' trip home popped up, Ax looked up from the plans of the Meyers' home he'd been studying.

"I got the flight delayed. I even got Meyers bumped, but he hopped on the next flight and it landed thirty minutes ago." Max looked over at Ax.

Now it was just a waiting game to see how long it took the motherfucker to pay a visit to his sister.

Chapter Thirty-Three

Nick

Dinnertime. It was dinnertime before Daniel Meyers made an appearance in Cherie's room. The house was probably too bustling for a rendezvous. The fact that he knocked on her door from the inside of the house and didn't sneak in from the back was also a good sign.

The guys had all taken turns getting a few hours' sleep. Ax was still down for the count after passing out from all his crying jags. Sam and Bray were sleeping as well. Mitch and Chase were on their way back to Texas with Ax's family. Clay was standing guard outside Ax's door to alert them if he woke up.

Max, Wade, Colt and Nick were the only ones still working, and they were all huddled around Max's laptop to watch what was happening. Cherie let Meyers into her room. She seemed nervous, and her focus kept darting to the plug where the camera was.

Meyers didn't seem to notice. He announced he was doing his rounds, checking the staff upon his return before closing the door and pulling Cherie in for a kiss. It was clear she was simply tolerating his attention, but he continued to kiss and touch her.

"I missed you," he said quietly. "I need to figure out a way to take you with me when I travel."

"I'm not sure your wife would believe you need a cook-slash-maid with you everywhere you go." Cherie smiled as she said it, but her eyes were so sad. She looked at the plug again and Meyers seemed to notice.

"Is everything all right?"

"Yes, I was just thinking about when you first…acquired me."

"It's not like that anymore, Cherry," he said.

All the guys looked at each other. *He called her Cherry instead of Cherie?* Nick knew it was probably a reference to him taking her virginity, and he was relieved Ax hadn't heard it.

"I may have had to coerce and even intimidate a little in the beginning, but now, we have something special. Bill was right. He found a rare gem in you."

"What about when I turn eighteen? Will you still want me then, or will you sell me to someone else?"

Nick looked up at Wade, who smiled wide. Not only could they trust Cherie not to tip Meyers off, but she was also getting incriminating evidence on him on the record. Nick could have sworn she was already eighteen, but he could have been wrong.

"Is that what you're worried about? Oh, baby, don't worry. I love having you around. I have no plans to pass you off. We have a deal, remember? I'm letting you work off what I paid for you. You'll be all paid off by the time you're twenty-one."

"And that's when you'll toss me out? When I'm twenty-one? Is that when I become too old for you?"

"Cherry, I thought you wanted to go back to your parents. It was the deal we came up with, and I plan on honoring it. I admit I like younger women. Usually, I like women under eighteen, but you're special. I want to keep you longer. Why are you worrying about this now? That's years away."

"I miss my family, but by then, what if they forget about me?"

"They haven't forgotten about you," Meyers said.

"How do you know?"

He hesitated for a moment, which Nick took as a sign that Meyers knew her parents were still actively looking for her.

"No one could forget you," he finally said.

Meyers grabbed her ass and pulled her in for a sloppy kiss. Everyone in front of the computer turned away in disgust. Everyone but Wade looked at each other rather than the monitor until Meyers said his goodbyes.

"I have to admit that I'm pleased you're hesitant to leave. We've come a long way from me having to hold you down when I first had you. We'll work something out. I have no intention of putting you out on the street."

Meyers gave her ass one final squeeze before leaving the room. Cherie collapsed on the bed and looked again at the camera.

"I hope you got all that," she said quietly.

"You bet your ass we did," Max said.

Leaving Cherie behind hadn't been the plan, but things might end up even better than they'd planned. A US Congressman admitting to trafficking and systematically raping an underaged girl? Now that was incriminating.

"What's the ETA on Ax's family?" Nick asked Max.

Max tapped on his keyboard. "Approximately three hours, depending on traffic. Oh shit."

"What?" Wade and Nick asked at the same time.

"We've got movement on Raymond Snow, AKA Robby."

"Fuck," Wade said.

"Where's Ghost?" Nick asked.

"He's on his way back to Campbell's vineyard," Wade said.

"He'll probably pass right by them," Max said. "You said they were sending him to Chicago? Let's see if we can find out what flight he's on. Wade, can you listen to their conversation and let me know if they mention a flight or time?"

"Sure. We can head them off at the airport. Ghost can handle this quietly."

"Or maybe he can head them off at the destination. I have an idea," Max said as he started typing wildly on his laptop.

Wade pulled up the video files before turning to Nick. "Nick, go tell Ax that his family is in the air and will be here in approximately three hours. Hopefully that will settle him a little."

"He's not going to back down on going back tonight." Nick said.

"I know. I've got a plan for that, too," Max said.

"Great. I'll go check on him and bring him back here so we can go over everything."

Max grunted in reply as he did something with the video they'd just recorded of Daniel Meyers admitting to all his crimes.

Nick left them to figure it out. When he walked down the hall, Clay was leaning against the wall by

Ax's door. He stood away from the wall and gave Nick a nod.

"Any signs of life in there?" Nick asked.

"I think I heard the shower go on, but I wasn't sure if it was his room or the one next door."

"I got this." Nick nodded at Ax's door.

"My turn for a nap then."

Nick watched Clay walk down the hall and turn a corner before he knocked. For a minute, there was no sound inside the room.

After a while, there was a thump and some groaning before the door was wrenched open. Clay had definitely been mistaken about the shower coming on in Ax's room.

His longish hair was sticking straight up on one side and flattened to his face on the other. Nick bit his lip to keep from smiling. If he thought the man's bedhead was cute and even a little sexy, he was in a lot deeper than he'd let himself believe. His stomach sank as he realized he'd fallen in love with the asshole in front of him.

Even now, when Ax looked like shit, Nick wanted him. Mostly he wanted to give him a hug, but that was even worse than wanting to fuck him. Ax's clothes were rumpled and wrinkled, as if he'd simply passed out and fallen asleep.

"Did something happen?" Ax blinked. Then he blinked again. He must have been out, because it was like he was still trying to bring the world into focus. Nick watched as the last of the sleepy haze left his eyes.

"Nothing bad. Your family is safe on a plane with Mitch and Chase."

"And Cherie?"

Nick looked left and right down the hallway. This wasn't a discussion they wanted to have where anyone could open a door or walk by. Ax must have gotten the hint, because he stepped back and opened the door wider. Nick stepped into his room. The door clicked shut and Nick turned to watch as Ax rubbed his hands over his face.

"Meyers paid a visit to Cherie—"

Ax interrupted Nick's sentence with a step forward. Nick held up his hands to try to calm Ax down.

"He just came to say hello. Nothing happened. We watched the whole exchange. But we know we can trust your sister."

"She got him to talk?"

"She was flawless, except she kept looking at the bug. She could practically work for the CIA, she was so smooth."

"Too smooth?"

"No. Perfect. When he left, she looked at the camera and said, *'Hope you got all that'*."

Ax looked out of the window. Nick knew exactly what he was thinking.

"We need the cover of darkness," Nick said.

"Do you think he'll wait for the cover of dark?"

"Yes. I think he probably waits until the whole house is asleep before sneaking into her room. Let's make sure your parents make it to the hotel and don't get stopped or waylaid."

Ax didn't say anything, but after a moment, he gave one sharp nod. The silence stretched out between them until it got awkward, and Nick felt like an intruder.

"Let me know if you need anything," Nick said as he turned to leave, but there was a hand on his bicep before he took one step.

"I need to get my sister away from that child molester."

Nick turned and saw the guilt and shame and torture in Ax's eyes. Nick let out a breath. He felt for Ax, but he wasn't totally sure how to help him.

"We will. Tonight."

"That's not soon enough. I feel like I want to crawl out of my own skin when I think about him even laying a finger on her."

"It may sound cold or even heartless, but, Ax, she stayed to keep your family safe. If you take her out of there before they're here under our protection and anything were to happen, her guilt would be as big as yours. At least let her feel like she sacrificed for a reason."

"That's hours away," Ax said. "What the fuck do I do for a few hours?"

Ax started to run his fingers through his hair but then stopped and pulled the thick locks away from his scalp as he groaned.

"I have an idea," Nick said.

Chapter Thirty-Four

Ax

Ax turned to Nick. A million questions ran through his mind about how to distract himself. *If I suggest punching a mattress again…* Ax stopped when he saw the wicked grin on Nick's face.

His cock began to thicken even as he shook his head. He couldn't sit here in a safe hotel room and fuck while all the members of his family were in limbo.

"I can't have my dick in you while Cherie is still with him," Ax said.

"You can't control that. If you went there right now, everything would fall to shit. Worrying about your family doesn't mean you're in control of this situation. It's out of your hands, whether you sit here and pace like a caged animal or let yourself forget for even just a moment. Besides, I think it's my turn to have my dick in you."

That last sentence had Ax groaning. It would feel amazing to let himself go, *if* he could let himself go. To just set all the decisions bearing down on him aside even for a few minutes sounded like heaven.

"I don't want to use you like that," Ax said.

He knew what Nick was doing. He was offering himself up as a distraction, even though Ax had been a total mess. He had continually fucked everything up between them, pushing too hard, losing his temper.

"You're not asking. I'm offering—or rather, demanding. I want all your clothes off. I want you on your hands and knees in the middle of the bed. Tell me where you keep your rubbers."

Ax swallowed past the desert in his throat. He nodded to the bathroom and let Nick know he kept condoms and lube in his toiletry bag.

Nick turned and headed for the bathroom, so Ax took a moment to pull himself together. It wasn't a question of whether or not he wanted to be with Nick. It was a question of whether or not it was fair to Nick.

Nick was... He was nothing like Ax had thought he was. Ax had figured he was spoiled, selfish and probably down for some no-strings fucking. But he was sweet and caring and thoughtful. He deserved a lot better than Ax would be able to give.

"I said clothes off and ass on the bed."

"I thought you wanted my knees on the bed."

"Fine. Knees on the bed, ass in the air. Is that detailed enough?"

With a smirk on his lips, Ax dropped his pants as he walked to the bed. He quickly pulled off the rest of his clothes and climbed onto the mattress. He'd just gotten into position when he felt a hand on his back. Nick's fingers were warm and firm when they cupped the back of his neck and pressed his cheek down into the sheets.

"Do I need to blindfold you, or can you just close your eyes and concentrate on the sensations?"

Ax groaned at the pressure of Nick pressing him down, even as his dick pulsed at the thought of just letting go and allowing Nick to do all the work.

"I'll keep them closed."

When Nick let go, Ax's shoulders tensed. Then Nick pressed both his hands into Ax's shoulder blades. With a deep breath, Ax did what Nick was silently demanding. He relaxed. He allowed himself to melt into the bed.

He concentrated on the muscles of his quads as they kept his ass in the air. Nick took care of that, though, as he grabbed all the pillows and stacked them under Ax's hips.

"Relax," Nick said.

The click of the lube cap opening echoed against the walls. Ax kept his eyes closed as he waited. The featherlight touch over his pucker had a shiver running up his spine.

"How much prep?" Nick asked.

His voice was a lot closer to Ax's ear than he thought Nick had been. He turned his head toward the sound but didn't open his eyes.

"None," Ax bit out.

"That's not an option. Acceptable answers are 'minimal' and 'copious'."

Ax wanted to feel the burn. He needed a little pain to take his mind off everything that was about to crash down on him.

"As little as you're willing," Ax agreed.

Another fluttering touch danced over his opening and his hole spasmed and twitched. When Ax pressed back, Nick removed the touch completely.

"Fucking tease," Ax grumbled.

Nick laughed. Ax smiled at the sound but then gasped when Nick not only touched him again but pressed one long finger all the way in, past Ax's tight ring of muscle. The burn pulled all the air from his lungs. It wasn't actually painful, but it had his focus narrowing on the place where flesh met flesh. It was exactly what he needed.

When the burn dissipated and the friction began to mount into something pleasurable, Nick pulled his finger out and pressed in not two but three fingers. Ax groaned as the burn moved back to the forefront. Again, as soon as Ax felt any pleasure build, Nick pulled free.

There was the crinkle and tear of a condom wrapper. In his impatience, Ax almost told Nick to forget the rubber, but he bit his tongue. He never fucked without protection.

"Fuck." Ax drew out the word as Nick pressed forward.

Nick didn't stop or slow down or even speed up. He didn't pull back a little to let Ax adjust or work more lube in. He just pushed slowly in until he bottomed out. Ax was on fire from the inside out, and yet, Nick wasn't hurting him. It was just enough pain to narrow his focus again.

"So tight," Nick whispered in his ear as he lay his chest across Ax's back.

"Fuck me," Ax demanded.

"This is my show. You're just here for the big 'O' at the end."

Ax let out a breath that was a laugh but turned into a groan as Nick pulled almost all the way out before slamming back in—then did it again and again. He built a steady pace, only to come to a jarring halt when Ax was close to coming.

After the third round of this, Ax lifted his hands behind him and tried to grab Nick so he could control the rhythm. Instead, Nick grabbed Ax's wrists and locked them together at the base of his spine.

Ax tried to thrust into the pillows supporting his hips, but Nick used his knees to spread Ax's legs wider. He couldn't get any leverage.

He lost what little control he'd had, and it made something inside him loosen and break free. He had no power over what was to come, and the feeling of letting go was so freeing that his balls drew up and the base of his spine began to tingle.

"Did you finally let go?" Nick whispered in his ear.

Tears sprang to Ax's eyes. He nodded but couldn't speak.

"No guilt, no shame, just pleasure. You deserve pleasure, too," Nick said.

Ax coughed out a sob. Nick pulled his hips up and ripped a few pillows from beneath him. Ax felt a firm hand grasp his cock and begin to stroke hard and fast. Nick wasn't slowing down this time as his pending release built up in his balls.

In fact, Nick sped up. His rhythm faltered and became chaotic. He squeezed Ax so hard that he would have been raw if his cock hadn't been leaking so much pre-cum. But it was perfect. Every move was exactly what Ax needed.

All it took was one last thrust of Nick's cock pegging his prostate and Ax exploded. Everything turned light then black. His muscles seized. Pleasure so sharp it bordered on pain arced through him from his core to his fingers and toes. It was like nothing he'd ever experienced in his life.

He was too far gone to even know if Nick had come as well. When he finally relaxed, Ax collapsed face first onto the bed. His breathing was loud and rough. He heard more than felt the *squelch* of Nick pulling out and disposing of the condom.

Ax rolled to his back, lying haphazardly across the bed and looked at the ceiling. The real world was trying to intrude on the pleasant post-orgasmic buzz he had going.

When Nick came into his vision again, he was dressed and held a wet washcloth in his hands. He rearranged the pillows so that Ax had one under his head. Ax's eyes burned. He couldn't remember the last time someone had thought about his needs like that.

Sure, his parents loved him, but they wanted him to come home and be the backbone of the family. At least that was what his mom wanted. He didn't think his dad knew what to do and Diego just wanted to be a normal teenager.

Nick threw the pillow covered in Ax's jizz on the floor then proceeded to clean him off with the little face towel. Ax felt like crying at the gesture, so he laughed.

"Why did you…? How…?"

Ax didn't know how to ask how Nick had known exactly what he'd needed. It was scary how well Nick had guessed what would crack him apart then seal him right back together.

"It's okay to just say thank you," Nick said.

Ax laughed. "Now who's being cocky?"

"I just wanted to help you let go." Nick said. "You keep the world on your shoulders."

"Not the world, just my family."

"Then after tonight, you can relax a little. You accomplished your goal. You'll have your sister back."

But there was still so much to be done, even after they got Cherie out. He needed to sell the house he'd bought his parents and see if he could get their things without anyone figuring out where they were going or even that they were related to him.

Cherie would need therapy. Diego would need therapy. Hell, they'd all need therapy. He'd have to relocate them and keep them afloat financially until things settled and his parents could find jobs wherever they landed.

"You don't have to figure it all out yourself, y'know." Nick said. "Those guys in there? They're great at logistics and I think they kind of like you, at least a little. I think I kind of like you, too."

Ax snorted. Maybe Nick was warming up to him, but he couldn't lay all his burdens on his friends. That just wasn't right. They all had enough to deal with. And Nick…

"I think—"

There was a pounding on the door. It was probably for the best. Ax had been about to say something stupid, something like 'I think I love you.'

"Loco," Wade called through the door, "your family landed safe, sound and early. ETA thirty minutes."

"Ten-four, Lamb," Ax said.

"Lamb?" Nick whispered.

"Yeah, but he won't tell anyone how he got his call sign. Since he was a SEAL, we don't know a lot of Frogmen, so we haven't been able to figure out what it means."

Nick got so quiet that Ax looked over to find his eyes downcast and his ears pink. Ax smirked. "So your call sign story is that bad?"

Nick shrugged.

Ax wondered again if it was an acronym for something that had happened in boot camp, or maybe just after. Ax was about to ask when Nick stood from the bed.

"I'll let you get ready. The sun will be setting by seven-thirty, so we can head out once you get your parents settled and updated on the situation."

Nick was embarrassed, and Ax didn't want to leave things like that. Nick had calmed him when he'd gone off the rails, soothed him when he'd been at loose ends, but the words that fell from his lips were the last words on Earth he should have spoken.

"I think I'm falling for you, Dash."

The shy smile that spread Nick's lips had Ax's heart stuttering. Letting Nick in on his feelings was probably a big, big mistake.

Chapter Thirty-Five

Nick

Nick was pacing back and forth in the main suite. Wade had pulled Ax aside to discuss something and the rest of them sat waiting for the arrival of the Guttierez family. Nick had just turned toward the door when it opened.

Nando and Cella came in together. Nando had a protective arm around his wife. Cella's gaze was pinging all over the room, clearly searching out Ax as she wrung her hands together. Mitch stepped into the room next, followed by a sullen Diego and finally Chase.

"Nick," Cella said, as she rushed over to him.

Nick gave her a comforting hug and she squeezed him so tight that he almost lost his breath. He heard a quiet sniffle, and it took her a minute to pull back.

"They said Ruby needed us here. Ruby called and asked us to go with his friends, so here we are. What is it? Where is he?"

Nick opened his mouth to respond but realized he couldn't and wouldn't put the words out there. Ax needed to explain things in his own way.

"He'll explain everything," Nick said as he waved Nando over. He asked Chase to show Diego how the TV worked. Diego huffed out a dramatic teenage sigh and plopped down on the sofa. He grumbled something about being treated like a baby as he settled in.

Not willing to let Ax's parents sit anxiously, Nick knocked on the door to the bedroom where Ax and Wade were talking.

"Enter," Wade said.

Nick opened the door. As soon as Cella saw Ax, she hurried in and attached herself to him. Nando chuckled at Nick's side. Cella started speaking a mile a minute, but all in Spanish.

Ax gave Nick a dark look, but he just shrugged. Ax would have been even more pissed off if Nick had told his parents what was really going on before Ax had a chance to.

"He found her, didn't he?" Nando said so low that only Nick heard him.

When Nando looked over at him, Nick gave a slight nod. Nando closed his eyes for a moment and simply breathed out.

"I'm relieved, ecstatic. But I hope he didn't sell his soul to the devil for this," Nando said.

Nick chuckled a little as he thought about Max's handle. He'd have to explain that to Nando later. For now, he just shook his head.

"I found her," Ax said.

Cella gasped. She grabbed Ax's biceps as her body began to sway. Nando rushed forward to help Ax as they moved her over to sit on a chair by the window.

"Are you sure?" Nando asked in a low brittle tone.

"I saw her, talked to her, touched her," Ax said.

"Where?" Cella stood and looked around the room as if maybe she'd missed her daughter standing there. "Where is she?"

The look of guilt and shame that pinched Ax's face had Nick's heart beating loudly in his ears. Ax opened his mouth but then closed it.

"She wouldn't come with us," Nick said before he could tell his mouth to stay closed.

Everyone turned to him. He swallowed down the apology that tried to burst out. He didn't want Ax to try to take on any more blame.

When Nick didn't say anything else, Nando and Cella turned and looked at Ax. He didn't look any less guilty, but at least the truth was out there.

"She's living in some rich guy's house. He's married and she's pretending to be part of his household staff. He…he's been keeping an eye on you and showing her pictures. He's made her believe that her staying with him is what's keeping you safe."

Nando collapsed down into the chair Cella had just vacated. His arms hung lifelessly over the sides of the armrests as he looked up at his wife.

"The white car," Nando groaned.

"What white car?" Ax said.

"Ever since we moved into that house, your mother's been pointing out this white car. She thought they were watching us. I thought… Well, we've all been a little on edge since Cherie disappeared. I told her it was just a neighbor or a friend of a neighbor, but she said she'd seen that car before we moved. I hadn't, so I disregarded it."

Nando stood and wrapped his arms around his wife. He whispered words of apology in her ear. He said something about Diego, but Nick couldn't hear exactly what he'd said.

"Cherie has surveillance pictures of you up all over her room. He's using your safety to keep her there, so once we get her, you can't go back. You can't go back to California at all."

"No. No, of course not." Nando confirmed.

"I want you to come to Virginia for a while until we figure out the safest route to move forward," Ax said.

"Virginia? Is that where you're living?"

There was no censure in Cella's statement, just curiosity. Still, Ax stiffened. Maybe it was the realization that he'd pushed his parents so far away that they didn't even know such basic things about him anymore.

"This is what you've been doing," Nando said. It wasn't a question but a statement. "This is why you left the military. You've been searching for her all this time."

"No," Ax said. "I do work with this consulting firm. It's just they tend to work on similar cases, so I was using those contacts and that experience to help me find her, but—"

Ax was cut off when his father squeezed him so hard that he let out a little grunt. After a moment, Ax wrapped his arms around his father as well. When he finally pulled back, Nando had wet tracks down his cheeks, and he shook his head.

"I really need to listen to your mother," he said. "She knew. She knew all along about the white car, about what you were doing, that Cherie was alive and that we needed to protect Diego." Nando turned to Cella. "I let you do what you wanted, but I didn't help. I didn't support. I closed off and assumed the worst when that's not me. That's not me at all. But when they took Cherie, I lost that part of myself, the part that looks for good."

Wade met Nick's gaze over Ax's shoulder and flicked his head toward the door. Nick nodded and they both quietly eased their way out of the room to give Ax and his parents some privacy.

When they'd stepped out into the main room of the suite, they both took a breath. There had been a lot of sorrow and unresolved issues in the bedroom. But the living room didn't seem to be faring much better.

"What's happening to Ghost?" Diego demanded.

Max was standing over his laptop as he typed, blocking the screen from Diego's view. Wade strode over and laid a gentle hand on Diego's shoulder.

"This intel is classified," Wade said in a gentle tone.

"But Ghost—"

"Can take care of himself," Wade interrupted. "The guy's more highly trained than I am, and I'm a former Navy SEAL."

Diego's focus moved again to where Max was standing in front of his monitor. After a moment, Diego looked up at Nick, as if waiting for confirmation.

"There's a reason we get handles. Some of us get call signs if we do something funny or stupid in boot camp. Sometimes it's a play off our real name. Sometimes, it's about a talent. They call Mitch 'Flash' because he's so quick on the draw." Nick nodded in Mitch's direction.

"They call Colt 'Reaper' because he stacked up a lot of..." Nick faltered. He didn't want to tell a sixteen-year-old kid that Colt had killed more with his rifle than most snipers combined.

"I get it," Diego said.

"Ghost never gets caught," Wade said. "He got his handle because he's in and out like a ghost, no sign he was even there unless he wants there to be."

Diego's Adam's apple bobbed as he swallowed. Eventually he nodded.

"Work to do," Max reminded quietly.

"Let's see what they have in the mini bar," Nick suggested.

Diego only hesitated slightly before walking in the direction Nick indicated. They raided the mini bar and took all the spoils back to the sofa. They were tearing into all the food when Diego finally spoke again.

"Is something wrong with Ax?" Diego asked then shook his head. "I know something's wrong, but I wanna know what it is."

Nick wanted to roll his eyes at all the precarious situations he was finding himself in recently. He had no idea what he was going to tell Diego. Luckily, he was saved from having to figure that out when the door to the bedroom opened and Diego's whole family filed out. He stood when he saw his brother.

"Rubio," Diego said as he ran to give his brother a hug.

"Who's Rubio?" Max asked.

Wade rolled his eyes. "Maybe you should use your mad hacking skills to find out who you're working with. Ax is Rubio Axel Guttierez."

"There aren't any electronic files on you guys. How the hell am I supposed to hack into something that doesn't exist?" Max grumbled.

"That's exactly why we don't have soft copies of the HR files." Wade smiled.

Max rolled his eyes and sighed as he went back to typing.

"I figured you'd take what you knew and pull the rest from other sources," Wade said.

"Maybe when you give me five seconds to breathe. I've been pulled in ten different directions since the day I started."

"And you wouldn't have it any other way," Nick said.

Max loved being useful, and even more than that, he loved being in demand. Max gave Nick a glare but just went back to typing.

Chapter Thirty-Six

Ax

Ax had agreed with his parents that they wouldn't tell Diego about Cherie until she was with the team. By the time his parents were settled, the sun had set and everyone except Wade, Max and Mitch was once again in the plumbing van on the way to Meyers' house.

This op was a little more fly-by-the-seat-of-their-pants, because though Max said he had a plan, he was furiously working to help Ghost save a little boy from an inhuman fate. So Ax had held his tongue when Max handed a bag to Nick and told him to wait for his go-ahead.

"What's in the bag?" Ax asked when they were on the road.

Nick unzipped it and pulled out a small box made of wood. It reminded Ax of a large matchbox, the kind that had about five hundred matches inside. On the back was what looked like a plug but was also made of wood, with just a tiny piece of metal at the end of one prong.

"It's light as a feather," Nick said.

He reached in and pulled out something else. It was one of those grill lighters with a long flexible neck. There was a small note attached to it that said *Backup*.

"We burning the place down?" Nick asked.

"If we have to," Ax said.

With a shrug, Nick put both items back in the little bag and slipped it into the pocket of his tactical pants. Ax tried to concentrate on his breathing. For some fucked up reason, knowing Nick had his back was the only thing that calmed him down.

When they pulled up to the side of the house, everyone put on one of the ski masks Wade had given them. Ax knew the masks meant the op tonight was riskier and that one of them might be seen or even get caught, but he couldn't allow himself to care. Every one of these guys knew how to handle himself. Cherie didn't.

"Sin, we're here," Sam said into the mic.

"Shit. Okay, let me have Wade take over comms with Ghost. He shouldn't need us for a while yet anyway. Let me check everything. Nick, you ready?"

"I'm ready" Nick said.

If Nick was doing his little thing, that meant Cherie wasn't in her room. She was somewhere else. Their stunt would unfortunately pull everyone from the house, but Ax couldn't wait around for Meyers to rape her one last time.

"I'm going to set off the fire alarm for the whole house, but Nick is only going to set a small fire. The house has a fire suppression system that should actually put the fire out, but the fire department will show up anyway. Once I trip the alarm, you'll have probably five minutes to get out of there before the place is crawling with cops and other first responders. So make sure everyone's in place before I trip the alarm."

"Ten-four," Sam said.

"Nick, I've unlocked the windows and doors to Meyers' downstairs office, room A34. Chances of him being inside the room at this time of day are slim-to-none, based on his patterns, but let me know before you go in, and I'll give the all clear."

"Not that I'd mind running into the guy," Nick grumbled.

The other guys chuckled. Once that died down, they all got out of the car except Sam and Bray. Mitch had stayed with Wade to keep watch over Ax's family, so this op wasn't quite as overstaffed as they had been last time. But this time they might actually need all the operators who were there.

They took turns jumping the fence then sneaking to their posts. Ax and Chase were spread out along the back of the house. Colt and Clay were in the front of the house in case Cherie ended up somewhere else, so they could snag her.

The lights along the back of the house flickered then went out. Ax saw Nick sneak up the small set of stairs from the pool and crouch down.

"Sin," Nick whispered over the comm, "I'm in place."

"Everyone is in place," Ax confirmed into his mic.

"All clear in the office." Max said. "Plug the box by the door. There's an outlet behind a curtain."

"Ten-four." Nick's low voice came over the comm.

Ax watched the lights from the pool reflect onto the glass of the door as Nick slowly opened it and went inside. When he saw Nick's dark form creep back out and close the door, Ax released a breath he hadn't known he was holding.

"Ten-twenty-four," Nick whispered, letting Max know he'd completed the task.

"Clear the area to be safe," Max said. "Fire alarm in five, four, three, two, one."

There was a flash inside the office where Nick had put the little box. The curtains in the room lit up and an alarm began to sound. Within ten seconds, people began flooding from the house. The staff who didn't live with the Meyers were obviously still there, because ten people filled the backyard.

Ax didn't pay attention to anyone but Cherie. She came rushing out from the where the kitchen was. She looked around at everyone, then began looking over to the wooded area of the property. He'd always said she was smart as a whip.

Crouching down, Ax moved forward, even as Cherie moved slowly toward the wooded area. No one was paying any attention to her, and Ax didn't see Meyers, so he must have evacuated out of the front door. Ax followed along the edge of the property until Cherie reached the edge of the trees. He came up behind her.

"Smart as a whip," he said in a low voice.

He heard Cherie gasp. Chase was right next to him. They were both scanning the area to see if anyone was watching his sister.

"Clear," Ax said.

"Clear," Chase confirmed.

Ax grabbed Cherie's wrist and pulled her down and out of sight. They crouched backward a few steps before Ax lifted his mask off his face and pulled her into his arms.

"Everything's in place. We're getting the hell out of here," he told her.

Cherie's face was pressed tightly against his chest, and he felt her nod. He took her hand and began to lead her through the trees. Chase covered them as they went.

"We've got the package. We're clear. Let's GTFO," Ax whispered in his mic to let everyone know to hustle back to the van.

Within seconds, Clay and Colt were letting everyone know they were in the van. Sam and Bray confirmed. There was only one voice missing. Everyone had checked in but Nick. Stopping, Ax turned and tried to look through the trees.

"What is it?" Cherie whispered.

"We're a man down," Ax said as he turned to Chase. "Can you get her to the van?"

Chase shook his head once. "Ax, I can go get—"

"This op is a favor to me."

Chase looked at Cherie before nodding. He pulled up his ski mask and gave her a tentative smile as he took her hand.

"Ruby," Cherie pleaded.

Ax looked at her. He tried to convey everything he wanted to say into that one look. They didn't have time to argue.

"I can't leave a man behind. You're safe. I promise Chase will keep you safe. I'd trust him with my life, and more importantly, I'd trust him with yours. There are four more of my men in the car waiting to protect you. He's *not* getting you back."

Cherie hesitated a moment before nodding. Ax gave her a last peck on the cheek then took off through the trees to the edge of the clearing. Crouching down, he scanned the area for Nick.

His heart was racing. He began to sweat as he moved his gaze over every inch of the backyard. Ax told himself Nick wasn't in that much danger.

The bodyguards had guns, but they obviously weren't the most astute. They should have been checking to make sure everybody was safe rather than watching the house with open mouths like everyone else.

After three passes over the backyard with no sign of Nick, Ax crept back around. The back part of the fence was the most dangerous, because there were large gaps with no foliage to hide behind.

Slowly, Ax made his way silently around the perimeter of the yard. There was still no sign of Nick anywhere. He checked every nook and cranny he passed. The only explanation for Nick remaining silent was that he was backed into a corner where he couldn't speak—or else he'd been compromised.

Ax was almost to the back corner of the house where he and Nick had waited the night before to get into Cherie's room. When he saw Daniel Meyers striding around the side of the house, Ax took a deep breath. He blocked out the sounds he could occasionally hear through his earpiece.

Every time Max unmuted himself to speak, Ax could hear his mother talking a mile a minute, pestering Wade and Max with questions. He finally heard his father tell her she needed to let them work.

Chase told Max he was safe in the van with 'the package'. Ax let out a relieved breath. Even if he got caught, Cherie was safe. His team would make sure she got back to his family, no matter what.

As he crouched, Ax saw something move along the ground. He knew where Nick was, and the asshole was risking his position to give them more time to get Cherie out.

Ax couldn't see him, but he knew Nick was hiding behind a bush because he slowly moved a large stick out onto the sidewalk. As Meyers walked past the bush, the stick lifted about two inches from the ground. Meyers stumbled and fell.

He landed on his hands and knees so hard that Ax heard his bones hit the pavement. Groaning and swearing, Meyers rolled to a sitting position.

"Firetrucks ETA less than one minute," Max warned.

"Go," Ax whispered into his mic.

"Ten-four," Sam said. "We're pulling out and moving exactly one block west."

Ax could hear Cherie crying in the background, but he couldn't bring himself to leave Nick twisting in the wind.

"What the fuck is that?" Meyers snarled.

Ax crouched on the balls of his feet, ready to pounce if Nick had been found.

"I pay those landscapers thousands a month to keep this place pristine. This fucking log shouldn't be here."

Sirens wailed in the background.

"Congressman, let me help you back into the front yard. The EMTs will want to take a look at you," said the guard who had been tailing him.

Meyers finally nodded. Meyers was looking over his shoulder the whole limping walk back to the front of the house, and Ax knew exactly who he was looking for.

When the coast was finally clear, Nick crept out from behind the bush. Ax couldn't see any of his features, only the movement. He sat back and waited for Nick to reach him.

"You should have gone," Nick whispered. "I would have caught up."

"How…by running? You gonna call an Uber?"

Ax heard the quiet, frustrated sigh and knew Nick was rolling his eyes under his ski mask as they made their way to the back corner of the yard. The smoking guard was there, holding a lit cigarette behind his back. Ax stayed far enough away so he could whisper without being overheard.

"Sin," Ax said, "we need a diversion. We need lights out or something to draw people toward the house."

"Diversion in ten-nine-eight…"

Ax and Nick both inched forward toward where the man kept sneaking drags of his cigarette. When Max ended the countdown, the electricity went out. Most importantly, the pool lights went out. The lights along the overhang at the back of the house began to flash on and off, drawing everyone's attention.

Ax and Nick ran at a crouch across the open area along the back wall. Once they reached the trees, they both yanked off their ski masks and vaulted over the wall into the neighbor's backyard.

Ax pulled off his black shirt. He was wearing a white tank underneath, but it was less conspicuous than all black at night. Nick was wearing a light blue T-shirt under his black top.

"We'll pretend we're jogging," Ax whispered.

Nick nodded. They both stuffed their masks into their pockets and held their shirts in their hands. The neighbors would likely know they didn't live on this block, so exercising would be more believable.

Ax jumped up and looked over the stone wall that separated the neighbor's backyard from the front. There were enough trees to hide them as they bounded over. Ax went first and Nick followed.

Quite a few people had come out of the other houses, but no one was looking at Ax or Nick because the fire truck was pulling up to Meyers' house.

"Do you think there's really a fire?" Nick asked.

The question was directed at Ax but loud enough that the group of people who were gathered at the end of the street could hear.

"Probably just an alarm malfunction," Ax replied.

No one turned their way. No one gave them a second glance. Still, they paused to gawk for a moment as most neighbors would before jogging away.

Chapter Thirty-Seven

Nick

When they reached the van around the corner, the door slid open. Ax's mouth dropped in horror at the sight of his sister blubbering on the floor of the van. He picked her up and held her in his lap like a baby, rocking her as they all piled in. He murmured to her in Spanish as they pulled away from the curb.

Nick imagined being rescued by her brother, only to be taken away again would be frightening. Guilt assailed him. He hadn't meant to get trapped, but as he'd made his way from the house, a security guard had come around the corner.

He'd been stuck in that bush for what had felt like forever. The guy had been the only competent one of Meyers' security, as he'd tried to keep his eyes on what was going on both in the front and the back of the house. His ass had been blocking Nick's vision, so he hadn't even risked communicating.

Max was chatting through the comm about how he was busy deleting any evidence of the op from all video surveillance. Nick smiled as he heard Ax's family peppering Wade with questions in the background.

"Make sure to check the neighbor's footage," Nick said. "We had to jump the fence of the neighbor to the back and then hop the fence into the front yard."

"I'm on it. There will be no sign of any of you. I can't remove all evidence of Cherie, though. It already looks like she backed into the trees. He'll just think she ran away." Max said.

"He'd be stupid to think she didn't have any help," Sam said as he pulled out of the back exit of the gated community.

Once they were past the gate, they all breathed a sigh of relief. They passed a few cops, sirens blaring, headed in the other direction, but they were home free. People needed plumbers all hours of the day, so they wouldn't be conspicuous.

"He'll probably turn on his security team and think it was an inside job," Bray said.

"Even when he realizes her family is gone, he'll probably just think whoever helped Cherie escape warned them," Nick added.

No one discussed the possibility of him trying to replace Cherie. They'd figure that when out she was safely reunited with her parents. The last thing she needed was any guilt about getting out.

By the time they reached the hotel, Cherie had calmed but was still in Ax's lap. They all piled out, and when Ax slowly and carefully scooted to the end of the bench seat and stood, Nick realized Cherie had fallen asleep. Ax carried her gently to the elevator and all the way to the suite.

Trailing at the back of the group, Nick lifted a hand to Ax so he'd hang back as the guys filed into the suite. He quietly slipped into the room to let everyone know they'd arrived. Cella was on him like a magnet.

"Where is she? Nick, I have to see her. Where — ?"

"Shh," Nick held his finger to his lips. "She's passed out. It's probably the first time in a long time she's felt safe enough to just sleep."

A quiet sob escaped Cella's lips, but she swallowed the next one back and nodded. Nando had his arm around her back and they both had tears streaking their cheeks. Diego looked shell-shocked, eyes wide and brimming with tears as his gaze ping-ponged between Nick and his parents.

"We'll take Cherie to the room Ax was in," Nick told Wade.

Wade nodded and gave Nick the keycard as he began speaking quietly with the team. Nick led Ax's family into the hallway. Cella let out a breath but no sob when she stepped out and saw Ax holding a sleeping Cherie. After a moment, she reached out and smoothed her daughter's hair.

Nick tilted his head toward the hall and Ax nodded. He hurried to unlock the room and held the door open for the quiet procession. As she passed over the threshold, Cella squeezed Nick's biceps and mouthed 'thank you'.

Fighting back his own tears, Nick nodded. Diego tentatively stepped into the room. He looked at his sleeping sister as if she were a completely unknown and novel object.

Ax gently laid her on the bed. She stirred for a moment, but as soon as she heard Ax's voice, she settled back into sleep, curled around him like a baby koala. Cella turned her face into her husband's chest and silently cried. Nando wrapped both arms around her and held her tightly.

Unsure what to do, Diego stood at the foot of the bed for a moment and watched his sister sleep. He kept licking his lips and swiping at his eyes. After a few moments, he turned and walked past his parents. Nick gave his shoulder a squeeze.

Diego looked up at Nick and there was such desolation in his eyes. Taking a deep breath, Nick tried to let it go. It seemed every member of the family was placing a heap of blame on their own shoulders for something that had been completely out of their control.

Nick looked back toward the bed. Ax was watching him as he cuddled his sister. Their gazes held across the room and Nick's heart kicked up. Ax's jaw ticked. Nick wasn't sure if Ax was grateful or angry, but he couldn't stand there all day wishing things were different.

Finally, Nick gave Ax a little smile and a nod. Ax nodded back as he ran his hand over his sister's hair. Backing out of the room, Nick closed the door without even a click. Taking a deep breath, he turned and headed back to the suite.

His urge to protect the broken family in that hotel room grew and doubled. *What the hell am I going to do with that?* he wondered as he let himself back into the suite.

"We have to let him know that we know what he did, or he'll just do it again," Max said.

"I'm not disagreeing with you, but we have to do it in a way that is completely safe for our group and for Ax and his entire family," Wade said.

"Agreed," Max grumbled.

"We need to get Ax and his family to Virginia ASAP. Mitch and Chase, you'll go with them. You've built trust with Ax's parents, and Chase helped with Cherie, so she'll trust you as well."

Both men nodded.

"The rest of us will hang back a few days and try to tie up loose ends — unless you need to get back, Sam?"

"I'm good for a few more days. Then I'll need to meet up with Jazz."

Wade nodded before rubbing his hands together. The corner of Nick's mouth kicked up a little. He looked over and found Bray making the same face. They were the newest on the team besides Max, but they'd both learned enough to know that when Wade got ready, things could get fun.

Chapter Thirty-Eight

Ax
Several weeks later

Another sleepless night.

Ax sat on the cool sand and stared out at the horizon as the sky began to lighten. Cherie wasn't talking, not about anything important. She seemed happy to be with their family and relieved to be away from Meyers but she wasn't talking about it.

She wasn't pretending nothing had happened or that she was the same Cherie who'd been taken, but she didn't discuss it, either. No one else dared bring it up after the first two meltdowns. The therapist couldn't tell him if she was actually talking about it in their sessions, but he hoped she was.

She met with the therapist three times a week and had for the past month since they'd gotten settled in at Dee's beach bungalow. His parents and Diego were also meeting with a therapist once a week. He'd gone a couple of times, but the anger burning inside him was growing, not shrinking.

Meyers was walking around like he'd done nothing wrong while Cherie was afraid of her own shadow. It wasn't fair, and Ax could have prevented it.

"You too?" Cherie asked as she sat beside him in the sand.

Ax wrapped an arm around her, pulled her in for a hug and breathed in her scent. She flinched when their father hugged her, Diego too. Ax didn't know why he was different. Maybe because he'd made first contact and had physically pulled her out. He still couldn't believe she was home safe.

"Me too, what?" He asked.

"You can't sleep. You're as restless as I am. You don't eat much more than me, either."

"You don't need to worry about me," Ax told her.

At first, she'd done nothing but sleep. She'd been so exhausted. But recently she'd been growing restless.

"You haven't cornered the market on worry," she said. "Everyone is hovering over me all the time. I know I was young when this all started — "

"You're still young."

"My age might be young, but I had to work like an adult, look after myself like an adult."

"If that's what you want, I'll tell Mom and Dad to back off," he said.

"No. That's not what I want. You think I don't know how lucky I am? You found me. Mom and Dad left their home and everything they knew, no questions asked. They moved to the other side of the country. If they want to hover, they can hover."

"Not if it slows your healing process."

"Is that what this is?"

Ax pulled her close again and kissed the top of her head. He didn't know how to help, so he just sort of stood back and watched, making sure his family had what they needed.

They sat for a few minutes in silence while the black sky became red and orange. As the sun crested, Cherie took a deep breath and spoke words Ax never wanted to hear in his life.

"It was my fault," she said.

"The hell it was."

"I went with him willingly," she whispered.

Ax didn't know who 'he' was, but he knew damn well that she hadn't known what lay ahead if she made that choice.

"So you knew," he said. "You knew they were going to sell you into slavery and you went anyway?"

"No. Of course not. This guy, Adam, he helped me out when a couple of guys were giving me a hard time."

"Danny Silva and Shawn Torres?"

She turned to look directly into his eyes. After a moment, she settled back against his chest and looked out at the ocean. It seemed easier for both of them to talk if they didn't have to see the other's face.

"Yeah. They kept harassing me on the way home from school. One day, this guy steps in. He introduced himself, but I could tell he thought he was hot stuff, y'know?"

Ax nodded. He didn't want her to stop talking now that she'd started. She didn't look at him, but she must have felt the movement, because she continued.

"I didn't give him the time of day, but from then on, he'd usually be there to tell those guys to back off. Sometimes he wasn't, but I handled it."

That last nugget made Ax want to scream and tear something apart. She shouldn't have needed to handle a couple of drug dealers harassing her.

"Then Adam started walking me home from school. He never tried anything or asked me out. He never even touched me. He was just there every day. He walked me to the corner of our building and watched me go in. Then he'd leave."

Emotional manipulation. Many traffickers used it. They pretended to be what the victim needed. Cherie had needed protection.

"One day, he wasn't there. I was…disappointed but not scared. Then, on the way home, Shawn and Danny started coming after me. It was worse than ever before. I…I was scared they were going to rape me. I remember thinking that would be the worst thing that could ever happen to me."

Cherie chuckled humorlessly and shook her head before continuing.

"Mom used the say that things could always be worse. In that moment, I couldn't imagine anything worse than being raped then having to go home and tell you guys. Then, a car screeches to a halt and Adam jumps out. He pushes both guys off me and tells me to get in the car while he fights them off. I did. I jumped right into that car."

Ax waited for her to continue. It was like she'd ended the story at the beginning. He wanted to know every fucking bad thing that had been done to her so he could exact his revenge.

"When do we get to the 'I went with him willingly' part?" Ax asked.

"That was it."

"No, *mija*. That was you being duped, manipulated, lied to. There was nothing about that you have to take responsibility for. You chose what you thought was the lesser of two evils. They set it up that way. It's what they do."

"You mean Adam was working with them? I wondered about that as I replayed it over and over in my head."

And that right there ripped what was left of Ax's heart to shreds. She'd been going over that again and again for three years, laying the blame at her own feet.

"I think the only thing that could have prevented it would be you not being there in the first place. I could have made that happen, and I chose not to. This is on me."

Cherie scoffed. "How is any of this on you?"

"I had the money. I could have moved you all out of there."

"Why is that your responsibility?"

"I was saving up. I saved every penny. I had enough to maybe buy a little two-bedroom condo in a decent neighborhood, but that wasn't good enough. I had to be the big man. I wanted you and Diego to have your own rooms. I wanted there to even be a guest room so I wouldn't be on the couch or the floor when I came home for a visit."

"Ruby, we never expected that from you. We expected you to build your own life. And you didn't get to. You spent all that time looking for me."

"I found you. That's all that matters," he said.

"But I'm not the same."

"I didn't expect you to be. My worst fear was that you imagined yourself in love with your captor."

Cherie snorted.

"I didn't expect it to take three years."

"So much guilt. The guilt is so thick in that house that I have to swim through it every day," Cherie said. "It's not your fault."

"But —"

"But nothing. If it's your fault, then is it Mom and Dad's fault too?"

"What? No, of course —"

"They had money too, Ruby. They scrimped and saved. They could have afforded a bigger apartment years ago, but they were saving for a down payment on something — anything in a better neighborhood."

Ax hadn't known. He'd known they were always squirreling money away, but he'd thought it was so Cherie and Diego wouldn't be forced to go into the military in order to get college paid for. Maybe if he'd actually had a conversation with his parents, he would have known and pitched in on the down payment. He realized the distance he'd put between himself and his family had started long before Cherie had been taken.

"If it's your fault for not moving us, then isn't it theirs too?" she asked.

"No."

He could logically see her point, but the guilt still sat in his gut like lead. They'd been saving for a down payment, but he could have paid cash for something.

"If I could go back..." Ax's throat closed and he couldn't finish the sentence.

"Me too, Ruby," Cherie said quietly. "Me too. But you found me. You got me out of there."

"Three years. It took me three fucking years, and I kept running into dead ends. Max had you located in less than twenty-four hours."

"But you found Max."

"No. No, I didn't. I was planning on asking him to help me. He'd just joined our team and I got sent to San Francisco on a job. I was going to ask him as soon as I got back. Then Nick just emails him a picture Mom showed him and said, 'Can you check facial recognition for this photo?'"

Ax still couldn't believe how simple it had been.

"I had no idea it could be so quick and easy. I would have found a hacker years ago and paid them every penny I had if I'd known. Once I knew where you were, I barreled in. I didn't stop and think. I didn't tell Mom or Dad. I was fucking selfish. Then I left you…" Ax wiped his eyes. "I didn't mean to traumatize you as soon as you were free."

"What are you talking about?"

Cherie pulled out of his arms and looked at him. She cupped each of his scruffy cheeks in one of her petite hands and looked him in the eye.

"How did you traumatize me?" she asked.

"As soon as I pulled you from that place, I passed you off to a stranger and went back in. When I got to the van and you were…" He couldn't even describe the sight of her dissolved into tears on the floor of the car.

"Is that what you think? If there's anyone I trust, Ruby, it's you. You looked out for me. You always had my back, always."

"Until I walked away and handed you off to a complete stranger."

"I knew what you were doing. You had to go rescue a certain rogue agent."

Ax laughed at the phrase she'd used. "We don't say that. I'm an operator and so is Nick."

"Nick." She smiled when she said it. "Mom thinks he hung the moon."

"Maybe he did. I was pissed at him for meeting with Mom, but that was when she gave him the photo. Even after I yelled at him, he contacted Wade and told him where you were, started the ball rolling to get you. God, he's so selfless and I just keep…" Ax stopped himself before he told his sister he'd shit on everything Nick had been offering.

"All the more reason to make sure he got out safe. When you walked away, Chase asked if I wanted to stay there and wait for you or go to the van. I asked him if our parents were safe. He told me they were at the hotel. Then he chuckled and he put an earbud in my…"

Cherie paused and blinked rapidly. She bit her bottom lip and took a few deep, cleansing breaths before she could go on.

"I heard them, Ruby. I heard Mom bombarding them with questions. I heard Dad trying to calm her and telling her to let them work so they could bring me back. I…I heard them, and I knew it was real. That was why I lost it."

Ax rubbed her arm and gave it a gentle, encouraging squeeze. *So she was crying because her freedom had become real, not because I left?*

"When you told me everything was in place and we were leaving," she said, "I was afraid to ask what that meant. The first time you came, I refused to go because I wanted to protect them, but I regretted it as soon as you were gone. I didn't ask you about them that second time because I wasn't going to refuse. Hearing their voices…" Cherie shook her head as a few tears finally slipped free. "You brought them out to Texas so I would be able to leave, and I love you for that, Ruby. You're my hero."

"Three years," he choked out.

"And you looked for me every one of those days. Mom told me so. No matter how many dead ends, you kept looking and so did she."

They both sighed, both wiped their eyes. He pulled her in for another tight hug. They stayed like that for a long while until she pulled back.

"I know how lucky I am, Ruby, but I'm restless. I need to do something. I can't just sit here and think about everything that happened while I was gone. I need to help get other people out. I need to be involved. I need to help people who don't have someone like you. I may not be educated, but —"

"You have something more valuable than an education. You have experience. I'll reach out to Wade. He's probably not happy with me, since I haven't been responding to his texts...or voicemails...or emails."

Cherie laughed, and the sound made Ax feel lighter than he had since finding out where she'd been. And yet the thought of going back to HC had dread lacing his veins. There were other messages, other voicemails he'd ignored.

He thought about Nick every day. He'd replayed their every interaction in his mind from the beginning, when they'd clashed, and he'd thought Nick was spoiled and entitled to the end, when Nick had risked his own safety to help get Cherie out.

There was one thing Ax knew about Nick. He was stubborn. The texts and calls had stopped after a month. That had been a few days ago. Ax had typed out a response to each and every one, but he hadn't been able to send them.

He had figured Nick deserved better than to play second fiddle to a fucked-up family situation. Ax hadn't been boyfriend material, even before Cherie had been taken, and he wasn't any better now. Nick deserved more.

Chapter Thirty-Nine

Nick

"Only one guard?" Wade scoffed.

Daniel Meyers cowered in a chair. He'd been surveying the damage to his home with the fire department now that the investigation was complete. The investigator had left long ago. Meyers had been gathering some things to take with him when his new security detail had become indisposed.

Meyers had fired his previous security company, claiming something valuable but very private was missing from his home, and he knew it was an inside job.

He'd kept a team of six men on him for the last month, but apparently his wife didn't like footing the bill for such a huge entourage, so they'd cut back to one guard each. It was the perfect time to let him know they were watching.

Meyers had been limping around the house. He'd broken a kneecap when he'd fallen that night, but Nick couldn't drum up even an ounce of remorse.

"What did you do to him? I know who you are. If you do anything to me—"

"Shut the fuck up." The mouthpiece in Wade's mask disguised his voice and made him sound robotic.

It reminded Nick of what he might sound like if he sucked helium out of a balloon, only not quite that high-pitched. *The big, tall guy with the tiny little voice.* They'd laughed their asses off when he'd tested the thing out.

"You think that thing disguises your voice?" Meyers sneered.

Wade got right in his space. Meyers shut his mouth and leaned all the way back, his hands shaking in his lap.

"What's my name?" Wade asked.

There was silence in the room. Wade took a step back and Meyers' shoulders slumped in what Nick was sure was relief.

"That's what I thought. You're just a coward when you don't have your armed guards at your side. We brought you a present."

"A present? Are you going to return what you stole?"

"Don't you mean what *you* stole? A person isn't a thing, and when you steal a person's free will, that makes you a monster."

"I didn't steal her free will. She wanted to be with me. She l—"

Wade leaned forward and Meyers again closed his mouth.

"If someone was with you of their own free will, you wouldn't have to threaten them to stay. They wouldn't run as fast as they could at the first opportunity."

Wade snapped his fingers, and Nick stepped up to his side. He'd volunteered for this. He'd wanted to see

Congressman Daniel Meyers' face when he realized he was the one who was trapped now.

He'd wanted to look into the man's eyes and make sure he understood that if he even tried to find Cherie, his career would be over, and if he continued after that, his life would be over.

The video was queued up and Nick pressed play. He watched the emotions move over the man—disbelief, anger, fear, resentment. Nick smiled behind his mask at the impotent rage that lingered long after the clip had stopped playing.

"No one will believe you," he said, but there wasn't much confidence behind his voice.

"Let's say they don't believe you bought her like cattle," Wade said.

"It wasn't like cattle. She was special, specific, exactly what I wanted."

Meyers was too stupid to realize he was still being recorded even now. He blubbered on about how much he loved his 'Cherry' and how he'd kept her much longer than he had planned.

"She got too old for you?" Wade asked.

Meyers stiffened. "I won't discuss my preferences with you," he said with a lift of his chin.

"That's fine. You can discuss them with your constituents," Wade said.

Finally, the congressman realized his situation. His Adam's apple bobbed as he assessed the three men in the room with him. Clay stood as a quiet, imposing presence behind them with his height of six-foot-three. Colt waited outside. He was the getaway driver and lookout.

"H-how much?" Meyers finally stuttered.

Wade laughed. The sound made Nick snicker a little and he imagined Clay was doing the same. It sounded maniacal with the voice disrupter.

"You think it's that easy?" Wade asked. "You think I'm going to take your money and let you do this again? Here's how it's going to go. We'll keep this from the press and your wife as long as you follow a few simple rules. The first is that you better not contact anyone for sex other than your wife."

Meyers choked.

"No hookers, no escorts, no buying another sex slave and especially no one under the age of eighteen. We're watching you, and if you make one wrong move, every piece of information we have on you—which is a lot more than this one tame, fully clothed video—will make its way to the press. Now, for number two as far as the rules go, you will not in any way, shape or form try to contact the girl who ran away."

Meyers didn't respond but swayed slightly like he was going to throw up or pass out—maybe both.

"If we find out you've hired a PI or made inquiries about her information in any way, we start releasing information, piece by piece. You'll be in the news for a long time with all the dirt we have on you. Do we understand each other?"

Meyers nodded, but there was venom in his eyes. If he could find a way out of agreeing, Nick had no doubt he would have. It all made him furious. He could literally reach out and snap the guy's neck, but he didn't.

"I'm glad we understand each other. It's really too bad about the fire, but at least it was electrical. It's not like anyone threw a match into your house."

Meyers' eyes widened then narrowed.

"It's also too bad your wife's screwing her golf pro. Less sex for you, I'm sure. You'll be hearing from us, Congressman. Have no doubt. If you get a call from *Sotiras*, you'd best answer it."

Wade turned on his heel and strode out of the room. Nick and Clay followed. They all piled into a large black SUV with no license plates and drove away. Meyers' entire house was now bugged, as were his DC residence and all his offices—even the one in the Congressional building. Max also had his cell phone set to alert HC if certain words were used by Meyers.

"What's *Sotiras*?" Clay asked as they took the long way back to the hotel as a precaution.

"It means 'Rescuer' in Greek," Max said through the Bluetooth speaker. "And Meyers is on his phone right now trying to figure out who you are."

"Yeah, well, tell me if he tries to find Cherie, orders an escort or contacts a seller. Otherwise, I don't care what happens to that fuck," Wade growled.

"He might come in handy someday," Nick mused.

Wade shrugged like it didn't matter. Nick wanted to ruin the man's life like he'd ruined an entire family, a family Nick was too attached to. A family he was going to have to let go of.

* * * *

Four weeks. Nick had been back in Virginia for a month with no word from Ax. The fact that no one had heard from Ax didn't make him feel better. When they'd arrived back, he'd texted Ax to check in and see how he and his family were dealing with everything.

Nick had called, too. Of course, Cella's phone had been disconnected. Nick knew because he'd tried that number as well.

At first, he had texted to keep Ax updated on what was going on with Cherie's case. Wade probably had too, but it had made Nick feel useful and gave him an excuse to keep on reaching out. But after a month with no reply, he needed to stop.

He knew where they were. Everyone at HC knew where they were. But he wouldn't impose upon the whole family just to tell Ax he was being a dickhead.

Deep down, Nick knew that assessment wasn't fair, but he felt cheated, cast aside. He'd known Ax's family was in the number one slot and he was okay with that. His family was a top priority as well. But he was willing to be an ear or a sounding board or whatever Ax needed.

Over and over, he kept hearing Ax saying he was falling for Nick. Apparently, he hadn't actually fallen as hard as Nick had.

Chapter Forty

Ax

"Six fucking weeks?" Wade demanded as soon as he walked into the reception area and saw Ax. "I don't hear from you for over six fucking weeks and now you waltz in here like you own the place?"

Ax rolled his eyes.

"And you bring a visitor without advance notice." Wade motioned to Cherie.

"She's not a visitor. She's family," Ax said.

Wade sighed. "Yes, she's family, but she's not part of the team. If you wanted to bring in your folks or your brother, I'd ask the same."

"I want to be part of the team," Cherie said.

Wade looked at her, assessed her. The fact that she'd asked herself impressed Ax and would impress Wade as well.

"Is that so?" he asked after a moment.

Cherie lifted her chin and nodded. Dee, who'd been chatting with Cherie, watched the interaction and smiled at Cherie's boldness.

"Well, technically you have more experience than our entire team put together—though we all wish you didn't." Wade said that last part quietly.

"I can't change what happened, but I need it to mean something. I need to help save people who don't have a family like mine."

Wade gave Ax a harsh look. Ax simply raised his eyebrows at his team leader.

"Cherie, we're not exactly vigilantes. I don't know what Ax told you, but—"

"He didn't tell me anything. I asked to meet with you, so he brought me here."

"And gave me the shit job, apparently," Wade grumbled. "Cherie, we try to take down the kingpin, the guy at the top. And sometimes, even though it's hard to stomach, that means leaving people in the hands of monsters."

Ax watched Cherie, but she gave no emotional response. The old Cherie would have been indignant and argued. This Cherie gave away nothing.

"We go in undercover to get intel. We're not the DOJ or the FBI. When we're undercover, sometimes we have to walk away from things that make us want to scream and tear our eyes out."

"I don't want to be undercover. I couldn't... I could never be around someone like...like... I just couldn't pretend I wasn't disgusted. I want to help here. I can research, or work with any people you do get out, or—"

"Or even help us profile," Wade said with a nod.

"Sure," Cherie said. "I just want to feel like I'm making a difference, pushing things forward. I understand that you have to leave one or two to try to save hundreds. I don't like it, but I understand it."

Of course she did. She'd been willing to stay in order to try to protect her family. Why was Ax surprised by her request to help?

"That's the way we all feel, Warrior Princess." Wade smiled.

"Well, I guess you're in, Sugar," Dee said. "The big man just gave you your handle."

"It's not that simple," Wade argued.

Dee scoffed and came out from behind her reception desk to give Cherie a hug and welcome her to the team. Wade rolled his eyes, but Ax laughed.

"I've had to delay an op for six weeks because you went AWOL. You're not out of the woods yet, Loco."

"You knew where I was," Ax said.

"Yeah, and I refused to be the dick who went and dragged you away from your family. A phone call would have been nice." Wade turned to the girls. "Dee, make Cherie a badge, level one only, and show her around. Buzz me when you're done, and Ax will come back down to meet her."

"Already on it, bossman," Dee said as her long nails click-clacked on the computer.

"Ax," Wade said as he held the door open for him.

Ax walked through and followed Wade up the stairs.

"I couldn't leave her," Ax said.

"Your family's welcome to stay here if you're worried about their safety."

"It's not that. I mean it is, but mostly it's her mental wellbeing. She's more relaxed with me than she is with anyone, even my parents or Diego."

"I get it, but technically you're undercover. You wanted to lead a team. You deserve to lead a team, but once you do, you're in it for the long haul. You can't ghost out. Campbell went nuts when he found out the doctor was snuffed. I can't just throw Nick in there as your assistant. You need to push this forward."

"I'm sorry. I know you can't exactly fire me right now, but—"

"I'm not firing you, Ax. I was actually worried you were done with this work."

"No. I'm still in. I still want to keep doing what we've been doing."

"Good," Wade said with a nod. "Let me round up Max and Jett. You're going to have to go in without a PA. Meet in the war room in ten."

Ax started to trip over his own feet but quickly recovered. Where was Nick? Had he quit? Had something happened to his father? Maybe if he'd responded to even one of Nick's messages, he'd know what was going on.

When he saw Sam, Ax made a beeline. Just as Ax approached his desk, Bray came around the corner into the bullpen. One look at Ax and he turned right around and walked away.

Ax ran after him, but the elevator doors closed as Ax rounded the corner. The arrow was going down, so Ax ran down the stairs and made it just in time to see Bray walk out of the elevator car.

"Where's Nick?" Ax demanded.

"Gone," Bray said.

Ax snorted. "Don't try that shit on me. I did that to Sam when you left, and within twenty-four hours, he was at your feet declaring his undying love."

"Is that what happened?" Bray smirked.

"Yeah, and now you're happily living together, so you owe me one. Tell me straight. Did he quit?"

Bray gave an impatient sigh. "No. He didn't quit, but maybe he should if you're going to keep being a douche-canoe."

"I can't believe that came out of your sweet little pancake-loving mouth," Ax teased.

"I cuss," Bray grumbled.

"So he went to visit your folks?"

"My dad had another mini stroke. I just got back from Orange County last night."

The news had Ax itching to do something, but he wasn't sure what. His chest burned a little as he thought of Nick staying behind alone with their dad.

"When's he coming back?" Ax asked.

"Not like he's had much to do around here without a team leader."

Ax huffed out a laugh. Bray sounded like an angry teenager when he tried to be pissed or intimidating. Shaking off the thought, Ax assessed Bray. He had a mulish frown on his face.

"Look, Bray. I get you're not happy with me because I...played with Nick's emotions or—"

The punch caught him by surprise and the strength of it took his breath away. Bray's fists were ready to go for another hit as Ax stepped back.

"What the fuck was that for?" Ax demanded as he rubbed his abs.

"Luckily I didn't hit your face. I will the next time you play with Nick's emotions."

"I wasn't playing with his emotions."

"You just said you were," Bray pointed out.

"I was going to say I know you're not happy I played with his emotions or whatever you think I did. I wasn't playing. Guess I could have phrased it better."

"Then why did you ghost him?"

"I ghosted everyone. I had some serious family shit to deal with."

"Yeah, well so did Nick and so did I, but I sure as hell texted Sam to keep him updated on what was going on."

"We're not you and Sam."

"That's for damn sure. I'd kick Sam's ass if he cut me off like that with no reason. It was a pure asshole move."

The thought of Nick needing someone to talk to when he'd reached out to Ax had guilt filling him from his gut to his chest. There he was, selfish again. Ax rubbed his hands over his face as he looked at everything from Nick's perspective.

Ax hadn't wanted to pull him in to his family drama, but what if Nick had needed an ear? Would he even have reached out to Ax for that? Did he know he could? Actually, he couldn't. How could Nick talk to him if he didn't respond?

Bray's shoulders deflated a little. "How's Cherie?" he asked. "We've all been worried about her."

"I get it. You all want updates."

"We helped get her out, too, Ax. We did that because we care about you and, by extension, your family."

"She's a fighter," Ax said.

"What does that even mean? When I was tied up on the floor of that room in the basement of some club in Kiev, I about shit my pants and no one even did anything to me. I can't imagine—"

"What do you mean no one did anything? They beat the shit out of you, Bray — and shot you."

"I think those kinds of wounds heal much easier than the kind Cherie has."

"Yeah." It was hard to get the one word past the lump in Ax's throat.

"I'll be okay," Cherie said.

Bray and Ax turned to find her standing at the entrance of the hall that led to the gym. Dee stood a few paces behind her. Ax wondered how much they'd heard. By the look on Dee's face, too much.

"I'm glad to hear it," Bray said.

"Why'd they tie you up?" Cherie asked.

"It's classified," Bray and Ax said at the same time.

"But if you ever want to talk," Bray said to Cherie, "my door's always open. I mean, well, you probably don't want to talk to a guy, but...well, anyway..."

"Thanks," Cherie said. "That's actually really sweet, considering you're so pissed at Ax you just punched him."

Well, that answered how much she'd seen. She and Bray both huffed out a laugh at her joke. A kernel of hope expanded in Ax's chest.

That was the first time Cherie had made a joke of any kind, even if it was a bad one. She assessed Ax for a long moment as if seeing him in a new light.

"I...uh...also know someone else who might need to talk," Bray said. "My new..." He hesitated and scratched back of his neck as he looked up at Ax. "My new sister could probably benefit from talking to someone, someone who'd also been taken."

"Your sister, too?" Cherie took two steps forward.

Bray looked at Ax. He must have been at a loss. Technically, Ramona and her history were classified.

Ax gave Bray a nod. Maybe this was what Cherie needed.

"We didn't meet her until she'd been pulled out of the, uh, situation. My mom and stepdad got custody of her and are adopting her, so now she's my sister. She's seeing a counselor, but—"

"Yes," Cherie said, "I'll talk to her."

"Great. Her name is Rosalia. My mom calls her Rosie. If you have a minute, I could call her and introduce you. She's a little shy."

Ax snorted. Ramona, or Rosalia rather, had not been shy in the least—although at that point she'd probably figured she hadn't had anything to lose. Now, with Bray and Nick's family in the mix, she had a lot to lose.

"Now?" Cherie's eyes widened.

"Or later if—"

"No. Now is good." Cherie cut Bray off before he could finish.

Cherie looked at Ax. He gave her his best smile, even if he was falling apart inside. He had no idea if this was what was best for her, but he let her make that decision.

"I have a meeting," Ax told her. "I'll be back down in less than thirty minutes."

Cherie nodded as she went with Bray and Dee into one of the private workspaces on the first floor. Ax ran up the stairs and headed straight for the war room.

Chapter Forty-One

Nick

"You already heard," Bray said as soon as he pulled back from giving Nick a hug.

Nick nodded. He had just started unpacking when Bray had knocked. He continued stuffing the clothes he'd washed at their dad's house into the drawers. He didn't look up as he spoke.

"I met with Wade as soon as I got back. Campbell's still in town. I guess he's staying away from San Francisco for a few weeks."

"Probably trying to give himself a head start in case they link him to the doctor."

"We have a meeting with him in a few hours. Seems urgent. He's been trying to get a hold of Ax for a few days."

"You think he has any idea?" Bray asked.

"I don't think so. He says he needs a favor. I was pushing him off, but he's getting more urgent."

Nick took a deep breath. Now he'd see if he could hack it working next to Ax after everything that had happened. Nick's role was superfluous. Ax could easily fire and hire a new personal assistant, but Ax was the main character, so to speak.

And yet he'd stopped all communication, not just with Nick but with the team as well. Wade and Sam had someone watching Dee's house around the clock, so they all knew the family was safe.

Wade had decided very early on to give Ax some space. Nick had had a harder time and continued to try to text and call a bit longer — not that it had done him any good — before finally giving up.

Bray told him Ax had been back for two days. So he was obviously communicating with the team, but he still hadn't reached out to Nick. That was telling, wasn't it?

"But you said you'd go," Bray guessed.

Nick nodded and pushed the drawer closed. "Y'know, I thought you were crazy to take this job? I thought I was crazy, too, but Dad thought it was a great idea. He hoped we'd all get close as brothers again."

Bray grunted but didn't otherwise respond.

"I figured I was doing this for you and for Dad."

"But…"

"But I feel valuable. I feel like part of the team, more so than I did in the army. Plus, I feel like we're really doing something here. I never really saw what was being done in the army. I was a peon. I didn't save anyone's life or feel like I really helped anyone, but here…we found Cherie. We got Ramona out. We're finding people who do bad things and taking them down. I mean, it's still slow, but I feel like…like…"

"It's making a difference?"

"Yes. And I'm not ready to let go of that, even if I feel more for Ax than he feels for me."

"If there's anyone here who gets that, it's me," Bray said.

Bray squeezed Nick's arm and patted his back. He probably could understand, but then again, Bray had gotten a happy ending out of it and Nick hadn't. But he still wasn't leaving.

* * * *

A few hours later, when he had to face Ax for the first time, Nick wasn't so sure he'd made the right choice. He had successfully avoided Ax all day. As he made his way to the second floor, he realized that probably hadn't been the best decision.

Seeing Ax for the first time in over a month felt like a lead ball pulling Nick's chest down to his stomach.

When he walked into the war room for a quick briefing before they left to meet Campbell, he stopped in his tracks when he saw Ax. Everyone turned to see who'd come in. Nick's gaze flicked around the room but settled on Ax.

Ax stared at him for a long moment before giving him a slow nod of recognition. Nick wasn't sure if he returned it or not as he hurried to sit as far from Ax as possible.

When he sat down, Wade stood from where he'd been hunching over Max's shoulder. He started pacing as he tended to do when he was in planning mode.

"I just wanted to make sure you four knew that Campbell is cracking. Between the doctor's elimination and the loss of two of his victims, he's become completely paranoid."

"How does Campbell know about Cherie?" Nick asked.

That's a new development.

"Less than an hour ago, Campbell got a call from Congressman Meyers via one of his new bodyguards' cell phones."

Nick rolled his eyes. When people told you they were watching you, they were also watching the people who were watching you.

"We've just leaked some information about the congressman having an affair. It will hit the online news sources in less than four hours. We've also sent him a message that this is a warning and the next time things will get real."

Nick nodded. He didn't like the idea of killing a US Congressman, but if it kept Cherie and others like her safe, it might be the only choice. A court case would expose Cherie and Ax. That wasn't an option.

"What happened to Raymond Snow?" Ax asked.

"His mom turned out to not be an option for reuniting. Ghost took him to Oregon to be with his grandmother. We can go over it in detail later if you'd like."

"Is his grandmother a safe place?"

"His grandmother has been advised not to post that he's been found on social media. She's been fully apprised of the situation. So far, Campbell thinks both are runaways. He did send someone to check on Raymond's mom, just like he sent someone to check on your parents' old apartment. They found Raymond's mom high as a kite and your apartment empty."

"Does Raymond's mom know he's been found?" Ax asked.

"No. The grandmother seems like a smart woman. Max sent a GPS tracker for Rain."

"Rain?" Nick asked.

Wade cleared his throat. "It's what she calls Raymond. We've started to use it as a sort of code name for him. Max has a trace on his tracker that will alert us if he goes outside a certain vicinity."

Ax nodded, seeming satisfied.

Wade clapped his hands then rubbed them together. "Now, on to the show. Campbell knows there are two escapees who have seen his face and probably know at least his last name. We have eyes and ears in Campbell's office and Max has tapped all his phones, but we don't have eyes and ears in his DC place. We're sending that with you. He's cut power to the security system in his home, so Max won't be able to see you, but we'll still hear you."

"Anything else?" Ax asked.

"Keep your eyes open. Something's going down."

When Ax stood, so did Jett, Nick and Brody, who was acting as their driver. They filed out of the room and the four of them headed for the elevator. Nick adjusted his leather satchel that held his tablet and a few other items a personal assistant would carry, as he studiously avoided looking at Ax.

* * * *

Campbell's DC place was nice, but nowhere near as lavish as his Napa vineyard. When Nick knocked on the door, they were all surprised when Campbell himself let them in.

"Campbell, having some problems with the domestic help?" Ax joked.

"I haven't brought anyone with me this time," Campbell said as he stepped back and allowed the three of them into his townhouse.

"Is this the home you share with your wife?" Ax asked.

"Yes. I also have a condo here in DC, but...there's not as much privacy there as I need this visit."

"You seem anxious," Ax said as he looked around the house as if for cops.

Nick and Jett took the hint and looked around as if more alert than before.

"Are you pulling us into something, Campbell?" Ax's question dripped with accusation.

"No, well..." Campbell took a deep breath. "I was hoping to meet with you in San Francisco, but I needed to come out east anyway and now...I need your help."

"I've been out of the country," Ax said. "But I have to tell you that this whole meeting seems a little fishy. This better not be some setup."

"It's not... I thought I had everything handled, but I'm trying to clean up a mess that just keeps getting messier."

"So you need our help cleaning up a mess?" Ax asked.

"Yes. You see, a client of mine lost their asset. Obviously, it's not the first time this has happened, nor will it be the last. I don't often personally handle assets. Most of them never see my face except in special instances."

"Like my gift?" Ax clarified.

"Yes. A few years ago, a connection of mine hinted about wanting a certain type of asset. He's a fairly powerful man here in Washington, so I handled the request myself. He's just informed me that after three years, she disappeared into the night."

Ax leaned forward slightly. Campbell would probably mistake the move for interest, but Nick knew exactly what it was. It was fury. Campbell was admitting to them that he'd had Cherie taken.

Ax's shoulders rose and fell a few times before he spoke.

Chapter Forty-Two

Ax

"So this friend of yours wants a new toy? I think we can help with that." Ax said.

Ax calmed himself with the knowledge that Wade and Max were already on this. He reminded himself that Mitch or Chase or one of the other guys was watching his family. He trusted his team.

"No, that's not what I need help with." Campbell said. "My friend is more concerned with any backlash and looking for protection against anyone finding out, though he did hint at missing his favorite…'toy', as you said."

"So he wants us to help protect him? I'm not sure someone with my background can help keep some DC player —"

Campbell waved away the suggestion.

"I told him I'd try to help where I could, but I know not much can be done unless she comes forward publicly."

Ax's heart literally stopped beating for a second before pumping at a breakneck speed. The scum before him was talking about Cherie as if she were some ant that needed to be squashed.

"I need something a little more complex from you," Campbell said. "I have a more personal problem."

"Did you lose your toy, too?" Ax joked.

"No, though I almost wish it were that simple." Campbell sullenly shook his head before looking Ax directly in the eye. "I need you to get rid of someone for me."

"Not that we haven't had to do that, but it's not exactly our line of work. Is it this DC player?"

"No. No, it's a little closer to home. You see, my personal assistant has stepped in where he didn't belong. He learned of my...side business, if you will, and must be dealt with."

Peter Thornton. The guy who'd been all over Nick when they'd visited Campbell's office. Ax had wanted to give the guy a fist or two, but he didn't want him dead.

"So you want me to take care of your assistant?"

"I need him to disappear," Campbell confirmed.

"Where is he? Still in San Francisco."

"No. I at least saved you the trouble of having to find him."

"I haven't agreed to anything yet," Ax said.

Inside, Ax was so glad Wade and Max were listening to every word being said...and recording it. No one could make this stuff up.

"Let's see what we're dealing with." Ax sighed as if put out.

Campbell led them through the house and down a flight of stairs to a basement area that looked almost like a small apartment. There was a little kitchenette to one side and a few doors off to the other side. In the dining area, two of Campbell's bodyguards were sitting at a retro Formica and chrome table as another paced behind them.

In a third chair was Peter Thornton. His mouth was covered with duct tape and his arms were pulled behind his back, presumably tied. Ax made a show of rolling his eyes.

"Your men can't handle getting rid of one little twink?" Ax held a hand out as if to showcase the bodyguards.

"This cannot be tied to me in any way."

Ax looked at poor Thornton. His eyes were red and bloodshot. Ax had seen hope flare when he walked into the room, and he watched it die as panic rose and Peter's breathing kicked up.

"Worried your guys will fuck it up?" Ax smirked at Campbell.

Both the guards stood from their chairs. Jett took a step forward and, in his peripheral vision, Ax saw Nick do the same. There wouldn't be a face-off. There was no contest and Campbell's yahoos knew it.

"Everyone, calm down." Campbell said.

His men grumbled but sat back down in their chairs. The third moved up to stand behind them. There were tears running down Thornton's face, and though Ax knew it was tough, he had to really sell this. Ax watched as Thornton turned his gaze to Nick, and the pleading in his eyes was so raw and so desperate that Ax hesitated.

Was there something between them? Had Thornton and Nick been in contact while Ax had been gone? Was that why Nick couldn't look him in the eye?

Ax had determined to let Nick go, to find someone better, but when faced with the possibility of it really happening, he realized he'd made another error in judgement where Nick was concerned.

"Now," Campbell said, "are you willing to help me?"

Ax sighed. He took a moment to look over at Jett, then at Nick. Nick was having a much harder time hiding his emotions, and that just made Ax more suspicious.

"I'm going to have to talk to Sam about this before I commit to anything. Even if we weren't on his side of the country, I'd bare minimum give him a heads-up."

"Fine." Campbell nodded.

"He's going to wonder why your men can't do it. Then he's going to ask me what's in it for us."

"My men don't have this type of experience. They make people disappear in an entirely different way. They don't know how to make things appear like…an accident, or perhaps a self-inflicted incident."

Ax nodded. "And the second question?"

"Connections. I can offer you some very valuable connections right here in DC, ones I would never dream of sharing, except that this is a desperate situation."

"What about that doctor?" Ax asked. He'd never asked for a meeting with the guy because he'd rushed off to Texas. "Can he be part of those connections? That 'insurance' seemed very interesting to Bernard."

Campbell puffed out a breath then rubbed his hands over his face. When he dropped his arms, he looked Ax in the eye. They guy was scared. *Good.* This was the man who'd taken Cherie and sold her like cattle, and he had no remorse. When this was all done, Ax was going to make sure he suffered greatly.

"I'm afraid that's no longer possible. My doctor friend met with a terrible fate. It's very unfortunate. He apparently could have used your business even more than I thought. He had debts to the wrong people."

"That's too bad. It might have worked for us. What other connections, then?" Ax pressed.

"Political connections. There's a club in DC."

"Cypher," Ax said. "We—"

"No, not Cypher. Everyone knows about Cypher. It's the worst kept secret in Washington. There's another club, an unknown one. I can get you in, and there you will make connections you have never dreamed of."

"An unknown club but one you can get anyone into? Sounds—"

"I can't. What I mean is, I can't get you a day pass or something like that, but I can sponsor your membership, and I'm on the membership board so..." Campbell shrugged.

"Unless you're passing these things out like candy, it'll be above my pay grade if I let Bernard know, but I can't cut him out of this."

"I understand. I can probably sponsor two people. There's an annual limit per member, but I have never sponsored another member, so they may allow me three."

Ax tapped his hand on his thigh as if nervous or apprehensive. "I need to make a call."

"Be my guest." Campbell lifted his hand and pointed to one of the doors along the wall behind them.

Ax told Jett and Nick to wait there as he entered the room. The call was just for show, and Wade posed as

Sam because Sam wasn't available, but the message was clear. Get Peter Thornton out of there.

When Ax stepped out of the room, everyone turned to him expectantly. Thornton's tears had dried up, but he was still aiming beseeching looks at Nick. Everyone else just looked curious.

"Well?" Campbell said.

"He asked the questions I predicted. He also suggested we send your assistant to a client of ours in London. He—"

"No. Absolutely not. I'm offering top notch connections. I want no loose ends."

"Fine." Ax sighed. "It would be a lot simpler, but..." Ax shrugged as if it didn't make a difference. "So how do we get him out of here without anyone seeing he's been to your place?"

"Have your driver pull around the back and into the garage. We'll put him in the trunk or whatever." Campbell waved his hand dismissively as if talking about a suitcase.

Ax nodded at Nick, who pulled out his cell phone and called Brody to instruct him. When he turned away and began speaking quietly, Ax turned back to Campbell.

"How do you want this to go? I can't exactly send you his finger, and it's not exactly newsworthy when a random guy disappears. I can't exactly coordinate when and where he'll be found."

Though that was probably exactly what his team would do. Ax had heard Max in the background. The plans were already in motion.

"I'll file a missing person's report when he doesn't show up for work. That way I'll likely be notified when he's found. I would prefer for him to be found. It would put my mind at ease."

Ax nodded once. "I'll see what I can do."

Nick tapped Ax on the shoulder and leaned forward to whisper in his ear that Brody was pulling up to the garage. Ax nodded and willed his dick to stand down.

It didn't seem to matter what situation they were in. Nick's breath on his neck, his low voice in his ear, cranked Ax from zero to sixty. Ax clamped down on the need building inside him. One look at Thornton's face did the trick.

"My driver's at the garage," Ax said. "Untie his legs," he told one of Campbell's men.

"We'll carry him as is," the man said.

Ax shook his head in disgust. "And let us take a chair from Campbell's house as evidence? Cut the ties on his legs, bind his hands in front instead of the back and bring us three new ties."

"Do as he says," Campbell said. "His forethought is why we need his help."

The guard clenched his jaw. He looked at Ax and snorted out an angry breath before doing as he'd been told. Thornton silently watched everything as they cut his legs free.

"I'll also need—" Ax was interrupted by Nick tapping him on the shoulder and leaning in again to whisper that he'd left his messenger bag up in Campbell's office.

"For fuck's sake," Ax grumbled, but the move had been genius.

They hadn't had a chance to place any listening devices around the house. They also knew Campbell had turned off the security system, so unless he ran into another of his men, Jett could place them all around the first floor. Ax turned to Jett.

"Run back up to Mr. Campbell's office and get Nick's bag."

Jett nodded and turned to take the stairs two at a time. Ax gave Nick a look of supposed frustration.

"I didn't know we'd be leaving out of another door," Nick said.

"Never leave your shit lying around," Ax said.

"Lesson learned," Nick said.

"It's fine," Campbell said. "Let's just get this handled." He nodded toward his men, who'd just cut Thornton's legs free.

"Right," Ax said. "We'll need some oil or petroleum jelly."

"What the fuck for? You gonna fuck him?" said the guard who'd back-talked.

"You wanna hand me the lube I know is in your wallet?" Ax asked.

The guy pulled his gun from the small of his back and took a step forward. Nick had his gun on the guy before he was able to take aim. Because Nick had his gun out, the guard pointed his weapon at Nick.

Ax's heart stopped. Panic rose inside him as he pictured Nick taking a bullet—a bullet that was meant for him. The urge to step in front of Nick was so strong, and his legs burned with the need to move. Instead, he pulled his gun out and pointed it at the guard as well.

Campbell told his man to put his gun away, but he only swung to aim at Ax. Ax gave him a bored look.

"Put that down, Jason," Campbell insisted. "We can't have my neighbors reporting a gunshot. The cops will be here in seconds."

"It has a suppressor on it," Jason told him.

"Mine doesn't." Nick's voice held satisfaction.

"We can handle this," Jason told Campbell.

"I told you it's too easy to tie you to me. We need to let Mr. Hernandez handle it."

If Ax really was what he was pretending to be, he'd tell Campbell to get rid of the hothead. But he wasn't a criminal, so if the idiot got Campbell caught, it was actually better for them.

They stood in silence and looked at each other. The two other guards didn't seem to know what to do. They probably had some loyalty to Jason but seemed to be listening to Campbell.

Jett would be coming back downstairs soon, and if he walked in on this scenario, his gun would be out and he'd probably —

There was quiet *pew* before a small explosion of blood on Jason's shoulder. Campbell was looking around, his mouth open. Ax didn't need to look to see what had just happened. He just aimed it at the remaining guards.

"My arm!" Jason screamed.

"What the hell's going on?" Campbell demanded.

"You'll learn that in this business, you shoot first and ask questions later," Ax said. "Anybody else want to ask any?"

The other two guards shook their heads and held their hands away from their bodies. Ax looked at Campbell.

"Tell your main man over there not to pull a gun on me unless he's willing to use it. Do you still want my help?"

Campbell looked over at Jason. The two other guards were ripping off his sleeve to look at the wound.

Campbell's gaze flicked over Ax's shoulder before he nodded.

"I just gave him a warning," Jett scoffed from behind Ax. "If I'd wanted him dead, he would be."

Jett's handle in the army was Hawkeye. The kid didn't miss unless that was exactly what he'd set out to do.

Ax turned to Campbell and quietly told him that if it was going to look like an accident or suicide, they'd need to get the duct tape off gently without ripping any skin. Campbell nodded and let out a relieved sigh before telling Ax that he appreciated his forethought, but they didn't have any petroleum jelly.

Jett handed Nick his bag then went over and pulled Thornton up from the chair. Jett dragged him by his bound arms, looking every bit like the enforcer he was supposed to be.

They opened the garage door then shut it once Brody pulled in. Jett got Thornton to the back of the SUV and tossed him in. Ax cringed internally but didn't say a word. He simply held out his hand for the extra zip ties.

Campbell watched as Ax bound Thornton's ankles together, then bound his wrists to his ankles. Finally, Ax bound Thornton to a small steel bar behind the last row of seats.

Campbell gave Ax a smile and a nod, then patted him on the shoulder. "Let me know who I'll be submitting for membership."

Ax nodded and shut the back of the SUV before climbing into the back seat next to Nick. Every window but the windshield was tinted, so no one would see their 'cargo'. Campbell was smiling easily now that he thought he was off the hook, but his men didn't look too happy as Brody backed out of the garage.

They were all silent as Brody drove out of the city. They couldn't exactly stop somewhere, pull Thornton out of the cargo area and move him to the back seat. They needed a secure location. When they approached Woodbridge, Ax told Brody to pull off. Jett turned and gave Ax a questioning look.

"I know a secure place."

Jett nodded and faced forward. Ax guided them to Z's workshop. When they arrived, Ax was surprised to see Z there, working on a vintage Harley-Davidson. They pulled into an empty spot in the garage before Ax got out to close the garage doors.

Chapter Forty-Three

Nick

"What the fuck, Loco?" demanded the man standing in the garage.

The guy was tall and built. He was in a pair of athletic shorts and a tank top, but Nick knew right away he'd been in the military. His low-sitting brows were pulled even lower by the thunderous look he was giving Ax.

"We just needed a secure location for a minute, Z," Ax said. He leaned back in the car and whispered in Nick's ear, "Undo the tie between his hands and feet only. I'm going to get something for the duct tape."

Nick nodded. Not wanting to open the back hatch, he climbed over the seat. He took his knife from strap on the inside of his ankle and did as he'd been instructed, cutting the zip tie linking Peter's ankles to his wrists.

Peter gave him a pleading look and said something that Nick couldn't decipher. They'd patted him down but didn't yet know if Campbell had placed any bugs or tracking devices on him, so they couldn't explain anything.

Nick looked up toward the front of the car then back at Peter before giving the man a meaningful nod. Peter's brows pinched together before lifting in question. Nick put a finger to his lips before mouthing, *I'll help you.*

Peter nodded frantically. *Later,* Nick mouthed. Peter nodded again before slumping in relief. Nick gave him a pat on the shoulder before climbing back over the seat.

Ax came back to the car with his friend trailing behind him. The guy had a strange gait that wasn't quite a limp.

"You gonna introduce me to your friends?"

It was more of a demand than a question. There was a defensiveness to his tone that said he was daring Ax to say no. Nick wondered if they had a history, or maybe they were currently...he shook his head. It was none of his business.

"Course." Ax pointed to each one of their team and told the guy their names. "And this is Zayne Archer. You guys met his sister when she went with me to the gala a few weeks ago."

"You didn't tell me you were taking her around other vets. You know she has a thing for military men — even former military men."

Zayne looked over each one of them as if wondering which of them had dared to look at his sister. Jett's Adam's apple bobbed.

"She's a big girl. She can take care of herself," Ax said.

"The fuck she can. Which of you flirted with her?"

"Two-thirds of these guys are gay. I'll let you guess who's who." Ax patted him on the shoulder and walked back to the car.

"This the team you've been wanting me to join?" Zayne asked.

"Not this op team specifically, but the team in general, yeah."

"Who's in the back of the car?" Zayne asked.

"It's classified. Thanks for the supplies." Ax held up a plastic bag and a small cooler.

"Classified," Zayne repeated.

"You want in, you gotta interview. Call me if you change your mind." Ax got back in the car.

Everyone else followed his lead. Zayne nodded as he went back to fixing the bike. Brody started the car and slowly backed out.

"Hold up a sec, Bro," Ax said.

Brody stopped the car. Ax leaned in and whispered in Nick's ear. "Cut off everything, even his underwear, and put it in this cooler. Then start working the duct tape off."

Nick nodded and climbed back over the seat and sat next to Peter. Within minutes, Nick had his clothes cut off and stuffed into the cooler.

"We need to dump this somewhere we can come back and pick it up later." Ax said as he pulled the cooler over the seat.

"I know a place," Jett said.

Nick covered Peter with a small blanket they had in the back. There was a pair of sweats in the bag, but Ax hadn't told him to free Peter's ankles to get them on. Next, Nick took the cotton swabs and the petroleum jelly and started working a little under the edge of the duct tape. Little by little, Nick began loosening the tape until he could see the corner of Peter's mouth. Peter let out a relieved sigh, even though Nick was sure it wasn't a pleasant process.

The car stopped. Jett got out but was back in less than a minute. When the car moved again, Ax pulled out his phone and called Wade.

"Cut him loose," Ax told Nick after a moment before returning to his phone conversation.

Nick had just gotten the tape more than halfway off Peter's mouth. He figured Peter would be more comfortable with clothes on, so he freed Peter's hands then gave him the cotton swab.

"Nickel, thank God I wasn't wrong about *you*," Peter rasped.

Nick patted his knee and cut his ankles free. He gave Peter the sweats then turned away to give him privacy to pull them up. They worked together after that, each taking a side of the tape and working their way toward the center with a cotton swab. They'd just gotten the whole thing free as Brody pulled into the underground garage at HC.

There was a flurry of excitement as they took Peter up to the fourth floor and had him checked out by Clay, who'd been a medic in the army.

"I'm okay," Peter said, but he didn't exactly push Clay away.

Peter kept looking to Nick. He did his best to send Peter reassuring smiles, because no one was talking very much or telling him that he was safe. Nick kept his mouth shut, trusting there was a reason. Every time Nick gave Peter a smile, Ax frowned at Nick.

"They didn't even put the zip ties against the skin of his ankles," Ax informed them with disgust.

"Would you prefer they'd torn his ankles to shreds?" Nick asked.

"I didn't correct them, did I?" Ax growled.

"You sure had fun correcting them at almost every other turn," Nick said.

"I did what—?"

"Out," Wade commanded.

Nick and Ax both looked at Wade then back at each other. Ax's jaw ticked. When neither of them moved, Wade grabbed each of them by the elbow and pulled them out of the room.

"Enough," Wade said.

"I'm sorry," Nick replied as he realized Peter would probably be more insecure without him. "Just let me sit with Peter while—"

"Go fix your shit. I really am going to have to institute a no fraternizing policy," Wade grumbled.

"If you do that, you can't drool over a certain cyber genius," Ax said.

"Don't put this on me, Loco. You can do what you want on your own time. Don't. Fuck. With an op."

Wade went back into the room and shut the door in their faces. Nick huffed out a frustrated breath. He turned and took a look at Ax, who was silently fuming next to him. With a shake of his head, Nick walked off toward his room.

"What's with you and Thornton?" Ax asked.

His voice was directly behind Nick, even though he hadn't really heard Ax moving. Nick whirled on him.

"Go away, Ax," Nick growled.

He turned and stomped to his door, keyed in his code and stepped inside. When he turned to close the door in Ax's face, Ax pressed him into the room before following him in and closing the door.

"What's the deal with you and Thornton?" Ax asked again.

"Peter and I had exactly—" Nick stopped himself. "Why am I explaining myself to you? I don't owe you anything. What the hell was that back there?"

"That was me asking a question."

"At Campbell's, asshole. Why were you egging on that meathead? He wanted to shoot you."

"I'll answer your question when you answer mine. What's between you and Thornton?"

"What do you care? You went dark on me."

"You're right. I shouldn't care," Ax said.

"Then why do you?"

Ax scrubbed his hands over his face. "I should go. I just wanted to apologize."

"Now that you're being nice, you're going to leave? Typical." Nick rolled his eyes.

"I'm not a nice guy, Nick."

"I know."

That startled a laugh out of Ax, but then the silence stretched.

"What exactly are you apologizing for?" Nick asked.

Ax looked at him for a long moment "First and foremost, I'm sorry for cussing you out about meeting with my mom. If you hadn't…" Ax shook his head.

"You would have found her," Nick said. "You would have asked Max, and you would have found her."

"But when? I didn't want to bombard him, and I waited. She spent more days in that hell because I hesitated. I shouldn't have fucking cared."

"I'm used to asking Max for favors," Nick said.

"I also wanted to apologize for not calling or texting you back. My life's pretty fucked up right now."

"Join the club."

Ax shook his head. "Another thing I'm sorry for. You were there for me, really there for me when I needed it. God, Nick, even when I was raging at you, you comforted me. You are so thoughtful, so selfless...with me, with your father..." Ax shook his head. "But I wasn't there to return the favor when your dad had another stroke. I wasn't there to listen to you talk about your worries or take out your frustrations. You deserved that."

Nick's eyes stung as he felt truly seen for the first time since all his dad's health issues had started.

"But what I'm most sorry for," Ax said, "is for what happened today."

"Today?" Nick asked.

"When, uh, when that guy pointed a gun at you..." Ax rubbed he back of his neck. "I was ready to break cover and step in front of you."

Nick's mouth opened, but nothing came out, because now his throat was burning along with his eyes. Ax had wanted to protect him? After leaving him high and dry?

"You ghosted me," Nick finally whispered.

Ax cleared his throat. "You should probably go check on your buddy Thornton," Ax said.

A frustrated breath burst from Nick's mouth with a loud *huh*. "Why do you keep bringing up Peter? You said you wanted to save lives. You helped save one today."

"Just be careful getting involved with a victim." Ax said.

"Involved? Until a few weeks ago, I was sleeping with you. I know we weren't exactly boyfriends or anything, but I don't typically jump from on guy's bed to another's."

"He knows your name, *Nickel*."

Nick huffed out a humorless laugh. *Ax is jealous of Peter.*

Chapter Forty-Four

Ax

"He guessed it." Nick said. "Peter and I had exactly one conversation at Campbell's office. He told me he was a con man and he guessed my nickname, along with my sexual preference and the fact that technically I'm a middle child."

"Nickel's not a common name. If he knew it—"

"He didn't know it. He listed like"—Nick waved his hand around—"ten nicknames for Nicholas and read my reaction until he narrowed in on the one my family tortured me with. There's no need to be jealous."

"I'm not…" Ax stopped and ran a hand through his hair.

He wasn't going to lie. He'd told himself he wasn't going to lie or make light of what had happened between them.

The truth was that he was jealous, so jealous that he was surprised his skin hadn't turned green, so jealous that every muscle in his body had been strung tight from the moment he'd heard Thornton whisper the endearment in the car. He didn't realize it until just then when his shoulders finally relaxed.

And yet, if Nick had moved on, no one could fault him, least of all Ax. He had bailed on him, and if Nick had needed someone, he would have had to turn to someone else.

So even though Ax was relieved that Nick hadn't jumped into another man's bed, it didn't change the fact that Ax had been and continued to be selfish.

He'd been giving Nick space, then he'd planned to apologize. Today had fucked everything up. Now he was even more sorry and more jealous.

"This was never what I wanted to happen," Ax said as he turned away.

Nick grabbed his arm and yanked him so hard that Ax spun around and almost fell into Nick's chest. Ax was surprised by Nick's anger. He pushed right up into Ax's space.

"What the fuck does that mean? First of all, that would have been nice to know six weeks ago so I didn't make a fool out of myself by texting and calling and hoping for a response. If this is some sort of 'it's not you, it's me' kiss-off, then—"

Ax grabbed Nick's biceps and jerked him forward until their lips met. Why did seeing Nick all riled up make Ax want to stick his tongue down the man's throat?

The kiss quickly spiraled out of control. There were teeth and tongues and moans. Nick held on to Ax's shoulders so hard that there would be finger-sized bruises there in a few hours.

Ax slid his hands down to cup Nick's ass. Instead of melting into him, Nick stiffened. He pressed his palms to Ax's chest and pushed him away.

"Was that a literal kiss-off?" Nick asked.

Ax laughed but quickly sobered.

"It's not a line, y'know," Ax said.

"What's not?"

"It's not you. It *is* me."

"That's bullshit," Nick said.

"Nick, you call your dad every day, even though he drives you crazy with his scheming."

Nick quickly looked off to the side, no longer meeting Ax's gaze.

"Hell, you even feel guilty about not wanting to call sometimes *because* of his scheming."

"I never told you that," Nick said.

"You didn't need to. Nick, you could barely handle saying no to my family. I realized I started pulling away from my parents long before Cherie got taken. You and Bray, you guys are doing all these crazy things to get your family back together."

"You just spent three years trying to get your family back together," Nick argued.

"Physically. But all three of those years, I kept everyone, especially my family, at a distance. I let everyone else suffer alone because I was so sure it was my fault. I was *so* sure." Ax shook his head in disbelief. "My folks were feeling that way too, but I wasn't there for them to talk to. Whether it was my fault or it wasn't, I was only concerned about myself, righting *my* wrong. The rest of my family, especially Diego, got lost in the cracks."

"That's not true. You love your sister, or you would have dumped her on your parents and walked away." Nick said.

"But I did walk away. I walked away from you without a thought as to whether *you* might need someone. I walked away from my team, my other family."

"A text would have been nice," Nick admitted.

Ax smiled at his honesty. He really wanted to kiss Nick again, but it wasn't a good idea. He put a hand on Nick's shoulder.

"I'm not good for you. Hell, I'm not even good for me. I yelled at you for meeting with my mom when that exact meeting instigated the request that found Cherie. And even after I chewed you out, you put together a team to save her. Nick, you deserve someone..."

Ax couldn't even describe the kind of man Nick deserved—kind, honest, selfless, loving. The list could go on for a mile.

"I guess the real question is, are you willing to put the work in?" Nick asked.

"The work in?"

"To be the guy I deserve? Y'know, instead of just giving up and walking away...again."

Ax shook his head, but he spread his lips out into a smile.

"I'd rather have a work in progress who thinks I deserve the best than someone who's amazing and thinks he's better than me. I'm not perfect by any stretch, Ax."

"I know you're not perfect, but I kind of like you how you are."

"Kinda? Is that like saying *'I think I'm falling for you'*?"

Ax snorted. "I'd already fallen at that point. Yet another white lie I told you."

Nick bit his bottom lip, but the smile that spread them pulled it out from under his teeth. He looped his arms around Ax's neck.

"What'll it be? You crazy enough to give it a chance?" Nick asked.

"If you're willing to give me a chance, a real chance, I'd be crazy to let that go."

"The fact that your handle is Loco sort of means you are crazy."

"Okay," Ax laughed, "I'd have to be stupid to let you go."

"I haven't heard anyone accuse you of being stupid, so I guess that'll work, but…"

Ax's heart dipped a little at the thoughtful, possibly unsure look on Nick's face. Ax licked his suddenly dry lips.

"But…" Ax encouraged.

"But you should be with someone who thinks you're amazing too," Nick said with his eyebrows pinched together. Then his face cleared and he gave a wicked grin. "Good thing you found me, then."

Nick laughed when Ax growled. This was the flirtatious Nick he'd heard so much about. He could get used to this.

Ax stalked forward as Nick moved back. Nick gave him a smirk as Ax maneuvered him back toward the bedroom. When the backs of his knees hit the mattress, Ax pushed his shoulders until he fell back. He spread out like a starfish on the bed.

"Someone's going to have to tell Wade we're together and not at each other's throats, at least for the moment. I call 'not it'," Ax said.

"That's bullshit," Nick said as he came up onto his elbows. "You're the team leader. The buck stops with you. You'll look like an asshole if I tell him."

"Fine. I'll tell him," Ax sighed. "Under one condition."

"What?" Nick smiled, curled his fingers around Ax's waistband and pulled him down onto the bed.

"Tell me what Dash stands for."

"You'll never get that out of me." Nick pulled him down for a kiss.

Epilogue

Ax
Three months later

"What took you so long?" Nick demanded when Ax stepped into the apartment they shared on the fourth floor of the HC building.

"It's debrief, baby. I have no control. Have you been up here pacing the whole time? You could have gone without me. I always know where you go as soon as debrief is over."

Nick shrugged. "The same place you go after debrief."

"I'm glad you waited for me, though." Ax needed to talk to him about something, preferably before they went to Nick's dad's house.

Nick bit his bottom lip.

Now that they were together, things had started to fall into place between them. They worked together all the time, so Ax had wondered if Nick would need space in their downtime. So far, that hadn't been the case.

"You know he's fine, right?" Ax cupped the back of Nick's head and pulled him closer. "If anything, he's getting spoiled rotten."

Nick smirked and gave a half-shrug, because he couldn't refute that. Their lives had become even more entwined than either of them had imagined, and yet it worked.

"So, we don't have to rush," Ax whispered before pressing his mouth to Nick's.

The kiss turned hot and hungry almost instantly. Whether it was angry sex, makeup sex or sweet, slow sex, it was still so hot between them.

"I think you need to relax a little before we go see your dad." Ax slid his hand down Nick's abs and grasped his erection through his jeans.

Nick groaned and punched his hips forward. "Does that mean I get to be on top?"

Ax chuckled. "But then you'd have to do all the work, baby. If I'm on top, you just have to relax. And when I'm done, you'll be all fucked out and relaxed."

Nick shook his head, but he was smiling.

"Or I could just do this." Ax lowered to his knees and unzipped Nick's pants.

Nick hummed his approval as Ax lowered the waistband of his underwear until his cock bounced free. Grasping the base, Ax leaned in and licked the pre-cum from the slit.

Ax's dick throbbed in his pants when Nick slid his fingers into the long strands of Ax's hair and gripped tight. That meant Nick was already good to go.

Because they'd started their relationship out with angry sex then moved to the slow, loving kind, they weren't afraid to let loose, and Nick needed to do that.

He didn't give Nick any warning, just swallowed him down all the way. When Ax's nose pressed against the neatly trimmed pubic hairs at the base of Nick's shaft, Nick sucked in a breath through his teeth.

Nick cursed when Ax swallowed around the sensitive head. Ax groaned when Nick pulled against his scalp and drew him back.

Ax's chest squeezed a little whenever Nick did that. He was worried about Ax not getting enough air, but Ax knew how to hold his breath long enough to give Nick pleasure. But this time Nick pulled him all the way off and used his grip on Ax's hair to tilt his head up.

"I want to be inside you," Nick said.

"You just were."

Nick huffed out a laugh. "Shut up and take off your clothes."

Before he was standing from his position on the floor, Ax had his jeans and underwear around his knees. He kicked off his boots as he watched Nick shed his clothes as well.

As Ax spread himself on the mattress, Nick pulled lube out of the drawer. Ax slowly stroked himself as he watched all Nick's muscles contract and release when he moved to the bed.

"Hard and fast or slow and easy?" Ax asked.

"How about hard and slow, but stay on your back? I want to watch you come."

With a smile, Ax pulled his knees up toward his chest. Nick licked his lips as his gaze dropped to Ax's opening. His hole clenched in response.

"Later," Nick said, as he flicked the lube cap open. "When we get home, I'll use my tongue to make you come."

Ax groaned.

Nick had a very talented mouth. Ax's dick throbbed when Nick brushed lubed fingers over his pucker.

"It won't take much for me," Nick admitted as he pushed a finger into Ax.

They hadn't been on the same op for the last week, so they were both on the knife's edge. It wouldn't take much for Ax, either.

"More," Ax said. "Fuck," he groaned at the stretch when Nick went from one finger to three.

"You okay?"

"I'm fine," Ax said. "Apparently my body is just as impatient as you are."

"Or you just like a little pain with your pleasure."

He wouldn't deny what they both knew to be true. It was Ax's turn to lick his lips as he watched Nick slather lube over his cock, then jack himself a few times to make sure it was covered.

Then Nick was there, the blunt head of his erection pressing against Ax's opening. He closed his eyes for a moment, relishing the feel, the stretch. When he opened his eyes, he looked up into Nick's blue gaze.

"I missed you," Ax said.

Nick's eyelids fluttered in ecstasy as he bottomed out inside Ax. "And I missed you...so much."

"Did you miss me or just my body?" Ax asked.

"Don't joke when I'm balls deep inside you," Nick groaned. "I missed all of you. I love you."

Ax took a deep, satisfied breath. He'd never get used to those words falling so easily from Nick's mouth.

Then his world narrowed to where their bodies met as Nick began to pump in and out. The friction was exactly what Ax needed and yet not quite enough.

He grasped the back of Nick's neck and pulled him down for a kiss. Ax groaned, as the benefit was twofold. Not only did he get to suck on Nick's tongue, but Nick's washboard abs rubbed along the underside of Ax's shaft.

Nick sped up his thrusts. He gripped Ax's shoulders to hold him steady as he pumped harder, practically fucking Ax across the bed. A week apart was clearly too long.

"Close," Nick panted.

Then Nick changed the angle of his hips. Ax shouted out a few curse words as Nick pegged his prostate. His spine tingled, telling him that he was close too.

Nick's thrusts came harder, faster. They slapped their bodies together in the quiet room. Sharp pleasure arced from Ax's balls and zapped up his spine. His body bowed off the mattress, slamming his chest into Nick's.

"Yes," Nick hissed when Ax clamped around him, spasming.

Nick's shaft throbbed and jerked inside Ax. An aftershock skittered up his spine at the thought of Nick shooting deep inside him, bare.

Ax released his legs as he fell back to the mattress. Nick collapsed onto his chest, their sweat-slicked bodies sticking together as they let their breaths calm.

"Missed this, too," Nick slurred, his cheek against Ax's chest.

"Yeah." Ax rubbed his hands up and down Nick's back, just touching him. "That was like a mad 'dash' to an orgasm."

Nick pushed up so he could frown down at Ax. "I never should have told you what my handle meant. I knew you were a merciless tease. And yet, I let you pull it out of me."

Ax laughed. "No, you didn't. You knew I was close to getting the truth out of Bray."

"That's not true. My twin would never betray me."

"He's the one who confirmed it was an acronym."

"But he never would have told you I shot myself."

Ax laughed. Every time they talked about it, he laughed so hard that he almost lost control of his bladder. He could just imagine a cocky young Nick twirling his gun around and shooting a little chunk of his toe off.

When a guy did something like that in bootcamp, a name like 'Dumb Ass Shot Himself' was sure to be shortened to DASH, so the recruit would never forget about it as long as he was in the army.

Nick rolled to the side and pouted.

"I'm sorry." Ax tried to curb his chuckles.

"I'm going to Dad's." Nick got up and headed for the bathroom.

Ax sighed. There was no way he'd be able to have a calm discussion with Nick now. He just had to hope his family could keep their mouths shut for a few hours. Ax would tell him when they got home and Nick had a chance to calm down.

* * * *

Laughter rang out as Ax shut the door. It was the loud, boisterous laughter of Ax's father. He'd recognize it anywhere. It made him smile as he and Nick made their way farther into Nick's father's home.

"And he still denied it," Russ said when they entered the den where he spent most of his time.

Mom and Dad were both there, laughing.

"Speak of the devil," Russ said when he saw us.

"Uh-oh," Nick said. "What are you telling them?"

"A story I will definitely need to hear," Ax said.

"Don't tell all my secrets. You might have them believing I'm a troublemaker."

"*Pfft.*" Russ waved his hands. "They'll never believe you're anything less than perfect."

"We know he's not perfect," Mom said. "Just perfect for Ruby."

Ax's cheeks heated a little at his mom's words, but they were also stretched with a smile. Who would have thought the best solution for everyone would be for Ax's parents to be Russ' caretakers?

Mom was studying to be a CNA, so she had the medical training to help Russ. Dad used his landscaping skills and his construction experience to make sure the house was in perfect condition.

And Russ loved having constant company. He'd gained a little weight and his color looked more peach than chalky.

Even Diego helped out around the house and would sit and talk with Russ. And Cherie felt safe there, even though she felt safest at HC.

Dee had taken Cherie under her wing and the two were thick as thieves. Mom felt a little left out sometimes, but Cherie seemed to know when that was happening and would come spend a few nights at Russ' before heading back to her apartment on the fourth floor of HC, the one not too close to the apartment Ax and Nick shared.

Thinking about their apartment had Ax swallowing and rubbing the back of his neck. He was regretting teasing Nick about his handle.

"I was just getting ready to serve dinner," Mom said. "I'll set two more plates. Everyone into the dining room. Soon we'll be having more family dinners, when you move in."

"Move in?" Nick asked, just as Ax swore under his breath. Nick must have heard it because he turned to Ax. "Is there something you need to tell me?"

"We'll be right in," Ax said as he took Nick's hand to hold him back as everyone else headed to the dining room.

Dad helped Russ stand, and Mom handed him his cane. Diego came in from the kitchen, where he'd probably been helping Mom cook dinner. He opened his mouth to say something to Ax, but Mom turned him around and pushed him from the room as she spoke to him in a low voice.

"What's going on?" Nick asked. "Are you moving and didn't tell me?"

Ax cleared his throat. His stomach tightened as he tried to remember what he'd thought about saying to Nick.

"I... uh... I was hoping we'd both be moving. I sold the house in Oakland. Mom and Dad won't take any of the money from it. I did set some aside for Diego to go to college, but... I bought a condo just down the street."

"From here?"

Ax shrugged. "Well, I figured we both spend so much time here."

"So you bought a condo?"

"Yeah, but then Mom said I probably should have asked you if you liked it before I bought it."

"She did, did she?" Nick rocked back on his heels as he watched Ax.

"But I was pretty sure you didn't care where you lived as long as you were close to your dad."

"So you're asking me to move in with you?"

Ax sighed. "We're already living together. I just figured we'd live together closer to where both our parents live. I mean, if you're willing to live in that tiny apartment in HC, the condo I bought will be a step up."

"Ax?"

He hadn't realized he was closing his eyes until Nick called his name and he opened them.

Nick gave him a lopsided grin. "I'd like to live closer to my dad. And I wouldn't mind living near your parents, but mostly I want to be where you are."

Ax's shoulders sagged as he let out the breath he'd been holding. "So you're not pissed?"

"No, but if I hate the place, you might be on your own."

Ax shook his head. "You won't hate it."

"I guess not. Besides, you can make it worth my while to stay."

"You already topped today," Ax said. "Tonight, it's my turn."

Nick covered Ax's mouth with his hand. "We talked about this — no hard-ons around our parents."

Ax kissed Nick's palm then took his hand and led him into the dining room where their two broken families were laughing. They could heal and grow and let go of the past…together.

Want to see more from this author?
Here's a taster for you to enjoy!

Hart Consulting: Savage
Rae Marks

Coming September 2022

Excerpt

Mase

"He's gonna kill you," Wade grumbled over the phone.

"He's gonna have to make me first," Mase said as he pulled up flights.

"He's an operator of the highest caliber. He'll probably feel it when you land at the same airport he did."

Mase rolled his eyes. There was no way Jazz would 'feel' when he landed. Then again, Mase felt it when Jazz entered a room. It was like the air changed. In the beginning, he'd tried to ignore it, but over the past decade, it had become a part of him. He was a sucker for Jazz.

"I'm plenty angry at him, too," Mase said. "I just might kill him for doing something so monumentally stupid."

Jazz wouldn't see Mase until he wanted Jazz to. And, at some point, Mase would want that. Jazz would learn he couldn't just go rogue at any time without being detected.

"Fuck," Max yelled as something crashed.

"Don't throw that keyboard. It belongs to HC," Wade chided.

A scraping sound followed by the clackety-clack of typing meant Max had made up with his computer and was once again working to find Jazz with his mad hacker skills.

"I can't find him. Why can't I find him? I have better facial recognition software than the government does," Max mumbled.

"Only because you took theirs and made it better," Wade reminded him.

"Why start from scratch when you can improve upon what's already there?"

"If it's so stellar, why can't you locate Jazz?" Mase asked.

There was a sigh and more typing on the other end of the line. Mase had three tabs open on his laptop, each ready to book a flight to a different city.

Jazz was already in the air, headed to some unknown destination. They were stuck trying to figure out which flight he'd boarded.

"This is ridiculous," Max said. "You can't wear a hat or a hood through security, so why can't I find him?"

Mase could tell that it was more of an ego thing than a general frustration on Max's part. Max never missed. He didn't screw up when it came to computers. He was a genius with both hardware and software, and Hart Consulting was lucky to have him.

Max had never been in the military, but he still had a call sign. His name was S.I.N. Some buddies in college had called him a Super Intel Nerd and the name had stuck and shortened to 'Sin'.

The description fit Max, but the acronym didn't. Mase only ever thought of him as Max, because if he looked at Max, his thoughts were more protective than sinful. Max was cute as a button...in a grumpy kitten sort of way. Sure, he was a good-looking kid—but he was still a kid.

He looked about sixteen, not twenty-four. And he was one of Mase's kid brother's best friends. Mase still couldn't believe that his younger brothers had sought him out after all these years. He shifted in the pleather airport seat as he thought about how much pressure Nick was applying to get Mase to go see their father.

"Is there another way to find him?" Wade asked.

"Of course there is, but I still need to figure out how he slipped past my facial recognition software. If it's a flaw in the program, I need to know and adjust for it."

"Fret over your precious program later," Mase said. "For now, find Jazz so I can get on a plane."

Mase kept his voice low. He was already at the airport, bag in hand, ready to chase after Jazz. No one was close enough to hear what he was saying, but he was still paranoid. It came with the job.

"Fine," Max sighed. "Let me follow his coordinates for a minute or two. I'll match the trajectory with tail numbers of planes and find out where he's going. If we didn't have a GPS tracker on him, this wouldn't be possible, so when you do see him, ask him how he slips past airport security cams."

And Mase sent a thought of thanks to Dee, Jazz's grandma. They'd all been worried about his erratic behavior over the past two months. Dee had helped them plant GPS trackers in items Jazz almost always had with him.

Mase would do everything he could to keep Dee's name out of it, but he'd have to give up at least one of the trackers when he confronted Jazz. And there would *definitely* be a confrontation.

He'd give up the disk they'd placed in his wallet first. It was something any of them could have put there. Max had tagged each tracker. Currently, Jazz had two of the trackers on him, the one in his wallet and the one in the watch that had been his grandfather's.

They'd put a third tracker in his favorite knife and a fourth in the knife that had been his grandfather's, but Jazz had left both of those behind. It would have been hard to get them through airport security.

"Is it some CIA trick?" Max asked.

"What?"

"Dodging my facial rec program."

"I'll ask him if I ever find out where he's going," Mase said.

"Yeah, yeah. Almost there. Got it. He's on a flight headed to Bush Intercontinental in Houston."

"Fuck," Mase said as he clicked on the tab with the flight to Houston.

"Houston's bad?" Max asked.

"Dee said his sperm donor lives in Texas, so not a good sign. Okay, flight's booked. I'm out for at least forty-eight hours."

"You're risking your cover, too," Wade warned.

"My job is to follow around Bernard. That's exactly what I'm doing."

Jazz was supposed to be undercover as a high-level French drug and human trafficker named Lucien Bernard. Mase had been rising in the ranks of a Ukrainian drug and human trafficking ring. Their covers were intersecting for the moment.

"We'll make it work if we need to." Wade sighed. "Texas is a believable place for you both to travel. I need you back by Wednesday, though, because Jazz has that meeting with Campbell, the lawyer from San Francisco. Though I'd prefer to have you back by Tuesday. Double-D is coming in to go over financials, and since you're Stateside..."

"I'll be back. In fact, both Jazz and I will hopefully return long before Tuesday. I need to go catch my flight. We'll talk when I touch down."

Mase disconnected the call and got in line for the TSA security checkpoint. Being back on American soil was great—and yet it wasn't. Wade wanted him to jump into a role he'd neglected three years before when he'd moved to Ukraine.

Hart Consulting had originally started as a joke. While he was being investigated for sedition, Mase started investigating the men accusing him, namely his commanding officer and teammates.

It hadn't initially worked out as he'd planned. Mase had been discharged, and two of the three men who'd testified against him were still in the army. But he'd done such a good job investigating his commanding officer that Captain Banning had been court-martialed and was still in jail. The assholes who had accused Mase of sexually harassing them were still serving their country.

Mase was no longer bitter, because he'd found his calling. The army had offered financial security when he'd had none. But Hart Consulting was his, and he was making a difference exactly where he wanted to.

He'd been cleared of most of the charges, though he hadn't received an offer to return to service. He could probably thank Major General Moore for that.

Mase shook thoughts of Blake and his father out of his head. Coming back to the US had his past bombarding him. It seemed Jazz was facing the same issues.

* * * *

Jazz was going to land soon. He could get in a hell of a lot of trouble before Mase touched down.

"Nervous flyer?" The woman next to him on the plane asked.

Realizing his knee was bouncing, Mase took a deep breath. He was an operator. He could be patient for the length of a mid-haul flight.

"Just in a hurry to get where I'm going," he said.

"Where *are* you going?"

The woman leaned forward and tilted her head to the side. She was young, beautiful and sultry, but Mase's mind was on Jazz.

"Meeting a buddy of mine so I can try to keep him out of trouble for the weekend," Mase said.

"That's too bad. I thought maybe you were looking for trouble."

She smiled. She was sexy, but Mase wished he'd brought headphones so he could block her out.

"No, ma'am," he said. "My wife would kill me if I got into any of that."

The flirtatious light in her eyes died at the word 'wife', and Mase was glad. If she'd continued to flirt, it would have made her so much less attractive.

Another time, another place, if he were going to meet anyone else, maybe Mase would have considered her offer of trouble. But he was going to find Jazz.

"Is your friend as cute as you?" she asked.

Mase raised his brows at how quickly she'd moved on.

She shrugged. "You already said he's looking for trouble."

"I'm afraid you're a little too feminine for him." Mase winked.

"Oh. Well then, I hope he doesn't find trouble." She lowered her voice. "Many Texans can be very closed-minded about certain things."

"That's why I'm flying out there last minute...to make sure he doesn't do anything stupid."

She nodded, and after a moment of awkward silence, changed the subject. But Mase's mind stayed on Jazz. It was not a coincidence he was flying to Texas after going AWOL.

There had been a change in Jazz since the incident a few months before. That night had been pure torture. It was the first time in three years they'd been in the same room together, and everything had gone to hell.

Even two months later, Mase started to break out into a sweat when he remembered walking into that hotel room to find Jazz unconscious on the bed.

After ten years, Mase had given up hope that what he felt for Jazz would diminish. He did his best to hold himself back, but that had been impossible when Jazz had been calling his name.

The things he'd mumbled had been just enough to twist Mase's guts but not quite detailed enough to let him know what he needed to do about it. Jazz had told him the man in question was untouchable.

Mase hadn't realized why until Max had helped them put the pieces together. *Martin Coleman.* US Congressman Martin Coleman had gone to college and been in the ROTC program with Jazz. And Martin Coleman had been at the gala that night. He also happened to live in Houston when he wasn't representing the great state of Texas in Congress.

Jazz had only been sixteen when he'd started college, so it didn't take a genius to figure out that the much older Martin had taken advantage in a way that had deeply affected Jazz — and was still affecting him to this day.

Mase's phone pinged — then it pinged again...and again. He was getting messages from Wade and Max. Jazz was at Martin Coleman's home. Max was working on accessing the security feed. He would remove any evidence of Jazz's presence.

Mase sat forward in his seat, only to lean back. Leaning forward again, he looked around until he realized he was looking for a quicker way to get to Jazz, and that just wasn't possible.

Jazz was on his own, no backup. He hadn't even told them where he was going, probably because they would have tied him down to stop him from making such a crazy decision. Mase didn't even try to stop his foot from bouncing on the floor of the plane. Jazz was the one person who could throw him into a tailspin.

"You're friend already find some trouble?" his seat partner asked.

"You could say that."

And there wasn't a damn thing Mase could do to stop the backlash that was sure to come.

About the Author

Rae has been secretly penning romances since high school. It started with short stories that grew into full-length novels. When she received her first Kindle and had thousands of books at her fingertips, she became a little distracted from writing. Then one day she read a book that she would have written a different way. She began writing again and hasn't stopped since.

When she's not writing, Rae can usually be found reading, walking along the beaches of Half Moon Bay, or taking her geriatric dog to the vet, yet again.

Rae loves to hear from readers. You can find her contact information, website details and author profile page at https://www.pride-publishing.com

PUBLISHING

Sign up for our newsletter and find out about all our romance book releases, eBook sales and promotions, sneak peeks and FREE romance books!